BRIGHT
STAR

BRIGHT STAR

ERIN SWAN

TOR TEEN

A TOM DOHERTY ASSOCIATES BOOK
NEW YORK

BRIGHT STAR

Copyright © 2019 by Erin Swan

A Tor Teen Book
Published by Tom Doherty Associates
120 Broadway
New York, NY 10271

www.tor-forge.com

Tor® is a registered trademark of Macmillan Publishing Group, LLC.

Library of Congress Cataloging-in-Publication Data

Names: Swan, Erin, author.
Title: Bright star / Erin Swan.
Description: First edition. | New York : Tor Teen, 2019. |
    "A Tom Doherty Associates Book."
Identifiers: LCCN 2018053119 | ISBN 9780765392992
    (hardcover) | ISBN 9780765393005 (ebook)
Subjects: | CYAC: Elves—Fiction. | Dragons—Fiction. |
    Revolutions—Fiction. | Magic—Fiction. | Kings, queens,
    rulers, etc.—Fiction. | Fantasy.
Classification: LCC PZ7.1.S9254 Bri 2019 | DDC [Fic]—dc23
LC record available at https://lccn.loc.gov/2018053119

Our books may be purchased in bulk for promotional, educational, or business use. Please contact your local bookseller or the Macmillan Corporate and Premium Sales Department at 1-800-221-7945, extension 5442, or by email at MacmillanSpecialMarkets@macmillan.com.

First Edition: August 2019

Printed in the United States of America

0 9 8 7 6 5 4 3 2 1

For my husband,

*who gave me a better love story
than I could ever write.*

BRIGHT STAR

1

The Choosing

Andra shrank deeper into the alcove, biting her lip as the young, sandy-haired man beside her peered out from their hiding place, his blue eyes alight, cheeks flushed. Her heart hammered in her ears, but not with the same excitement so clear on his face. She swallowed hard, trying to keep the anxiety from her voice as she spoke.

"Talias," she whispered as quietly as she could, "we shouldn't be here. I could get in serious trouble for this. We *both* could." She added the last part in the hopes that it might frighten him into changing his mind about the scheme, but they both knew that Andra's punishment would be much greater than the kitchen boy's if they were caught.

Still, Talias seemed unfazed. He looked at her with a mischievous quirk at the corner of his lips that made her stomach lurch. "Have I ever led you astray, Andra?" he asked. "Besides, I know you're just as curious as I am. There must be a reason they keep everyone out of the arena during the Choosing."

"Exactly," Andra hissed. "There *must* be a reason, so why are we breaking the law and hiding behind this statue to watch?"

The young man was spared from a reply as a rumbling sound echoed through the great space before them. Andra forgot her nerves, curiosity overtaking her, and peered out from around the marble statue at the large indoor arena. The open, dirt-floored space was large enough to put some town squares to shame, and steep benches lined the walls, though they were empty for now.

At the center of the arena stood a tall man in the blue-striped robes of a judge, his long brown hair tied with a cord at the nape of his neck. Those cold eyes that made Andra cringe were now looking down on a dozen twelve-year-old boys, all of whom were shifting and bouncing in their well-polished boots.

Andra saw why. Directly across from where she hid, a pair of enormous wooden doors were being hauled open by a half dozen thick-armed men. As the gap widened, a reptilian head appeared, blue scales glittering with the sunlight that streamed in from outside. Andra's breath caught, but not with fear. Awe filled her as the dragon slowly stepped through the open doorway, sharp azure eyes measuring the twelve boys before her.

"She's beautiful," Andra whispered.

Talias exhaled slowly. "'Terrifying' is more accurate."

The young girl looked at him, brow furrowing. "We've seen dozens of dragons, Talias," she said. "Surely you're not scared of this one."

"This is different," her companion answered. "That's no Paired dragon, Andra. She doesn't have a Rider. That's a *wild* dragon."

Andra knew this, of course. Paired dragons didn't breed; nesting would take them from their Riders for weeks on end, and that was something no Paired dragon would stand for. All the eggs for the annual Pairing came from wild females, who willingly gave their children to be partnered with human and elven Riders. It was something that the dragons had done for the better part of a thousand years—excluding the few hundred years of war that had briefly wiped Riders from the land—honoring the pact that had been forged among dragons, elves, and humans so long ago.

Each year, the humans and elves selected a few of their own to meet with the wild female who would give her eggs to the Pairing. Exactly what happened in that meeting, Andra wasn't sure, and neither was Talias. And that was how he'd persuaded her to crouch in this corner, behind the statue of the Guardians, and spy on the proceedings. She knew the moment he'd suggested the idea that it was a bad one, but she'd had a hard time saying no to the handsome kitchen boy from the day she arrived at the Hall of Riders as a child. And her own curiosity had pressed her into finally agreeing to follow him into the arena.

The two hidden figures watched as the great sapphire dragon stepped up to the collection of boys and Judge Dusan, the master of the Hall. Even from this distance, Andra could see some of the boys cringe backward nervously, and she suppressed a small laugh. These twelve were supposed to be some of the most promising young men that the land of Paerolia had to offer. Though she knew most of them were the sons of high-ranking officials, or even judges, they were thoroughly trained and tested before being selected for the Pairings. They included boys of both human and elven blood, as well as some of mixed races, and they all would have been exposed to dragons many times before this moment. And yet, she could still see a few shaking in their shiny boots.

Judge Dusan's voice reached her ears, speaking aloud to the dragon, as propriety demanded. "Welcome, once again, to the Hall of Riders, Ena. It is a great pleasure to see you once more." He gave a deep bow, and the dragon inclined her head politely.

Andra knew that Ena must be replying to the greeting, but the dragon spoke only into the judge's mind, and the girl felt a pang of envy. What must it be like to have a dragon speak to your mind? Most people in the Hall had experienced it at least once. Even Talias had spoken to dragons during his service. But not Andra. It was forbidden.

She watched silently, her green eyes riveted on the sleek, scaled shape before her as Ena turned her attention to the boys chosen for the Pairing. Andra saw some of the boys flinch and recoil, and she heard Talias snort with amusement.

"What's so funny?" she whispered.

"She probably just touched their minds to speak to them," he said. "I think that one on the end there may have soiled his britches."

Andra gave a small smile and shook her head, turning her attention back to the dragon. The wild creature was closing her shining eyes, and the girl thought she heard a deep, thrumming sound coming from the scaled throat. Suddenly, a warm presence pressed itself against Andra's mind, and she gasped. Instinctively, she began to pull away, putting up the walls to protect her thoughts as she had been taught since childhood.

But there was something so gentle, so reassuring about the presence that she stopped. After a pause, Andra lowered the walls around her mind and let the presence in. It was like sinking into warm water after a hard day of work. The dragon's mind enveloped Andra's like an invisible embrace, and she felt joy swell inside her at the touch, her eyes closing as she savored this strange and wonderful contact.

Then, as abruptly as it had come, the touch was gone. Andra opened her eyes and looked at Talias, a smile on her lips. But the look on the servant boy's face was far different. His eyes were wide, his face pale, making the freckles stand out on his skin.

"Are you all right?" Andra asked quietly.

Talias looked at her. "Did you not *feel* that?" he whispered tensely.

She nodded, smiling again at the thought of the mental embrace. "Yes. It felt . . . beautiful."

Her friend gave her an incredulous look, but any reply he might have given was interrupted by a shout from Judge Dusan.

"Three?" he asked loudly. "When I was a boy, there were at least six Riders chosen every year! And yet, each year, we see fewer and fewer Pairings!"

Andra heard Ena give a low growl in her throat as she made some silent reply to the judge. The lanky man let out a huff, but gave a small bow. "Of course. My apologies, Ena. So you will bring the three eggs, then?" A pause as he listened to the dragon's silent reply; then he nodded. "Yes, one month's time. We will ensure the Hall is prepared for the Pairing."

With that, the dragon turned, narrowly missing the line of boys with her long tail, and lumbered back out the open doors. Andra leaned around the large statue, straining to watch through the doorway as Ena spread her brilliant blue wings and, after several laborious beats, took to the sky.

Talias's hand abruptly seized her arm, yanking her back behind the statue. She suddenly found herself pulled close to him, her chest pressed against his, one of his arms tight around her waist. Her heart stuttered at his closeness, the warmth of his arm around her obvious through the thin brown wool of her dress. But he wasn't looking at her. He was peering carefully around the statue, watching as Dusan and the twelve boys filed past. He had pulled her back behind the statue just in time to keep her from being seen.

When the candidates and the judge had exited the arena, Talias let out a heavy sigh, and he finally looked down at her. His blue eyes caught her pale green ones, and he seemed to realize just how close he held her. There was a brief pause, and Andra thought she heard his breath catch for a moment. Then he smiled, relaxed and easygoing once again, as he always was. He gave her short brown hair a playful tug, and the arm around her back fell away.

"Come on," he said with a smirk. "We need to hurry before

anyone notices we're missing. They'll be starting the Riders' banquet soon."

Andra swallowed hard and stepped back, nodding in agreement, and Talias turned away, by all appearances unaffected by the moment that had passed between them. She fought back the disappointment, the lingering hope that he would have kissed her in that moment, and followed him as he hurried to the doors that connected the arena to the rest of the Hall of Riders. The kitchen boy cracked the doors, checking the hallway for any passersby, and Andra glanced back at the statue that had hidden them.

It was beautiful, carved of sparkling white marble. At the center was the great dragon, Oriens, his wings outstretched over the two figures beside him. The stories said that his scales had been as golden as the sunrise, and his children had been the first dragons Paired with Riders in three centuries. To one side was the shape of an elven man with a slim build and pointed ears, his smooth face carved into a serious expression. Caelum, prince of the elves and general of the elven armies at the end of the War of Races. To the other side of the dragon stood the marble shape of a woman.

Andra knew the stories about her—Eliana of the Two-Bloods, the first halfblood to be born in three hundred years, in a time when humans and elves were still at war, Oriens's Rider. The girl stared for a moment at the graceful, shining face of the long-dead woman, a strange feeling of longing in her chest. To be a Rider . . .

"Let's go."

Andra jerked her attention away from the statue and back to the doors, where Talias was hurrying through into the empty hallway. She followed quickly behind him, and they made their way briskly to the kitchen. As they stepped into the Hall's enormous kitchen, the cacophony washed over Andra, breaking the spell that seemed to have been lingering over her mind from Ena's touch.

2

The Riders' Feast

"There you are!" a shrill voice called.

Talias and Andra jumped guiltily and turned toward the sound to find Talias's mother, the head cook of the Hall, moving toward them.

"Where have you two been?" the gray-haired woman asked in a harried voice. "You should be putting the trays together for the banquet. The Riders will be in the dining hall any moment."

"Yes, Mother," Talias said briskly. He grabbed Andra by the hand and pulled her toward the tables where servants and contracted workers alike were piling food and goblets of wine onto serving trays. They joined the commotion, falling into their duties with natural ease. This was routine, something they did every year.

The Banquet of the Choosing was a tradition that dated back to the time of the Guardians, when the first candidates were selected to become the first generation of new Riders. Eliana herself had chosen them, the finest soldiers from both the human and the elven armies, and they'd held a celebration to honor the coming together of three races who had been at war for three hundred years. And the tradition had continued each year, with the Riders from all over Paerolia returning to the Hall to honor the ones who could join their ranks.

Of course, unlike that first generation, not all the selected candidates would join the ranks of the Riders. Only three this year, Andra thought, remembering Dusan's agitated words. But still, it was a night for all twelve boys to be celebrated for their hard work and training. A night for them to dream of what it might be like to become a Rider like the other men around them. For now, they all held on to that dream, but when the Pairing came, only three of them would be chosen by the hatchlings.

"Something on your mind?" Talias asked suddenly, as they carried their trays down the corridor to the banquet hall.

"Oh, it's nothing," Andra said with a shake of her head.

"Come on," the kitchen boy urged, nudging her elbow and almost upsetting the tray of goblets in her hands. "You can tell me."

She looked at that disarming smile and, as she so often had in the past, surrendered to its persuasion. "I was just wondering . . . why are all the Riders men now?" She asked the question quietly, afraid that she pushed the boundaries by questioning the tradition.

Talias made a thoughtful face for a moment, then shrugged. "I don't really know, I guess. It's just the way it's been done for so long."

"But Eliana was the one who restored the Riders to Paerolia after the War of Races," Andra pointed out. "She was a woman. There were women in the first several generations of Riders after her, weren't there? Why did it stop?"

Talias shrugged again. "I guess the judges just decided it was better that way," he replied. "The humans and elves each only get six candidates a year. There had to be some way to limit the selection pool. Making it only twelve-year-old boys just simplifies it, I suppose."

Andra suppressed a sigh and nodded in agreement. The judges had been established by the Guardians as well, after the emperor was overthrown. They knew what was best for Paerolia. She pushed her questions aside as they arrived at the banquet hall, joining a long line of servants and indentured workers waiting to enter.

They all stood silently, waiting for the signal to begin serving. After several minutes, the large doors at the end of the hallway opened, and the line of servers streamed into the noisy dining hall. There were three long tables that filled the length of the room, and all were filled with chattering men and boys who ranged in age from the new, twelve-year-old candidates to gray-haired Riders with heavily creased faces.

Clustered at one table were the younger Riders, the current residents of the Hall. They stayed at the Hall until they were seventeen, receiving formal training from the elder Riders on magic, swordplay, and, of course, dragon-mounted combat. Andra knew most of their faces, as she had served many of their meals to them during her five years of service at the Hall. There were only eighteen of them, filling a small fraction of the rooms that the Hall contained.

The remainder of the dining hall was filled with the fully fledged Riders, who came from all around the land to attend this banquet and the Pairing that would be held in one month's time. Andra knew, of course, that these were not all the Riders. There were several hundred of them across the land, and many of them would have to remain at their assigned posts, regardless of the current celebrations.

As Andra carried drinks to the noisy Riders, slipping almost imperceptibly among them, she listened to their conversations. "Finally off the Range, eh?" one asked his neighbor with a knowing grin.

The other Rider let out a sharp laugh. "Mercifully, yes. I did my year of service, and now I can move on to an easier assignment."

"It can't be that bad," a younger man chimed in. Andra recognized him as a recent graduate from the Hall. "Most creatures from the Mordis Range don't venture out of the mountains anymore, right?"

"Ah," the first man laughed, holding out his goblet. Andra refilled it deftly, never drawing the Rider's attention. "Still haven't been called up for Range Duty, eh?"

The young Rider shook his head, and the others around him laughed.

"Just wait, lad," another said, slapping the young man on the shoulder. "Whether you end up having to drive back some of them Mordis wolves or not, you'll learn right quick why all Riders dread going on Range Duty."

"Those mountains . . ." The Rider who spoke gave a shiver. "Well, they'll drive you half mad just having to be in 'em for a day. Spending a year there . . ."

"Your dragon keeps you sane," another agreed with an affectionate smile. "I'd swear on the Stone Table that's why only Riders monitor those cursed mountains. Less to do with our magic and our dragons' strength, and more to do with us having our dragons as our mind mates."

Andra smiled softly to herself as she listened. Riders always talked like this about their dragons, with this note of affection that sounded as if they were talking about a sweetheart back home. She envied the closeness they clearly felt to the beautiful creatures she'd glimpsed so often at the Hall, and her mind drifted back briefly to the sensation of Ena's mind pressing against her own.

In her distraction, Andra didn't notice the Rider who began to stand from the bench, swinging his leg out in front of her. She collided with him, the tray of goblets she held careening to the stone floor with a cacophonous clatter. Andra landed heavily on her backside while the burly, broad-shouldered Rider gave a shout of outrage. Red wine stained his fine yellow tunic.

Andra leapt quickly to her feet and bowed low, avoiding his gaze and muttering apologies under her breath. With her eyes on the floor, she didn't see the strike coming. The man's large hand collided with her jaw and sent her back to the floor in the puddle of spilled wine.

"You stupid, clumsy idiot!" he shouted. "Look what you've done!"

The Rider stepped toward her, and Andra instinctively tensed, her hand curling into a fist before she caught herself. *Your willfulness will get you killed, just like your father.* She bit her tongue and unballed her fist. But the blow she expected didn't come. Another Rider stood from the bench, stepping between Andra and the wine-covered Rider.

"Now, now, brother," he said in a soft, calm voice, placing a hand on his fellow Rider's shoulder. "It was an honest accident. No harm done, see?"

With a wave of his slim hand, the wine seemed to draw itself off the large man's silk tunic, leaving it as spotless as it had been before. He huffed and, without a word, stormed out of the dining hall. The Rider who had interfered turned now toward the girl on the floor. She looked up at him, taking in his moonlight-blond hair, blue eyes, pale skin, and pointed ears—one of the elven Riders. He bent and held out a hand to her.

"Are you hurt?" he asked.

Andra shook her head slowly, then took the hand, feeling the soft, supple leather of his black Rider's gloves in her grasp. He pulled her easily to her feet, then handed her the tray. There was a flurry of wind around them, and the spilled goblets gathered themselves off the floor, settling back onto the tray Andra bore.

Before the girl could mumble her thanks, a familiar figure hurried to her side, taking her by the arms and beginning to turn her away from the fair-haired elf. "Thank you, Master Rider," Talias said with a brisk nod. "Thank you for your help. Please, enjoy the rest of your meal, and allow us to attend to the mess. Thank you."

As he ushered Andra quickly down the aisle toward the doors, she heard one of the other Riders chiding the elf. "You know you're not supposed to do magic in front of them."

Talias hurried Andra out into the hallway and shut the doors behind them before taking the tray from her arms and setting it on a table beside the doorway. His hands suddenly cupped her face, tilting it to look up at him. His expression was concerned, and his eyes seemed to be searching her for some sign of injury.

"Did he hurt you?" he asked softly.

Andra didn't dare shake her head, for fear the movement would cause his hands to fall away from her skin. "No," she whispered softly.

His hands tilted her head to one side, and she felt his fingertips graze the right side of her jaw, where the Rider had struck her. "You're a terrible liar, Andra," he replied.

"It's—it's not so bad," she stammered. "I'm sure I just . . . look a fright from all the wine."

Talias sighed, and his hand slid down to her shoulder, leaving a trail of tingling skin down her neck. "Right," he said with a forced smile. "Go get cleaned up, then. I'll get some new goblets and wine. Hurry up, now."

As badly as she wished to linger in that moment, to bask in the look of tender concern in his eyes, she knew that punishment would be waiting for her if she shirked her duties for too long. So Andra nodded and regretfully stepped away from his touch, then turned quickly on her heel and hurried toward the servants' quarters. She bounded up the steps two at a time, threw open the door, and rushed to her cot.

Dropping to her knees, she opened the small chest that contained her spare uniforms and pulled out an identical brown wool dress. She stripped off the wine-soaked clothes she wore and tugged on the clean outfit, then hurried from the room, combing her hair into place with her fingers as she did so. Before she reached the dining hall, she paused before a mirror that hung on the corridor wall, inspecting her reflection.

Part of her hair looked damp from the wine still, but aside from that, she looked as she ought—an unassuming, pale-faced girl who was meant to be seen and not heard. She sighed and touched the leather collar on her neck, wondering what she would look like without it there, its silver lock shining in the torchlight. What would it be like to be just another servant, like Talias, instead of having a labor contract hanging over her?

She drew a breath. Ten more years, she thought. Ten more years, and she would have repaid her father's debt to the judges. The collar would be gone, the contract ended, and she would be free to choose for the first time in her life. She shook her head sharply, forcing the thoughts aside, and began to run again, arriving at the dining hall doors just as Talias arrived bearing a new tray of goblets and a decanter of fresh wine.

"Quick as always, I see," he said with a crooked smile.

She smiled back and took the tray from his hands. "Thank you, Talias," she replied quietly.

"You know I'd do anything for you, Andra." The words were spoken lightly, playfully, with that same teasing quirk on his mouth, but they made Andra's heart stutter. Then he turned and pulled open the dining hall doors. "After you," he said with a small bow.

Andra smiled at him and stepped inside, back into the noise of the banquet, blending back into her place among the silent servants who continued to serve the Riders.

3

The Pairing

"Andra!" a woman's voice called.

The girl looked up from the book in surprise. She had thought she was alone. She glanced back down at the book's beautiful illustrations of Iterum, then shut it and returned it to its shelf in the library. The voice called again, and Andra hurried out of the room, shutting the door quietly behind her.

Footsteps echoed down the hall, and a rotund woman in an apron appeared from around the corner. Andra jumped away from the library doors, trying not to look guilty.

"Andra!" the woman snapped, marching forward. The girl bowed her head and gazed at her feet. "What are you doing, you lazy girl? How many times have I told you that the rafters in the dining hall need to be cleaned? I can see the dust from the doorway! Now, you get up there and get those clean, understand?"

"Yes, ma'am," Andra muttered, still not meeting the housekeeper's gaze.

"And you had better get it done quickly. The Pairing will be starting soon, and we need to prepare the dining hall for the feast."

"Yes, ma'am."

Andra listened as the footsteps faded away before looking up. Filled with relief at having avoided punishment for the moment, she raced toward the dining hall. When she entered the room, she found it filled with both indentured laborers and servants, all bustling around, cleaning one thing or another.

Talias trotted up to her, smiling brightly. "There you are, Andra," he called.

Andra smiled back at him, her heart leaping joyously at the sight of him, as it always did.

"Shall we start on those rafters before the housekeeper starts scaring the dragons?"

She gave a small laugh, but before she could reply, the kitchen boy said, "I'll race you up!" Talias darted toward where a ladder leaned against the lowest rafter of the ceiling, moving before the words had even left his mouth.

Andra smiled again to herself. It was the only ladder in the room, but that didn't matter to her. She ran toward one of the supporting beams of the wall. Leaping upward, she grabbed a wide peg in the wood and pulled herself up. Placing her foot on the narrow hold, she leapt confidently out over the dining hall and grabbed a low rafter. Swinging around it once, she released herself into the air and landed astride the beam.

She grinned at Talias as he scrambled up the last steps of the ladder. He laughed and shook his head in amazement. "I shall never understand how you do that," he said, grabbing a rag from a bucket resting on the beam beside him. He wrung the water out of it, then tossed it to her. She snagged it easily out of the air. "Now, let's make this shine," he said.

They set into wiping down the tops of the rafters, removing a year's worth of dust from their surfaces. The rafters were cleaned only on the day of the Pairing each year. Andra moved easily across the narrow beams, while Talias wobbled and wavered as he removed the dust. Andra had finished her half of the rafters and was beginning to help Talias with his when cheering reached her ears.

The shouts were coming from the arena. The Pairing was beginning. Though she had never seen one, she knew from what others had said that the Riders would be marching in now, followed by the Riders in training, then the candidates for this year. Last of all, Ena would enter, with the eggs she sensed would bond with the candidates carried by servants. She sighed longingly, thinking of the beautiful blue dragon who had touched her mind a month ago, then looked back down at the gray dust that awaited her.

Talias looked up at her sigh. "You've never seen a Pairing, have you."

She shook her head. "It's not allowed," she whispered. "Not so long as I remain under a contract."

The boy glanced around, then whispered with that familiar mischievous look in his eye, "Only if you get caught. Sneak in the back and climb to the large beam in the center of the ceiling. No one will see you there."

Andra looked at him in surprise, trying to determine if her friend was serious.

"Go on," he urged. "Just be careful."

She smiled at him and swung down from the beam, dropping the twelve feet to the floor without hesitation. She crouched on landing, absorbing the impact of the drop, then stood and ran from the room. The other workers watched her go in confusion, but returned to their work without a word.

As quietly as possible, Andra slunk through the halls and down the stairs to the corridor that connected to the arena. The cheers of the spectators grew louder, and she knew that Ena and her eggs must be entering at the end of the procession. She hastened her step, not wanting to miss the Pairing. She climbed several flights of stairs and stepped out onto the upper benches of the arena where the Pairing took place. The seats beneath her were all filled with eager spectators gazing down at the floor far below.

The twelve candidates were stepping toward Ena, who stood over her eggs in front of the marble statue of the three Guardians. The crowd fell silent. One young girl glanced over her shoulder at Andra, frowning in distaste at her dirty face and leather collar. Andra darted back into the shadows and glanced up. The rafter was not far above her head. She found a hole in the wall where a loose stone had fallen and used it to lift herself up toward the rafter. She wrapped her arms around it, then swung her legs up and twisted herself to the top of the wood.

Sliding quietly on her belly along the wide beam, Andra shimmied out toward the center of the arena. Finally, she was looking almost directly down at the dragon, her three eggs, and the twelve hopeful young boys. A low humming echoed throughout the silent arena as Ena touched her nose to each egg in turn—an emerald green egg, a rich brown egg. A quiet gasp rippled through the crowd as Ena touched her nose to the last egg. It was a deep, shimmering purple, the rarest color among all dragons, save gold. No one had been a Rider of a violet dragon since the very first generation of Riders taught by Eliana herself.

The eggs began to tremble, humming in response to their mother's voice. Even from her height, Andra heard the faint cracking of the stone-hard dragon eggs. A golden light streaked through the cracks of the shells. Andra held her breath as she watched the light growing brighter until, at last, all three hatchlings tumbled from their shells at once. Andra gasped. They were beautiful, like living jewels sparkling on the sandy floor. The tiny dragons shook their heads, licking their hides clean of the sticky membranes before turning toward their patient mother. She touched their snouts and hummed again, giving her permission for them to leave her.

The hatchlings turned to the twelve waiting boys, making soft cooing sounds as they approached them. Jealousy ached in Andra's chest as the brown hatchling headed straight for a young boy at the end of the line. The boy, who bore markers of elven heritage, knelt down and extended his hand hopefully toward the little dragon. It turned its head from side to side, studying him curiously—then, closing its eyes, touched its nose to the boy's hand. There was a flash of light. The newest Rider lifted his little dragon to his shoulder and turned toward the crowd, beaming widely, displaying the fresh, flame-shaped mark on his hand.

The walls began to echo with a chant from the spectators. "Veholum! Veholum! Veholum!" Andra recognized the word, a sacred word from the elven language. It was used to address a Rider and his dragon, a single word for the pair—Sky Riders.

The boy stepped away from the other candidates, joining the line of Riders in training, who stood against the walls. They greeted him warmly, with jostling pats on the back and firm handshakes.

The other two dragons were studying the line cautiously, staying close together, as if afraid to venture forward alone. At last, the green hatchling stepped slowly forward, approaching a boy in the center of the line, making a questioning mewing sound. Andra saw his moonlight-blond hair and the points on his ears. The young elf crouched as the green dragon stopped before him. He held out his hand as the other boy had. The hatchling blinked once at him, then closed its eyes and marked his hand. He lifted the dragon to his shoulder, and the crowd cheered the sacred name once more as he joined the ranks of Riders.

Silence fell again quickly as they all turned their eyes toward the violet hatchling, which still stood in the center of the arena. This was the one they had truly been waiting for. Who would be chosen to Ride such a rare and beautiful creature? It didn't move. The little dragon looked around, squawking in fear and confusion.

Ena rumbled in her throat and the hatchling glanced back at its mother, making a pleading sound, as if asking for help in making the decision.

"Poor thing," Andra whispered to herself as she gazed down at the little dragon.

Suddenly, the hatchling looked up at her and squawked again. Andra froze in surprise. Could it have possibly heard her? It mewed loudly and opened its still-wet wings, flapping them clumsily as it gazed up at her, still raising a chorus of noisy protestations. Andra tried to make herself invisible, but it was too late. Ena turned her large head upward, gazing at Andra with surprised blue eyes. She made a noise in her throat, then several more pairs of eyes looked up at her.

"Get down from there!" Judge Dusan cried.

Andra jumped to her feet and raced along the beam, back toward the benches on the wall. Shouts of surprise and anger swarmed up at her. Andra swung down from the beam and took off running the moment her feet hit the ground. She didn't get far. A man wearing a contract collar grabbed her forcefully by the arm, stopping her in her tracks.

"Sorry, Andra," the man whispered to her, then marched her down a corridor to where Dusan was waiting, tapping his foot angrily. She could still hear the purple hatchling mewing and squawking, and Ena's answering hums as she tried to soothe the startled infant. Andra grimaced inwardly with guilt; she had frightened it.

Dusan stepped forward. She barely registered that he had lifted his hand before it slammed into her cheek. She bit back a gasp of pain and looked down at her feet to hide the tears.

"Do you know what you've done?" he raged at her. "For the first time in over a century, a Rider was chosen by a violet dragon, and you have prevented it from bonding! The disruption you created has so upset the creature that Ena has refused to allow the Pairing to continue! You have prevented the training of a Rider! What do you have to say for yourself, Andra?"

"I'm sorry," she whispered, the only response she could think of.

"Your apologies repair nothing," he hissed back at her. His voice continued to rise as he spoke, until he was spitting the words in her face like venom. "I won't have someone so irresponsible, so flagrantly disobedient, so entirely *disrespectful* anywhere near this Hall! You are to leave at first light, and I never want to see you near the Hall of Riders again! I am reverting your contract to Chief Judge Castigo, and adding five years to your service."

"You can't do that!" she shouted, the words almost reflexive.

Dusan merely raised an eyebrow at her, as if her inappropriate outburst were more of an interesting oddity than an outright violation of her station.

Andra checked herself, reining in her tongue, her mother's voice in her head. *Think before you speak, Andra. Your willfulness will get you killed. Just like your father.*

In desperation, she threw herself to the floor at Dusan's feet. "Please," she pleaded, fighting back the tears. "Please, my lord, I will accept my added years. I will accept your punishments as you see fit. But please, don't send me back there. I beg you."

He didn't reprimand her for her words. He didn't strike her or shout or order another punishment. Judge Dusan merely turned and strode away down the corridor as if she had not spoken at all.

4

Judgment

Andra sat on the hard wooden bench inside the enclosed cart. The walls were made of rough wooden planks, and the two small windows had iron bars. She didn't try to look out of them. She didn't want to see her life disappearing into the trees.

To distract herself from the crushing loneliness, Andra turned her mind to the one good that came from her return to Castigo's manor—her mother. She had accepted four additional years on her contract to have Andra transferred to the Hall. The Hall of Riders was a highly coveted service among those with contracts, but Elysea had won it for her daughter. And now, Andra would be able to see her again for the first time in five years.

As the cart continued on, Andra fingered the braided leather bracelet on her wrist. Another indentured girl had slipped it to her as she had headed toward the waiting cart. As she pressed it into her palm, she had whispered, "Talias says goodbye." Andra had not been able to see her friend again, a fact that pulled at her heart. But he had managed to give her this last parting gift.

Her heart ached at leaving him. From the time she'd arrived at the Hall, Talias was the dream she'd held on to. She could finish her contract, then become a servant at his side in the Hall. He'd fall in love with her. They'd be married, and she would be happy. But that dream was as near to dead as it could be now. She was being sent away from him, and she had five additional years on her contract. She would not be free until she was thirty, and she knew that he would have found another to love long before she was free to love him.

After another hour of bumping and rumbling along, the cart slowed, and Andra heard the distant lowering of a drawbridge. They had reached Vereor, the capital city. The cart moved more smoothly as it rolled off the rough path and onto the cobbles of the city's streets. Curiosity took her, and Andra finally stood on the bench and peered out the narrow window. Tall buildings slid past; barefoot children darted through the streets, dirty dogs barking at their heels. A crush of people seemed to surround the cart, a larger crowd than she could ever remember seeing. Indentured workers were almost never allowed to leave the compounds where they served; for Andra, even being permitted outside had been a rare occurrence.

Then Andra spotted the manor. It loomed over the city, its golden dome and spire piercing the sky. The walls shone white, making the building seem like a beacon in the crowded, dirty streets of the bustling city. Though she knew the manor would be as good as a prison for the next fifteen years, even Andra had to admit that it was beautiful.

They drew up to the manor, and there was the sound of footsteps, the jangling of armor, a man's voice, and then the turning of the lock. The door opened, and an armored soldier stood before her, gazing at her with stern brown eyes. "Get on out of there, girl," he commanded her gruffly.

Andra quickly and obediently grabbed her bag and stood, stepping carefully down from the cart. She glanced around her, taking in the massive stable in which she now stood. The room held several elaborate carriages, each of them large enough to hold at least eight people and be drawn by a team of four or more horses.

The soldier grabbed her roughly by the arm and led her out of the stable and across the courtyard. Andra tried to appreciate the brief walk across the grass, feeling the wind and tasting the fresh air. But soon enough, he led her through a pair of doors at the rear of the manor, and inside what had once been the palace of the emperors.

After Emperor Nocens's fall at the hands of the Guardians, it had been converted into the court and council chambers for the judges. Several of them had lived in certain wings of the palace as well. But slowly, the judges had moved outside the palace into great manors of their own, with some like Judge Dusan— moving to new cities to attend to duties there. Now it was home to only the Chief Judge and his family, and they lived much as the emperors had.

The soldier led Andra down a long corridor, where several servants and slaves glanced at her curiously before returning to their work, then down another corridor and up two flights of stairs until they were standing in front of a simple wooden door.

"These are the quarters for indentured workers," the soldier told her. "The others will instruct you from here on out. Stay out of trouble, and your stay here should be peaceful."

He disappeared down the stairs without another word, his armor clanging noisily as he went. Andra looked back up at the door, then cautiously pushed it open. It looked like the quarters at Judge Dusan's manor, only much larger. Sitting on a cot at the end of one of the long rows of beds was a woman with light brown hair streaked with gray. It was cut short, like all indentured women's, to make care of it simple. Her face showed lines of pain and fear, and she was dressed in the same type of simple brown dress Andra now wore. The little lock on her leather collar was tarnished with age.

She stood as Andra entered the room, a smile on her lined face, and stepped slowly forward. "Andra," she said quietly. "I would have hardly recognized you had I not been expecting you."

Andra smiled back and hurried forward into her mother's waiting arms. The woman embraced her gently, then released her and held her at arm's length, studying her face.

"My, how you've grown," she told her daughter softly, pushing a strand of dark brown hair behind her ear. "You're as tall as I am now. And so very pretty. You have your father's beautiful green eyes. And, of course, a little bit of his ears too," she laughed, touching the very slight point at the tip of Andra's ears.

Andra laughed quietly. "I've missed you, Mama."

"And I have missed you, my dear," the woman replied. "Tell me, was the Hall as wonderful as they say?"

Andra smiled again to herself, thinking of the stories she'd heard as a child in Castigo's manor—that the Hall was an easy assignment for a contracted servant, that the work was light and the servants were never abused. It hadn't been the paradise others had made it out to be, but her mother had sacrificed for her to be sent there, and she had escaped the abuse she'd faced here as a child for a short while.

"It was," Andra answered. "I'll miss it, but I'm glad to be with you again."

Her mother smiled once more. "Well, are you ready to reacquaint yourself with the manor? You probably don't remember much of it."

Andra nodded and trailed her mother down the stairs to the main level of the manor. She followed silently, taking in the halls she had grown up in, and yet remembered so little about. The children of indentured servants were often seen as being in the way, so they were usually confined to back rooms and hidden corridors until they were old enough to take on some of the remaining years of their parents' contracts. She followed her mother through room after room, listening as the older woman explained which areas Andra would be responsible for cleaning.

Suddenly, a man with graying hair, dressed in finely woven, brilliantly colored robes, stepped out of a nearby corridor, appearing immediately before them. He frowned at them, and they took a step back, giving him a more respectful amount of space. Andra recognized him immediately—Chief Judge Castigo.

Castigo pointed a long finger at her and asked sharply, "Who are you?"

"Andra, my lord," she whispered, giving a small curtsy.

"My daughter, sir," her mother added for clarification.

"Ah yes," he mused. "The girl who disrupted the Pairing. And a willful servant by Dusan's word. I'm not sure why I should be saddled with someone who causes so many problems by her mere *presence*, but I suppose it's better you're here than anywhere near the dragons or Riders."

He seemed about to dismiss them when footsteps rang down the hallway from which he had just appeared and a male voice called, "Father! Father!"

Andra stiffened as a young man with dark blond hair appeared from the corridor. She recognized him immediately. How could she forget the boy who had kicked her whenever he saw her, simply because it amused him? He jogged up to his father and opened his mouth to deliver whatever message he had come to give, when he spotted them.

His mischievous hazel eyes fell on her immediately. Andra saw her mother make the tiniest of sidesteps to try to block her from his view. But Ledo frowned at her and made a quick motion with his hand for her to move.

"Step aside, Elysea," he said sharply.

Slumping her shoulders submissively, the woman moved aside, leaving her daughter in Ledo's full gaze.

He studied her for a brief moment before repeating his father's earlier question. "Who are you?"

She was spared having to answer by Castigo himself, who said, "Elysea's daughter, Andra, the girl that Dusan banished for interrupting the Pairing ceremony."

"Ah yes. They said you were here before." His eyes seemed to study her for some memory of the ten-year-old girl who'd been sent away to protect her from his hands. Then he shrugged indifferently. "Don't remember you. But don't you worry, pet." The smile on his face did nothing to soften his angular features as he took her chin in his hand, holding it much too firmly. Andra stood rigid, fighting the urge to pull back, reminding herself to be still, be calm, be obedient. "I'm certain we'll make plenty of new memories together, now, won't we?"

Andra clenched her jaw, holding back the words that swirled inside her, the furious fire that burned at her throat, urged her to scream. After the torment he'd put her through as a child, he didn't remember her? After pushing her down stairs, kicking her, slapping her, and chasing her through the halls just to blacken her eye, he didn't know who she was?

"Pig."

The word seemed to crawl from her lips of its own will. The moment it was free, she felt the blood drain from her face, and saw the blood rising into Ledo's.

"What . . . did you say?" Ledo asked, his voice low, tense, and dangerous.

As quick as that word had been to leap from her tongue before, Andra had no words now. She merely stared at Ledo's blood-hungry hazel eyes, her heart hammering in her ears, her mouth as dry as the Burning Sands.

"She didn't mean it, my lord," Elysea stammered at Andra's elbow. "She's just . . . just a girl. She's been coddled at the Hall. She's forgotten her place."

"Indeed she has," Castigo interjected in a blustering voice. "I will not allow a servant in my household to speak to my son—the heir to the judgment seat—in that way! After the trouble you've caused, girl, it's time that you—"

Ledo raised a hand, and to Andra's surprise, the Chief Judge immediately stopped speaking. A smile was twisting the young man's lips now as he looked at Andra. "Please, Father," Ledo said silkily, "allow me to deliver the punishment, will you? After all, I am the one she insulted."

Castigo nodded obligingly. "Very well, my boy." He put a hand on his son's shoulder for a moment and added, "I'll leave you to pass judgment on the girl."

"Thank you, Father."

The Chief Judge strode off down the hall, apparently indifferent to whatever Ledo's sentence might be. Andra's palms felt clammy as they grasped the front of her brown dress, her mind running through a list of punishments he could inflict upon her.

"Guards."

Andra looked up again as Ledo spoke the word in a calm, even tone. He said it so casually that the soldiers standing nearby exchanged a look, apparently uncertain if they were being ordered to Ledo's side or not. Finally, they stepped up behind him.

"Yes, m'lord?" one asked.

"Take the servant to the dungeons," he replied calmly, still smiling softly. "She's to be hanged at first light."

Andra felt her knees go weak. Her mother grasped one of her arms in a protective motion, as if she meant to hold her daughter back from the two guards, a single unarmed woman defying two armored soldiers.

"My lord!" Elysea cried, her voice desperate. "Please, she meant no harm!"

But the guards still stepped forward. One pushed Elysea back, easily breaking her grip on Andra's elbow, and they seized the girl roughly. But she didn't fight against them. Shock weighted her limbs, turned her mind sluggish.

"No, not her." Andra blinked at Ledo's words, her numb mind processing them slowly. His hazel eyes didn't leave her face as his lips curled in what should have been a handsome smile. He tipped his head slightly, indicating the woman who still stood behind Andra, trying to take hold of her daughter's elbow again. "Her."

There was a brief stillness, Ledo's single word hanging in the air. Andra felt the guards' gloves leave her skin, heard the metallic shifting of their armor as they turned. Then the reality of that single word struck her like the fall of a headsman's axe, and she spun.

"No!" she screamed, her hand lashing out and clinging to her mother's wrist, even as the guards' hands closed around the woman's forearms. "No! No, please, don't do this!"

The guards tried to pull Elysea away, but Andra fought and clawed, shrieked and kicked. A guard seized her, and her fingers clawed at his face, making him scream in pain and release her, allowing her to grasp her mother's hands again. A third guard finally hurried from down the corridor and wrapped his arms around the girl's torso, pinning her arms to her side and lifting her from the ground as she screamed and kicked. The other two began to pull Elysea away.

"No!" Andra howled, tears streaming down her face. "No, Mama! Mama! Please, no!"

Over the sound of her shrieking, she heard her mother saying softly, "Don't worry, darling. Don't be afraid. You shall be fine. Be good. Be safe."

The guards pulled Elysea down the corridor toward the dungeon, and Andra had a final glimpse of her mother's face. Her eyes were filled with fear, and tears streaked her cheeks. But there was a gentle smile on her face as their eyes met. Then she was gone.

———◈———

Ledo made her watch. The following morning, a guard came to the servants' quarters in the dark hours before sunrise, as the workers were all leaving to begin their duties. He escorted Andra to an empty corridor and stood her before a narrow window overlooking the courtyard. In the gray predawn light, Andra saw the black silhouette of the gallows, and two small figures marching toward it.

A pair of soft footsteps echoed down the corridor, but Andra didn't look away from the small form that she knew was her mother. She felt his presence at her side, knowing who it was without looking away from the window.

The two figures ascended the steps. The rope was lowered, then slipped around the small, dark figure's neck. Andra stood stiffly, her face rigid and emotionless, her heart screaming inside her chest.

His breath was hot on her cheek as he whispered words in her ear, low and harsh. "This is what comes of speaking out of turn, Andra," Ledo rasped. "I want you to watch. I want you to see what your words have done."

She didn't hear the hatch drop open. Suddenly, the rope was taut, and the small black figure that had been her mother fell through. Her eyes closed, and tears began to fall down her cheeks, leaving hot, silent trails on her skin.

"You did this, Andra," Ledo reminded her, his lips nearly brushing her skin as he spoke. His hand closed tightly around her forearm, his soft nobleman's hands somehow rough on her skin. "You are the one who sentenced her. I want you to remember that, if you dare to speak again."

But Andra knew that she wouldn't. She had spoken a single word, and that word became a death sentence. She wouldn't allow it to happen again.

5

Outlaws

Andra silently scrubbed the floors of Castigo's manor. The other servants around her chatted idly as they pushed the soap and water around the stone floors. They didn't try to include her in their conversation. They knew she wouldn't speak to them. She hadn't spoken for over a year, since the day her mother was hanged.

They said she'd attacked the Chief Judge's daughter. "So unlike Elysea," the others had muttered when they thought Andra wasn't listening. "She was always so careful, so obedient."

She was, Andra thought, *but her daughter was not.*

As Andra scrubbed, she allowed her mind to drift to Talias, as it often did. She imagined once more that he came to rescue her, carrying her away from this place to a faraway village. She clung to that dream like a drowning woman, clutching the single piece of driftwood in the raging sea. She lived in that dream, far from thoughts of her mother, far from Ledo.

Familiar footsteps echoed down the corridor. Andra didn't look up at their approach. She knew whom they belonged to and what they were coming for. The chattering around her stopped, as did the sound of the brushes on the stone. Only the gentle *swish swish* of Andra's brush remained as the footsteps drew to a halt beside where the servants scrubbed.

"Andra," Ledo's sharp voice said.

She fell still, the brush going silent. Without further command, she stood and dropped her brush in the bucket beside her. The metallic *clang* echoed through the foyer. Ledo's hand firmly seized the back of her neck and began to steer her down the hall, soap suds still clinging to her arms and legs.

Andra felt the pitying gazes of the other women on her back as they watched her go. As she rounded a corner, she heard the gentle swishing sound of the women returning to their work. It was all a part of the routine.

Andra closed Ledo's bedroom door behind her, not looking back at his form asleep on the tousled bed. Her slippered feet made no sound on the stone floors as she walked through the dark corridors, wandering without purpose, her mind as numb and empty as it had been since the day her mother died—since the day she sentenced her mother to death.

She didn't know how long she wandered before the silence of the sleeping manor was shattered. A scream echoed from another hall, then the sound of footsteps racing down the corridor. Andra froze, suddenly alert and on edge. Another scream, a crash, a door banging. A kitchen maid appeared, running at full speed down the hall, her skirts flying around her. She grabbed Andra by the arm, giving her a rough shake as she looked down at her with wild, terror-filled eyes.

"What are you doing?" she asked sharply. "Run! There are murderers in the manor!"

The kitchen maid ran on, leaving Andra behind. The girl paused briefly, her mind turning. Then she bolted, heading toward the dungeons. Those would be safe. Whoever was here, whatever their reasons, there would be no reason for them to go into the dungeons. If she could just get to the dungeons, then— With a bone-jarring crash that made her ears ring, Andra collided with a solid body.

She was thrown to the stone floor with a force that sent the air rushing from her lungs. She shook her head, trying to clear her vision, and looked up at the dark form above her. He held a shining red blade in his hand, dripping blood onto the floor. She felt the urge to scream, but couldn't seem to make the muscles of her throat cooperate. It was as if she had forgotten how to make the sound at all. He gazed at her with narrowed eyes, as if deciding what he should do with her. Andra braced herself for the piercing pain of steel.

The shouts and metallic footsteps of approaching soldiers made the man look away from her, toward the source of the noise. He glanced back down at her frantically, then seized her by the hand and yanked her to her feet.

"If you scream," he growled, "I will kill you."

Of course, he couldn't know that there was no danger of that. Still, Andra nodded in understanding. Holding her tightly by the wrist, the man raced down another empty corridor and up a flight of stairs. Andra stumbled after him as he dragged her through an empty guest room, where a window stood open to the cool night air.

He shoved her toward it. "Go," he ordered quietly. Andra stared at him in surprise. "Go!" he snapped. The sound of soldiers was drawing nearer.

Andra peered out the window. Thick vines grew on the wall below her, forming a natural ladder. At the base of it, two men were gazing upward, obviously waiting for their third companion. The man in the room pushed her again, and she swung her legs over the window ledge, shimmying down the ladder easily. The moment her feet touched the grass, the two men grabbed her by the arms, making sure that she didn't run. The third man was beside them in moments, and soon they were running away from the large palace. They darted behind a building that backed up against the city wall.

"Climb," the first man ordered her, pointing toward the roof of the house.

She paused, uncertain what to do. But the three armed men stood behind her, their shadowed forms filling her with fear. With nowhere else to go, Andra stepped onto a barrel beside the house and leapt toward the wall, using it to push off and get herself high enough to land on the roof of the house. The three men were close behind her. The other two gave her looks of surprise, but the first remained unimpressed. He grabbed her by the arm and dragged her after him as he jumped from the rooftop to the top of the wall, then down nearly twenty feet to the grass below. He released her on impact, and they both rolled into their landing—he springing back up to his feet immediately, Andra tumbling and landing on her backside.

The other men landed on the grass as well, and Andra noticed the three horses tethered to a nearby tree. The animals snorted and stamped their feet as the four figures raced toward them, Andra still being dragged along by the man with the blood-covered sword.

As they reached the animals, the man holding her wrist turned to one of his companions. "Colmen, hold on to her for a second," he said brusquely, giving her a small push in his direction. One of the other men placed a gentle but firm hand on her shoulder as the first swung up into the saddle. "Pass her up to me."

"Pardon me, miss," the one called Colmen said, putting his hands on her waist and lifting her upward.

The first man received her, pulling her into the saddle so that she was sitting sideways in front of him. Despite her fear of him, her fear of falling off and being trampled by the impatient animal beneath her was greater, and she held on to the man tightly.

"Let's go," he ordered sharply.

The three men kicked their horses forward, and the animals immediately stretched their strides into an earth-eating gallop. Andra clung tighter to the stranger as she watched the earth fly away beneath her, and she quickly clamped her eyes shut to block out the dizzying sight. The man held on to the reins with only one hand, the other wrapped firmly around her waist.

They raced on for what seemed like hours to Andra. At last, they slowed their heaving horses to a brisk walk, and she ventured to open her eyes again. She could hardly see a thing. They had entered the woods, and the slim moon in the sky could hardly pierce the thick canopy of the treetops. She could hear the heavy breathing of the horse beneath her, as well as the two behind her. One of the horses moved forward until she could see the dark shape of another horse and rider beside her.

"What were you thinking, Kael?" the rider snapped. "Why did you take her?" As Andra's eyes adjusted to the darkness of the forest, she began to make out the features of her three abductors.

"She saw me, Alik," the man holding her responded. She turned her head so that she could see the face of the man who still held her firmly in the saddle. His black hair was tousled from the frantic ride, his square jaw clenched in agitation. The sharp angle of his cheekbones cast shadows on his face in the dim light, making him look ominous and threatening. "What was I supposed to do? Leave her behind and let her identify me to the soldiers?"

"You could have killed her," Alik growled angrily. Andra turned sharply toward the man, suddenly much more wary of him than the one whose horse she shared. He was thick of build, with a short beard and close-cropped hair. An axe glinted at his waist.

"You think you would have been able to kill an innocent

bystander?" Kael shot back. "It's not as simple as you might think, Alik."

"I would do what's necessary to further our cause. You just created a very serious complication. One that endangers the lives of people we care about!"

"Now, now, gentlemen," Colmen said calmly from Andra's other side. "Let's not frighten the poor girl with talk of killing her. The fact is that Kael decided to spare her, and so she shall travel with us until Kael decides otherwise."

Alik grumbled under his breath and trotted his horse forward, taking the lead as they wound their way through the dark woods. Colmen remained silently riding beside them. Andra studied him in the shifting light between the trees. His black hair was cut short, exposing a perfectly pointed ear—an elf. He caught her scrutinizing him, but when he looked at her, it was with a gentle, reassuring smile.

"My name is Colmen," he said kindly, apparently not bothered by her studying gaze. "And you are?"

Andra blinked at him, chewing the inside of her lip. A part of her wanted to respond; there was something kind about his face, a friendliness in his voice that she had not heard in a long, long time. But her voice was gone, and she did not know how to bring it back.

"Is she deaf?" the elf asked, looking at Kael.

"Of course not," he answered in irritation. "She's understood every command I've given her since I ran into her in the manor."

"Maybe she's just mute, then," Colmen pondered aloud. "Can you speak?" he asked her.

Andra made no response. Could she? She felt that she *must* still have the ability in her. One couldn't simply forget how to speak, could they? And yet, words still fled from her, still afraid of what horrors they could bring.

Apparently the elf decided to let the issue rest, because he asked no more questions. The forest lapsed into a silence punctured only by the soft treading of horses' hooves and the occasional snort. Andra felt fatigue seizing her body. The warm breeze and the rich scent of earth were foreign to her, but they calmed her somehow. The steady rhythm of the horse beneath her began to feel like a rocking chair, and Andra soon found herself drifting into sleep.

6

Watching and Waiting

When she awoke, Andra was lying on a blanket on the hard earth, sunlight warming her bare legs. She sat up, startled and confused, and looked around. In front of her, a low fire was sputtering into ash. The three horses grazed freely in the clearing, restrained by neither tack nor harness. On either side of her, a man lay sprawled out on another blanket. The third man, Kael, was nowhere in sight.

Andra looked down at her own body. She was not bound. Glancing at the men beside her, she quietly stood and slunk toward the edge of the woods. She paused to look at the horses. It would be faster to take one of them, but she had absolutely no idea how to ride. On foot, she started for the woods.

"Where do you think you're going?" a voice asked quietly.

She jumped and spun around to see Kael standing at the edge of the trees, watching her with narrowed eyes. Andra darted for the other side of the clearing.

"Stop!" Kael shouted, and she heard his footsteps racing after her.

Two more voices joined Kael's as Colmen and Alik awoke,

roused by their leader's shouts. Andra glanced over her shoulder. They were close. Finally reaching the edge of the clearing, Andra jumped for the lowest branch of the nearest tree. She grasped it with both hands and swung herself upward to the next branch, then the next, until she was several feet above their heads. When she was certain she was out of their reach, she stopped and looked back down at them.

The three men gazed up at her with varying expressions on their faces. Alik looked angry and irritated, Colmen looked amused, and Kael watched her blankly, clearly still unimpressed.

"She's a spry one, isn't she?" Colmen chuckled, his pale violet eyes crinkling with his smile.

"I told you to watch her," Kael grumbled.

Colmen shrugged. "So I fell asleep. No harm done."

"Fine, you have fun sitting here until she comes down. Alik and I are going to hunt."

"Have fun," Colmen answered lightly, waving them off.

The other two men shook their heads and disappeared into the woods on the opposite edge of the clearing. Colmen sat at the base of the tree and gazed up into its branches. Andra peered down at him around the large branch she sat on. Was he really going to sit there and wait for her to come down?

"Tell me," he said, leaning back on his hands, "where exactly were you planning on running?"

Andra frowned down at him and stood on the branch, looking to either side of the tree. She hadn't paid much attention when she darted up it, but now she realized that there were no other trees within jumping distance. She was truly treed like an animal.

Colmen continued his one-sided conversation. "I hate to point it out, but you are quite obviously under a contract of servitude. It's hard to run away with those enchanted collars they make you wear. Were you really planning on running back to the people who have turned you into a near slave?"

Andra scowled and shook her head at the absurd question.

"Sorry, what was that?" Colmen asked, tilting his head to one side and squinting up through the leaves of the tree. "I can't really see you all the way up there. You'll have to come down a bit."

She paused, studying him carefully. But she was still far from his reach. Slipping down a few branches, she settled herself where she could see him more clearly.

"That's better," he said with a smile. "So you were going to run away, then? A little girl all by herself in the woods could get hurt. Do you even know where we are?"

Andra paused, glancing around. Reluctantly, she shook her head again.

"Then that's not much of a plan, is it," Colmen pointed out. "How would you know where to go? Do you even have a place that you can go?"

Andra didn't reply, looking down at the bracelet on her wrist. There was only one place—only one person—that she knew she could run to.

"So why don't you speak?" Colmen asked, apparently unperturbed by her lack of reply. "I believe you can."

Andra just shifted to a more comfortable position on her branch. They were quiet for a long moment and Andra studied the tree she sat in. She ran her fingers across the rough patterns in the bark, touched the soft, vibrant green leaves beside her. Colmen watched her quietly.

Andra ran her thumb along a deep groove in the tree branch, suddenly aware of a quiet, humming energy beneath her. She knew that the unmoving tree was very much awake and aware of her presence. She looked back down at Colmen as he moved toward the camp. Quickly, hoping to reach the ground before he returned, Andra slipped down several more branches. But he merely retrieved something from a rough brown pack and returned to the base of the tree. She stopped her descent, only eight feet above the ground.

"Now, you weren't trying to slip away when my back was turned, were you?" he asked, his voice more playful than accusing.

Colmen sat on the ground again, holding out a small instrument for her to see. It was a hand-carved flute, much like the one her father had taught her to play. After his death, his belongings were destroyed, including the flute. Andra stared at the instrument longingly.

"You like music?" Colmen asked.

Andra nodded. He put the flute to his lips, bent his head of black hair, and began to play a bright, lilting tune that wove its way through the trees. She thought she felt the tree beneath her tremble with delight. The music danced through Andra's mind, conjuring up a desire to dance through the clearing. A small smile pulled up the corners of her lips, and she slipped down another branch to be closer to the music.

Colmen stopped playing and looked up at her, grinning. "Ah, the lady smiles," he said joyfully. Andra pointed at the flute. "You want me to play some more?" he asked. She nodded. Obligingly, he lifted the flute again, closed his amethyst eyes, and played another song, this one slower and more enchanting. Andra felt as if she knew the tune, though she was not sure how she could, and she slipped down yet another branch, now well within Colmen's reach if he stood.

But he didn't. When he stopped playing, Andra pointed at the flute again, but he shook his head. "I'd rather not," he said. "Those are the only two songs I can play well." Andra frowned in disappointment. Still sitting, he held the flute out toward her. "Do you know how to play?" he asked.

Andra paused, then nodded slowly.

"Here," he said, still holding it out as he sat on the grass. "You play for me now."

Andra held out her hand for the flute, but he remained seated and shook his head once more.

"I don't want my flute up in that tree. You might drop it. Come down here."

She felt her mouth quirk slightly in amusement. He was certainly charming, but not as clever as he thought. Colmen continued to hold out the flute, his kind face patient. Finally, knowing she had no way of escaping anyway, she slipped down the last few branches and landed beside him. He made no move to restrain her, but handed her the flute and patted the ground beside him.

"Have a seat," he said. "Let's hear a tune."

Andra sat on the grass beside him and put the wooden instrument to her lips. She placed her fingers carefully over the holes and blew into the opening, producing a soft and pure note. The instrument was beautifully crafted, and Andra felt a thrill at the perfect sound it made at her bidding. She began to coax a song her father had taught her out of the instrument, closing her eyes in simple happiness as she played.

Her song was interrupted by the sound of footsteps. She opened her eyes and looked up as Kael and Alik approached, each carrying several rabbits and a basket of roots and berries.

"I see you got her to come down from the tree," Alik muttered, dropping his load beside the dwindling fire. In the sunlight, his short hair and beard burned a deep red.

"She likes music," Colmen said, "and she's quite good at the flute."

"Did you get a name from her yet?" Kael asked.

Colmen shook his head. "She still won't speak, but I've gotten a few nods and headshakes from her, which is progress I suppose." He pushed himself up off the grass and brushed off his trousers. "Come on," he said, holding out a hand to pull her to her feet.

Andra took the offered hand, standing and giving Colmen back his flute. The three of them moved toward the fire, and Andra no-

ticed for the first time that Kael held several papers wadded in his
fist. Colmen seemed to notice as well.

"What do you have there?" he asked, nodding at the group's
leader.

"Kindling," Kael grumbled roughly, tossing the papers into
the fire.

"Ah," the elf answered, as if the word were sufficient explanation.

Andra tilted her head, squinting into the flames as the crumpled papers began to catch fire. One of them had unfurled enough
to show her a rough sketch of a square-jawed man with black hair
and flat, dead eyes. She looked up at Kael, then back at the paper,
realizing what it must be—a bounty poster. Though it wasn't a perfect likeness, it was close enough for Andra to know it was meant
to be Kael.

A pile of wood landed atop the smoldering coals and burning
papers, and Andra jumped in surprise, looking up to see Alik's hard
gaze on her. She met his eyes, trying to remain calm as he studied
her, then with a huff, he turned away again.

Colmen appeared at her side, setting a black pot over the wood.
"Don't worry about Alik," he whispered conspiratorially. "He's not
nearly so rough as he acts."

Andra smiled, still surprised that this elf could so easily coax
such a reaction from her. She shouldn't be so quick to trust him.
Water suddenly appeared from the air around her, breaking her
from her thoughts. She watched, wide eyed, as the droplets swirled
together into a liquid orb, then drifted into the waiting pot, landing with a quiet splash. Flames immediately roared up around the
pot, the smoldering embers springing to life again.

She heard the elf laugh, a light and musical sound, and she
looked at him.

"Never seen magic before?" he asked.

Andra shook her head. She had, of course, seen a few acts of
magic occasionally—it was bound to happen when you served in

a Hall filled with Riders in training—but they were rare occasions. She had certainly never seen such an open display of elven magic before.

"You're not supposed to do magic in front of contract servants," Kael said gruffly, his eyes not leaving the bow he was restringing.

"Truly?" Colmen asked, sounding surprised.

"The judges are afraid they'll learn," the young man went on. "Many have elf blood, so elven magic may be within their reach. And there is always the possibility of a human with the ability to be a sorcerer. The last thing the judges want is for an indentured servant to arm himself with a few spells he overheard and learn how to fight back. You can't force a magic-wielder into many things, much less a contract of servitude that's little better than slavery."

There was a roughness in the man's voice that surprised her. Kael almost sounded angry about the labor contracts. But why? Contract labor had been an initiative started by the first Chief Judge to provide work and opportunities to the poor. Work for a given number of years, and receive a home and land when you had served your time. It was a chance many had taken over the centuries, including Andra's father—though of course, his contract had been extended many times, and passed on to Andra and her mother after his execution.

Alik leaned over the now boiling pot. "It's ready," he said, ending their conversation.

The men immediately produced bowls and scooped themselves out large helpings of the concoction. Andra stared at the fire, trying not to smell the aroma of stewed meat and vegetables. Despite the elf's kindness, she knew she was a prisoner, and she didn't expect to receive a portion until they had eaten their fill—if she received one at all. A wooden bowl filled with a steaming liquid abruptly appeared before her downcast gaze. She looked up in surprise.

Kael was standing before her, silently holding a bowl toward her. She stared at him in confusion. Kael rolled his eyes and pushed the bowl into her hands.

"Just take it," he said. "It's not going to bite you."

Andra took the bowl, watching him as he returned to the fire and sat with his companions. Then she slipped away, several feet from the fire, and settled herself on a rock with her back to them.

She could feel their gazes on her back, and she pretended not to listen, acting like the dumb and docile servant she was trained to be. "Shall we discuss the horrendous failure of last night?" Colmen asked. His tone was cheerful, but she detected a hint of bitterness at the edges of his voice.

Someone let out a soft growl—Alik, she assumed.

"I didn't expect him to be awake and armed," she heard Kael reply. "He was supposed to be asleep, easy to subdue without magic. He wasn't supposed to fight us."

"That filthy jackal nearly got his knife in me," Alik barked. Then, in a lower voice, "If you hadn't drawn your sword when you did, Kael . . ." The gruff man let out a huff of frustration. "You should've just used your magic from the moment we entered that room."

"You know I couldn't, Alik," Kael replied, his tone impatient. "Castigo has halfbloods and sorcerers amid his soldiers. They could have sensed me."

"Then we should've taken Colmen in with us!"

"I needed to keep watch," the elf answered with a sigh. "If I hadn't been doing that, you two never would've known those guards were coming."

"I just don't understand it!" Alik barked. "Astrum came to Bellris—the Seer himself!—and told us that going to the Chief Judge's manor would be the key to winning this rebellion."

"Well, technically, he said that retrieving the *power* that Ledo held was the key," Colmen interjected. "And yet, here we are . . . rather Ledo-less, and quite powerless."

"We can talk about this all day," Kael snapped. "It doesn't change the fact that Ledo is now dead, and we have nothing to force Castigo's hand."

Andra stiffened, her bowl resting in her lap. Ledo was dead. . . . She heard Kael swear softly; then he called out, "Girl!"

She turned quickly toward him, trying to look calm, as if she had not heard anything. His gaze was sharp on her, and she noticed for the first time that his eyes were a pure gray color, like iron or stone, hard and unyielding.

"You heard us, didn't you."

She thought of denying it, but she could see in his expression that he already knew the truth. So she nodded once, her hands clasping the bowl in her lap tightly.

Kael swore again, running one hand across his jaw. Andra met his gaze, trying to keep her hands from shaking. He had spared her before. But would he do it again, now that she knew what they'd done? Finally, the young man sighed.

"She'll have to come all the way to Bellris with us," he said decisively.

"To Bellris?" Alik shouted, standing so quickly that his half-eaten stew fell to the grass.

"She knows what we've done, Alik," Kael replied in a hard, commanding voice. "Right now, she's the only person outside the rebellion who knows, and we can't let her tell anyone else."

"So do what you should have done last night!" the bearded man roared.

Kael stood as well, meeting the larger man's eyes with the confidence of an army general. "I've made my decision, Alik. I won't play executioner to an innocent girl! She is coming with us. That's final!"

"Both of you, shut up!" Colmen cut in.

The two men turned angry eyes on the elf, but he raised one finger to his pointed ear and another to his lips. Their expressions immediately became attentive, and Andra found herself listening as well. At first, she heard nothing. Then, distantly, she heard the snort of a horse. It came from somewhere in the woods.

She turned toward the sound, her senses piqued, her body tingling in anticipation. Someone was there. Something in her mind screamed it at her, the same sense that always knew when Ledo approached. There were men in the woods, and they were watching them.

7

The Arrow

Her abductors seemed to sense the watchers as well. From the corner of her eye, Andra saw them slowly reaching for their weapons. Then, with a burst of noise and motion, a cluster of men streamed from between the trees. They wore no armor, but Andra saw the familiar crest of the judges, a crossed sword and olive branch, emblazoned on their tunics—scouts, likely searching for the men who had murdered the heir to the judgment seat.

Andra found herself rooted to where she stood, watching in shock as the soldiers charged at the three men by the fire. Kael raised a black-gloved hand, and the flames beneath the black pot roared high, then surged at the men like a burning wave. Three of them were caught in the flames and dropped to the grass, shrieking in pain.

Colmen seized a sword from the grass and Alik retrieved his axe just in time to deflect the swing of a sword. Kael leapt over the fire, unsheathing his sword and bringing it down in a single motion, an arc of red metal cutting through the air. Andra realized then that the red color of his blade she'd noticed the night before had not been entirely from blood, as she'd assumed. Kael's red sword met the gray steel of the soldier's blade with a crash. Andra stared at the battle roiling before her as if it were distant, her mind surprisingly numb to the chaos mere feet away from her.

Suddenly, a sword came swinging toward her. Andra reacted before she could even form the thought to do so. She dropped to the grass and rolled away from the attacker, springing quickly back to her feet and turning her eyes on the soldier. He was charging at her again, and Andra realized with a shock how defenseless she truly was in her thin wool dress and shabby slippers.

There was a sudden roar of wind, and the man charging her tumbled to the side in a flurry of air. She looked toward the source of the magic and saw Kael hurrying toward her. Alik and Colmen had already mounted their horses and were charging away into the woods. Kael seized her arm and turned to pull her toward his tethered, rearing horse as two soldiers fell upon them.

He shoved Andra back and crossed his arms above his head. The soldiers' swords seemed to strike a wall just inches above Kael's arms, and they jumped backward again. There was movement at the corner of her vision, and Andra turned her head toward the abandoned camp, strewn with the men's belongings. One of the soldiers who had been injured in the battle was on his feet again, bow raised, arrow already on the string.

Almost as soon as her eyes had found him, the man released the arrow, and it streaked toward Kael, who faced the two sword-wielding men before him. Andra placed a hand on Kael's back, pushing him a single step forward as her other hand swung outward. She felt a stinging sensation on her palm; then her fingers snapped closed around the wooden shaft of the arrow.

Kael turned toward her, rage burning in his eyes. His gaze fell on the arrow in her hand, then darted toward the archer several yards away. And then the two soldiers were upon him again. He beat back their attacks for a moment, then seemed to gather himself and shoved his hands forward, his palms directed at the earth. Grass and soil rose upward, encapsulating the soldiers' legs to their waists. They shouted and struggled, but were unable to break free.

Kael turned sharply toward the archer, but the man was fleeing into the woods, and some of his wounded companions were beginning to struggle to their feet again. Without a word, Kael grasped Andra by the arm and dragged her toward his frightened mount. He released her briefly to cut the horse's tether with his red blade, then leapt expertly into the saddle. Leaning down from the horse's back, he seized her arm again and yanked her unceremoniously up in front of him. She didn't fight him, and he lifted her easily into the saddle before slapping his heels to the horse's flank and sending it charging into the woods.

Andra held on breathlessly as the air tore at her face and stung her eyes, trees rushing past, terrifyingly close. They charged on for several minutes, Andra's heart pounding, wondering if they were being followed. Then Kael pulled back on the reins, slowing the horse to a jarring trot, then to a brisk walk.

"Steady," Kael said, leaning around Andra to pet the animal's foaming neck. "Steady, boy. You did well. Are you hurt?"

It took Andra a moment to realize the question was directed at her. She swallowed hard, then shook her head, her heart still racing in her throat.

"Good," he said. "Alik and Colmen should be here any moment."

The words had hardly left his lips before Andra felt someone approaching, like the breath of a breeze on her mind. She turned her head toward where she sensed the presence, and a moment later, Alik and Colmen appeared, their horses blowing hard from their mad dash. They fell into stride alongside Kael, following a worn track through the trees.

"Well, that was simply delightful," Colmen said with a sigh.

"Are either of you injured?" Kael asked in a brisk tone that was all business.

Alik shook his head. "Nothing serious. I took an arrow to the shoulder as we were fleeing, but Colmen had time to Heal me before you caught up to us."

"Where'd you find the arrow, darling?"

Andra looked up to find that Colmen was looking at her, an interested expression on his narrow face. She dropped her gaze to her hand to find that it was still clutched around the arrow.

"She caught it," Kael answered slowly, as if he knew that the words would be difficult to believe. "An archer fired it at me, and the girl caught it from the air before it reached me."

The elf let out a sharp, disbelieving laugh. Then, seeing the expression on Kael's face, his brow immediately furrowed. "You're serious? How is that even possible? I don't even know of any full blooded elves who can manage that."

"I haven't a clue," Kael replied.

Colmen held out his hand, riding close beside them. "May I?" he asked politely.

Andra held the arrow out to him, and he took it from her hand. He looked down at the weapon, as if it held the answer to his earlier questions. After a moment, he asked, "Whose blood?"

Kael looked over at him with a frown. "What?"

"You said it didn't hit you," Colmen explained, holding the arrow up for Kael to see. "But the shaft is covered in blood."

Andra saw that he was right. Fresh, wet blood painted the wooden shaft, from arrowhead to fletching. She looked down at her own hand and realized abruptly that a deep cut ran across the palm, and blood ran down her fingers.

"You said you weren't hurt!" Kael snapped, startling her with the ferocity in his voice.

He pulled the horse to a halt and grabbed her hand. She flinched reflexively, expecting his touch to be as rough as his tone. But his hands were surprisingly gentle as he spread open the injured hand, examining it. She winced as the wound flexed from the movement, and wondered how she hadn't felt the pain before.

"It's deep," Kael muttered, sounding like he was talking to himself. "I can Heal it well enough, but it will scar without a proper Healer who knows what they're doing."

Without waiting for any sort of response, he pressed his gloved palm over hers. His fingers, which were bare, slid between her own as if in a gesture of tenderness. Andra felt a sudden tingling in her hand, as when she slept on top of it in the night, and the skin slowly came back to life. She drew in a sharp breath at the sensation, but didn't try to pull her hand away. The tingling lasted only for a moment longer; then Kael removed her hand from his.

He wiped the remaining blood away with his thumbs and lifted her hand to the level of his eyes, inspecting his handiwork. Andra looked as well. A raised, white scar now ran from the base of her little finger to the flesh inside her thumb. She stared at the scar, dumbfounded. She had known that magic could Heal, but she had never seen it for herself.

"Don't lie to me next time I ask if you're injured," he said gruffly, releasing her hand.

She looked up at him, her brow furrowed, her lips parting to tell him she hadn't meant to lie. But her voice still seemed to be hiding somewhere inside her, and the words never came. She turned away and looked down at the drying blood on her hand.

"We're going to need new supplies," Alik said as the men kicked their three horses into motion again. "We left half our things in that camp."

"We'll be passing near Vegrandis in a few days," Kael replied with a sharp nod, making it clear he'd already considered this. "I'll go meet with the rebel supporters there and see what they can spare while you set up camp."

"You'll need to be careful," Colmen remarked. "Those scouts saw your face, Kael. They'll be looking for you."

Kael turned his steel eyes on the elf. "Everyone's looking for me, Colmen," he answered flatly. "That's never going to change."

Eithne

They continued traveling through the nights and camping during the day, eating from what little supplies they carried with them as they rode. Andra was surprised at how readily Kael shared his canteen and his rations with her, but she accepted them gratefully. The long hours in the saddle were entirely unfamiliar to her, and they left her with a constant feeling of hunger and exhaustion.

On the third day, when they at last stopped to make camp at sunrise, Kael offered his hand and helped Andra down from the saddle, then dropped the small pack he carried to the grass beside her. He looked at the two men, who were dismounting and unsaddling their horses.

"Keep an eye on the girl," he told them. "I'll be back by midday."

Alik and Colmen nodded in understanding; then Kael turned and trotted his horse back through the trees. Andra watched him go, then looked toward the two remaining men. Colmen was laying a traveling cloak on the ground as if it were a blanket, obviously intent on getting some sleep.

"Girl."

Andra looked up at Alik. The man reached into his belt and pulled out a long hunting knife. Andra stiffened as he stepped toward her with it, but then he turned the blade in his hand, holding the hilt out to her. "You should have some sort of weapon," he said gruffly. "Traveling with us is dangerous. You need to be able to protect yourself."

Andra hesitated, eyeing the knife. It was forbidden for indentured workers to carry any sort of weapon. She knew all too well what the sentence was for carrying a knife—death. Her mind flashed briefly back to her father, watching him hide the dagger under his brown wool tunic.

"What are you doing?" she'd asked him frantically.

"Protecting my family," he'd answered, his pale green eyes, identical to hers, burning with anger. "I should have every right to defend myself and those I love. And if that blasted boy hurts you again, I'll be certain that someone finally teaches him a lesson."

"Well, are you going to take it or not?" Alik asked irritably.

Andra blinked, and her hand quickly rose and closed around the hilt of the dagger. *I should have every right to defend myself,* her father's voice repeated in her mind. She took the knife from Alik's large hand, then looked up at him. His brown eyes were on her, intense and tinged with uncertainty, as if he already regretted giving her the weapon. Andra nodded at him in gratitude, and he returned the gesture, then turned and strode over to a large stone, where he sat and settled his axe across his knees.

"Kael has a cloak in that pack there," Alik said, nodding at the bag the man had left. "You can use it to get some rest."

Andra hesitated, eyeing the pack. She was wary of digging into the gray-eyed man's things. She'd been with him for only a few days, and she could already see that his temper was quick and hot. Finally, she bent and untied the traveling cloak from around the bundle.

As she prepared to lie out on the grass, Alik's voice called quietly, "Girl."

She looked up at him, but he was not looking at her. He continued to stare out into the woods, as if he were speaking to the trees.

"What I said before . . . I didn't want to kill you. Not really. I'm just . . . trying to protect someone. That's all."

He glanced at her, and she nodded in understanding, realizing that she and the big, gruff man had something in common—they were both afraid, and trying hard not to let it show.

Andra lay on the grass and stretched the cloak out over her, pulling it up to her nose. She stayed there for several minutes, listening to the sounds of the forest waking up to the day. She wondered briefly if she could escape while Kael was away, if she could find her way back to the Hall and to Talias. But exhaustion quickly took hold of her, and the thoughts were snuffed out by deep slumber.

She dreamed about her parents. She was a child, playing in the servants' quarters with her mother. Her father stepped through the front door with a smile on his face, and he scooped her into his arms. She giggled and pulled at the lock around his neck, as she had done so often as a child, when it was still new and interesting, before she'd been given her own.

Then suddenly, the lock turned into a rope in her hands, and she was a child no longer. She stood holding the knot of a noose, and it was around her mother's neck. Her mother looked at her with her patient, kind eyes. "Be good. Be safe," her gentle voice whispered in Andra's mind.

And then her mother was falling, and Andra was screaming, afraid to seize the rope and stop the fall, afraid to let her mother tumble into the great nothingness below. She continued to scream in her mind, helpless as the rope slid through her useless fingers.

"Girl," a quiet voice said. "Girl, come on. Wake up."

Andra's eyes flew open with a gasp and she sat bolt upright. Her head slammed into something above her and she heard someone groan in pain, then curse. She blinked, looking around her, disoriented. Her gaze fell on Kael, who had a hand pressed to his forehead. He gave her an agitated look as he rubbed at the spot where their heads had collided.

Then he sat forward again, frowning as he studied her face. "I think you were having a nightmare. You were whimpering and thrashing around in your sleep."

Andra hugged her knees to her chest, trying to hide the trembling in her limbs from those searching eyes. Kael stared at her silently for a moment, then sighed and shook his head.

"I really wish you would talk," he muttered. "It would make things much easier." He sat back on his heels and pushed a hand through his shaggy black hair. His gray eyes fell on her again, and she thought that perhaps their color was not so hard as iron. Perhaps they were the color of rain clouds. He looked down at the grass before she could decide. His voice was low and gruff as he spoke again. "If it was about us—the nightmare, I mean—you don't have anything to worry about. We won't hurt you. You're safe with us."

With that, he turned his back to her and moved to the stone that Alik was occupying when she'd fallen asleep, laying his red sword across his knees. The burly man and the elf slept on a new pair of blankets nearby.

"I brought you back some clothes," Kael added without looking back at her. "They're over there." He gestured at a traveling pack that rested close to where she'd been sleeping. "You should get changed. The things you're wearing won't last long with the traveling we have to do."

Intrigued, Andra moved to the pack and pulled it open. Inside, she found a pair of trousers, a deep green tunic, a rough gray tunic, and a pair of leather boots. Andra pulled them out one by one, studying each in amazement. For as long as she could remember, she'd worn only the brown wool of an indentured worker.

She glanced up at Kael once, ensuring he wasn't looking in her direction, then turned her back to him and quietly pulled her dress over her head. She reached for a pair of trousers, holding them up to her bare legs, gauging their size.

Before she could even step into the trousers, she felt a firm hand grasp her shoulder. She went rigid, her body bracing itself for the rough hands and hungry mouth. But the voice that spoke from behind her was not Ledo's.

"What did they do to you?" Kael asked, his voice laced with anger.

Andra pulled away from his grasp, holding the trousers to her chest and staring at him with wide, terrified eyes.

"Will you calm down?" he snapped angrily. "I'm not going to hurt you, I just want to see. Now, stand still."

He grabbed her shoulder once again and turned her around so that he could see her back. She knew what he must see, what had caught his attention and ignited his anger. Her skin was crisscrossed with scars, from her shoulders to the small of her back. They had been a part of her for so long, she rarely thought of them.

Kael sighed and turned her around so that she faced him. Andra stared at him in wide-eyed uncertainty. He gently removed the trousers from her hand so that she was standing before him in nothing but her underclothes. She held her breath, waiting for the demanding touch she knew so well. But it didn't come.

Kael raised her arms, inspecting the fading bruises on her wrists and upper arms, her stomach and waist, the red marks on her collarbone. He scowled as he saw the bruises on her thighs, a sharp curse hissing from between his teeth.

Andra continued to stare silently, still unsure of what Kael intended. He lifted his gaze to her frightened eyes, then quickly handed back the trousers he had taken from her.

"Here," he muttered.

He turned away again, returning to his post without another word. Andra quickly pulled on the clothes, slipped her feet into the boots, then stood looking at Kael's still back. Cautiously, she stepped up behind him, then sat a few feet away in the grass.

He glanced at her from the corner of his eye, then looked down at his sword, turning it over and over in his hand. Andra watched the red blade shimmering in the sun. Its hilt was onyx black and embedded with a large ruby at the base. Kael ran his hand along its length, shining it with the soft leather of the short riding gloves he never seemed to remove.

He looked up at her again. "I . . . apologize," he said quietly. "I merely looked back to see if you were still there. You're always so quiet. When I saw the scars I . . ." He clenched his jaw. "I'm sorry I frightened you."

He went silent, staring at the trees around them. Andra watched him for a moment, considering his words. Then, cautiously, she touched his hand, drawing his gaze back to her. She gave a small, cautious smile, then dipped her head once in an understanding nod. For half a breath, he seemed to study her, then he nodded in return, and she thought she saw him nearly smile as he turned back to his watch.

⋙◆⋘

The small band continued traveling, the same plodding of horses each night, the same small camp each day. A week into their journey, Kael was seated by the fire, drumming his fingers against his leg and glancing repeatedly at the sky. Andra watched him from a distance, wary of his suddenly foul mood.

"Don't worry about him, darling," Colmen said quietly from where he sat beside her, cleaning his bow. "He's just eager to see Eithne."

"I don't think we should wait for nightfall to move out," Kael announced, looking up at the sky again. "The sooner we can get to her, the better. I'm starting to worry."

Alik gave a short chuckle. "I pity any man who thinks he can give battle to Eithne."

"Nonetheless," Kael said decisively, pushing himself to his feet, "we're moving out in an hour, so prepare yourselves."

Colmen and Alik both sighed, but obediently rose as well, beginning to break camp. Who was Eithne? And why was Kael so eager to reach her? Clearly she was important to him. He couldn't have been more than twenty, younger than most married men, but it was possible that this Eithne was his wife. If not that, possibly a mother or sister. He seemed deeply concerned about her well-being.

The sun had hardly passed its peak in the sky when they rode out. They had rested for only six hours after the previous night's twelve-hour ride. Kael believed that they could reach wherever Eithne was by nightfall if they kept a good pace. In her new trousers, Andra sat easily astride Kael's horse, her hands on the saddle horn. It was much more comfortable than it was when she had been forced to ride in her worker's dress, and she no longer felt that she would fall at any moment. Still, Kael kept one arm loosely about her waist.

They kept up a brisk walk through the woods, breaking into a loping canter when the trees opened up into a clearing. Andra glanced around her, searching for any sign of where they might be. But her single week of experience outside the stone walls of a manor did not offer her many skills in discerning direction.

Their journey continued into the evening. As the bottom of the sun touched the distant horizon, Andra smelled something strange in the wind. She frowned and inhaled deeply. The scent tickled her nose. It smelled like salt. Then she heard a distant sound that she had never heard before, like water from the pump splashing into a wooden pail. The horses stepped out of the woods, and Andra had to shield her eyes. The deep orange of the sinking sun was reflected against an endless span of water. Andra gasped in surprise.

"The ocean," Colmen explained from the horse beside her. "Eithne should be nearby."

Kael jumped down from the horse without bothering to help Andra down and ran toward what, to Andra, appeared to be the edge of the earth itself. As he ran, he shouted, "Eithne! Eithne!"

Then the earth shook, startling Andra and sending her tumbling from the saddle. She clapped her hands over her ears as the earth-shaking roar continued. And yet, somehow, she could tell that there was a great joy in that sound. A massive shape rose between them and the sun, casting a shadow over the cliff. Andra scrambled backward as a towering red dragon rose above the edge of the cliff and landed before them.

Kael ran straight toward the enormous creature, and as the roar ended, Andra could hear him laughing. The dragon gave another short bugle and lowered its head as Kael threw himself at the creature. He wrapped his arms around the great face, laughing still. The dragon gave a joyful thrum deep in its throat, the same kind of sound that Andra had heard Ena make toward her new hatchlings during the Pairing.

Andra stared in amazement. The man who had entered the Chief Judge's manor, who had killed the Chief Judge's heir, who had kidnapped her and threatened her with her life, was a Rider.

And Eithne was neither wife, mother, nor sister. She was his dragon.

Andra shakily stood. A hand landed on her shoulder, and she looked up. "Would you like to meet Eithne?" Colmen asked, smiling down at her.

She blinked at him. After five years in the Hall of Riders, watching dragons train with their partners, she had never approached a dragon before. The indentured workers were kept away from them, just as they were separated from magic.

"It's all right," Colmen continued, pressing her gently forward. "She's very kind."

Cautiously, Andra moved forward. Kael and Eithne were staring into each other's faces, and she knew that they were having one of those mysterious, silent conversations that she had heard of. Though Ena had entered her mind once, she had never actually spoken with another creature's mind. She knew she must have the ability to do so—virtually every human and elf did, as a result of the contract written on the Stone Table of Myli Ondo, and the magic that bound humans, elves, and dragons together. But it was a strange and sacred thing, one of the many forbidden to her, because it was too close to magic.

Eithne focused her great brown eyes on the approaching pair. Kael turned toward them and smiled. It was an unusual expression for the usually stern face, and Andra felt certain now that the color of those eyes was not of iron or stone, but of rain. He motioned Andra forward, and she cautiously took another step toward the dragon. She now stood only six feet from Eithne.

"This is Eithne," Kael said, placing a hand on the scaly nose, "my dragon."

The large brown eyes stared at her for a moment, then turned back toward the Rider. Kael shrugged in response to a silent question. Eithne looked at Andra again, and she suddenly felt a great mind prodding her own. She gasped and slammed the doors around her mind firmly shut. The dragon gave her a startled look, then turned back to her Rider.

Kael frowned and looked over at Andra. "Are you forbidden from speaking to dragons?" he asked her.

She nodded slowly.

"You don't have to worry about that here," he told her. "You can speak to her."

She shook her head firmly.

Kael sighed, showing an unusual amount of patience toward Andra's stubborness. Then he spoke, directing his words at Andra. "Eithne will carry us down to a cave in the cliff. We stay there during the night."

Andra stared in shock. They couldn't possibly be serious. She couldn't ride on a dragon. And yet, Kael was climbing up the dragon's massive foreleg, settling astride the great spine, and reaching a hand down for her. Andra shook her head frantically and started to back away, but Colmen seized her and began pulling her toward Eithne's leg.

She tugged against him, still shaking her head as she tried to turn in the other direction. Colmen sighed and pulled more firmly. Then a pair of strong arms seized her around the waist and carried her forcefully up to the dragon. Alik shoved her up the leg until she was within Kael's reach. Then Kael grasped her arm and pulled her up in front of him.

Andra anxiously tried to scramble away again, but Kael wrapped his arm tightly around her, holding her in place. "Let's go, Eithne. Before she makes a run for it."

The dragon lifted her great wings and beat them against the air, lifting them from the ground. Andra felt a scream build in her throat as she saw the ground pulling away from underneath her, but it came out as only a squeak. Kael tightened his arm around her waist. She grabbed the arm, digging her fingers into it, afraid to actually reach out and touch the dragon beneath her. Eithne tilted one wing and turned back out over the ocean. Andra glanced down briefly, saw the foaming sea churning against the rocky shore, then determinedly closed her eyes to the terrifying scene.

A moment later, the light on the other side of her eyelids disappeared and she felt cool, damp air against her cheeks. Andra opened her eyes to see that Eithne had landed in a large cave in the cliffside. Her large head was turned back toward them, gazing at Andra with one platter-sized eye. Once again, Andra felt the gentle brush of the dragon's thoughts. She could feel the kindness of the presence, and she hesitated briefly, allowing the presence to slowly slip into her mind.

"What is your name?" a tender voice asked in her thoughts.

Andra gasped and resolidified the walls around her thoughts, forcing Eithne's consciousness from her mind. The dragon looked away, and Kael slipped off the dragon's back. He landed on the foreleg and turned back toward where Andra still sat uncomfortably on Eithne's bare, scaly back.

"Well, come on," he said impatiently, holding his arms out toward her.

She grasped his forearms as he seized her by the waist and lowered her down to Eithne's crouched foreleg. He slipped down to the stone floor of the cave and helped her down after him. The dragon returned to her full height and turned back toward the cave entrance. Andra watched as Eithne dropped out of the opening, then rose up toward the cliff top again.

Andra wrapped her arms around herself and gazed uncertainly around her at the massive cavern. There wasn't much to see; there were a few supplies stockpiled in a corner, some cots, and a charred spot in the center of the cave, where a fire had clearly been built in the past. Eithne dropped back into the cave after a few minutes had passed, Alik and Colmen on her back, holding their supplies. The two men slid off the dragon and dropped the packs and bundles on the ground.

Colmen gave a great sigh and stretched happily. "Home at last!" he cried, a large smile on his face.

Andra frowned at him. Home? Kael had mentioned a place called Bellris. But this couldn't be it, could it?

The three men silently unrolled their packs. Colmen dragged dried wood from a corner of the cave and piled it in the center of the charred circle. Then, another spontaneous fire sprang to life, fueled by the elf's magic until it took hold of the wood.

With a low fire glowing, the men tossed blankets onto their cots. Andra watched them for a moment. There were only three cots. Andra moved toward the pile of supplies, searching for her blanket to lay in a corner. She found her bundle with her spare clothes, but no blanket.

"Girl," Kael said shortly. Andra looked up at him. He was holding a folded blanket under one arm and pointing back over his shoulder to where a blanket covered the third, unoccupied cot. "That's yours."

Andra stared at him in surprise as he moved over to where Eithne was settling down onto the hard stone. She rumbled a greeting to him as he laid his blanket out on the floor next to her warm side. Kael stretched out on the blanket and Eithne surrounded him with her body, lifting a wing over him and shielding him from view.

"You coming to bed, darling?" Colmen called to her.

Pulling off her new boots, Andra climbed under her blanket and curled up into a warm ball. Sleep overcame her almost immediately and she slipped into the comfort of a dreamless night.

9

Tiri

Andra awoke several hours later in the quiet of the predawn hours. A lifelong habit of rising before the sun was not easily broken. Alik and Colmen slept in the cots beside her, while Kael remained hidden underneath Eithne's outspread wing. The dragon herself was breathing evenly and deeply, her heavy eyelids closed. Andra could only assume she was asleep as well.

Cautiously, she slipped off her cot and pulled on her boots. She glanced briefly at her blanket and spare clothes. She wouldn't be able to carry anything if she was going to make it up the cliffside. She silently tiptoed past the snoozing dragon. The hulking form remained still, save for the steady rise and fall of her sides.

Reaching the mouth of the cave, Andra turned and gazed up toward the cliff top. It was farther than she had thought it would be. Taking a deep breath, she found a handhold and began the treacherous climb to the earth above her. The sea splashed noisily against the jagged rocks below as she heaved herself from one ledge to another.

Her legs began to shake, her arms screaming in pain, her breath labored from the effort. Twice, she slipped, losing the precious ground she had gained, and was forced to climb the distance again. At last, feeling certain that she would not have been able to climb another foot, Andra scrambled onto the flat earth at the top of the cliff. She lay panting for a long minute as the first rays of dawn crept across the top of the forest. She had to move. The men could be rising at any minute, and they would be after her the moment they realized she was gone.

She heaved herself to her feet and trotted into the trees, hoping that they would shield her if Kael and Eithne flew above. The sun continued its climb and Andra continued jogging pointlessly into the wilderness. Perhaps it had been stupid to leave. All that she knew was that they were on the western cliffs somewhere near Vegrandis. She didn't really have much chance of finding the Hall on her own, and with the collar around her neck, she couldn't stop and ask for directions without being seized and taken back to Castigo's manor. But the thought of finding Talias again pulled her forward.

Touching her bracelet, she silently prayed, *Help me, Talias. Help me find you.*

Then she heard a distant shout. "Girl! Where are you?"

She ran faster into the trees as Colmen continued calling out for her. She knew he would be fast—she'd seen elves in combat training enough times to know that—and she couldn't risk him catching up to her. The trees ended, and she found herself standing at the bottom of a sharp rise in the earth, one of the steep outcroppings that covered the edge of the western cliffs. Colmen called for her again, and Andra glanced frantically over her shoulder, then up at the sky. There was no sign of Kael and Eithne.

Jumping on top of a large boulder, she bounded up the cliff. Colmen's voice grew closer. Nobody else seemed to be shouting for her, but she didn't doubt that they too were searching. The rocky outcropping was not so tall as she had expected, and she reached the top quite abruptly, stumbling forward onto the flat top of the rock. Two large shapes lifted their heads to stare at her.

Andra yelped and jumped away from the two massive creatures before her, tripping over a small boulder and landing on her backside. Both dragons quickly rose to their feet, the larger of the two stepping in front of the smaller, violet-colored dragon and snarling deep in its blue-scaled throat. Andra raised her hands to shield her face. Rocks clattered aside as both creatures moved forward to stand in front of her. The snarling unexpectedly stopped, and Andra felt something pressing against her mind.

Instinctively, she resisted the forbidden touch of the dragon's mind, but something inside her stirred, like an unknown part of her mind had suddenly awoken. She lowered her hands and stared up at the smaller dragon, who was gazing down at her with curious amethyst eyes. The larger sapphire dragon stood close by, studying the other carefully. Cautiously, Andra opened her mind to the thoughts that pressed against her.

The dragon's consciousness flooded her own and Andra gasped. It felt like something had fallen into place, a piece of her own mind that she didn't know she had been missing.

"*Who are you?*" a musical voice asked. The presence was very distinctly female.

Andra stared at the dragon, her mind a swirling mess of confusion.

"*Can't you speak, two-legger?*" the voice asked.

Just then, a great roar shook the rocks beneath them. Andra and the two dragons quickly turned their attention to the sky as the towering red form of Eithne dove toward them. The violet dragon hunkered low to the ground, snarling as Eithne landed hard in front of them. The blue dragon, on the other hand, rose to its full height and roared back the challenge, positioning itself in front of its violet companion. Something in the way the dragon moved, in the graceful way it extended its wings, seemed familiar to Andra, and recognition flickered in her mind—it was Ena, the dragon who had touched her mind at the Hall a year ago. Kael leapt from his dragon's back, his red sword flashing in his hand.

"Get away from her!" he snapped at the dragon beside Andra.

Ena roared, which drew a growl from Kael's companion. Andra didn't doubt that Eithne could have overcome the smaller violet dragon, but Ena was much larger and seemed deathly determined to defend the other. Kael eyed the situation, gripping his sword firmly as he tried to find a path to where the frightened girl lay in the dirt behind the two serpents before him.

"*Leave in peace, Rider,*" a fierce female voice snarled. Andra knew that the words were directed at Kael, but with the barriers around her mind down, she could hear Ena's words in her own mind. "*We mean no harm to you or your dragon.*"

"We will not leave," Kael answered sharply. Eithne echoed the sentiment with a vicious snarl.

"*Very well,*" Ena's angry voice responded.

The sapphire serpent drew herself up, smoke rolling from between her teeth. Kael quickly raised his hand. A blazing inferno blasted toward him. Andra saw the Rider brace himself on the stones; then he was enveloped by flames. Behind the rock, Andra threw up her hands, guarding her face from the raging heat. The violet dragon remained crouched before her, watching the battle, an angry rumbling echoing deep in her throat.

The fiery deluge ceased, and Andra lowered her hands to see that the flames had parted around Kael, leaving him and his dragon unscathed. Eithne immediately lunged forward, fangs and claws scraping against Ena's tough, scaly hide. Both the wild serpents roared in rage, the larger quickly tossing Eithne away. The red female opened her wings, pulling herself into the air. Ena crouched, then launched herself after the other dragon. Eithne agilely maneuvered away from her oncoming assailant and bolted toward the ocean at full speed, the blue dragon in pursuit.

Kael turned toward the smaller dragon, who was now regarding him with fierce eyes. He twirled his sword in his hand and took a step forward. The dragon snarled and sank low to the ground. Suddenly, there was the sound of shifting rocks, and Andra looked over to see Alik and Colmen scrambling to the top of the mountain.

"Grab the girl!" Kael called to them. "Get her out of here!"

The two men obeyed without a word, darting over to where Andra was crouched, and seizing her by the arms. She saw Kael shifting his stance, sword at the ready. She pulled against the men's strong hands, frantically trying to get away.

"What is wrong with her?" Alik growled, trying to strengthen his hold on her. "Does she have a death wish?"

"Hold still," Colmen told her, and she could hear irritation in his voice too.

With one last twist, Andra escaped their grasps and bolted toward where Kael and the violet dragon circled each other. She saw Kael's legs tighten as he prepared to lunge at the dragon, blade first. With one last burst of speed, Andra threw herself between the dragon and the blade.

"Don't!" she cried, throwing up her arms. "Don't hurt her!"

Kael stumbled as he ceased his forward momentum and lowered his sword, staring at Andra in shock.

"P-please," Andra pleaded, lowering her arms and stepping toward Kael. "Please, don't hurt her, sir. She meant me no harm."

Colmen gave a sharp, disbelieving laugh. "You can speak!"

She glanced at the elf, then looked back at Kael.

Kael paused, looking for a moment toward where Eithne and the blue dragon had disappeared before he looked up at the dragon, still obviously very confused. "Who are you?" he asked the dragon.

"I am Tiri," the dragon's voice said, reverberating in Andra's mind, "daughter of the Rider-bonded dragon Juran and the wild dragon Ena."

"And do you know this girl?" he asked, pointing at Andra with his sword.

Tiri turned and looked down at Andra. *"I do not,"* she said slowly. *"Yet her mind is familiar to me. . . ."*

A great shadow covered them, and Andra looked up to see Eithne and Ena descending from the sky. She could only assume that Kael's brief glance in their direction had been him sending his dragon the message to stop fighting. She shielded her eyes as the two pairs of massive wings kicked up dust in all directions. Then, with a brief trembling of the earth, the two settled.

There was a pause as the two dragons turned toward their respective companions. Ena nuzzled at Tiri, searching for injuries, while Eithne hummed over Kael, who patted her snout and told her reassuringly, "Yes, yes, I'm fine. And you?" Once the inspection was over, Kael looked at Andra. "Now that you've apparently found your tongue, do you have an explanation for this?"

Andra hesitated under her suddenly much larger audience. Finally, she swallowed and stuttered quietly, "If she is the daughter of Ena, I think I may know why she recognizes me. I—I interrupted a Pairing a little over a year ago. There was a young violet hatchling who was never Paired. I think that it might have . . . been Tiri."

Ena was staring down at Andra with deep, penetrating eyes that made the girl tremble. *"I do remember you,"* she said slowly. *"I know your mind from when I met the candidates. But you could not have been there. Your judges no longer permit females to Ride."*

"I . . . was spying," she admitted sheepishly. "I wanted to see what a Choosing was like. I didn't know that you would touch my mind."

"Hmm," Ena mused, withdrawing her mind slightly.

Tiri looked back at Andra, and the girl found her eyes glued to the immense amethyst one that gazed upon her. Again, she felt that warm, stirring sensation in her mind, and somewhere deep in her chest, a profound longing coupled with an inexplicable joy. The eye blinked.

"I feel that this is more than a memory," Tiri said quietly.

Ena touched the young dragon's shoulder with her snout, drawing her attention away from Andra. *"Come,"* Ena said gently. *"We must discuss this privately."* She then turned toward Kael and Eithne. *"I apologize for the confusion. May the wind carry you safely home."*

Kael and Eithne nodded in unison, returning the blessing. Mother and daughter ruffled their wings, preparing for flight. Andra quickly stepped forward.

"Wait!" she cried, and they looked over their shoulders at her. She hesitated under their intense gazes, then, after clearing her throat, asked quietly, "Will you come back?"

Tiri looked up at her mother, who rumbled thoughtfully before looking back at Andra. *"We have much to discuss, but will return by midday tomorrow."*

"I hate to interrupt," Colmen said, raising a hand, "but am I the only one who notices that we are missing a very important point in this story?"

They all turned to gaze at him with a curious frown.

"Her *name*?" he asked, exasperation in his tone.

They looked back at her, waiting for a response.

"I—My name is Andra," she answered with a slight bow.

Colmen smiled and held out a hand toward her. She cautiously took it, and he bent over it, briefly pressing his lips to the back of her hand. "A pleasure to meet you, Andra," he said, looking up at her with a smile.

She heard an amused chuckle in her mind and turned toward the violet dragon. A smile curled up the corner of Tiri's mouth. *"I will see you tomorrow, Andra,"* she said gently, and Andra felt a thrill at hearing the dragon speak her name.

She nodded silently and watched as the pair of dragons crouched at the edge of the cliff, then launched themselves into the early morning sky. A pang of longing pulled on her, and she felt the piece that had clicked into place tear away and disappear as Tiri's form dropped below another cliff top. She sighed, and turned toward Kael, only to find him glaring at her angrily.

"Are you insane?" he snapped, and she flinched at the anger in his voice. "Where do you get off, disappearing into a wilderness that you know nothing about? You could have been killed! You're lucky those dragons happened to be somewhat gentle, or they would have eaten you without a second thought. You're not in Castigo's palace anymore. You could get hurt—"

Kael seemed as if he had more to say, but stopped quite suddenly, and Andra somehow knew that he was thinking of the scars and bruises he'd seen. The wilderness was not the only place she could be hurt. He clenched his teeth and turned away from her. "Never mind," he muttered, pulling himself up onto Eithne's back. "Pass her up here, Colmen," he said shortly.

Colmen helped Andra up onto Eithne's leg, Kael pulling her the rest of the way up. The elf smiled up at her and patted her on the leg. "I'll see you later, Andra," he said.

Eithne opened her wings and lifted them off the cliff top, carrying them back toward the seaside cave. Kael remained silent, and Andra sensed that he was still angry with her for endangering his dragon. She bit her lip and pulled at the hem of her tunic. His smoldering anger set her on edge, making her expect an explosion at any moment.

They landed in the cave, and Kael hopped down, helping Andra down after him. She watched him as he quietly rooted through all three of the men's packs, pulling out three bows and three quivers. At last, he looked up at her, a frown still on his face.

"We're going hunting," he told her curtly. "Eithne will stay with you to ensure that you don't do anything else reckless. We'll be back before sundown. *Stay here.*" He emphasized the last two words, his gray eyes boring into her.

She nodded quickly. "Yes, sir," she answered. "And, I'm sorry. I didn't mean to cause you trouble."

Kael nodded brusquely and scrambled atop Eithne's bare back again. Without another word, the dragon turned and dropped out of the cave mouth before lifting upward again, carrying her Rider to the top of the cliff. Andra sighed and glanced around the room, feeling truly alone for the first time in her life. She felt . . . empty. And somehow she knew it was because Tiri was gone.

Her eyes drifted over the men's things strewn about the cave, landing finally on a bulky heap in the corner. She stepped closer, trying to discern what it was, stowed away in the shadows. At last, she began to recognize the shape, the tangle of complicated straps. She tugged it out into the light, brushing the dust off the seat of the saddle. She realized quite suddenly that she had never seen Kael use it. Probably just as a matter of convenience. She had seen him Ride only a few times, and every time it had been in a hurry.

She turned to her own pack and rummaged through it until she found her old, rough dress. She held it up, examining it with a half smile. She seized a small tear at the collar and pulled at the cloth. It gave way with a satisfying ripping sound. She bundled the torn piece of cloth in her hand and poured some of their drinking water onto it.

Kneeling beside the saddle, Andra began gently polishing away the dust that had settled on the smooth, supple leather. She looked up as a shadow blocked out the light and Eithne landed at the edge of the cave. Andra shrank back instinctively as the gentle mind brushed her own, but then she forced it open, allowing the dragon to speak to her.

"That is very kind of you to clean Kael's saddle," Eithne told her.

Andra paused, trying to decide how to respond, if she should respond at all. She felt that Eithne wanted a response, but she was still not comfortable with speaking.

"You can speak to me with your mind if you wish," the dragon said, sensing her discomfort. *"Just think the words to me. I shall hear them."*

After another hesitation, Andra thought, *"It is the least I can do for him."*

She saw a smile turn up the corner of Eithne's mouth as the dragon settled down against a wall of the cave, watching the girl polishing the leather. *"My Kael may come off as rather curt at times, but he has a kind heart. He is simply impatient."*

Andra gave a small laugh as she ran the cloth along one of the leather straps. *"Yes, I have noticed."*

"Perhaps he'll be less impatient with you now that you will speak."

Andra paused. Though she had finally spoken to the three men who had been her companions for over a week, the thought of making a regular habit of it seemed impossible to her. When she'd first spoken on that cliff, it had been out of desperation. She'd needed to protect Tiri, and the words had come without thought. But now that the moment had passed, she once again feared what her words could do.

Eithne sensed the tone of her thoughts. *"Why is it that you wish to remain so silent?"*

Andra pressed her lips together, trying to suppress the painful memories. *"Speaking has consequences. It can bring you pain. It can cause death. Sometimes, it's better to remain silent."*

She felt warm breath on her back as Eithne touched her muzzle to the girl's shoulder. *"You poor child. You are safe. You can speak now."*

Andra flinched away from the strange touch, and Eithne withdrew her head, watching her with sad brown eyes. She could feel Eithne still lingering on the outskirts of her thoughts, waiting for some kind of response. But Andra had nothing more to say on the topic.

"Will we be staying here long?" Andra asked. *"Colmen called it home."*

Eithne chuckled deep in her chest. *"Colmen has a tendency to be a bit overzealous. We have made camp here for several weeks as we solidified our plans. We shall soon be returning to our friends and fellow Freemen in Bellris. It's the closest thing to a home that Kael and I ever had."*

Andra pondered on this. Where was *her* home? Though she had grown up at Castigo's, the place now held only memories of her parents' deaths. She thought of her years at the Hall, which had been the closest to happiness she had ever been. She thought of Talias's kind smile and warm laughter, even when she said nothing. But her home was not the Hall. Her home was Talias, wherever he may be.

"Who is Talias?" Eithne asked suddenly.

Andra jumped. She had not been aware that Eithne had still been listening to her thoughts.

"My apologies," the dragon said quickly, *"I didn't mean to pry. I am so accustomed to always hearing what Kael, Colmen, and Alik are thinking that I didn't even consider that I might be invading your privacy."*

Andra nodded curtly as she polished the last strap and carried the saddle over to a corner of the cave. She remained silent, feeling vulnerable and exposed. She had not meant for anyone to know about Talias, or her intentions of returning to him. Now Eithne knew, and no doubt Kael would know soon enough. Then he and the others would be watching her even more closely for signs of another escape attempt.

Eithne sighed, apparently giving up on continuing a conversation with the girl. *"I enjoy speaking to you, Andra,"* she said as she lowered her head and closed her eyes. *"You are a fascinating girl. Your mind burns as brightly as the morning star. You should not be afraid to show that."*

Then Andra felt the dragon's mind pull away, and her breathing deepened as she drifted into a light sleep.

10

Missing Fate

Andra was sweeping the ash out of the mouth of the cave when Eithne lifted her head and looked up, as if seeing through the stone roof. Andra glanced at the dragon questioningly.

"Kael," she said in explanation, standing and shaking herself slightly. *"They're back."*

Andra nodded, and watched as the dragon lumbered to the entrance of the cave and dropped out of sight. Andra set aside her makeshift broom of sticks and waited for the dragon's return, staring out at the orange sun sinking down into the endless sea.

Eithne settled back into the cave several minutes later, laden with all three men and several carcasses. As they scrambled down, carrying their food with them, Colmen glanced around the cave admiringly. The cots were made, the blankets folded neatly at the foot of each, their other belongings folded and stacked beside each bed. All the tack had been polished, the floor swept, and the fire was ready to be lit—products of the long, empty hours of her day.

The men set their kills down, and Colmen quickly lit a fire without any effort. Alik sat down beside the flames, pulled out a hunting knife, and began to skin a wild pig. Along with the pig, they had bagged several rabbits, a small deer, and a large wild bird that Andra did not know the name of. They would have enough meat for over a week.

And then Kael dropped his deer down at Eithne's feet and she swallowed it in a single mouthful, the bones crunching between her teeth. Well, they would have enough meat for several days. As Colmen settled down and grabbed a rabbit to skin, Kael moved over toward the cots, a deep scowl on his face. Andra watched him, wondering if she had done something wrong.

He seized his blanket from off the third cot and wheeled on her. "I told you this was your cot," he said gruffly. He picked up his pack from beside the cot and dropped it against the wall where Eithne lay. Snagging Andra's own blanket and belongings from the corner where she had deposited them, he dropped them unceremoniously on the now-empty cot, then snatched up another rabbit and began skinning it.

Andra watched the back of his head uncomfortably as he bent over his work. She had annoyed him again. She hadn't meant to, but she just hadn't felt comfortable placing a Rider's belongings on the floor while hers were neatly stacked on the cot. She shifted her feet, unsure of what to do.

Kael glanced over his shoulder at her, then grabbed the wild bird beside him and held it out toward her. "You know how to pluck a bird?" he asked.

She nodded. "Yes, sir."

She took it from his hand and settled down beside him, beginning to expertly pluck the feathers from the large fowl's body. Colmen hummed quietly to himself as he worked, the rest of them lapsing into silence. Andra continued glancing deftly at her companions' faces, trying to discern their thoughts, as was habit—reading people's moods made it easier to anticipate trouble.

Colmen looked simply content, while Alik scowled fiercely down at his work, as if the pig had personally offended him. Kael's expression changed so frequently—from thoughtful frowns to slight smiles—that Andra couldn't help but think he was having a silent conversation with Eithne.

She glanced around the loose circle again, wondering how much they would tell her if she asked. She gnawed at her lip, trying to muster the courage to make her lips form the words. It was difficult after such a long habit of silence, but she finally managed, "May I speak?"

They looked up at her, frowning. After a pause, Colmen said, "Of course."

"You said you came to the manor to kidnap Ledo, to use him as leverage against Chief Judge Castigo. Why?" she asked.

The three men exchanged looks, as if gauging how much she could be told. Colmen shrugged; Alik's eyes narrowed and he shook his head. At last, Kael sighed and said, "You're going with us to Bellris one way or another, so I suppose you might as well know the reason we were there. We wanted to use Ledo to force Castigo to step down as Chief Judge. If he did, the law would require all of the judgment seats to be vacated and reelections to be held. We want every judge replaced."

Andra frowned. "But the Guardians established the judges themselves. Why would you want to replace them?"

"The judges are no longer what the Guardians intended them to be," Kael said, and his normally flat tone began to take on a fervent note. "They manipulate the Riders, blackmail and bribe them. They drain the people to fund their own coffers." She thought she saw his gaze flicker to the lock on her neck. "They've corrupted the labor contract to turn indentured servants into slaves. They are an infection, and in order to remove that infection from the land, we need to remove them entirely and begin again."

"It's more than that, though," Alik added, his tone gravelly with the same passion Andra had seen in Kael's eyes. "They don't intend to remain judges for long—at least, not all of them."

"What do you mean?" she asked.

"There's a group of men who call themselves the Kingsmen," Colmen said. "They want an emperor over Paerolia again. And Castigo is the one they plan to put on that throne."

Andra blinked in surprise and disbelief. "I've lived all my life in judges' manors," she said, shaking her head, "and I've never heard any of this."

Alik snorted. "Wouldn't be much of a secret plot if they told every servant in every manor, now, would it?"

"And *all* the judges want to make Castigo their emperor?" Andra asked.

Colmen shrugged. "We don't really know. We have only a few contacts in the manors, and it's hard to get information out without detection. But we know many of them have agreed to the plot for one reason or another. Judge Caedo is his most fervent supporter and—"

"That's enough," Kael said sharply, cutting off the elf. Andra turned to the Rider and was surprised to see his face flushed with anger. "The girl doesn't need to know every detail of the rebels' plans. She's learned enough. We'll leave for Bellris tomorrow, after Ena and Tiri have completed their visit. We can tell her more when we get there."

Andra felt a thrill at the thought of the violet dragon returning, distracting her from her confusion over Kael's sudden anger. She again became acutely aware of the empty feeling at the back of her mind, where a piece had fallen into place the moment she felt Tiri's mind. It seemed to ache, longing to feel that piece again.

"Do you know why Tiri knows my mind, Rider Kael?" Andra asked. She thought that if anybody knew about a dragon's mind, it would be Kael.

He measured her with those gray eyes before answering, "I have my ideas, but I'm much more interested in what Ena thinks." Before she could ask another question, he pulled the rabbit from its spit over the fire and began to divide it up, handing Andra a plate of the roasted meat. "Eat," he commanded. "Then we all need to get some rest for the journey."

They ate in silence, then slowly began drifting to their beds one by one. Andra didn't feel as if she could sleep, her mind brimming with excitement and thoughts of Tiri. As Alik and Colmen settled into their cots, and Kael nestled down next to his dragon, Andra drifted to the edge of the cave. She stared out at the dark, churning sea for a long time, until she heard the heavy breaths and soft snores of the men and dragon inside the cave.

The words of a song her father had often sung to her came into her head—a song about forbidden love. Somehow, though, with thoughts of Tiri in her mind, the words seemed to have a different meaning. She began quietly singing the words to herself as she gazed out at the ocean, her arms wrapped around herself against the cool, damp breeze that blew in from over the sea.

The sight of the endless water was still strange and daunting to her, but something about it appealed to her as well, and she briefly wondered what it would be like to wake every morning to the smell of salt and the view of the sea reaching to the horizon. Maybe, she thought, if she were ever truly free, she could live somewhere near the sea.

Suddenly, a voice said softly near her shoulder, "My mother used to sing that to me." She jumped and turned toward the voice to find Kael standing beside her, his chest bare as he gazed out at the stars above the sea.

"I—I'm sorry," Andra stammered. "I didn't mean to wake you."

"You didn't," he said. "I hadn't fallen asleep yet. You should . . ." He seemed to hesitate, then sat at the mouth of the cave, legs dangling out over the deadly drop below him. "You should finish the song."

Andra gazed down at him, brow furrowed, but he didn't look up at her. After a moment, she sat beside him and continued with the final verse of the song.

> And so beneath the sycamore tree,
> I'll wait for you if you'll come to me,
> and to the mountains we will flee,
> where you and I can both be free.
> For I have loved you
> and you have loved me,
> both knowing that it should not be.
> We have found what they cannot see,
> under the branches of the sycamore tree.

The final words of the song seemed to disappear beneath the crash of the waves below them, and a heavy silence fell around them.

"It's a sad song," Kael remarked. "I never understood why it's a lullaby for children."

"It's not sad," Andra replied with a laugh. "They run away together. They find happiness, even when everyone told them they couldn't."

"But at the expense of the only lives they'd ever known. Did you ever wonder how much they had to give up, how much they had to leave behind for one another?"

Andra hesitated. "I suppose . . . I didn't. But I imagine that when you love someone, little else seems to matter. When you find that person—"

"Your heart-song." The words were spoken softly, as if he said them only to himself, but she caught them before they drifted away on the sea breeze.

"Heart-song?" she repeated.

"Nothing," Kael said briskly, pushing himself to his feet again.

"You should get some sleep. The journey to Bellris is a long one, and you'll need your strength."

Without another word, he turned away from her and strode back to Eithne's side. Andra watched him disappear beneath the dragon's wing. Then, with a sigh, she stood and returned to her cot, lying down and pulling the blanket to her nose. She drifted into a quiet slumber, with a smile on her lips and thoughts of Tiri in her mind.

———◦◈◦———

The first gray rays of dawn were barely touching the sea when Andra awoke, her heart already racing with excitement. *Tiri . . .* She swung out of bed and made her way to the edge of the cave, peering out at the dim sky, hoping to see some sign of the two dragons. There was none. She sighed and turned back toward the cave, where a few embers glowed amid the ash.

As quietly as she could, she pulled more branches into the fire, feeding the embers until it sparked to life and burned steadily again. The dancing light flickered throughout the room, and Eithne stirred, lifting her head to peer sleepily at Andra.

"I'm sorry," Andra whispered. "I didn't mean to wake you."

Eithne yawned, her long forked tongue curling slightly, then shook her head as if trying to chase away the sleep. *"We should all be rising soon anyway. There is much to do today."*

Her triangular head disappeared underneath her wing for a moment. Andra heard Kael grunt and roll over. A chuckle rumbled in Eithne's chest. There was a pause; then Kael yelped in surprise and tumbled out from under the red wing, scurrying away from his dragon. Eithne laughed until smoke rolled from her nostrils, and the sound awoke the others. Kael stood, scowling at the dragon's mirth, rubbing his arm across his face repeatedly.

Colmen was glancing frantically around the room, still trying to get his bearings, his hand on his bow. "What's happening?" he asked, his voice slurred slightly.

"She licked me!" Kael cried, pointing an accusing finger at Eithne, whose laughter simply continued. And then Colmen was laughing too, then Alik. Andra covered her mouth, trying to suppress her own laughter, but a small chuckle escaped her. Kael scowled at them momentarily, but she thought she saw a hint of amusement in those stern gray eyes. "Glad you're all so entertained," he grumbled, snatching his blanket up from the ground, "but I suggest you stop giggling and start packing."

Still holding back laughter, Andra turned toward her cot and began folding up her belongings. For several hours, the cave was filled with sounds of packing and cleaning, removing all signs that anyone had ever been there, erasing their trail as much as possible. By the time the sun had climbed near its peak, no trace of their camp remained.

Then Eithne carried them two at a time to the top of the cliff to wait for the pair of wild dragons to return. Andra sat, fiddling anxiously with the edge of her tunic, while the three men loaded their food and packs onto the horses. She watched as, for the first time, Kael strapped the saddle onto Eithne's broad back. He swung expertly about her legs, chest, and neck, securing the straps tightly in place. Then he loaded the larger belongings—the ones that they would not need on the coming journey—onto the saddle and patted her large leg.

Andra saw the dragon's red chest heave with a sigh as she pressed her snout to the Rider's chest, and somehow she knew that they were saying a silent farewell. Kael would be riding on the ground with them, while Eithne would stay high overhead. They would not be able to Ride together for several days.

Andra felt her before she saw her. Warmth crept through the girl's body, filling first that cold, empty place in her mind, then creeping into her chest and along her limbs. She leapt to her feet and looked up at the sky. The men cast her curious, confused glances, then followed her gaze as a large blue dragon and a smaller violet one appeared over the edge of the low mountain beside them.

They circled slowly downward, throwing up eddies of warm air as they lighted on the green grass; the horses gave startled snorts. Andra had to fight back the urge to throw her arms around Tiri's long, amethyst neck. But she couldn't suppress the smile that lit up her face as she gazed up at the beautiful creature who, she was quite certain, was smiling back at her.

"Andra," Kael said from behind her, "did you feel Tiri coming?"

She forced herself to look away from the dragon and nodded at the Rider who was addressing her. "Yes, sir," she answered briefly before looking back up at Tiri.

Kael frowned in thought, then looked up at Ena. "I suppose you have come to the same conclusion that Eithne and I have come to?"

Ena nodded her large head. *"I believe so,"* she answered, projecting her thoughts to the rest of them. Tiri seemed to drop her head slightly, and Andra felt a faint twinge of sadness that was not her own. She turned toward Ena, waiting for an explanation. The mother dragon drew a deep sigh before continuing, allowing the others to hear her, though her eyes were solely on Andra.

"As you know, Andra, every egg has one destined Rider. Only one on the planet that it can bond with. And so Fate plays a heavy role in the bonding of dragons and Riders. A role that is further magnified by the limitations that time places on the process. A hatchling has only a matter of hours to meet that destined partner and form the Bond that intertwines their two lives.

"Your judges have placed restrictions on what cannot and should not be restricted. Fate does not follow these restrictions. An egg's Rider can be anyone, regardless of age, gender, or status. But because of these limitations, many eggs miss their opportunity to be Paired."

"I understand that," Andra said as the dragon paused, "but how is this related to Tiri's knowing my mind?"

"You, Andra, were her destined Rider."

Andra blinked disbelievingly. "Me . . . ?"

"Yes. When I sense the souls of the chosen candidates, I do not see which soul belongs to which child. I cannot explain it precisely, but it is like seeing many glowing lights, all close together. Their colors and rays blend with one another, and though you can see each color distinctly, it is impossible to see where one begins and another ends. When I touched the minds of those candidates a year ago, Andra, I touched yours as well. I sensed your soul, and I sensed that you were meant to be Tiri's mind-partner.

"Yours and Tiri's case is a rare one indeed, because you came so very close to being Paired, missing each other by so small a distance. I believe your minds know each other because you so narrowly missed your Fate. Your minds briefly touched at that time, but the Bond was not truly forged. And so you know one another. But you can never truly know each other's souls as you should."

Andra stared at Tiri, who looked back at her with large, violet eyes full of sadness and longing. Andra's heart ached at the thought of how close she had come to being permanently connected with that beautiful mind. She quickly looked down at the grass, trying to blink away the tears of frustration.

"Is there nothing that can be done?"

She looked up at the sound of Tiri's voice. The young dragon was gazing up at her mother, and Andra again faintly felt Tiri's emotions, this time a feeling of pleading. She too turned hopefully toward the blue dragon.

Ena sighed and shook her head. *"I am sorry, dear one,"* she answered, *"but the moment of Fate has passed. It cannot be re-created. There is nothing to be done."*

Andra felt that her heart might break, a feeling that was magnified by Tiri's own sadness, which tickled at the back of her mind like the faint touch of a feather. The purple dragon turned toward her again and heaved a great sigh that washed warm air over Andra's face.

"*I wish . . .*" Tiri started, then paused, shaking her head slightly. "*I wish there were a way that we could have been Paired.*"

Andra felt that this statement had been spoken only to her, so she answered silently, "*As do I. I . . . I would have very much liked to be your Rider.*"

Tiri nodded once, then looked back up at Ena. "*I'm ready to go now, Mother.*"

Ena looked down at them and bade them farewell, preparing to take flight again. Tiri turned her eyes on the men and fixed them with a stern gaze. "*You protect her, understand?*" she said sharply.

They nodded, and Kael answered, "We will, Tiri. Fair winds to you."

Ena took to the skies, and with a final glance back at Andra, Tiri followed. Andra tried desperately to cling to the warmth that had crept into her limbs, but as she watched Tiri disappear back over the mountain, the feeling slowly ebbed away, until her mind felt cold, empty, and lonely once again. She bit her lip, fighting back the tears. Tiri could have been her dragon, partner of her heart and mind. They could have flown together, learned to fight together. But it was too late. They had missed Fate, and there was no getting it back.

Feeling the eyes of the dragon and the three men on her, she turned to them, forcing her face into the blank, obedient mask she had worn for over a year. "Is there anything else that needs to be done to prepare for our journey?" she asked.

Alik and Colmen shook their heads, while Kael and Eithne continued to watch her, their eyes full of pity. She thought she saw Kael's chest rise and fall with a quiet sigh. Then he spoke, his tone as brisk and commanding as ever. "We should head out. We'll ride through the rest of the day and through the night before stopping.

It will be a long ride, but we have a long ways to go. Andra, you'll ride with me again."

She nodded, and Kael swung up onto his horse. He held out a hand for her and pulled her up in front of him before turning to look at Eithne again.

"Are you ready?" he asked her.

She flashed her razor teeth at him in a dragonish grin. *"Since the day I hatched,"* she answered.

He nodded. "Off you go, then."

Her muscles coiled, making the red scales ripple as she crouched low, then sprang upward, snapping her wings open. With several fierce beats that tossed Andra's short hair about her face, she lifted herself into the sky, disappearing against the blinding light of the setting sun.

Kael turned to the other men. "Let's head out."

The men turned their horses back into the woods, starting forward at a quick walk. Andra watched the form of the nearby mountain until it became invisible behind the trees. She saw no sign of Tiri. With a sigh, she looked forward again, preparing herself for another very long journey.

11

Worth Fighting For

As the sun began to rise the following day, the band stopped to camp between a pair of rolling hills. Eithne landed in the small clearing carefully, and Kael and Alik unloaded the supplies from her back as Andra helped Colmen unsaddle the horses. Then Alik and the elf disappeared into the trees to gather firewood.

"Andra."

She looked up at the sound of her name and found a wooden staff soaring toward her. She caught the staff with both hands, looking down at it in surprise. It was shaped from a branch, stripped of twigs and leaves, and was nearly as tall as she was. She raised her eyes and found Kael watching her with a hard expression, a similar weapon in his own hands.

"Come stand here." She paused for a moment, uncertain, before moving to stand in front of him in the center of the meadow. "You're not physically strong," he said. "If it came to a test of pure strength, you would probably lose every time. But your speed will be your greatest weapon."

"Weapon, sir?" she asked, holding the staff uncomfortably in her hands.

"Yes, weapon. Do you want to defend yourself or not? And don't call me 'sir.'"

Without warning, he swung his staff at her side. She started to lift her staff, then hesitated, remembering the consequences of trying to fight back. The wood landed on her side with a solid *thwack,* and she flinched. Kael scowled and marched up to her, taking her staff and yanking it from her grasp. He seized her hands and forced her to grasp the wood tightly, holding it up in a defensive position.

"I saw you start to raise it," he snapped. "I know you could have blocked that. So do it. Do not let me hit you again. Understand?"

She nodded silently and he stepped away, lifting his staff again. He paused, then lunged forward and swung the staff at her legs. The long staff in Andra's hands flashed downward, parrying his attack, knocking it away from her body. The moment she had blocked it, Andra stepped back and looked up at him with wide eyes, waiting for his reaction.

Kael gave a small nod. "Good," he said. "Keep doing that."

Andra smiled slightly to herself, then repositioned her hands on the staff as Kael had shown her. She watched him eagerly. She'd felt a rush of excitement blocking that single blow, stopping that strike—stopping the pain. For the first time in as long as she could remember, she felt powerful. She saw him move forward again, swinging his staff with his full strength behind it, aimed at her left shoulder.

She turned toward the blow and lifted her own weapon, his striking hers just between her hands. He didn't stop this time. He took another step and swung again. Andra jumped quickly backward, and the wood hissed past her waist. Kael continued advancing, aiming at her legs, arms, torso, and head. Andra continued avoiding the attacks, blocking, dodging, and prancing backward to stay out of his reach.

After several minutes, he stopped. Andra was panting and smiling to herself, sweat beading on her forehead. He hadn't hit her once. Kael looked down at her, and she thought she saw a hint of approval in his eyes. "Good," he said briefly. "Now I want you to fight back."

A flash of surprise went through her, and she opened her mouth to reply. Kael swung his staff at her head again, and she jumped, raising hers just in time to block the blow.

"Keep your weapon up at all times!" he barked. He jabbed at her again, and she spun out of the way, her eyes on him, still retreating. "You can't always back up, Andra," he said firmly, continuing the attacks. "Sooner or later, you will get backed into a corner. Then what will you do? You can't just defend. You must *attack*!"

He swung his staff straight down at the top of her head and she raised hers with both hands, the two pieces of wood colliding with an echoing *crack*. Breathless, she stared up at him as he glared back down at her, his face only a few inches from her own.

"Now what will you do?" he asked quietly.

It was only then that she realized her back was against a large oak tree, its branches too high to climb. He held her in that position for what felt like a long moment, his gray eyes never leaving her face. She could feel the heat from his body, hear his heavy breathing. She stared back up at him in silence, with no answer to offer. She knew she should fight, but fear gripped her insides.

"I can't," she finally whispered.

Kael stepped back with a sigh, dropping his staff to his side and running a hand through his hair. Andra lowered her staff as well, but stayed where she was, watching him pace agitatedly before her. After a moment, he turned to her, throwing a hand in the air in exasperation.

"Why?" he demanded. "Why will you not raise a hand to defend yourself? Would you rather always be at someone else's mercy? Do you *want* to always be the victim, Andra?"

"No," she answered quietly.

Kael swung the staff in his hand, and it struck the side of the tree with a *crack,* making her flinch. "Then tell me why!" he snapped.

"Because the last time I fought back, my mother was executed for it!"

Andra immediately clamped her lips together, her heart racing in her ears, a lump rising in her throat. She swallowed it down quickly, refusing to let it choke her.

Kael blinked, his intense gaze softening. "What?" he asked in a low voice.

She licked her lips and went on in a whisper, "I tried to stand my ground with him—with Ledo. My first day back in the manor, I insulted him when he dared to put his hands on me." Her hands tightened around the staff at the memory, her knuckles turning white. "In punishment, he had my mother hanged. He said it was to teach me what happens when I speak out of turn, when I try to fight back."

The flame in his eyes was gone now. "And that's why you stopped speaking," he said softly.

Andra nodded, looking back at the ground. She heard the rustle of grass as he stepped forward, and his black boots entered her range of vision. Softly, almost hesitantly, he touched a finger to her chin. She allowed him to lift her eyes to his, and she was surprised by the tenderness in his gaze.

"Those days are behind you, Andra," he told her, his voice soft yet firm. "You've left that life behind you now, and you don't ever have to go back to it. You have my word. Do you understand?"

Andra swallowed, then nodded. Kael stepped back from her, his gaze hardening again, a soldier once more.

"In this life," he said, "your new life, it is *not* fighting back that has deadly consequences. If you refuse to defend yourself, then you are no freer now than you were inside those walls."

Kael seized his staff in both his hands and pressed it across her chest, pinning her to the tree as he stared down into her face. Her breath caught at the sudden return of his closeness, at the fire that burned once more inside the iron of his eyes.

"Answer me now, Andra," he demanded, his voice low and rough, "because if you don't care to learn how to defend yourself, then tell me, so I don't waste my time trying to teach you."

Andra paused, staring at the dark gray eyes that so reminded her of thunderclouds. Looking at him, seeing the ferocity in his expression, she felt a sudden desire growing in her chest. She wanted that ferocity herself. For so long, she had held it down, been silent, been obedient. She wanted to lash out, to rage against something, to fight as she had been told she should not do. She wanted the fire that she saw in Kael's eyes for her own.

Firmly, she nodded. "I want to learn."

Kael studied her face for a moment, searching for signs that she meant what she said. Then he took a step back and lowered his staff. "All right," he said, pointing with the staff to the open field behind him. "Back to the center of the meadow."

She walked to the middle of the clearing, and Kael followed, placing himself before her. "Take a defensive stance," he instructed, demonstrating the position. She mimicked him, widening the set of her feet, gripping her staff firmly. He straightened and shook his head. "No, no. Bend your knees more," he said, tapping his staff against the back of her kneecaps. She obeyed. "Back straight, eyes on your opponent at all times." When he was satisfied with her stance, he returned to standing before her. "Now," he said, raising his staff, "this time, if you see an opening, take it. Attack with as much strength as you can."

Kael launched himself immediately into a series of complicated attacks, testing her to see just how fast she really was. Andra parried and dodged, spinning out of his reach, dancing around his attacks on fast feet. Her eyes never left him, watching his movements at every moment, like partners in a dance. At one point,

Andra registered that Colmen and Alik had returned, and they were watching the sparring with interest, but Kael never paused to acknowledge them.

She saw him drop his guard on his left side, and she quickly swung the end of her staff at his waist. It connected with a solid sound, and Kael jumped back with a grunt, a wince of pain flashing across his face.

Andra gasped and covered her mouth with both hands, letting her staff fall to the grass. She hadn't meant to strike him that hard. She started to step forward, saying, "I'm sorry, sir! I—"

Kael straightened suddenly, his staff whistling through the air toward her head. She froze, and he stopped, the staff hovering within an inch of her ear. "I told you," he said slowly, "to always keep your weapon up. Now, pick up your staff and take position. And *don't* call me 'sir' again."

She hurried to obey, but her eyes were still wary as she watched him. "Are you sure you're not hurt?" she asked cautiously as she widened her stance and gripped her staff.

"Like I said," he told her dismissively, "you're not that strong."

Kael pushed her through the motions again and again, forcing her to move as fast as she could, darting away, blocking his blows, and occasionally making attacks of her own. He didn't allow any more to connect, blocking them all carefully with his staff. He would stop her frequently, correcting her stance, her footwork, her grip, or her movements. The lesson continued until the sun had fully risen, and Kael looked up at the sky as if surprised by the brightness that had crept in around them.

"That's enough for today," he told her, taking the staff from her hand and laying it beside the fire. "Eat, then get some sleep. You did well."

Andra felt a glow of pride at the compliment, and nodded. She quickly ate the familiar stew, then removed her boots and settled onto her cot, her body sore with the exertion of the ride and the sparring. But unlike the exhaustion that had always followed her around the manors where she'd served, the heaviness in her body was a pleasant weight. She had fought back, and it had felt right.

But before she could drift to sleep, Kael's voice spoke again. "Andra."

She lifted her head and turned to look at him as he sat by the fire. The sun reflected off his black hair, and his head was tilted back, his eyes on the sky.

"You have a visitor," he said.

Andra looked up as well. In the growing light, she could make out a dark shape spiraling high above them, coming slowly lower. She sat up abruptly, suddenly aware of the warm glow that was spreading through her mind. She had thought it was merely pride at what she'd accomplished, but she now recognized it for what it was—the feeling of Tiri returning.

She was on her feet immediately, a tingling sensation spreading from her scalp to her toes as the shape circled lower, and she was able to identify the dragon's violet scales. Finally, Tiri landed carefully in the clearing beside Eithne. The dragon's amethyst eyes settled on the girl, and Andra had to keep herself from rushing to the dragon's side.

"Hello again, Andra." The voice in her mind sounded like a low, soft flute.

"Hello," Andra breathed quietly.

Kael glanced at her, then back at Tiri. "Tiri," he said, "where's Ena?"

Tiri sighed and shook her head. *"She advised me not to come, but I told her I would not be deterred."*

"Deterred from what?"

The dragon looked down at the entranced girl and hummed softly. *"From traveling with Andra."*

Andra blinked. The men and Eithne turned and stared at her in surprise.

"Traveling with me?" she stuttered. "I don't understand. You're a *wild* dragon."

Tiri nodded. *"Yes. But I enjoy your mind greatly, Andra, and I'd very much like to know it more. Fate may have passed us in the opportunity of Pairing our minds, but it cannot prevent us from traveling together."*

"But how did you find me?"

Tiri laughed, as if the question amused her. *"I followed your mind, of course. It is very easy for me to sense. Even my mother can feel you. You have a very bright mind."*

Andra frowned slightly. "What does that mean?"

"Nothing particularly," the dragon answered with a scaly shrug. *"You simply have a presence about your mind that draws me. I am sure Eithne can feel it as well."*

The larger dragon nodded. *"I told you before, Andra. You have a bright mind, and it is not only dragons who can feel it. Kael has felt it, as has Colmen. It is like asking the meaning of the morning star, and why it burns longer and brighter than any other star. Nobody truly knows—and yet, it still outshines all the others."*

Tiri shook her head. *"For as long as I can remember, I have had vague memories of your mind, from that moment when we nearly met. After meeting you and feeling the brightness of your mind again, the desire to be near your thoughts is even stronger. I feel as if I should know every part of your life and mind, because that was how we were destined to be."*

"What do you mean?" Andra asked

"That's what happens when minds are Paired," Kael answered from behind Andra. She could feel his eyes on her, as if he were studying her reaction to this strange development. "The minds of the dragon and the Rider are melded so that it is very difficult to keep anything from each other. The moment the Pairing happens, they know everything about each other—past, temperament, dreams. Everything."

Andra considered this for a moment. She had spent her entire life guarding every part of her heart and mind. The idea of being unable to hide any part of herself, even from a dragon, seemed impossibly foreign to her.

"How long will you stay?" she asked.

Tiri paused. *"I do not truly know. For as long as I feel that you need me, I suppose."*

"For now," Eithne interrupted, *"we must rest. We have had a long journey and must resume it in the morning."*

"Yes, please rest," Tiri insisted. *"I can keep guard if you'll permit me, Eithne. I have not traveled far today and do not need the rest."*

The red dragon nodded. *"Very well. Thank you."*

Alik and Colmen immediately flopped back onto their cots and quickly began snoring. Kael seized his blanket and dragged it to Eithne's side as his dragon settled with some difficulty into the small clearing. Tiri moved to the other side and managed to find enough space to lie with her tail curled around her body. Andra sat on the edge of her cot and stared at the violet dragon for several minutes.

Tiri turned her head toward the girl. *"Will you not sleep as well, Andra?"*

"I'm not tired," she answered.

Tiri gave a snort, sending a small trail of smoke into the air. *"I may not be able to sense your fatigue as I should be able to, but I can still see that you need rest. You should sleep. I will not have my destined Rider falling off one of those pack beasts of yours from exhaustion."*

Andra smiled, but looked away from the dragon without replying.

The dragon tilted her head sideways, an oddly birdlike gesture. *"Have I said something to upset you, Andra?"*

The girl shook her head slowly. *"You . . . shouldn't call me your Rider, Tiri. I'm not. I'm just a servant who happened to get in the way during a Pairing."*

"You were meant to be my Rider," Tiri answered firmly, her violet eyes seeming to glow, *"and so 'my Rider' is what I shall call you.*

Whether you were in the way that day over a year ago or not, you are still the partner of my mind."

Andra smiled at the dragon's use of the term. *"You're very kind."*

"Kind?" she retorted. *"Am I kind for saying what I think? You were meant to be a Rider, Andra, and if not for your petty laws, you would have been one."*

Andra felt a tingling of bitterness in the back of her mind.

"Now," the dragon went on, *"I insist that you sleep. We all have a long journey ahead."*

She obeyed and lay down on her cot, pulling her blanket up to her nose and closing her eyes. Tiri's presence was a warm pressure against her thoughts, a comforting companionship that was somehow both unfamiliar and a part of her.

"Sleep well, my new friend," Tiri whispered to her mind.

Andra smiled, and drifted off to sleep.

Kael stared up at the deep red color of his dragon's wing for a long time, listening to the sounds of morning around them. Eithne was awake as well, her mind mingling with his, sensing his thoughts.

"You were too hard with her during the sparring," Eithne said, her voice gentle but reprimanding. *"You must have more patience."*

The Rider sighed. Eithne frequently warned him of his short temper, and he often wondered if she knew just how much shorter it would be without her constant, calm presence in his mind. She said he was like the West Wind, always rushing on, howling when he could not move quickly enough, raging when anything stood in his way. And she was not wrong.

"You're the one who said I should teach her to fight," Kael answered.

"Yes, but I didn't expect you to undertake the task with such . . ." Her words drifted off in his mind and were replaced instead with the image of a snarling dragon, smoke rolling between bared teeth.

He pushed the image away. *"What was I supposed to do, Eithne? She wasn't fighting back. She'll never learn if I don't push her."*

The air beneath the wing rustled with a dragon-sized sigh. *"And you need her to learn,"* Eithne said softly.

He sensed that there was more than one meaning behind the words. He could feel it in his thoughts—in her thoughts. *"Don't try to guard your true meaning from me, Eithne,"* he said, his thoughts teasing.

"You feel responsible for her safety," Eithne said. *"You need her to learn to fight, because you need to know she is safe."*

Kael didn't reply with words, but she sensed the admission in his mind. He had taken her from the manor, dragged her into a rebellion that she hadn't even known about, and put her life in danger once already—and he knew it was bound to happen again soon. No matter how little he wanted more responsibility heaped on his shoulders, the girl was another burden that was his to bear.

"She is more than that," Eithne said in his mind. *"You would not feel such pain for her suffering if she were only a burden."*

Kael let out a puff of air, blowing his black hair away from his forehead. Though he made no verbal reply he knew Eithne could sense him turning her words over in his mind, thinking on how the girl tried his patience with her absurd subservience, how she had forgiven him so quickly when he'd forced her to stand nearly naked before him, how she still seemed to find reasons to smile at mundane things even when he knew the darkness in her past. She was, indeed, his responsibility to carry. But perhaps Eithne was right. Perhaps Andra was something more as well.

12

Hiding

Kael closed his eyes, relishing the cold wind on his face, the scales under his fingers, the well-worn dragon saddle between his knees. Eithne's warm contentment spread through his mind, sharing in the joy of flying together. It had been several days since they left the cliffside cave, and this was the first opportunity he'd had to Ride with her.

They drifted through the eddies of air for several minutes, and Kael allowed his mind to mingle more closely with Eithne's, feeling the subtle changes in the air, the way she shifted her wings and tail, tasting the wind on her tongue. Finally, he drew back into his own mind, to his own dull, human senses. This flight had a purpose.

Kael surveyed the land below them, searching the landscape for some source of water. Their canteens would be empty soon, and he didn't want himself and Colmen constantly draining their magic just to keep their party from dying of thirst. That was a task to be saved for when they had to cross the Shesol Mal. His eyes scanned the expanse of land below him. A low, hilly ridge occupied the eastern edge of where the others were camped, but aside from that landmark, there was nothing but dense forest pocked by a few clearings, as far as he could see.

Eithne tugged on his mind and he surrendered immediately to the pull as she shared her senses with him again. He could smell water in the air. Without any spoken direction, she tilted her left wing down and turned northwest. She dropped lower over the canopy of trees, and it was only a few minutes before Kael could see the distant glint of water between the branches. Eithne turned along the path of the stream, following its narrow length as it curved through the forest.

"The stream flows relatively northward," Kael remarked. *"We could follow it for a fair distance. It'll spare us from having to search for water."*

"And I'll be able to see you more clearly from the sky if you travel along the riverbank," Eithne added.

"Let's head back to camp."

She turned back in the direction they had come from, then pulled back suddenly. The abrupt jolt and his dragon's sudden alertness in his mind immediately set Kael on edge. He looked around, trying to find some source of disturbance, but he saw nothing.

"What is it?" he asked.

She pulled him into her mind again, and he could see the forest more sharply. Through her eyes, he could see the leaves of every tree below him. And then he saw it too—a brief glint of reflected sunlight through the trees, then a pause, then another glint of light on metal a few feet away. It could mean only one thing. Soldiers.

"Something is wrong."

Alik, Colmen, and Andra turned their eyes to where Tiri lay in the grass. Her head was lifted, eyes on the sky, and they followed her gaze. Andra spotted Eithne immediately. She was descending rapidly, diving toward the clearing instead of circling down slowly as she normally did. The two men hastily stood from where they'd sat eating, and seized their weapons. Andra's hand closed on the knife at her belt—the one Alik had given her.

Eithne snapped her wings open and gave one heavy beat with them, nearly knocking Andra over with the force of the wind she created. Then her clawed feet struck the grass with a rumbling sound. Kael vaulted from her saddle.

"Start packing," Kael ordered, pulling his horse's saddle from the ground and heading toward the animal. "We have to leave immediately. There's a small band of soldiers marching a mile to the east of here. It looks like they're headed toward the village on the other side of the hills. They'll probably just pass right by us, but I don't want to take the chance. We need to move."

The camp became a flurry of motion as hands and magic were used to quickly break down cots, gather supplies, and stamp out any sign of their fire. Within a matter of minutes, all trace of their passing was gone, and the men were mounted.

Kael grasped Andra's forearm and pulled her up into the saddle in front of him. "Eithne," he said, turning toward the dragon. "You and Tiri get as high up in the air as you can. Don't let the soldiers see that you are carrying any gear. Let them think that you are wild, if they see you at all."

Eithne nodded and leapt quickly into the air. Tiri paused for a moment, watching Kael closely.

"You will keep her safe?" she asked, glancing at Andra worriedly.

"You have my word," Kael answered. As if to demonstrate, Andra felt his arm go around her waist, holding her firmly in the saddle, though he knew that she was more than capable of maintaining her seat now.

Tiri nodded, then leapt into the air, following Eithne, who was steadily climbing higher into the sky. Tiri paused once more, circling them for a brief moment. *"I will be back, Andra,"* she said gently. *"That is a promise."*

Andra gave a brief smile. *"I believe you."*

Then the purple dragon turned her nose skyward and began to rise, following the diminishing red form above her. Kael turned his horse's nose to the narrow path at the edge of the clearing.

"Let's go," he said. "And double pace."

The three men kicked their horses into a brisk trot, the fastest pace they could maintain through the dense woods. Andra tightened her legs around Kael's horse and clutched the mane in front of her, trying to maintain her seat through the horse's jolting strides. Kael kept his arm tightly around her, his other hand on the reins as he followed after Colmen.

They continued quickly through the dense undergrowth, the soft earth muffling the sound of the horses' hooves. Then Colmen held up a hand and pulled his horse to a sudden stop. The others halted behind him. He silently tapped his pointed ear.

Andra sat perfectly still, listening for something that would signal danger. Birds chirped and insects hummed. A pair of squirrels chattered at each other in a nearby tree. Then she heard something different. A metallic sound that she recognized reached her ears— jangling armor.

Her heart leapt into her throat. They were close. If they were discovered, if the guards saw the contract collar around her neck . . . Fear gripped her chest and a whimper escaped her. Kael's arm pulled her closer to him, and she felt his breath against her ear.

"It's all right," he whispered. "Nothing's going to happen to you."

He kept her close to his chest with one arm, putting his opposite hand on the hilt of his sword. She could feel his heartbeat against her back. It was slow and steady, as was the rise and fall of his chest behind her. He didn't seem to be afraid. Andra took a shaky breath and steadied herself. If Kael was not afraid, then she had nothing to fear either.

The three horses stood silently, their riders unmoving as the sound of the soldiers drew closer. She could hear one of them grumbling quietly, cursing the dense forest, the insects, and the long march.

"Boy!" a deep voice barked. "If you do not stop complaining, I will leave you in the forest to find your own way back."

"Yes, sir," the young soldier muttered.

And then she could see them through the trees, brief glimpses of soldiers on horseback and on foot. If any of them were to move, they would be spotted. Andra held her breath.

"Hold on," a third voice said quietly. "I sense someone."

Andra started to tremble again.

"Where?" the deep, commanding voice asked.

"Over there." And she could see the finger pointed in their direction. "Three—four?—no, three people, I believe. I'm . . . having a hard time separating them. One of the minds is very . . . bright."

Behind her, Kael whispered a curse. "Alik," he snapped quietly. "Ride forward and speak to them. Delay them for a few moments. Assure them there are only three of us."

The man nodded and nudged his horse toward the soldiers.

"Identify yourself!" the officer barked.

"Just three travelers, sir," Alik said in a calm voice. "We're heading toward Aethoa."

"Remain where you are! We will approach you."

The solid presence of Kael behind her suddenly disappeared, and Andra looked over her shoulder frantically. He landed silently on the ground and quickly unclasped his cloak from around his neck.

"Here," he whispered, throwing it around her and clicking the clasp closed again. "Keep this around your neck," he instructed, arranging the fabric around her and tugging the hood up over her short hair. "Do *not* let them see your collar, do you understand me?"

She nodded.

"And sit sideways," he hissed. "You're a girl, for the gods' sakes."

She obediently swung her right leg onto the same side as her left leg. His eyes darted over her again; then, apparently satisfied, he disappeared into the trees. Andra tried to follow him with her eyes, but he was already gone. She looked back at Alik, who was speaking to the commanding officer.

"Yes, sir," he said pleasantly. "The village is not far. Just over the hills."

The armored man, who had brought three armed soldiers forward with him, nodded, then looked past Alik toward where Andra and Colmen sat on their horses.

"Come forward, please," he said. His voice was calmer now, less threatening.

Andra looked at Colmen. She had never directed the horse herself before.

"Just give him a nudge," he whispered. "A *small* one."

Andra touched her heel to the horse's side and it started forward, following Colmen the few yards to where Alik spoke with the soldiers. When they reached them, she pulled back slightly on the reins, as Colmen was doing, and the horse came to a stop. She breathed a small sigh of relief.

The commander was sizing them up, searching for any sign that they were not who they said they were. Andra felt as if his eyes were lingering on her neck, and she pulled the cloak closer around her. At last, he looked back at Alik.

"And it is only you three?" he asked.

"Yes, sir," Alik answered. "We were merely visiting some friends and are on our way home."

The commander looked at the soldier on his right, a thin young man with distinctly elfish features, though his eyes were deep brown. The young soldier scanned the woods momentarily, then looked up at his leader and nodded. The man looked back at the three of them.

"Well, a safe journey to you, then," he said.

"And to you and your men as well," Alik answered with a nod and a friendly smile.

The group of soldiers turned and headed back to where the rest of their troop waited on the narrow forest path. Once they had rejoined the contingent, the march forward continued, and the soldiers disappeared from view. Andra, Colmen, and Alik remained still, waiting for the sounds of the band to fade. Suddenly, a figure dropped from above them, landing beside Andra. She gasped and jumped in the saddle, making the horse toss its head.

Kael looked up at her with a cocked eyebrow. "You are really bad at pretending to be calm."

She let out a nervous laugh and tried to steady her racing heart. "Were you above us the entire time?"

He nodded as he pulled himself back up behind her and took the reins from her hands. "I had to stay close to cloak my presence from that half-elf soldier. Seems that bright mind of yours can prove useful for that."

His arm went around her waist again, and she felt it draw her closer to him, as if he were trying to stop her trembling with the steadiness of his own body. She took a slow breath and tried to settle her nerves. The soldiers had passed. She would not be taken back. She took another deep breath and relaxed into the saddle.

"Now that we're clear of the soldiers, turn northwest," Kael instructed. "Eithne found a stream in that direction. It heads mostly northward, so we can follow it for a day or two and have clean water."

Colmen nodded and turned his horse's head. The party fell silent again and plodded onward.

13

Burning Sands

Andra woke to Kael's voice. "We're stopping," he told her quietly. She groaned and opened her eyes, her body stiff from drifting off to sleep in the saddle. It was still dark, but the moon was already fading. Nearby, Eithne and Tiri were landing and stretching their weary wings. The trees of the forest had disappeared during the night's ride, replaced by low brush. Ahead of them stretched an endless plain of emptiness.

"Is that the Shesol Mal?" she asked as Kael helped her down from the saddle.

He nodded. "That's it. Two days' worth of nothing but hot sand."

"Did the dragons of the first days really create it?"

Eithne answered, *"The First War between dragons and men caused much destruction. My kind showed themselves to be very powerful, but it was at great cost. This land was once beautiful, rich, and fertile."*

"It's shrinking, though," Kael added. "The edges of the Burning Sands recede every year, and more green appears than ever before."

116 · ERIN SWAN

"Why has it taken so long?" Andra asked. "Why can't the earth heal itself as it does after a forest fire?"

"Dragon fire is difficult to counter," Eithne explained. *"When it burns, it burns away life itself. The flames of the old ones still smolder deep within the earth. It keeps the land from growing again."*

"And makes it insufferably hot," Kael muttered.

"I've heard it was farmlands once," Andra remarked.

Kael nodded, his eyes on the endless stretch of sand before them. "It was. When the dragons destroyed this land, they destroyed the livelihoods of thousands of men and women. It's the primary reason that men began to hunt the dragons, back in the old days before the treaty was written at Myli Ondo. But even after the treaty, many of the men and women who lived here couldn't let go of what the dragons had done to their ancestors."

"What do you mean?" Andra asked, looking at him. There was a distance in his eyes, as if his mind were far from where they stood.

"You've heard of the wandering clans?"

Andra nodded.

"They're the descendants of those farmers—descendants of the first men to come to Paerolia. When their ancestors arrived in this land, the elves ruled the forests, the dwarves ruled the stones below, and the dragons had the mountains and the skies above. The humans were given the fields for their own, in agreement with the elves and dwarves. But the dragons did not agree. These were their hunting lands, and the dragons retaliated by killing the men's flocks. The men retaliated by killing several dragons and destroying their nests. And the First War began.

"Before the elves intervened and proposed the treaty and the Bond contract, the dragons completely destroyed these lands with their fires. Many had moved on to other lands, and they accepted the treaty, but those who remained here refused to forget what the dragons had done. Their descendants continue to live in the desert, refusing to leave the land that they consider to be their birthright. And they continue to hunt the dragons."

She blinked at him. "They still hunt them?" she asked in disbelief.

Kael nodded. "Not often, but if they cross paths with a dragon, they'll kill it. And once a year, they hunt and capture a dragon to sacrifice to their gods, in retribution for the loss of their homelands."

Andra heard Tiri growl softly, and she couldn't help but silently agree with the sentiment. This was certainly not a part of Paerolia's history that they spoke of openly in the rest of the land. She looked back at Kael's face, taking in the hardness around his eyes. But there was sadness in the expression as well, a pain in those gray depths. And then she realized something. She'd seen that strange color in people's eyes before—when nomads had come to trade at the Hall.

"You're . . . one of them, aren't you," she said quietly.

Kael glanced down at her from the corner of his eye, his jaw tightening before he looked back out at the desert. "My mother was," he said, "before she met my father. I've been among them a few times in my life, but I'm no longer welcome there. As a Rider, I've betrayed all that they believe. I am the mind-partner of a dragon—the descendant of a home-burner."

Andra regarded him silently for a moment, then cautiously touched his arm. "Perhaps they will understand . . . someday," she said quietly. There was no conviction in her voice.

"Perhaps," he repeated flatly, and turned away.

Alik and Colmen were unloading things from Eithne's back, and Kael joined them. Andra continued to stare out at the empty desert. In the moonlight, it looked eerie and foreboding, and a shiver ran down her spine. She rubbed at her arms, trying to chase away the goose bumps, but they remained.

---◦❦◦---

Andra slept fitfully, slipping in and out of sleep, until she finally awoke with a start, her heart racing with panic, though she wasn't sure why. She looked frantically around her, but all was silent. Alik was still sitting with his back to the campsite, facing away from the desert. The others, including the two dragons, slept deeply.

Alik glanced over his shoulder at her. "You've been thrashing around like a landed fish."

"Has anything happened?" she asked hesitantly, going to stand beside him.

He glanced up at her with a frown. "No. Been quiet except for you. Why?"

Andra shook her head. "I just had a strange feeling. Like something was wrong."

Alik gazed at her for a long time, studying her. "Well, as far as I can see, everything seems just fine around here."

She sighed and ran a hand across her face, wiping off the sweat that beaded on her forehead. "I suppose it was just a dream. Is it all right if I take a walk?" she asked.

He shrugged again. "I don't mind. Just stay within shouting distance."

She nodded and tiptoed quietly out of the campsite. She walked briskly toward a nearby stand of trees and ducked thankfully under their low, spiny branches. The canopy was not so thick as it had been in the forest, and sunlight still shone through in ample amounts. Andra sat with her back against a tree, trying to stay in the shade as much as possible.

She leaned her head back and closed her eyes as her head throbbed with heat and exhaustion. When she opened her eyes again, she jumped in surprise.

A pair of large eyes was staring at her from a nearby tree. It was a dragon. A small one, no bigger than a new hatchling. But it was like no dragon she had ever seen—white, with golden eyes filled with centuries of wisdom. Andra stared back, wide eyed and uncertain.

Then the dragon opened its mouth and spoke. "Hello, Andra."

Andra gasped. "You . . . can talk? How?"

"You have spoken with dragons before, have you not?"

"Well, yes, but—but with my mind. And you're just a hatchling. Hatchlings can't speak."

The dragon ruffled its wings and gave a small chuckle. "Oh, I am certainly not a hatchling. I am much older than I look, Andra."

"How do you know my name?"

"I know many things," it answered, its voice as soft and golden as its eyes. "And I know many things about you."

Andra didn't know how to respond, so she remained silent.

The dragon continued, "Fate has not completely abandoned you, Andra. There is still hope, if you should choose to have it. But if there is to be any true hope, when the moment comes, you must stand, and you must fight."

"I—I don't understand."

"You shall—soon. Do not forget what I have said. You must fight, Andra. It is far more than your own life that depends upon it." The creature dipped its small angular head in a bow; then with a few silent beats of its snow-white wings, it was gone.

Andra leapt to her feet and raced out of the canopy, heading straight back to the camp. Alik saw her hurried approach and stood, his hand on the handle of the axe at his hip. He scanned the trees and everything around for signs of a threat.

"Is everything all right?" he asked her as she drew closer.

"A dragon," she panted, pointing back toward the copse of trees. "A small one. It talked to me. It knew my name!"

Alik stared at her as if she were mad as she continued to rattle out everything that had happened in the few short minutes she had been gone. Her frenzied explanation woke the others, who looked around in some irritation for the source of the noise. Kael rose and came to stand beside Alik.

"What's going on?" he asked.

Andra began her explanation over again, Colmen joining them, the two dragons listening carefully. The three men traded concerned looks, and Kael frowned at her.

"You're flushed," he said. "It must be the heat. You should get in the shade and lie down. Have some water."

Andra blinked at him, realizing that he thought she was reacting to the blazing sun overhead. Her shoulders slumped slightly in defeat. Perhaps he was right; the haze of her restless sleep still lingered, and even she realized how impossible it all sounded. Maybe she drifted off for a moment while sitting in the shade of the trees. Kael led her to where Eithne's hulking form lay, casting a long shadow on the ground. "Here," he said, handing her a skin of water. She took a long draw from it and held it out to him. He pushed it back at her. "More," he ordered.

She took several more long, slow drinks until Kael looked like he was satisfied. Then he pulled her cot into Eithne's shadow and pointed at it. "You should lie down."

"I'm fine," she answered irritably.

He shook his head. "You're not used to this heat. You should rest."

Andra sighed and dropped down onto the cot as he walked around to Eithne's other side. She lay on her side, staring out at the desert. In the light of day, it seemed less eerie, and more threatening, as though it were waiting for some foolish traveler to try to traverse it. She could easily imagine several people losing their lives to the heat and the endless sands. And she couldn't help but wonder if she would join them.

Kael sighed and ran a hand across his face. The sun was glaringly hot, keeping them all from sleeping. Colmen and Alik spread out on their cots, using their blankets to shield their faces from the sun overhead, while Andra sat with her back against Tiri's side, eyes closed and head tilted back. Her skin had a purple hue from the wing that was spread over her head. The horses were pawing at the sand, and Kael could sense their thirst.

He cast his mind downward, searching for the underground stream that he knew they were traveling along. He sensed it below them and squatted on the ground, placing his right hand on the sand. The water began to pool almost immediately. The horses whinnied excitedly and hastily plunged their noses into the water. Kael maintained the pool until the thirsty animals had had their fill.

"If you want a drink, come get it now. We should reserve our skins for when we're traveling." Alik and Colmen stood from their cots and scooped water into their mouths with their hands. Kael looked at Andra, who was gazing down at the clear pool of water that swirled atop the sand.

"How are you doing that?" she asked.

"Magic," he answered shortly. "There's water under the earth, and I can draw it up for a short time. But holding it for too long is difficult, so I'd appreciate it if you would get your drink quickly."

Andra hurriedly bent and cupped the clear liquid into her mouth before topping off her own waterskin.

Then Kael looked up at the dragons. "You too, Eithne, Tiri. Come drink."

Tiri lumbered to his side and dipped her nose in the water, drawing deeply, forcing Kael to pull more water up from the underground spring. Eithne refused, saying she would be fine until they reached Bellris. He knew she felt his fatigue from drawing on so much magic, and she wouldn't make him use more to sate her thirst. Kael released the flow of water, letting it seep back into the ground. As he did so, he felt his energy slipping away as well, and he sank to the sand, sitting with his head on his knees.

He heard the sand shift as a pair of light footsteps approached him, and he looked up at Andra. "Are you all right?" she asked, an expression of concern on her face.

Kael drew his forearm across his forehead, wiping the sweat from his brow, and nodded. "Magic is simply a bit draining if you use too much of it."

Her brow furrowed, her lips pursing slightly. She always made that face when she was thinking hard on something, and it amused him. Finally, she asked, "Do you think . . . that I might have magic?" There was a hesitancy in her voice, but a hint of hopefulness as well.

Kael shrugged. "It's possible. Colmen said he thought you had elf blood?"

Andra nodded. "My father was half elf."

"Hm. Likely not enough elf blood in you to give you much nature magic, then . . . But it's always possible that you have some sorcery in you as well."

She looked a little deflated, and turned her eyes to the wet sand where the pool had been.

"Would you like to try?" he asked.

She looked back up at him, those strange, pale green eyes alight with excitement. "Yes," she answered with an eager nod.

Kael paused, thinking for a moment. He was no instructor. "Well," he said, "there are two main kinds of magic—nature magic and word magic. Word magic is what sorcerers use. They have spells, words of power that allow them to harness control over an object or an element. Nature magic is elven magic, and is based on the four elements—earth, wind, water, and fire. All nature magic is some combination of those four elements."

"And what of Dark magic?" Andra asked.

His eyes narrowed slightly as he looked at her. "Dark magic calls upon the power of the dead. They say it uses the energy of the departed's souls, but it's impossible to say for certain if that's true. It's the most powerful form of magic there is, and is free of many of the limitations of word and nature magic, but Dark magic has an effect on the one who uses it. Touching the souls of the dead binds them to you, and it makes you something less than human. By using their souls, you lose your own. The Guardians banned the use of Dark magic when they established the judges' rule, but there are always a few sorcerers who practice it, hiding the true source of their power for as long as they can."

She nodded. She'd heard rumors of Dark sorcerers and sorceresses during her time serving the judges, but it was difficult to prove the exact source of a person's magic.

"What kind of magic do Riders use?" Andra asked.

"Riders can use both nature and word magic," Kael replied, "but we primarily use nature magic. Dragons are connected to the energy of the earth, and so nature magic comes more naturally to us, through them."

"And what do you think I will be able to use? If I can use any, I mean," she added hastily, as if she didn't want to get her own hopes too high.

Kael shrugged. "We can try a little of both. Here." He picked up a stone that rested on the ground nearby and held it in his palm. "Focus your mind on the stone; then say, 'Concalo.'"

He watched her brow furrow, her eyes intent on the stone in his hand. She held out her own hand, palm up, then said in a clear, confident voice, "Concalo."

The stone didn't move. He immediately saw the disappointment in her eyes, and she gave him a sheepish smile. "I really thought it would work."

"We'll try nature magic instead. It's a bit more difficult to explain, but you need to focus on the wind. Close your eyes."

She did so.

"Focus only on the feel of the breeze on your skin. The movement of the air has an energy to it. You need to find that energy."

Her face was calm and relaxed as she focused on the slight breeze that stirred the sand around them. He watched her, noticing for the first time how her skin had darkened from her weeks sleeping in the sun, her brown hair attaining streaks of auburn that burned to life in the sunlight. Much about her had changed since he first found her in those dark corridors.

"Now what?"

Her words jolted him from his study of her, and he answered quickly. "Try to bring that energy to you, make it collect in front of you." He saw her brow furrow slightly and he added, "Stay relaxed. Nature magic is connected to your emotions. You can't force it to obey. You have to guide it to your will."

Her brow smoothed again, and she remained still for several long seconds. Finally, she sighed and opened her eyes. "I guess I just don't have the ability," she said. Her voice was calm and indifferent, but he saw definite disappointment in her eyes.

"Maybe not," he answered with a shrug. "But it does take time to learn, so it's still possible."

This earned him a small smile from her. They were both silent for a moment; then Andra asked quietly, "Could I see it?"

Kael looked back at her. "See what?"

She nodded at where his right hand rested on the sand between them. "Your mark. All the years I was at the Hall, I never saw a Rider's mark. It seems that all Riders always keep their gloves on."

Kael tugged off the fingerless black gloves and held his hand out between them, palm up. He heard her let out a quiet gasp, and her hands immediately seized his, bringing it closer to her so she could examine the flame-shaped mark more closely. It shimmered in the desert sun, reflecting the light in a reddish hue.

"It's beautiful," she breathed. One of her fingers touched the shape, softly tracing the edges of the flame. "Why is it red?"

Kael swallowed hard, watching her finger continuing to trail across his palm. "A Rider's mark reflects the light in the color of his dragon's scales," he answered.

"And your magic comes from the mark?"

"Not exactly. My magic comes from Eithne. The mark is my strongest link to her, so my magic is strongest when I channel through it."

She looked up at him then, her green eyes meeting his, and she released his hand with an embarrassed smile. "Sorry. I shouldn't have presumed—"

"It's fine," he answered briskly, pulling the glove back on.

He felt a tickle at the back of his mind—his dragon's amusement—and he pushed it away with a flash of irritation at her. This only made the amusement flare brighter for a moment before she drew it back.

"You should try to rest," Kael said. "We need to set out again at sunset."

Andra sighed and stood. "Seems impossible in this blasted heat," she muttered.

He nearly smiled at hearing the curse coming from the normally quiet girl's lips. "You should try nonetheless," he answered.

She strode back to Tiri's side, and he watched as she settled onto her cot beneath the dragon's wing. Eithne was prodding irritatingly at his mind again, her presence all satisfied amusement.

"Something funny, dragon?" he asked.

"Still think the girl is only a responsibility?" Eithne asked in a teasing tone.

"And what else would she be?"

He could feel her rolling her eyes inside his mind, though her head rested under her wing in the sun. *"Kael, even I can still feel her touch on your skin. You are dwelling on the sensation quite intently."*

He hurriedly slammed his mental walls down around the

memory of her fingertips grazing over his mark, the shiver that had run across his skin despite the day's heat.

He heard her chuckle in his mind. *"Ah yes. That is very convincing."*

14

Bellris

Andra leaned forward eagerly in the saddle, her eyes on the line of trees that she could now see on the horizon. The Burning Sands were almost behind them, and ahead of them lay Bellris.

"You seem excited," Colmen remarked, drawing up beside her on his horse.

She glanced at him and smiled. "Well, I suppose I am."

"Why?" Alik asked from Colmen's other side. "You're not exactly a Freeman—no offense intended, of course."

Andra shrugged. "I don't know, really. I suppose it's just . . . the idea of it." She continued to stare wistfully at the tree line, and the sky-reaching mountains behind them. "So many people, coming all this way because they believe the same thing. It's so . . ."

"Completely insane?" Alik suggested.

Andra laughed. "Brave," she finished. Her voice softened a little as she went on. "I think . . . I think my father would have joined you, if he hadn't been killed. He was brave too."

She felt their eyes on her, and they were silent for a long

moment. Finally, Kael spoke quietly from his place in the saddle behind her. "What happened to him?" he asked.

"He fought back," she said. "He did it to protect me when I was a child. He purchased a dagger and turned it on Ledo for pushing me down the stairs. He only managed to cut Ledo's hand before he was taken by the guards and executed."

Colmen rode up close beside her so that their knees brushed. His hand reached out and briefly touched her leg. "I'm so sorry, Andra," he said. His light violet eyes were filled with compassion and empathy. She could see in his face that he understood—he had lost someone too.

She felt Kael's arm move from around her waist, and his hand covered hers where it rested on the pommel of the saddle. She looked down at the leather-covered hand atop hers, surprised as his fingers curled briefly, tightening around her own. The gentle gesture was very unlike him. And then the hand was gone, returning to its position around her waist.

"Well," Alik said, "it won't be long now. At sunrise, you'll be able to see the village. And then it will be only a few hours until we're home again."

Andra heard a hint of wistfulness in the normally hard man's voice, and she thought back to what he had said about protecting someone. She had a feeling she would meet that person soon.

———◦◈◦———

When the sun began to rise over the desert, they didn't stop and camp as they normally did. They pushed their tired mounts onward, the dragons hovering overhead on the warm currents of air. As the light fell on the tree line, still several miles ahead, Andra's breath caught in excitement. There, nestled among the trees that boldly grew up to the edge of the sands, were rough huts—dozens of them.

Kael abruptly pulled his horse to a halt, and Eithne landed in the sand beside them, as if replying to a silent signal from her Rider. He swung down from the saddle, and Andra looked over her shoulder at him.

"What are you doing?" she asked.

"They'll be able to see us soon enough," Kael replied. "And they'll expect to see me with Eithne."

He climbed expertly into the saddle atop the red scales, and she saw the slightest change in his posture, a slight lift in his chin, a leveling of his gaze, and a straightening of his back. She thought for a moment that he looked like a hero returning from war. And then Eithne leapt into the sky, and Andra had to shield her eyes from the sand.

They continued on, with Andra bringing up the rear. Though she'd caught on enough to know how to lead her mount in a slow walk, she was far from confident in the saddle, and preferred to allow Kael's horse to follow the others.

She kept her eyes on the village as they slowly drew nearer. Suddenly, the shapes of two dragons appeared over the tops of the trees, soaring out toward them. The three men each lifted a hand in greeting, and Andra saw Riders astride the serpents return the gesture. They circled above Eithne and Tiri, then fell into flight alongside them, an emerald escort.

Andra stared up at the four dragons that flew above her, excitement bubbling inside her. A new sound reached her ears, and her eyes returned to the village, which was now in full view. There were people streaming out from between the trees and huts, and they were cheering, chanting that sacred word.

"Veholum! Veholum! Veholum!"

The four dragons soared ahead of the horses, and Colmen and Alik kicked their mounts into a slow canter. Andra tightened her knees and clung to the horse's mane as it followed the others' pace. Hundreds of people now stood along the edge of the sands, arms raised, waving and shouting in joyous greeting. Eithne and the two green dragons landed before the gathering crowd, while Tiri settled some distance away.

As Andra and the others loped up to the crowd, she heard that the chant had changed. Hundreds of voices now shouted, "Kael! Kael! Kael! Kael!"

She drew her mount to a stop outside the swarm of people. Colmen and Alik quickly dismounted and joined the throng, the crowd absorbing them into their midst with shouts of welcome and familiar embraces. Kael slipped from Eithne's saddle, and was pulled down from her leg by adoring hands.

Tiri spoke in her mind. *"Did you know he was their leader?"*

"No," she answered, shaking her head. She watched as Kael shook hands and accepted embraces and rough pats on the back. His expression was kind, his countenance steady, but his eyes looked weary. *"They seem to love him,"* she remarked to Tiri.

Before the dragon could respond, Kael broke from the crowd and came to her side. Without a word, he held a hand out to her, and she accepted it, slipping from the horse's back. He led her into the crowd, the sheer press of bodies overwhelming her instantly. She tightened her hold on Kael's hand to keep from being lost in the mass of hundreds of unfamiliar faces. He held on tightly in return, drawing her confidently through the crowd, which seemed to part for him.

Colmen fell in at her side, helping to give her some distance from the excited throng. The elf grinned at her happily. "Welcome to Bellris, Andra," he said with a chuckle.

She smiled back. "They all seem very happy to see you," she remarked.

"Of course," he answered. "Kael is the symbol of their revolution, after all. They're always happy when he returns safely from a mission."

Andra's brow furrowed, but Kael had thrown an irritated look over his shoulder at Colmen's remark, so she didn't question the elf any further. The crowd followed Kael between the huts and into the trees. Andra stared upward at the canopy in wonder.

Wooden bridges connected the trees and curved around the trunks in wide balconies. Rope ladders ran up to the balconies, and Andra could see windows and open doorways high up in the trees' trunks, level with the wooden walkways. They came to a place amid the trees that had been cleared of undergrowth, a large firepit in the center.

Kael released her hand, leaving Andra standing beside Colmen, and hopped up onto the stone wall that surrounded the pit. He raised both his hands, and the crowd quickly fell silent. Andra gazed up at him, as did the rest of the crowd.

"As you all know," he began, "we went to Vereor to capture Ledo, to use him against his father and prevent the rise of a new emperor."

A sharp voice spoke from the crowd. "And we can all see that he is not here."

Andra turned toward the voice, as did most of the others, and her gaze landed on a brown-haired young man with blue, blood-shot eyes. His arms were crossed over his chest as he stared steadily at Kael, and Andra recognized him as the Rider who had dismounted from the larger of the two green dragons.

Kael didn't seem fazed by the edge in the other Rider's voice. "You're right, Egan," he replied, "he's not here. Ledo is dead."

"So we have nothing to use against the Kingsmen!" Egan shouted.

"No," Kael answered evenly, "we don't."

The crowd had gone silent, their jubilation quickly stamped out.

"But . . ." a hesitant voice said from the crowd, "Astrum said that Ledo was the key to winning the rebellion. Without him . . ." The voice drifted off to anxious murmurs among the onlookers.

Kael's gray eyes seemed to scan each of their faces, and he spoke evenly, calmly. "We don't know what Astrum's words meant," he said simply. "We had begun to piece together this plan before his arrival in Bellris. When he delivered his message, we took it as confirmation that we had chosen the correct path, and so we followed through. But the Seer's words often have a different meaning than we first believe."

"We still have nothing from your little expedition," Egan snapped, arms still crossed over his chest, his blue eyes bitter on Kael.

Kael met his gaze, and Andra thought she saw a flash of fire in his gray eyes. But his voice was even when he spoke. "We have nothing more than we had before, but we still have something— hope." He didn't raise his voice, didn't shout his words to the crowd. But there was a fervency in his voice that filled Andra with strength, passion, and the very hope of which he spoke. "There is not one among us who joined this cause because it was a certain and swift victory. We all came to Bellris because we had hope. Hope that we could restore what the Guardians sacrificed so much to build. Hope of rebuilding a land that we love. Hope for something better. And we still have that hope. This is not the first plan that has failed, and it may not be the last. But we must hold on to that hope. We *will* find another way. We are Freemen, and we *will* make Paerolia free again."

The gathered rebels cheered loudly, fists thrust into the air, the failure of their plan forgotten, and Andra found herself shouting along with them. Kael looked down at her and her upraised fist, and she smiled at him broadly. She thought she saw the hint of a smile on his lips.

Then he looked up at the crowd again and called, "Captains, gather for a full report!" before hopping off the stone wall and landing beside Andra.

She beamed at him. "That was incredible."

He gave a snort and a dismissive shrug, then said, "I'll need to meet with the other leaders to give them a full report of the mission. Colmen is one of my captains, so he'll have to come as well." Kael raised a hand and made a gesturing motion. A woman with soft brown skin and dark hair, which hung in a thick braid over her shoulder, stepped up beside Andra. "Andra, this is Amala, our Healer. Amala, this is Andra."

The Healer nodded at her, and she thought she saw the woman's dark eyes flash to the contract collar around her neck. But Amala smiled at her kindly. "Welcome to Bellris, Andra. Did you flee to join the rebellion as well?"

"It's a bit more complicated than that," Kael muttered. "Amala, is the room near yours still empty?"

Amala nodded.

"Will you see to it that Andra is comfortable here?"

"It would be my pleasure," she answered with another flash of a smile at Andra. She gestured with her head toward the trees. "This way."

Andra hesitated, looking back at Kael once more. But he was already turning away, and so Andra trotted off after the Healer, going deeper into the forest.

Kael pinched his nose wearily. "That won't work," he said, trying to keep his tone even. "The elves can't support us outright, and our forces are too small without their armies. A direct attack on Vereor would be a failure that would wipe out the entirety of the rebellion."

Egan looked sharply at Colmen. "Then you and the other elves here need to speak to King Vires. We need the elves' numbers."

Kael frowned at the elder Rider. "King Vires?"

Egan gave a short nod. "We received report of King Raegin's death a fortnight ago," he answered quietly. "Vires has now ascended the throne, though he has assured us that the elves' support of our cause has not changed."

Kael saw Colmen briefly bow his head, lips moving in a silent prayer for his king's soul. Then the elf looked up, glaring at Egan. "Regardless of who may be king now, you know as well as I do that the elves attacking the judges would start another race war. The last one lasted for three hundred years, and it took the Guardians to end it. Do you really wish to start another?"

Egan sat back with a huff, crossing his arms over his chest and falling silent.

"What about the dwarves?" another at the table chimed in. Kael looked at Janis, the other Rider in the camp. He was only fourteen, but as a Rider, he had the right to be a part of these meetings. His hazel eyes were filled with a hopeful expression in his dark, youthful face. "Surely they'll support us. They supply us with weapons and armor. Can't they fight with us?"

Kael sighed and shook his head. "Dwarves aren't much for fighting. They're craftsmen. They may have fought in the last battle of the Great War, but in this battle, we must stand alone."

The room fell silent for a long moment, the gathered captains mulling over the difficulty of their situation. Once again, they were trying to fight a raging current with nothing but sticks as paddles.

"What of this girl and that wild dragon you said she was destined for?" Egan suddenly asked. "Does she know anything that could help us?"

Kael shook his head once more as he picked at a chip in the wooden table before him. "It's doubtful. Andra had never heard of the Kingsmen when she joined us."

"Wouldn't hurt to ask her, though," Colmen added with a shrug. "Maybe she has information and doesn't know it."

The rebel general let out a puff of air, blowing a black strand of hair away from his eyes. "Perhaps. For now, let's move on. Any news from our scouts and spies while I was away?"

Egan, second-in-command whether Kael wished it or not, nodded. "It seems Judge Caedo has taken up with a sorceress as his bedmate, and there are rumors that she uses Dark magic."

Kael's hand reflexively gripped the arm of his chair at the name, his teeth grinding together.

Egan went on. "There have been soldiers filtering slowly into Vereor, but they're not going to the Chief Judge's palace as we thought at first—they're going to Caedo's manor."

His black brows drew together, eyes narrowing. "Anyone inside his manor who can give us more information?"

Egan nodded. "We have one source. His last report came shortly after you left on your mission, and he merely said that Caedo was gathering forces to support Castigo in his bid for a throne."

"But nothing on when that might happen?"

The elder Rider shook his head of brown hair. "No. But with a Dark sorceress in his bed and that many soldiers at his side, Caedo alone will be a force to be reckoned with. Combined with Castigo's armies . . ."

Kael nodded. He knew what the numbers meant. "So we have to move first," he said decisively. "We have to strike before they combine their forces and eliminate the judgment seats completely."

"Obviously," Egan answered with a less-than-subtle eye roll. "It's the *how* of it that makes things difficult."

Kael's fingers twitched toward the dagger in his boot, but Eithne pushed against his mind, holding his hand back.

"Slow yourself, my West Wind," she said. *"You may hate him, but this rebellion needs him."*

He sighed and rested his closed fist on his knee. There was a long pause as he mulled over the information. He stared at the table, imagining his army and the armies of the judges as pieces in a game of stones—only they had ten times the number of stones that he had. He saw their movements in his mind, and played out each scenario to an unsuccessful ending for the Freemen. Finally, he ran his hand wearily across his eyes.

"Insarius," he said, addressing the man who had remained silent for most of the meeting. The head of their spy network looked up at him with flat, emotionless eyes. "See if you can't get us one more source inside Caedo's manor. And get another report from our spies in the Hall of Riders. We need to know whom the Riders will back if Castigo does make his bid for an empire."

Insarius nodded silently.

"We'll break for tonight," Kael went on. "Perhaps sleep will bring us a little more clarity."

With that, the others stood and departed, likely in search of food. Kael dropped his head into his hands with a quiet groan. He felt Eithne at the back of his mind, trying to soothe him, but even her calmness and confidence could not push out the growing feeling of hopelessness inside him.

"We will overcome this, Kael," Eithne said softly. *"We have what is right on our side. And light will always banish the dark."*

He tried desperately to believe her.

15

Making Acquaintance

Andra stood at the edge of the wooden railing, gazing down at the forest floor below her. It was truly amazing. Though many of the Bellrisians lived in huts, the vast majority of the rebels lived in trees. Her room—which she was amazed to learn she shared with no one—was simply a round room in the center of a tree, as if the inside of the tree had been hollowed out, leaving a smooth floor, curved walls, a window, and a doorway.

She sighed contentedly as she watched the early risers in the camp move about on the forest floor. There were many women and children in Bellris, and she couldn't help but wonder what had driven them to cross a desert and join a rebellion.

Across the wooden bridge beside her, she saw a curtain draw back from the open doorway, and looked up to find Kael stepping out. He had dark circles under his eyes, and his hair was disheveled from sleep. His tunic was in his hand, his torso bare, and she caught a glimpse of several white scars on his olive-toned skin before he pulled the fabric down over his head.

She straightened and lifted a hand at him in greeting. He raised one in reply, rubbing at his eyes as he crossed the bridge to her.

"You're up early," he remarked, his voice still thick and hoarse with sleep.

"As are you," she replied.

Kael shrugged. "There's too much to do most days to let myself sleep past sunrise."

She looked at his weary appearance with a feeling of pity. Their journey had been long and taxing, but she was able to retire early the night before. Kael had been in his meeting with the army captains when she went to sleep, and she felt certain the meeting had continued long into the night.

"You need rest," she told him. "You look half dead."

"Only half?" he grumbled.

She laughed, and he shot her a sideways glance, sharing in the joke, though he didn't smile.

"Kael, can I ask you something?" she asked hesitantly.

The Rider suppressed a yawn. "Go on," he said with a nod.

"Why did Colmen say you were the symbol of the rebellion?"

Kael pressed his lips together, the weariness fading as a hard edge touched his features. "Colmen was being his usual absurd self," he muttered.

Andra shook her head slowly. "I don't believe that. I saw the way these people received you yesterday. I know you're their leader, but they treated you with more than just respect toward an army's commander."

He sighed, running his hands over his face before leaning forward on the railing beside her. He was silent for a long moment, watching his fingers entwining with each other. Finally, he said, "I am their symbol, Andra, because of who I am. Not only the first Rider to abandon the Hall to join them, but the son of a judge as well."

Andra leaned forward, certain she'd misheard him. "Your father is a judge?"

"Was," he corrected. "He died when I was sixteen, just before I left the Hall. They said he fell ill, but I'd seen him the day before, and he was in perfect health."

"You think he was killed? By whom?"

"My brother," he answered. She heard his voice go immediately hard with hatred. "Caedo."

Andra drew in a breath at the name. She knew Judge Caedo. She'd seen him many times at the Hall of Riders. He seemed to come every month, watching the Riders train as if he were a general overseeing the training of his personal armies.

Kael went on, "Caedo hated me from the moment Eithne chose me. He'd always been so certain that he would be a Rider, but was passed over at a Pairing when he was twelve. So when I was Paired with Eithne six years later, he was furious. It was as if my becoming a Rider was a personal slight to him. He became obsessed with becoming a judge, with taking my father's judgment seat someday. I think it finally reached a point when he could wait no longer."

"Why did you flee the Hall?" she asked.

"I grew up in my father's house, Andra," he said, looking at her. "I saw everything that happened there. I saw the corruption in the judges' councils, the bribing and the blackmail in the Hall, the misuse of the labor contracts to subject entire families to a lifetime of servitude. By the time I became a Rider, I'd heard whisperings of a rebellion, and I always listened for word of their movements. And when Caedo took my father's judgment seat, I knew it was time to abandon the Hall. So, when I was sixteen, Eithne and I left and followed those whisperings I'd heard until we found the Freemen. And within the year, they chose me as their commander."

"When you were seventeen?"

Kael shrugged. "I was a Rider. I was young, but I'd been receiving combat training at the Hall since I was twelve, while most of the other rebels were farmers or former contract laborers. And, as the son of a former judge, I knew the way the government worked. Plus, as Colmen was so shrewd to point out, I made a good symbol."

Andra was silent for a moment, but he didn't give her long to consider his words. He straightened from the rail and turned down the walkway. "We should get our morning rations before the rest of the camp wakes."

She trotted after him, across another bridge between the trees. She could tell his recent confession made him uneasy, so she took up a new line of questioning, hoping to distract him. "How was this place built? The rooms in the trees, and the bridges, I mean."

"Bellris is built from a combination of human construction and nature magic," he answered. "In Iterum, the entire city is sung from trees—rooms, stairs, balconies, bridges. But that's a form of nature magic that takes time, and we were in a hurry here, so those with enough elven blood to sing to the trees created rooms in them. The rest of the villagers built the ladders and bridges around them."

"It's incredible," she whispered.

He descended a rope ladder and she clambered down it after him, jumping confidently to the ground from several feet up the rungs. He raised an eyebrow at her, and she smiled in return. They headed toward the central fire, where Andra could smell something cooking and hear the sound of chatter and laughter.

The two approached the small cluster of people that had begun to gather around for breakfast. As soon as they came within sight, someone descended upon them, sweeping Andra into an eager hug.

"Andra!" Colmen cried. "You're awake!"

She laughed as he set her back on her feet.

He smiled down at her, his hands on her shoulders. "It's wonderful to see you again."

"It hasn't even been a day since I last saw you," she replied laughingly.

"Yes, well, I've spent the last three weeks with you almost constantly at my side, so being separated from you for even that long is liable to make my heart break," he said, putting an arm over her shoulders in a familiar way. Somehow, it didn't bother her. The feeling of companionship was comforting.

Two more people stepped forward from the group, the movement drawing Andra's eyes. Alik mumbled a greeting to her, and the young woman beside him offered her a hand in greeting. Her hair was a red-gold color in the morning sunlight, and freckles spattered her cheeks, making her look almost childlike. Andra was quite certain she was meeting the woman for whom Alik would kill to protect.

"Hello, Andra," she said. "I'm Syra. It's wonderful to finally get to meet you. Alik has told me so much about you."

"He has?" Andra asked, looking at Alik in surprise. Though the man had been companionable enough in recent weeks, it was far from the outright fondness that Colmen had shown, and certainly not close enough that she thought he would have talked about her to others.

Syra laughed. "Well, you needn't sound so surprised. He may pretend to be very gruff," she said, slipping her hand softly into Alik's and looking up at his face, "but he's not so hardened as he likes to appear."

"Come on," Kael said, gesturing toward the fire and drawing Andra's attention away from Alik and Syra. "We should find some breakfast before the rest of the camp starts coming for their rations."

"Of course!" Colmen cried, taking Andra by the hand. "Come, I'll introduce you to some of the others."

Andra tried to protest, but Colmen didn't seem to hear. He dragged her toward the fire, where she was immediately surrounded by faces—some friendly, some curious, some very guarded. Colmen started pointing to people and stating their names so quickly that Andra had no hope of remembering a single one.

"I said *food*, Colmen, not introductions to the entire camp."

The elf looked up at Kael, who was standing nearby, watching him with very stern gray eyes. Colmen grinned dismissively. "You know me, can't wait to show off a pretty girl."

Kael rolled his eyes as he began to turn away. "Just feed her, will you? I have someone I need to see."

Colmen nodded. "Can do."

Andra watched as Kael's back disappeared through the small crowd, wishing she could go with him; the closeness of so many people was making her uncomfortable. But to her great relief, Colmen soon removed her from the nearby bodies and sat her on a fallen tree that had been cut and placed to serve as a bench near the fire.

"Just wait here," he told her. "I'll get you some food."

He disappeared back into the mass of people vying for their rations. Andra sighed and rested her chin in her hands. A few people separated from the group, plates with servings of food in their hands, and sat on logs scattered around the firepit. Andra looked up as a young man sat a few feet away from her. He didn't look in her direction, but she felt that he was very much aware of her.

Colmen returned a moment later with two plates and handed one to her. She took it, but before he could sit beside her, a voice shouted over the rising noise of the growing crowd.

"Colmen!" someone called from somewhere near the huts. "Come here!"

He turned to Andra. "I'll be right back. Don't go anywhere, okay?"

She nodded and watched him disappear through the people. As

soon as he was out of sight, an uneasy feeling settled in her stomach, a feeling she knew all too well—the feeling of someone watching her. She immediately looked to her right and found the young man who had sat nearby staring openly at her as he took a long draw from his flask.

He smiled, a gesture that seemed friendly enough, so Andra relaxed slightly and offered a small smile in return. Taking this as permission, he moved closer, still maintaining a respectful distance. She recognized him now as the Rider of the large green dragon. His eyes were as bloodshot now as they had been the previous day, when she'd first arrived.

"Andra, right?" he asked conversationally.

She nodded. "Yes."

"I'm Egan," he responded.

"A pleasure to meet you."

He simply smiled and turned his eyes back to the fire. Andra watched him cautiously from the corner of her eye. He had light brown hair and a lean figure. He was dressed in the usual tunic and trousers, with high boots and a sword strapped to his waist. On his hands, he wore a pair of short-cropped Rider's gloves.

"You're a Rider, correct?" Andra finally asked, breaking the uncomfortable silence.

Egan gave her a sideways glance. "Oh, yes. I was Paired with Calix when I was twelve. Two years before Kael was Paired with Eithne."

"When did you join the Freemen?"

"About three years ago now. Just a year after Kael. But it was long enough that they'd already elected him to lead."

Andra could feel the bitterness in his voice. "Oh, I see," she muttered, turning her eyes away from him.

There was a brief silence; then Egan held out his flask to her. "Care for a drink?" he asked.

Andra looked down at the metal container in his hand, then at his bloodshot eyes. She may not have been able to smell the spirits on him at this distance, but she knew precisely what the flask held.

"No, thank you," she answered politely.

Egan shrugged and pulled the flask back, taking another sip from it. "So, if Kael took you from that manor and dragged you across half of Paerolia against your will, then why are you still here?"

She frowned at him. "What?"

He met her eyes again. "It doesn't seem like you're a prisoner."

"I'm not," she answered immediately, confident in the truth of her words.

"But you didn't come to the rebellion by choice. So why don't you leave?"

Andra fell silent, her fingers drifting to the leather bracelet on her wrist. She had intended to leave. She'd tried twice, but been stopped. And then she hadn't tried again. She felt that Kael now trusted her enough that he would let her go without fear of her betraying them. So why did she stay?

"Are you finished?"

She looked up to find Kael standing nearby. His gray eyes were tinged with suspicion as he glanced between her and Egan. The tension between them set her nerves on edge, and she stood.

"Yes," she replied quickly.

"Good. There's someone I wanted you to meet."

He turned and started away from the fire, and Andra hurried to follow, not bothering to say any kind of farewell to Egan. Kael led her through the trees on the eastern side of the camp, and they stepped out onto a meadow that stretched to the base of the mountains. A lake lay a hundred yards from the tree line, sparkling in the sunlight as the two green dragons splashed about in the water. The lake stretched toward the enormous mountains to the north, jutting out into a narrow spur of water where the dragons cavorted with bugles and snarls.

Eithne and Tiri rested close by, and Andra heard Tiri hum a melodic greeting as she and Kael approached the pair. The dragon nuzzled her shoulder in an affectionate way, and Andra smiled, stroking the violet scales between Tiri's eyes.

"Are you taking her to Setora now?" Eithne asked, projecting her thoughts to Kael and Andra alike.

Kael nodded once, his expression tense. "Based on what she told me, I thought it best she meet her right away."

Eithne nodded her agreement, and Andra glanced between them with a frown on her face.

"Who's Setora?" she asked. "Why do I need to meet her right away?"

"You'll see soon enough," he replied, already striding away from the dragons. "She's just on the other side of the lake."

She gave Tiri a pat of farewell, then hurried after the Rider. As she fell into step beside him, she spotted a low, rough hovel on the far bank of the narrow spur of water, a dark tendril of smoke curling skyward. "Why isn't she with the rest of the encampment?"

"She likes her privacy," Kael said with a shrug. "I went and spoke to her a moment ago, after I finished reviewing the rations report. When I spoke of you, she insisted I bring you as soon as possible."

"Is she a friend of yours?" Andra asked, studying the odd building.

"Not exactly," Kael sighed. "She's my mother."

Andra fell silent in her surprise. He'd always seemed so distant, so isolated from everyone but Eithne, that she'd somehow never considered he might have a family. Aside from Colmen, there didn't seem to be another person in the world who could crack through his steely façade.

They gradually rounded the narrow point of the lake and approached the little brown hut that she had spotted from across the water. Stacks of wooden cages stood against the walls, all of them different sizes. Most were empty, but a few held wild animals that stared warily up at the two approaching figures. Andra drew cautiously closer to the cages, studying the animals with curiosity. She looked over her shoulder at where Kael stood, watching her.

"Why are they here?" she asked.

He shrugged. "This is part of what my mother does. She finds most of them, injured in one way or another. She heals them."

Andra's brow furrowed. "Your mother is a Healer?" she asked, her fingers reaching out toward the cages.

"He wishes I were something that noble," a rough voice squawked.

Andra jumped and quickly clasped her hands behind her back, but Kael merely sighed and turned toward the voice. A woman hobbled around the corner of the shack, her withered arms full of herbs. She wore a rough brown dress, and her hair was a tangled mess of pale gray.

"I see you actually took my advice this time," the woman muttered, pushing bunches of herbs into the animals' cages; it seemed as if she was speaking more to them than to anyone else. "Brought the girl over here in quite the hurry."

Kael sighed. "You said it was important, Mother, so I brought her."

Setora continued feeding the caged animals herbs until her arms were empty. Then she dusted the dirt from her dress and finally looked at them. Her eyes immediately locked on Andra's. They were the same steely gray as Kael's, and her skin held the same golden brown tones as her son's, though a shade darker. Setora smiled crookedly at the silent girl.

"Andra," she said, the smile growing. "Come inside. I've been waiting to speak to you."

16

Setora

Andra peered cautiously around the dim, dusty room. Behind a curtain of beads, she could hear Kael's mother mumbling to herself as she searched through her things. Andra sat on a rough stool at a low wooden table in the middle of the room. Kael sat beside her, looking irritated.

"I shouldn't have brought you here," he grumbled, more to himself than to Andra. "I knew she was going to do this."

Andra didn't respond, but continued gazing around the room, listening to the shuffling of the woman behind the beaded curtain. A fireplace on the nearest wall was still filled with ashes from the winter. Books and several odds and ends were scattered about the room—books stacked on chairs, herbs hanging from the ceiling— all with a fine layer of dust. There were more cages inside as well, each holding an animal that peered at them quietly from between the bars of the cage.

The beads parted and Setora emerged, a heavy book in her arms. "I found it," she announced with a small smile, lifting the book slightly. She shuffled to the table and set it down, pulling up another stool. "It's been many years since I've done this. It helps to have a little bit of a reminder. As I am quite certain my son failed to mention, I'm a witch. And telling fortunes is one of the many things that I can do."

"Is this really what was so important, Mother?" Kael asked irritably.

His mother fixed him with a stern gaze. "Practice, patience, Kael," she said in a stern voice. "There are ways to do things, and this is the simplest way to begin."

Kael sighed and sat back without another word. Setora held out her hands toward Andra. Andra looked down at the extended hands, which were withered with age, then cautiously placed her own hands in her waiting palms. The moment her skin touched the wrinkled hands, the woman gasped and pulled away as if she had been burned, and Andra jerked her hands back into her lap. Kael frowned at his mother in confusion. Then Setora smiled as though she found something deeply amusing.

"Kael," she said softly, "I think you should leave me and Andra to speak alone."

Her son's frown deepened. "Why?" he asked sharply. "What happened?"

Setora simply continued smiling, her eyes on Andra. "This is something between Andra and myself."

Andra looked up at the Rider, who was gazing back down at her uncertainly. After a moment, he sighed and pushed himself up off the stool.

He gave his mother a stern look and said, "Try not to scare her."

Again, Setora smiled. "I can make no promises."

Kael looked down at Andra. "I'll be right outside," he told her.

Andra gave a small nod, then watched him walk out the door and close it behind him with a snap. She looked back at Setora, who was watching her with that slight smile still on her lips, though her eyes were guarded.

"Did I do something wrong?" Andra asked cautiously.

"Not at all," Setora answered, holding out her hands again. "You merely startled me. I knew from what Kael told me that you had a great amount of magic about you, but I wasn't expecting quite so much."

"Magic?" Andra asked in confusion. "I—I can't do magic. Kael had me try when we were crossing the desert."

"We all have magic within us," Setora replied. "It is our very energy. However, not all have the ability to release that magic. Some, like myself, have found other ways to release our magic. Witchcraft gives us that ability, but there is a consequence for it." Setora sighed and looked down at her withered hands. "We cannot replenish that magic as sorcerers and Riders can. By using magic, we sacrifice a part of our energy, and thereby, a part of our lives. So we must be very careful with how we use it." She looked back up at Andra. "But you possess more unreleased magic than most. Even more than Kael. It is in your eyes."

Andra blinked. "My eyes?"

"Yes," Setora said with a nod. "They are a very strange color. Something you got from one of your parents, I'd wager?"

"Yes. From my father. Mother always said I had his eyes."

"Then he would have been powerful too. You, my dear, still can be. You see, there are a few in this world—a very few, mind you—who possess a special ability to replenish their magic very quickly. Among the witches, we call them Siphons, because they can take energy from anything around them, without any effort. You, Andra, are a Siphon, as was your father. Nobody is certain what gives so few people this ability, but it is always those who have some combination of both elven and human ancestry. I believe it is the mingling of earth magic and word magic that helps to bring this ability to light, and though it has become more common as the two races have mingled, it is still exceptionally rare.

"You see, most sorcerers, Riders, and even elves have a limit on

150 · ERIN SWAN

the amount of magic they can draw into themselves. But a Siphon has nearly unlimited potential. They can draw in power slowly, over many years, and their magic will continue to grow, their coffers of energy stretching to greater and greater limits. The magic within you has built to extraordinary levels. And because you never learned how to release it, it grows still."

"How do you know all this?"

Setora gestured to the books around her. "Reading helps. But life is the greatest teacher. I met a Siphon, and he had those same pale green eyes that you have. I saw him create a thunderstorm that nearly leveled an entire forest, and it hardly taxed him at all."

"But if I can't release my magic . . ."

Setora simply smiled once more. "Yet."

The woman held out her hands again. Cautiously, Andra placed both her hands in the woman's. The witch turned the girl's hands so the palms faced her.

"Ah," she said, seeing the scar that marred her left hand, left by the wound from catching the archer's arrow. "I should have guessed that something would make this difficult for me. Well, I suppose I shall just have to settle for a small part of your future, as will you."

She released Andra's left hand, which the girl placed back into her lap, then began running one withered finger along the lines of her other hand. Setora paused, frowned, and released Andra's hand to open the book beside her. She flipped through several pages, then took Andra's hand again, glancing back and forth between the upturned palm and the book, as if comparing two texts.

The smile returned to her face. "Yes, I thought this was coming."

"What?" Andra asked, suddenly feeling eager.

"Here," Setora said, tracing two lines across her palm. "Your life intersected with someone whom you came to care about deeply." Andra's heart fluttered at the thought of Talias. "It is one of two major love lines that I can see," Setora continued. "Here, the first line drops away from yours—"

"Why?" Andra interrupted.

Setora lifted one thin shoulder in a shrug. "Palm readings can't give that much detail, I'm afraid. But it falls away just as another love line crosses your life line. Well, not really crosses so much as merges. It does not drop away." She paused as she looked over at her book again, flipped a few pages, then turned back to Andra. She ran her finger across another line, which almost ran perfectly vertical over Andra's hand. "This is a mark of great strength and power, just as I suspected," she said with a new self-satisfied smile. "Kael has the same line on his palm. You shall be a leader, just as he is."

Setora's face suddenly turned into a frown as she touched a short line on Andra's palm. "Ah, well," she sighed, "I suppose it should be expected for someone with so much before her." She took a deep breath and said, "Death. The death of someone very close to you, someone you care about."

Andra's heart seemed to stutter to a stop. "Do you mean in the past?" she asked breathlessly. "Because my parents have both died."

Setora pursed her lips and shook her head. "No, this is certainly in the future. Yes, someone you care about will die. I suspect—"

Andra quickly pulled her hand away and stood. "I'm sorry," she stammered, "but I need to go."

The witch seemed about to protest, so Andra darted out the door, throwing it open with more force than was necessary. It banged against something, which yelped and swore. Andra quickly turned around, wide eyed as Kael pushed away the door, rubbing his arm.

"You know," he grumbled, frowning at her, "you seem to bruise me a lot."

"Oh, I—I'm sorry! I didn't know you were—I was just . . ."

"Leaving in an awful hurry," he finished, taking a step toward her. "What did she do?"

"Oh, no, it—it wasn't anything. I just—"

Kael didn't let her finish; scowling furiously, he stomped into the doorway of the hut, glaring at his mother, who was still sitting at the table, looking surprised. "What did you do to her?" he snapped.

Setora held up her hands in a motion of surrender. "I just told her what I saw."

Kael stared at her disbelievingly.

"Really," Andra interrupted, placing an unsure hand on his arm. "It was just . . . I don't think I'm ready to know my future just yet," she said with an uncomfortable laugh.

Kael looked down at her, as if trying to read her expression, but she dropped her gaze. Finally, he sighed. "Mother, we're leaving."

Andra heard Setora huff in annoyance. "Very well. But you know she will need to come back here. I didn't ask you to bring her simply so I could say hello, Kael. Andra has great power within her." The witch looked at Andra, her expression earnest. "You need to control that power, my dear. It is essential—to everything."

"I'll discuss it with her," Kael said brusquely. "But I think you've given her enough to think about for one day." With that, he turned and strode away from the hut. Andra paused, looking back at Setora.

The woman reached out and seized her hand briefly, giving it a squeeze. "Promise me you'll return," she whispered quietly.

Andra nodded, returning the pressure of her hand, then hurried after Kael's retreating form. She fell into step beside him again, her steps quick to keep up with his long strides.

"Has your mother always been a witch?" she asked, wanting to end his brooding silence quickly.

Kael glanced down at her from the corner of his eye. "No. She took it up when I was about six."

"And . . . you do not approve?" she guessed.

He sighed and ruffled his own hair. "Not after seeing what it's doing to her. I've asked her to stop, but she won't."

"You mean how it ages her?" Andra suddenly felt as if she could see through his hostility toward his mother. "You only act angry with her because you hate seeing what she's done to herself."

Kael was silent.

Eithne and Tiri lifted their heads and bugled in unison at their approach. Both Andra and Kael lifted their hands in greeting. Kael stepped up beside Eithne and began scratching her jaw. She hummed with delight.

"Did anyone tell you of the celebration tonight?" he asked without looking away from his dragon.

Andra nodded as she sat in the grass beside Tiri. "Colmen said it's to celebrate your safe return."

Kael scoffed. "Don't see much reason to celebrate," he muttered. "It was still a failed mission."

"But you came back alive," Andra said. "That matters."

He looked down at her, his expression curious, but quickly looked away again. "I have tasks to tend to the rest of the day. I'll let Colmen know you're out here. I'm sure he'll come visit you when he gets a moment."

Andra watched Kael as he turned toward the village and strode back between the trees. When he disappeared, she looked down at the line on her palm, tracing it with her index finger, trying to suppress the sadness creeping into her heart. Who else would death steal away from her?

17

Celebrating

"Andra," a teasing voice called. Someone prodded her shoulder. Andra groaned and turned away. She heard a quiet, amused laugh. "Andra!" the voice called more loudly, shaking her slightly.

Andra sat upright, seized by the horrible feeling that she was back in the manor, and had overslept. She looked frantically around to see a pair of amethyst eyes, much the color of Tiri's, smiling down at her.

"Well, hello, sleepyhead," Colmen said with a grin.

Andra smiled. "Hello, Colmen."

"Kael told me I might find you here. Syra wanted me to fetch you to help you prepare for tonight's celebration."

"Prepare?" Andra repeated.

"We don't often have reasons to celebrate around here, so people tend to make it into a bit of an affair. Syra has a dress for you and is ready to help with whatever else you girls do for these sorts of things." Colmen seized her by the hand and pulled her to her feet. "Follow me. I'll show you Syra's place."

Andra said her farewells to Tiri and Eithne, and followed Colmen back toward the village. They passed through the trees and approached the northern side of the camp, close to the edge of the desert. They stopped in front of a little hut nestled in the center of the others.

"Here we are," Colmen declared. "You go on inside; Syra's waiting for you. I'll see you at the celebration!"

With that, he trotted back toward the tree line, disappearing between the low huts. Andra sighed and turned toward the hut she was standing in front of. Cautiously, she rapped on the rough wooden door. Almost immediately, it was thrown open to reveal the curved form of Syra, beaming excitedly down into Andra's face.

"Andra!" she cried, seizing the younger girl by the hand. "I'm so glad you're here! I'm all ready for you. Here, have a seat." She pulled a chair away from the low dining table. "Just let me grab my mirror for you."

She turned and disappeared momentarily behind a curtain of sackcloth and appeared again with a silver-framed looking glass in her hand. "Here you go." She held out the mirror to Andra. "You can watch me work if you'd like."

Andra carefully took the mirror from Syra's hands and held it up in front of her face. She frowned slightly as she studied herself in the mirror. There was a bit of dirt smudged on her cheek from sleeping on the ground, and her hair was rumpled from the same. Her face was tanner than she remembered it being. She looked into her own eyes, thinking about what Kael's mother had said. Did she truly have great magic inside her, building up because she could not free it?

Syra started combing out Andra's hair. "I just can't figure out what we're going to do with your hair," she muttered, frowning at the brown locks, which fell only to the middle of Andra's neck.

She began pulling at locks of Andra's hair, braiding them, then unbraiding them, twisting and untwisting. They both lapsed into silence for several minutes.

"You're very quiet, Andra," Syra remarked at last.

"I was just . . . thinking," Andra answered.

"What about?"

"Kael."

The older girl laughed slightly. "Really? What about him?"

"Why do you think he brought me here?"

"I . . . suppose I don't know. I only really know what Alik has told me, and he thinks that Kael must feel some responsibility for you, since he took you from the palace."

Andra pressed her lips together, trying not to feel irritated by the statement. She was not a child who needed to be watched over.

"Do you think he would let me leave if I wished to?"

Syra's hands fell still. *"Do* you wish to leave?" she asked quietly.

"I . . . I don't know."

"Well," Syra sighed, grabbing a few items that Andra didn't recognize and pulling up a chair beside her, "I don't see any reason why he should stop you."

Andra twisted the leather bracelet, thinking of Talias and that short line on her palm, as Syra began to apply a strange collection of powders and paints to her face. After several minutes, Syra sat back with a satisfied smile. "There. All finished. Have a look."

Andra had forgotten about the mirror in her lap. She picked it up and held it before her, immediately smiling too. "Syra . . ." she sighed in wonder. Then she laughed. "I look like a judge's daughter!"

Syra chuckled softly. "I think you look like a woman of Bellris. Now," she added, clapping her hands together, "time for your dress."

⟡

Andra laughed as she spun, watching the hunter green dress fan out around her legs. "Isn't it wonderful?" she asked of the dragons before her.

Tiri chuckled. *"It hardly seems like a practical thing, but if it makes you happy, sister, then I suppose it is wonderful."*

Andra smiled at the dragon, adjusting one of the thin straps that rested on her shoulders. "Some of us don't have glittering scales to always make us beautiful," she replied. "We must find other ways to accomplish it."

Eithne laughed at this as well, then touched her snout to the silver brooch that sparkled on the dress's bodice. *"And this is your glittering scale, I presume?"*

The dragons' rolling laughter made Andra chuckle, but before she could answer, Tiri and Eithne looked toward something over her shoulder, and Andra followed their gaze, turning around. Her eyes fell on Kael, and she smiled at him in surprise. "I didn't hear you approaching," she said.

He didn't answer her. She saw his eyes move over her, from the soft slippers on her feet to the plaits and curls Syra had put in her hair. She pushed aside a few stray pieces and shifted uncomfortably under his gaze, feeling her cheeks grow warm.

"Is everything all right?" she asked.

"Yes," he answered, seeming to pull himself back from some distant thought. "Eithne told me you were out here, so I thought I would come and take you to the celebration." Then, as if it were an afterthought, he added, "You look beautiful, Andra."

She felt her blush deepen and she smiled, dropping her gaze. "Thank you," she said. "You look wonderful as well."

And he did. She had grown used to seeing him in worn traveling clothes, but now he stood before her in a pair of clean black trousers and a white tunic, belted in black leather. The light from the setting sun darkened his gold-toned skin and seemed to reflect off the gray in his eyes, turning them to fire.

Kael held his arm toward her, distracting her from her study of him. "Ready?"

She looked at the arm, then cautiously slipped her hand into the crook of his elbow. They started toward the trees, where the orange glow of the fire was growing brighter, and she called a silent goodbye to the dragons as they walked away.

Andra turned her eyes upward, on the bright balls of colorful light that hung in the tree branches, casting dancing shadows all around them.

"They're beautiful," she sighed. She looked over at Kael to find he was already looking down at her. "Do you know how to make them?"

He nodded. "They're one of the first things you learn how to make when you start practicing nature magic."

They finally drew up to the bonfire. Music was already being loudly played, and people of all ages were dancing around the small clearing, laughing and twirling together. Food was roasting over the fire, and the smell permeated the air. The noise and the movement of hundreds of bodies both thrilled and intimidated her.

"I can stay with you if you'd rather avoid the crowd," Kael said, seeming to notice her hesitancy.

Andra smiled and shook her head. "I wouldn't want to keep you."

He shrugged. "From whom?"

No sooner had he said the words than a form extracted itself from the crowd and hurried toward them, calling, "Kael! There you are!"

A young blond woman drew up before them. She smiled coyly at Kael, then turned her attention to Andra. "Hello," she said in a not unfriendly voice, "you must be Andra. I'm Aylea."

Andra released Kael's arm and dropped a small curtsy. "A pleasure to meet you, Aylea."

Aylea's smile widened but her attention quickly turned back to

Kael. Seizing the arm that Andra had just released, she said in a coaxing tone, "Come on, Kael. Dance with me. I don't think you've ever danced a day in your life!"

Kael didn't move. "I told Andra I'd stay with her."

Andra shook her head. "I can manage."

"There," Aylea insisted, still tugging on his arm, "you heard the girl. Now, come on!"

He glanced at Andra once more, then allowed himself to be pulled toward the dancing, laughing crowd. Andra watched him disappear into the mass of bodies. She sighed and wrapped her arms around herself, suddenly feeling very alone. She glanced around her, searching for Colmen. Or Syra. Or even Alik. They were nowhere to be seen.

Cautiously, she began to work her way around the edge of the crowd, watching it with curious eyes. Those who weren't dancing were spread out across the clearing, sitting on logs, leaning against trees, and lying out on the grass. Some were eating, while others were simply talking, trying to make themselves heard over the noise.

Finding a vacant log, Andra sat with a sigh, resting her chin in her hands. As her eyes continued to scan the crowd, she managed to find Kael and Aylea. She was dancing. He wasn't. He seemed uncomfortable, and kept glancing over his shoulder as if looking for a means of escape, but Aylea had her hands on his shoulders, and she didn't seem intent on letting go anytime soon.

Sheltered by the shadows of the trees, certain that nobody would notice, Andra studied Kael in the firelight. His tunic was stark white, making his soft golden skin look even darker, turning his eyes the color of molten lead. His black hair reflected back the orange hues of the fire. She smiled slightly to herself, realizing that he appeared so very intimidating—his dark coloring, his odd gray eyes, the grim lines of his mouth, and firm set of his jaw.

Of course, he had terrified her at first, and in those moments when he became angry, he could frighten her still. But she had realized that he was not quite so coarse as he appeared to be. Beneath the assumed roughness, there was a gentleness to him she had not expected to find.

A motion in the corner of her eye caught her attention, and she turned to see a tall figure standing beside her, gazing down at her. He was clad in a gray tunic and black trousers, and he was holding a hand out toward her, palm up. The mark of a flame glinted up at her from his hand, reflecting the firelight in a greenish glow.

"Care to dance?" Egan asked with a crooked smile.

Andra paused, then slowly placed her hand in his. He smiled slightly again and pulled her to her feet, leading her to the fire amid the crush of bodies. He abruptly pulled her body close to his, making her breath catch. She tried to draw back, but his hand was firm on the small of her back, holding her torso against his own.

She glanced around, noticing that many other pairs were dancing in this way, and tried to force herself to relax. It was only a dance. But something in the pit of her stomach churned with a familiar discomfort.

He smirked slightly as he looked down at her. "Nice dress," he remarked.

"Thank you," she answered, her voice flat.

The smirk widened into a grin. "I scare you," he said. "I kind of like that, scaring Kael's new little pet."

Andra stiffened, her jaw clenching. She could clearly smell the spirits on his breath now. His bloodshot eyes had a wild, angry look to them.

"You see, Andra," Egan continued in a low voice, as if conspiring with her, "I don't like Kael much. The people here practically fall down to worship him. And why? Because he was the first Rider to get here. That's the only reason he leads."

"That's not true," Andra answered through her teeth.

He raised his eyebrows at her in surprise. "Oh, it's not?"

"No. Kael leads because he is brave, because he is strong, and because he cares about these people and this cause."

Egan laughed, a sharp and bitter sound. "And you are just like the rest of them already. So prepared to lick his boots if he demands it. Tell me, Andra, if he ordered you to his bed, would you go?"

She shoved herself backward, pushing against his chest, but his hands still held her firmly in place. "Let me go," she snarled.

"And what if I ordered you to mine?" he continued, his eyes never leaving her face. "Would you obey me as you would obey him?"

Suddenly, his hand went to the back of her neck. He grabbed it tightly, digging his fingers into her skin as he yanked her roughly forward. Egan's mouth covered hers with a hard, vengeful kiss. She continued to shove against him, trying to break away from his grip. Anger coursed through her veins, burning away the cold fear she'd felt. No. This would not happen to her again. This part of her life was over, and she would not go back to it.

In the back of her mind, there was a furious roar, and fire consumed her thoughts—angry fire, enveloping her, protecting her. There was a yelp and Egan leapt backward, swearing and cradling both his hands against his chest.

Around them, the Freemen fell abruptly silent, the music halting. Andra opened her eyes and found the silent crowd staring at the pair of them—at her. She looked down at her hands and found blue-violet flames flickering over every inch of her skin. She felt a shock of surprise, and the flames immediately vanished.

Amid the silent crowd, Andra heard one voice. "I said *move!*"

The crowd shifted and Kael forced his way among them until he reached the small circle that had cleared around the girl and the Rider. He glanced once at Andra, then turned a furious glare on Egan, who still cradled his hands to his chest. With an incomprehensible shout, Kael threw himself at the other Rider.

There were several gasps of surprise as the two men—the two

leaders of the rebel army—rolled across the forest floor. Andra heard the sound of flesh connecting with flesh, a sickening crunch; then the two tumbled apart, both gasping. Egan stumbled backward, one of his hands still held to his chest, the other pressed to his nose, blood dripping between his fingers.

Kael leapt back to his feet, apparently unharmed. Andra saw his legs coiling, ready to throw himself at Egan again, who was busy trying to Heal his broken nose. Andra jumped in front of the younger Rider and placed both her hands on his chest.

"Please don't," she pleaded quietly, glancing around at the bewildered Freemen.

Kael looked down at her, his gray eyes hazy with rage, then back up at Egan, who was now wiping the blood from his face, his nose straight once again.

"Please," Andra repeated. "You can't do this. Not here, in front of everyone."

He seemed to realize quite suddenly how many eyes witnessed the scene he'd just caused. He fixed Egan with a gaze that threatened bloodshed. "You shall answer for this," he said in a low, growling voice.

Egan met his gaze steadily, unafraid.

Kael seized Andra's hand and led her quickly through the crowd, which seemed to part for them, and into the darkness of the trees. When they were well away from the light of the fire, he stopped and made her turn to face him. She flinched slightly as he placed a hand on her shoulder, then gently took her chin in his hand. He lifted her head, turning it from one side to the other, inspecting the dark red fingerprints near the back of her neck, then took her arms and examined the marks there.

She saw his jaw clench, but he drew a breath, and when he rested his hands on her shoulders, they were soft. He looked down at her, his eyes swimming with a number of emotions she couldn't name.

"Andra," he said softly, "I'm sorry."

"Why are you sorry?" she asked. "Egan is the one who—"

"I'm sorry," he repeated, cutting her off. "This shouldn't have happened to you. I shouldn't have left you."

Syra's words from earlier in the evening came back to her, and she stepped away from him, avoiding his gentle gray eyes. "You're not responsible for me, Kael. I'm not a child. I don't need to be tended to."

He was silent for a long moment; then he stepped toward her again. His fingers touched her chin, turning her face softly back toward him. When she finally met his gaze again, his expression looked sad, somehow, a yearning look in his eyes.

"I . . ." he started, then stopped, as if he were choosing his words with extreme care. "I don't care about you because I feel that I *must*, Andra. I just . . . do."

She stared at him for a moment, taking in his words, reading the soft expression on his face. Then she wrapped her arms around him, pressing her face to his chest. For a single heartbeat, he was very still, then she felt his arms fold around her, and his head rest atop hers.

"Thank you," she said quietly. "For . . . everything."

She didn't know if he understood the true breadth of her meaning, but it didn't matter. She stayed there in his arms, listening to his heartbeat, feeling the warmth of his embrace for the first time. And she couldn't help but think that this was what it must feel like to be home.

18

Rain

Andra wiped the sweat from her brow, breathing heavily as she circled her opponent—a young man a little older than she, who wielded a staff identical to her own. The boy was watching her, an eager glint in his eyes, and she knew immediately what he would do.

As she'd guessed, he attacked quickly and fiercely, swinging straight at her head. Andra ducked the blow, stepping inside his reach, and jammed the end of her staff into his ribs. He grunted and stumbled forward as she darted past him. She swung the wooden staff at his back, and it made a satisfyingly solid sound as it connected. He grunted and turned toward her again.

She couldn't help but smile a little at the anger and frustration in his eyes. The other young men she'd sparred with that morning had the same expressions when she bested them. Her smile seemed to inflame his anger, because he rushed her again, swinging at her knees.

Andra dug the end of her staff into the ground, and his swing made a cracking sound as the two staffs connected. She pushed herself upward, both hands gripping the staff, lifting her feet from the ground. Her right foot swung outward, her boot connecting with the boy's shoulder, making him stumble. She could have struck his head, but she didn't want to injure him.

The momentum of the kick swung Andra around the staff, and she landed lightly on her feet, raising the weapon up into a defensive position again, ready for the next attack. Before her opponent had a chance to collect himself, Colmen stepped into the meadow.

"All right, that's enough," he called. Andra looked up to see a smile on the elf's face as he stepped up to her. He put a hand on her shoulder, pride clear in his expression. "Well done, Andra. That was truly exceptional."

She beamed back at him. "Thank you," she panted.

Colmen turned toward the young man, who was rubbing at his shoulder with a bitter expression. He smiled at him and patted him on the back. "Try not to let it bother you," he chuckled. "Remember, she did the same thing to four other soldiers this morning."

"Well," the young rebel grumbled, "I suppose it helps that she had private lessons from you and Kael for the last two weeks."

"Precisely," Colmen laughed. He turned back to the other soldiers who had gathered for their daily training in the meadow and called loudly, "You're dismissed! Tomorrow, we work on our hand-to-hand combat."

The soldiers began filing away, dropping their staffs into the large barrels that had been dragged out onto the grass for the training session. Andra remained where she was for a moment, reveling in what she'd accomplished. After all that had happened with Egan last night, fighting today felt like a release. All the anger, frustration, and even the fear had been washed away by the feeling of fighting back, of besting every opponent Colmen set before her. She might not have been able to fight Egan—to fight the memories his kiss had brought to the surface—but she could fight these boys, at the very least.

She looked toward where Eithne and Tiri rested nearby, watching the training. Tiri touched her mind, sending a sensation of pride, and Eithne nodded her angular head in approval. The rest of the trainees had almost entirely disappeared, and as Andra dropped her staff into the waiting barrel, she looked up to find that Kael was there.

She smiled at him in surprise, and a half smile touched his lips in return. "What are you doing here?" she asked.

"I watch the soldiers train whenever I can," he said. "I like to know how they're doing."

"How long have you been watching?"

There was a glint of amusement in his gray eyes. "Long enough to know that there are now several embarrassed young men in my army."

Andra laughed, but quickly fell silent at Kael's somber expression.

"Something the matter?" she asked.

"No," he replied with a brief shake of his head. "I just . . ." Kael broke off, and Andra was surprised to see him at such a loss for words. Finally, he went on, "I wanted to speak to you about what happened last night. With Egan, I mean."

Andra felt her jaw clench, and she looked away from him, toward the shining surface of the lake. "There's nothing to speak of," she said, keeping her tone level.

She heard him step closer and looked toward him again, now barely more than a foot away. His hand lifted briefly, as if he intended to touch her, then fell back to his side. She wrapped her arms tightly around herself.

"Andra," he said, "I'm no fool. I know what Ledo did to you. And I know that what Egan did . . ."

Andra pressed her eyes closed. "Please stop." Her voice was barely above a whisper, but Kael quickly fell silent. She could feel tears burning in her eyes, the familiar pain rising in her throat, threatening to silence her voice again. She would not let it. She swallowed hard and forced the tears away.

She felt a soft touch on her arm and opened her eyes to find herself staring into the astounding depths of Kael's gaze. She saw a deep sadness there, and a longing she didn't understand.

"Andra," he breathed, "I wish . . ." He trailed off again, his fingers trailing up to her cheek, and she found herself turning her face toward his touch, not knowing why.

"I tried to fight him," she said quietly, not expecting him to finish telling her what he wished for. "I tried so hard . . ."

"And you *did*," he told her firmly. "Somehow, you did."

"But it just . . . made me remember . . . It made me remember all the times I didn't fight. All those memories I thought I could just put behind me . . . But I can't."

His other hand rose to her cheek now, cradling her face between his black gloves, his exposed fingers warm on her skin. "Nobody expects you to simply move on from what happened to you, Andra."

Slowly, she nodded. "I know. I just . . . wish that I could."

He stared at her for a moment, her face still held between his hands, as if searching for a response in her eyes. Then a drop of water struck Andra's cheek, and she looked up at the sky. Heavy clouds the color of Kael's eyes had rolled in above them, and the raindrops began to fall more rapidly on her skin.

Kael glanced up at the sky. "We should head back," he remarked, his hands falling back to his sides.

Andra continued to look up at the clouds, feeling the rain's caresses. Kael turned and started in the direction the others had gone. She touched his hand, stopping him. "Wait," she said.

Kael frowned slightly at her as the rain began to fall more heavily. "Why?" he asked.

Andra closed her eyes at the soft, cool sensation, which seemed to cleanse her somehow. The sting of her memories was, for a moment, soothed. The anger and pain quieted under the rain's touch.

"It feels . . . good," she answered with a small smile, the water trickling across her mouth. She stood, eyes closed, face upturned, arms raised slightly, feeling the rain fall on her. Rain. It was so simple, so ordinary. But suddenly, standing there in an open field, feeling the moisture pressing her hair to her skin, her tunic to her chest, the rain became something beautiful, something that could make it easier to forget, if only for a little while.

"Come on," Kael said softly, his hand touching her arm, as if he intended to steer her toward the camp. "You'll get sick."

Andra pulled away from him, yanked off her boots, and took off at a dead run toward the lake, kicking up mud with her bare feet.

"Andra!" he called after her. "Where are you going?"

She didn't answer, but continued running until she reached the edge of the lake. She dropped onto the grass and tipped her head back, staring up at the rain and breathing heavily. She heard his boots squishing through the mud until he stopped beside her, his face looming above hers.

"Hello," she said, a little breathless.

"Is there a reason why you've decided to lie in a mud puddle in the rain?" he asked, cocking a black eyebrow at her.

"Yes," she answered simply.

"And that reason would be . . . ?"

"Because it feels easier to forget here."

He was silent. Then, Kael turned and dropped down into the mud beside her. She stared at him in surprise as he scooped up a handful of mud, weighing it between his hands. "I may not understand why," he said quietly, dropping the mud back to the ground and wiping his hands on his trousers, "but if sitting in a mud puddle in the rain brings you some measure of comfort, then we can sit in mud puddles in the rain."

She stared at his face in silence for a moment. He didn't look at her, just stared at the surface of the lake, which was dancing from the impact of the raindrops. Andra closed her eyes and rested her chin on her knees, listening to the sound of the rain on the lake, Kael's silent presence somehow adding to the soothing sensation of the rain on her back, washing everything away, if only for a moment. It wasn't long until the brief downpour began to let up— one of those heavy, short-lived summer rains that she had watched countless times from behind windows. When it was just a soft sprinkle on her back, she looked at Kael.

He was standing, pulling his soaked tunic over his head.

"I want to wash off some of this mud before we head back," he said.

"*I agree,*" Eithne said jubilantly. She leapt into the air, then dove into the lake with a massive splash.

Andra covered her eyes against the spray, and when she opened them again, Kael was sprinting toward the water. He dove off a stone ledge after his dragon, disappearing beneath the surface. After nearly a minute, Andra stood and walked to the edge of the shelf, peering into the lake's depth.

Then she saw the shadowy shape racing toward the surface. Andra stepped back just as Eithne surged out of the water, her red wings snapping open, sending droplets out into the air. Kael was clinging to her back and pushing his wet black hair off his forehead. Then Eithne pulled her wings to her sides, diving back toward the water. Andra thought she heard Kael whoop with laughter; then there was another enormous splash and the pair disappeared again. They stayed under even longer this time, until Andra began to worry.

Then Eithne's head broke the surface, Kael clinging to her neck. She bugled happily as Kael patted her scales. Andra sighed and sat back down on the smooth, stony shelf, her arms around her legs as she watched the pair diving and resurfacing, dancing together across the lake's surface. When Eithne sprang from the water again, hovering several feet above the lake, Kael stood on his dragon's back and jumped toward the water. He plummeted into the lake, disappearing again in a mass of swirling bubbles.

Eithne chuckled and landed beside Tiri, shaking the shimmering droplets from her red scales. *"He always was a show-off,"* Andra heard her say.

A moment later, Kael resurfaced several yards away. Andra watched him as he struck out strongly toward her on the shore. Watching him move through the water so easily gave her a pang of envy. He seemed so relaxed, so free in the water.

Cautiously, she slipped her feet into the lake as she sat on the rock shelf, watching Kael turn on his back and kick slowly toward her. The water felt good against her skin. At last, Kael reached shore and rested his arms on the ledge, breathing heavily.

"Kael?" she said quietly.

He turned his eyes toward her, his chin resting atop his arms. "Yes?"

"Will you teach me?"

"Teach you what?"

"How to swim."

He paused, regarding her for a moment. Finally, he said in a slow voice, "If you're certain. But the water here is a bit deep; I can barely reach the bottom and there aren't any shallows nearby. If you get too far from me even for a moment . . ."

His steel gray eyes were dark with worry and uncertainty. Andra placed a hand on his arm. "I trust you."

His eyes narrowed slightly, meeting her gaze and holding it, as if he could find the meaning of her words there. Then he nodded and slid over so that he held to the shelf beside her, standing on his toes to keep his head above the surface. "Put your hands on my shoulders."

Andra obeyed, her hands falling on his bare shoulders. Kael's hands took her gently by the waist and lowered her into the water. She drew slow, deep breaths as the water rose around her, keeping herself calm.

"It's all right," Kael said quietly. "I won't let go until you tell me to."

He had one arm around her waist, holding her against him and keeping her head just above the water, his other hand holding the bank for balance. Andra found herself caught in his gray eyes, and he gazed steadily back at her, his expression somehow both gentle and intense.

She swallowed hard, breaking her eyes away from his with great effort and looking down at the water. "I'm ready," she said.

He looked briefly startled, as if he had just remembered the reason he was standing there, holding her in the water. "You're sure?"

She nodded.

Kael kept his hands loosely on her waist, hers still placed on his shoulders as she slipped a little deeper into the water. At his instruction, she took a deep breath and let her head slip below the surface. She came up again almost immediately with a gasp, and wiped the water from her eyes.

"Good," Kael said, his features softening into a near smile. "Let's try again."

They repeated the process until she felt comfortable holding her breath under the water; then he showed her how to hold her body so that she could float along the surface. Kael treaded water beside her as she floated on the surface, trying to keep her close to the bank. After several minutes, she slipped back under the water, letting it swirl above her head. She felt the muddy lake bottom beneath her feet. Kael's hand was touching her arm gently, ready to seize her and pull her back up if he felt something was wrong.

She peered upward through the murky water, and could just make out the features of his face, his eyes still staring intently down at her from above the surface, watching over her.

When she started to feel the need for air, she pushed up off the bottom and surfaced in front of him, smiling. "Well," she said, "I'm not drowning."

"True," he answered with a nod, his hand on her forearm, helping to keep her head above water. "But you're not exactly swimming either. Here, I'll show you." He gently guided her onto her stomach, then showed her how to move her arms to pull herself forward through the water. "Keep kicking your feet," he instructed, swimming closely alongside her. "Yes, like that."

Andra gave a slight laugh as she pulled herself slowly but surely toward the bank where Tiri and Eithne were still watching them. She grasped the slick stone ledge with one hand and thrust the other into the air with a joyous laugh. "I did it!" she cried.

Kael looked as if he were working at not smiling as he leaned against the bank beside her. "Yes, you did. You are very adept at not drowning."

This drew another laugh from her and she turned toward the dragons on the shore. "Tiri, did you see—!" The sudden motion made her hand slip from the lip of shale, and she disappeared beneath the surface.

Kael's hand lashed out immediately and took hold of her arm, pulling her back up. She reemerged, surprised but unharmed. He slipped his arm around her waist, holding her to him as she gave a few startled coughs, wiping the water away from her face.

"Are you all right?" he asked.

She gave a small smile and nodded. "Yes, of course. You pulled me up so quickly. . . ."

"I told you I'd take care of you," he said quietly.

Andra fell silent, looking into his stormy eyes again. The expression in them was soft, kind, caring—but she saw something more behind it, a desire she knew too well. The memories that the rain and the lake had so recently washed from her came flooding back all too clearly. His arm seemed to tighten slightly on her waist, and she could hear him draw a slow breath, feel it caress her cheek as he exhaled. Her heart hammered against her ribs. She couldn't breathe. She felt as though she had slipped back beneath the water and was drowning.

"K-Kael . . ." she stuttered breathlessly.

The Rider closed his eyes momentarily, his jaw tightening as if in frustration. When he opened them again, the emotion she'd seen was gone. His gaze was as steely and impassive as ever.

"We should go," he said in a calm, even tone. He helped her to the ledge, then pulled himself out as well. He walked the few yards to where his tunic and boots lay, then snatched up her boots and returned them to her. He pulled his clothes on without a word, then helped her to her feet.

"Andra," Tiri prodded her, and she realized the dragon had been trying to get her attention for a while now.

Kael strode on ahead of her, his form dark and brooding again as he led the way back to Bellris. *"Yes?"* Andra asked without looking back at her.

"Your mind . . . It's very strange to me right now. I can't tell what you're thinking."

"Nor can I, Tiri. . . ."

Tiri paused, then said, *"My mother always told me that there would come times when my mind could not tell me what I should do. And when that happened, I should let my heart guide me."*

Andra was silent, watching Kael moving on ahead of her. Then she looked back down at the bracelet on her wrist. She touched it, twirling it gently around as she studied the intricate braids in the leather, considering the time and care that had gone into creating it.

She sighed and ran a hand across her face. *"And what if my heart is as lost as my thoughts?"*

"Your heart can never truly be lost, Andra. You must simply choose to see where it is leading you."

19

Intelligence

For once, Kael was thankful for his schedule. It didn't give him time to think about Andra and what had passed between them the previous day. The memory of her warm skin in the cool water was still all too vivid in his mind, bringing that ache back into his chest. He pushed it away. Andra was a distraction, a liability. First he'd started a brawl with Egan in front of the entire camp, and now, when the Freemen were relying on him to see them through this forsaken rebellion, all he could think about was how close he had come to kissing her. He marched across the clearing in the early morning light to the hut where he and the other leaders of the Freemen met. They were already waiting for him.

Egan was staring resolutely at the wooden tabletop, where he was carefully gouging a hole with his knife. Both his hands were bandaged, which gave Kael a bitter sense of pleasure. Andra's magic had burned him, and injuries caused by magic couldn't be Healed by it; he would have to wait for the burns to heal naturally.

Colmen and Janis were laughing together at something the elf had said, but they both fell silent when they saw their leader's brooding face. The two scouts who had just returned from their mission nodded at him, and Insarius looked up briefly before turning his eyes back to the stick he was whittling.

Kael threw himself into an empty chair. He turned to the two scouts. "What did you learn?" he asked without ceremony.

"Well," one of them started, "something is certainly happening."

"What do you mean by 'something'?"

The other scout picked up his companion's story. "There is odd movement throughout the land. We received word from many of the outlying towns that the judges' soldiers are withdrawing. Of course, some of the larger strongholds, such as Thys, have retained their soldiers, but those in the smaller towns are leaving."

"Gathering to Vereor?" Kael asked.

"That's just it," the man replied. "Nobody seems to know. It's as if the soldiers are just vanishing. They're not showing up in Vereor or anywhere else."

Kael's brow furrowed. "How do thousands of men just disappear?"

"And why?" Egan added.

"You think they're gathering an army?" Kael asked in concern.

The first scout shrugged. "It would appear that way, but where they're gathering to, none of our sources can tell."

"If they are gathering, it doesn't mean it's against us," Egan pointed out. "We've been here for years and have never had any reason to worry about being discovered."

"Still," Kael sighed, "we should be prepared." He looked at Colmen. "Is the stronghold stocked with sufficient supplies?"

He shrugged slightly and shook his head. "There are some supplies there, but not nearly enough should all of Bellris need to retreat there."

"Gather a crew and collect any supplies you can—blankets, healing supplies, weapons, any spare clothes, and any extra food that can be stored. If Castigo has somehow found where we are, we should have several weeks before they can mobilize from anywhere near Vereor, so we should begin our preparations immediately."

"So that we can retreat to our little hole in the mountains and hope they don't find us there?" Egan scoffed.

Kael turned his sharp gray eyes on him. "No. So that we can send those who cannot fight there while we try to fend the Kingsmen off. And so that, should we fail, those who survive have a safe place to fall back to."

"You know that cave won't be large enough for our dragons," Egan said flatly.

"I know. Eithne and I will fight until we fall. And I expect you and Calix to do the same."

"And Janis?" Egan asked. "Will you ask him and Tildin to fight to the death as well?"

Kael narrowed his eyes, but any response he might have given was interrupted. Janis slammed his black-gloved fist on the table, drawing the attention of the entire room. His expression was fierce.

"Kael doesn't have to ask me to fight," he said ferociously, his hazel eyes burning as he met Egan's gaze. "I came to Bellris by choice, by myself. I chose to join the rebellion, and I didn't do it so I could hide when a battle came. Tildin and I will fight."

Egan fell silent, and Kael gave Janis a nod of approval. "Thank you, Janis," he said. "We'll need every dragon we have." With the elder Rider effectively silenced, Kael turned his attention back to the rest of the group. "What do we know of the elven nation? What are their intentions?"

"We spoke to them," one of the scouts said. "They say they still can't declare their support for us. They'll continue allowing elves who want to fight with us to come to Bellris, but they won't send their armies to help us. The risk of another race war is too great; relations with Vereor are already tenuous."

Kael nodded slowly in understanding, then sighed and moved on to discussing the rations. They had a small plot of crops, and were in the process of clearing more land to increase their yield. The few livestock they had were beginning to dwindle, and the farmers who supported them couldn't spare them more at the moment.

"And the dwarves?" Kael asked. "Any word from them?"

Colmen shook his head. "Nothing new. We requested more weapons as soon as they are able to craft them, and they sent us the gold they've been mining several weeks ago. I spent it in my last trade with the nomads a few days back. It will be some time before they can send us any more funds."

"And they still won't fight."

"No," the elf sighed. "It is not their battle."

Overall, it was the usual bleak situation for the Freemen. The rest of the camp had long since gathered around the firepit when their meeting finally concluded and they began to filter out to collect their breakfast rations. As Insarius moved to go, Kael placed a hand on the spy's arm. The man turned his weathered face back toward him.

"Any word yet on that trade I asked for?" Kael asked.

Insarius shook his head. "Hasn't come through yet. Should be any day now."

"You're certain your courier can be trusted."

The older man nodded. "He's good for it. He'll send it along soon, if there's not already a bird on its way to Bellris."

"All right," Kael said, releasing Insarius's arm. "Let me know the moment it arrives."

The intelligence officer touched two fingers to his brow in a small salute, then left the hut. Kael followed the man to the central fire. His eyes were quick to locate Andra. She was sitting on a log, staring at her bowl of stew. Syra was sitting beside her, talking, but Andra seemed to be only half listening. She would nod occasionally, but her face remained drawn in a look of deep thought, as if thoroughly preoccupied with something.

Kael retrieved his stew, then sat next to Colmen, who was chatting with several other elves who had traveled with him from Iterum when he first joined the rebellion. His friend turned to him as he sat.

"You saw Andra's sparring yesterday?" the elf asked.

Kael nodded. "The end of it, yes."

"She's really remarkable," he laughed. "I've never seen someone learn to fight so quickly. That speed of hers . . ." He paused, shaking his head. "I don't think there's any elf in Iterum who can move so quickly."

This drew the interest of the other elves, and they turned their eyes to the pair; elves prided themselves on being far faster than humans.

"Whom are you discussing?" one of them asked, her blue eyes curious.

"Andra," Colmen said, nodding across the fire to where the girl sat. "The one with the contract collar." He began to explain to the other elves how Andra had caught an arrow in full flight, but Kael stopped listening, his mind turning. Eithne listened to the spinning of his thoughts, her own emotions and instincts swirling with his.

"Her magic . . ." he said quietly.

Colmen looked back at him. "What?"

"Her magic," Kael repeated, more loudly now. "When I spoke to my mother about Andra that first day, she told me that she thought Andra had the potential to be powerful, and that it was likely she'd been using magic without intending to throughout her life." He met the elf's eyes then, eager. "What if her speed is a part of it? What if her magic is the cause?"

"Is that even possible?" Colmen asked.

"Why not? They say that elves' connection to the energy of the earth is what makes them so much faster than humans. They have that natural source of magic in them that's harder for humans to access, and it somehow offers them greater speed and endurance," Kael replied. "And you know as well as I do that her speed can't be natural."

The elf shrugged in admission. "I suppose after that magic trick of hers at the celebration, anything is possible."

Kael felt a flicker of agitation at Colmen's words. Amid all the noise and riotous dancing, it seemed that Kael had been the only one who saw what Egan had done—because his eyes had been on Andra, as they so often were. The other Freemen had seen only Andra's skin dancing with blue-violet fire, followed by a brief brawl between their two leaders.

As much as Kael wanted to skin Egan for daring to touch Andra, he knew there was little he could do openly. Punishing the Freemen's second-in-command would not be good for morale. So, he'd told people that there had simply been a misunderstanding, and all was well. Then he'd promptly cut off any trade of spirits into the camp; he would enjoy watching Egan squirm when his stores ran out.

Eithne prodded at him gently, drawing him back to the situation before them. Kael sighed and stood, handing his unfinished breakfast to one of the elves. "Well," he said, "my mother did say Andra would need to go back to her. I suppose now is the time."

"You think Setora can teach her?" Colmen asked curiously.

"I don't know," Kael said with a shrug. "Both nature and word magic failed to work when I tried to show her how, but maybe Setora will have another way. She said she's known someone with powers like Andra's before. If anyone in Bellris can teach Andra, it's she."

Andra looked up in surprise as Kael appeared before her. Immediately, she felt a flush climb up her neck as she looked at him, thinking of the way his bare skin had felt beneath her fingers in the lake.

"Have you finished eating?" he asked without greeting.

Andra glanced down at her half-eaten stew, then looked back up at him and nodded. She offered the bowl to Syra beside her, who took the extra food eagerly.

"Good," he said. "I have something I want you to do today."

Her curiosity stirred, and she raised her eyebrows. "What is it?"

"I want you to go back to my mother's."

She tilted her head to the side, brow furrowing. "Why?"

She saw his jaw tighten briefly before he said, "After the magic you demonstrated at the celebration, I think it's important that you learn to harness it, to use it. You're doing well with your combat training, but fast as you are, nobody can outrun an attack from a sorcerer. If you have magic—and it's clear now that you do—then you need to learn to use it."

Andra felt a flare of excitement in her chest, and she stood immediately. "Should I go now?" she asked eagerly.

Kael nodded. "She'll likely be home. She usually is. And . . ." He paused. "You'll have to tell her about what happened, so she knows everything about your abilities."

Andra drew a breath but nodded in understanding. Little as she wished to discuss her encounter with Egan, if it meant that Setora could teach her how to make the flames on her skin reappear, she would do it.

"I'll go with you," a voice said near her shoulder, and Andra turned to see Colmen smiling next to her. "I could use a walk before I start gathering supplies for the fallback point."

"Fallback point?" Andra repeated, looking between Colmen and Kael in confusion.

Kael shook his head. "Something for another time. Colmen,

take Andra to Setora's—then come see me before you start working on the supplies."

The elf nodded, then started away from the fire, Andra following. The two walked side by side out of the village and into the
open meadow around the lake. All four dragons were lying out on
the grass, and they lifted their heads to peer at the two shapes
emerging from the trees. Calix and Tildin quickly returned their
heads to the grass. Eithne and Tiri stood, stretching their wings
as Colmen and Andra approached them.

When Andra told them where she was going, Tiri joined them,
and the three of them headed around the banks of the lake. Andra
sighed with contentment as she took in the deepening color of the
sky and water, and the deep green of the grass and trees.

"Colmen?" she asked.

"Hm?"

"Are you a full-blooded elf?"

He gave her a curious look. "Yes. Why do you ask?"

"I was just wondering if you had ever been to Iterum."

He laughed. "I was born there, as were my mother and father, and
their mothers and fathers. Elves are very much creatures of habit. We
don't change much, don't travel much. We're very like the trees we
love so much. We put down our roots, and are content."

"Then how did you come to be in Bellris?"

"It must have been about . . ." He paused, calculating in his head.
"Eight years ago, give or take. The rebels didn't even call themselves 'the Freemen' yet. They were just a handful of men and
women who were tiring of the judges' corruption and were removing themselves from it. They came through Iterum and asked
King Raegin for safe harbor. He gave it to them, but he couldn't
offer it for long. The judges weren't happy about the rebels. They
were calling them traitors and conspirators. Obviously, with the
Hall and Vereor being so close by, they couldn't stay in Iterum long.
But they intrigued me, and when they left, I went with them."

"Have you been back since then?"

"Only once," he answered, his voice quieter now. "When my little sister, Andimea, died."

"I'm sorry . . ." she whispered. A silence stretched between them. She wanted to ask more, but feared prodding too deeply into something that so clearly pained him.

Colmen sighed and took Andra's hand, as if he needed some sort of contact. Then, to her surprise, he went on in a slow, deliberate voice, "It was about a year after I left. Just one of those random, unpredictable accidents. A horse got spooked, and she thought she could calm it, but she couldn't. It panicked. The blow to her head killed her instantly."

"You were very close with her." She could hear it in his voice, the tenderness and sadness, even after so many years.

He nodded. "She would've been about your age now. You actually remind me of her." He gave a small smile and squeezed her hand slightly. "Especially when you play that flute I made for her." He sighed and looked ahead of them again, the sad smile still on his lips. "If it weren't for finding you, Andra, that mission would have been a complete waste."

Andra joined him in the brief laughter, then sighed herself. "I don't know that I'll be much good to the Freemen," she said. "But I do know that they've done much good for me."

They were drawing up on Setora's hut. Smoke was curling from the crumbling chimney, but the house itself was silent. Colmen released her hand.

"I should head back to Bellris," he said reluctantly. He pulled her into a tight embrace, then turned back the way he had come, waving a hand over his shoulder. "Good luck!"

She waved back, then turned to the door before her and drew a breath. Then she knocked.

20

Magic

"Just a moment!" she heard Setora call.

There was shuffling, then the sound of many objects being moved around. Finally, the door opened. Kael's mother looked briefly surprised when she saw Andra standing in the doorway; then she smiled broadly, her prematurely aged face looking, for a moment, much younger. "Come in, come in!" She gestured for Andra to step inside. She did, and with a nod of acknowledgment to the dragon outside, Setora closed the door behind them. The woman stepped immediately to the shuttered window beside the doorframe and pushed it open. "So that you may watch as well," she explained.

"*Thank you,*" Tiri said. She moved so that one large amethyst eye peered at them through the window.

Setora turned back to Andra. "I must say that I am surprised Kael actually sent you back to me," she sighed, moving quickly about the room and pulling the occasional book from the many piles around them. "It is no secret to me that he does not approve of my magic."

"He said it's important that I learn to use my magic," Andra responded, standing uncomfortably in the middle of the hut. "Something . . . something happened the other night." She explained to Setora in detail about the moment Egan had kissed her, the rush of anger, the flames that suddenly engulfed her.

The witch listened, her dark gray eyes fixated on Andra's face. When the girl had finished with her story, Setora looked through the window at Tiri.

"And what did you feel in that moment, Tiri?" Setora asked.

"Me?" Tiri asked with some surprise.

"Did Andra reach out to you in her distress?"

"I . . . don't know," the dragon replied. *"I know I felt her touch my mind, but it was so brief that I didn't even have time to sense her emotions, only her presence."*

"Did you feel anything drawing on your energy, on your magic?"

"I did feel . . . something. It felt like something pulling at my heart, but I did not know what it was. I certainly didn't think it was connected to what happened with Andra."

Setora seemed excited, smiling as she looked back at Andra. "What Tiri felt," she explained, "was you drawing on her magic, just as a Rider would have done."

Andra's eyebrows rose, her eyes widening. "But how?" she asked eagerly. "How could I do that without being Bonded to Tiri?"

The witch sighed and shook her head at the question. "That is one question that I can't answer. But the fact that you are able to draw on her is an important element we shall need to consider in your training."

Setora set the books she had gathered onto the table. She pulled her long, gray hair back, knotting it at the nape of her neck, and motioned at one of the stools by the table. "Sit, sit."

Andra obeyed, and Setora sat in the chair opposite her. "But I never meant to use magic," Andra said. "It was only an accident. And it was only once."

Setora waved her response away with a flick of her wrist, turning her attention back to her book. "Intention makes no difference. On the contrary, it makes you that much more powerful." She stopped looking at the book again and turned her gray eyes on Andra. "Tell me, what did it feel like when you summoned the fire to your skin?"

Andra frowned, struggling to remember. "I just remember wishing for something to happen. I was angry. I wanted to fight him, but he was stronger than me, and I just wished I could do something to fight back. And then . . . I don't know how to explain it. It was something in the back of my mind, something like when I sense Tiri nearby. Not really a tingling . . . But a feeling that something is there, and it grew until . . . Well, until what I wished for happened."

Setora was smiling at her. "That's the wonderful thing about magic, isn't it? True magic—not the kind that I use, but the kind that true sorcerers and sorceresses use—is not a skill of the mind, but a strength of the heart." She pushed the book toward Andra. "Here, read this. It was the only thing I could find that was at all close to your situation."

Andra looked down at the passage Setora had indicated. She paused, sounding out a few words in her mind before beginning; she had not had much reliable schooling as an indentured worker. "Unlike other magic-wielders, a Siphon's ability to accumulate magic is not predetermined. It is something that can be expanded in the right situations. If the Siphon is willing to abstain from the use of magic for long periods of time, their power will continue to grow to previously unattainable limits, giving the Siphon even greater power."

When Andra looked up from the passage, Setora elaborated, "Most children are given the opportunity to attempt magic at a very young age. Those who exhibit the ability go on to train in it. You, of course, were never given that chance. And because you also happened to be a Siphon, you were given an ability that most don't have the patience to reach for. Your magic has grown within you for more than sixteen years, and is now greater than anyone's I have ever heard of. You are capable of spells that no one would even dream of attempting."

"What about my father?" Andra asked. "If he had the same abilities you believe me to have, why am I demonstrating the magic when he never did? I never had any more training than he did."

"The reason," Setora said, holding up one gnarled finger, "is exposure. Kael has told me that magic-wielders are told not to practice their magic in front of indentured servants. Is that correct?"

Andra nodded.

"And there is good reason for it. If someone has the latent ability within them to practice magic, that ability can be awakened with enough exposure to it. Your father never had the necessary exposure to begin to manifest his abilities. But because you have now spent more than a month in the company of an elf and a Rider, and are now among many other magic-users, your powers are beginning to stir."

Andra was silent for a moment, thinking of her father. What would he have been able to accomplish if his abilities had been awoken? She'd always thought him far braver and stronger than she ever could have been. What would he have done with magic as a weapon?

She forced herself to focus again on Setora and asked, "But the book said that refraining from using magic is what makes a Siphon so strong. If I start using my magic, won't my abilities become weaker?"

Setora shook her head, releasing Andra's hands. She turned and grabbed a sheet of parchment, a writing quill, and a bottle of ink from a nearby chair. Dipping the quill in the ink, she said, "It works like this." She drew a square box on the paper and tapped it with her finger. "This is what I am like, and what Kael would have been like if not for Eithne. My mind is a closed system, with no way for energy to get in or out on its own. I can create ways to force it out, with my potions and incantations, but there is no way to force it back in. It will naturally diminish within the system on its own until I die."

She drew another picture—a square with two sections missing from its sides. In one opening, she drew an arrow pointing in, and on the other, an arrow pointing out from the square. "This, Andra, is you, and any other sorcerer, sorceress, dragon Rider, or elf. Dragon Riders, like Kael, have these openings created when they are Paired. Sorcerers, sorceresses, and elves are born with the ability. You can gather magic just as easily as you can release it. Releasing that energy does not tax your body as it does mine."

"Then what causes death?" Andra asked. "If they can regenerate that energy, why do they die?"

"Magic-users do generally live longer than those who don't have that ability; it's why elves live longer than most humans. But over time, the mind weakens, just as the body does. When you are sixty, you will not be able to run as fast, or lift as heavy loads as you could in your youth. Eventually, the mind's capacity for magic diminishes, and the person dies."

Andra was silent for a moment, considering. "What about dragons?" she asked.

Setora glanced out the window at Tiri's watchful eye. "Their capacity for magic is much greater than ours," the woman said. "However, they have no natural ability to release it on their own. Or at least, not usually. There are occasions when a dragon can perform magic by instinct, such as when they mark their Rider, but for the most part, their magic stays within them. When they are Paired, the Rider can then call upon his dragon's magic to strengthen his own. A wild dragon will live for centuries, because the source of magic within her is so great. However, like me, they cannot regenerate it. So, a Paired dragon makes a great sacrifice in allowing a Rider to use her magic, because it takes as many years from her as it does from me." She looked back at Andra and added, "Not that it ever comes to that. Their supply is so great that the Rider's life span ends long before that, and a dragon never lives long after the Bond is severed."

Andra had heard that much before.

Setora took a deep breath and rubbed her hands together. "Well, then, shall we begin?"

Andra felt her heart leap with excitement, and she nodded again. Setora stood and Andra followed her to the door. They stepped out into the late morning sunlight beside Tiri. Setora paused, looking around her with a thoughtful expression.

"I haven't really had time to prepare," she muttered, more to herself than to Andra. "And this is such a unique situation. . . . It's hard to know where to start." She sighed, and spoke in a normal tone again. "Well, you said that you were able to use your magic when you truly wanted something." She bent and picked up a small stone by her feet.

Andra tried not to smile; Kael had tried the same tool to teach her in the Shesol Mal.

Holding the stone flat in her palm, Setora said, "An elf would summon the wind to bring them the stone. A human sorcerer would use a simple spell to command the stone to him. But I won't teach you that, Andra. I want you to *want* the stone."

Andra frowned at her, doubtful. "Just . . . want it?" she asked skeptically.

Setora nodded. "Yes. With all your heart. *Want* this stone to be in your hand."

She gave a shrug of resignation. "Very well." She held her hand flat out in front of her, like Setora's, and frowned in concentration at the stone in the woman's palm.

Almost immediately, Tiri said in her mind, *"You're concentrating too hard. Magic is in your heart, not your mind."*

"Well, I don't know what else to do," Andra replied in irritation. *"How am I supposed to want a stone?"* She scowled more deeply at the little rock. It was an unremarkable thing—small, smooth, and plain gray. Why would she want that stone at all?

Setora noticed the difficulty she was having. "Try not thinking about the stone itself," she said. "When you retaliated against Egan, you weren't focused on summoning fire to your skin, were you?"

"No," Andra answered, looking away from the stone and up at Setora for a brief moment. "I just wanted him to let go of me. And . . ." She paused briefly, then confessed, "I wanted to hurt him."

Setora didn't seem bothered by the admission, but simply said, "And because you wished for him to release you, your magic found a way to make it happen. So think, not of the stone coming to you, but rather of the end result, of having it in your hand."

She stared at the little pebble, imagining holding it in her hand, trying to make herself want it. She remembered the way the flames had danced on her skin, consuming her without burning, blue-violet flames protecting her. Suddenly, a blue-violet spark exploded beneath the pebble, making it leap from Setora's hand. The woman jumped and let out a small yelp. Andra quickly snagged the pebble from the air and looked down at it, resting in her palm, with mild surprise. She looked up at Setora, who was holding her hand to her chest. And Andra realized what she had done. She dropped the pebble and hurried to the woman's side.

"I'm sorry!" she cried. "Are you hurt?"

Setora laughed and shook her hand out, as if she were shaking away a writing cramp. "No, no, I'm fine. That was . . . unconventional. . . . But you did it, and that's what matters. You got the stone into your hand, one way or another."

Andra laughed as well. "I . . . I did, didn't I."

The witch smiled at her. "It was a good beginning. Now," Setora continued, "shall we try something a bit more challenging?"

———⋖⊰⊱⋗———

The lesson continued until the sun had set fully and darkness fell over the meadow. Andra struggled with most of the tasks Setora tried to get her to complete. She managed to throw the same pebble at many objects, with less than perfect accuracy. But it was the things that required sustained concentration that taxed her. No matter how many times Setora asked her to try to make the pebble hover over her palm, she couldn't do it. Either it would remain perfectly still, or a blue spark would make it leap into the air and it would quickly fall back down again. Setora had released her reluctantly, and only because Andra was weary from the full day of lessons.

With a feeling of great relief, Andra stepped out of the hut into the silver glow of the moonlight. Tiri was still waiting for her, and the dragon stood and stretched when she stepped out of the hut. Andra sighed and stretched as well, feeling elated at the knowledge that she could now return to Bellris.

"Free at last, are you?" Tiri asked teasingly.

Andra smiled. *"Yes. At last."*

"You do know that you will have to come back tomorrow."

"I know," she answered with a nod. *"And that's all right. I want to learn. I'm just ready to go home."* Even thinking the word sent a feeling of warmth through her chest.

"Well, then," Tiri said, lifting her wings, *"let's not waste time. I'll race you."*

Andra laughed in disbelief. "Race you?" she asked, speaking out loud in her amusement. "You want me to race a dragon?"

Tiri heaved herself into the sky with a beat of her wings, hovering only a few feet over Andra's head. *"The longer you stand there and laugh at the thought, the farther behind you will fall!"* And she turned toward Bellris.

Andra laughed once more, shook her head, then sprinted as fast as she could go. She knew Tiri was holding back, toying with her as Andra coaxed every bit of speed she could from her legs. The dragon would occasionally tip one wing downward, nearly knocking Andra over, or teasingly grab at her with her front claws, making Andra laugh and race harder. As she neared Bellris, Andra saw a tall, familiar figure step out of the trees. He took a few steps in their direction, then stopped, apparently spotting them. Her eyes fixed on the figure, Andra raced faster toward him.

The silhouette didn't move, watching her race at him at full speed. She thought she saw him stiffen, as if searching for some threat that would cause her to run at such a speed.

And then she crashed into him, nearly bowling him over. He steadied himself on a tree with one hand, steadying her with the other. Kael looked down at Andra in surprise as she laughed against his chest.

Then, turning her face toward the dragon who was just settling herself on the grass outside the tree line, she called, "Ha! I win!"

Tiri made a chuckling sound deep in her throat. *"Very well, I concede,"* she responded.

Kael looked down at her again. "Is . . . everything all right?" he asked, clearly confused.

"Of course," she answered with another laugh. "I was racing Tiri, that's all."

"Racing?" he asked, and she was certain now that a small smile was pulling on the corners of his mouth. "You were racing a dragon?"

She turned back toward Tiri with a triumphant grin. "Yes, and *winning!*" she called.

Tiri laughed, a throaty yet pleasant sound.

"So, how were your lessons?" Kael asked. "Was my mother able to teach you anything?"

Andra's face immediately lit with an excited smile, and she recounted her day to him, telling in detail every task she had succeeded and failed at. He listened intently, his eyes never leaving her face. When she had finished, his gaze drifted out to the moonlit lake, but he said nothing.

"Is something wrong?" she asked, her brow furrowing.

Kael drew a breath, then said slowly, "I wanted to ask you something."

"What?"

He turned his eyes back to her face, and in the darkness, they looked nearly black. "Why did you stop trying to run?"

Andra blinked at him. "What do you mean?"

"When I first took you from the palace, you tried twice to get away. Then you didn't try again. Why? Did you give up? Or was it because you found Tiri?"

"I . . ." She stopped, breaking her gaze away from his and looking toward the dragon, who was still watching her, listening with curiosity. "I did decide to stop running on the day that Tiri joined us. But . . . that wasn't the reason I chose to stay."

"Then what was?" he asked.

She looked back at him again. For some reason, the answer seemed very important to him. Her voice was low as she replied, "You taught me to fight." She saw his brow furrow in confusion, and she went on. "That day, when you forced me to spar with you, when you told me that I had to learn to defend myself, I realized something. In the past, I felt that running away was my only choice, the only way to protect myself. But you showed me that I could fight back, that I could be strong. And I knew then that I didn't want to run anymore."

Kael's heavy gaze had softened as she spoke, and she noticed in the moonlight just how long his lashes were. "So, you would stay here?" he asked quietly. "Even if you could leave, if you had no con-tract. If . . . If you had a way back to Talias. Would you go?"

Andra looked up at him in surprise. "How did you . . . ?"

"Eithne told me. She said she overheard your thoughts about him, and could tell that you cared for him. And I've seen enough of your attachment to that bracelet to guess that he gave it to you." He nodded down at the braided leather around her wrist, and she put her hand over it, hiding it from view. There was a brief silence; then Kael said again, "So, if you had a way back to him, would you go?"

"I . . . I don't know," she said, feeling a pang in her chest as she remembered Setora's palm reading, the lines of love and death. She wanted to fight, but something still drew her toward Talias—a warm, comfortable familiarity that promised safety.

Slowly, Kael nodded, and she saw that mask falling back into place—the mask of the soldier. "You should get to bed," he told her. "It's late, and you have training with Colmen and with my mother tomorrow. Good night, Andra."

Without waiting for a reply, Kael turned and walked back into the camp, disappearing in the shadows under the trees. Andra watched him go, wishing that she'd been able to give him a better answer.

21

A Broken Contract

The days that followed were much of the same routine—combat training with Colmen in the mornings, magic training with Setora in the evenings. Occasionally, Kael or Egan would step in and direct the morning sessions as their other duties allowed. When it was the latter, Andra felt herself fighting with increased vigor. Whether it was because of the anger that arose in her at the sight of him, or because she wanted to show him she was not someone to be trifled with, she couldn't be certain. Nevertheless, the Rider seemed to steer clear of personal contact with her during the sessions, never offering her direct criticism or feedback.

The evenings were more enjoyable. Andra was learning quickly to locate that well of power in the back of her mind. She knew now what it felt like, and how it felt to draw upon it, so summoning the magic was becoming easier. Setora watched her with some amusement as Andra directed the same pebble they'd been using to hover in the air, then weave circles around both their heads.

"Very good," the witch laughed. "You're learning to sustain

your use of the magic. That's a vast improvement in very little time."

Andra allowed the pebble to drop into her palm. "What should we try next?" she asked eagerly.

Setora pursed her lips, tapping a finger against her chin. "I am certain that Kael would like me to teach you more combat-focused uses for your magic. . . ." She sighed, letting her hands fall to her lap. "But I am not a soldier, nor a sorceress. I'm not terribly familiar with using magic as a weapon. Witchcraft tends to focus on more mundane things—divination, healing, spells of protection. It's not often we use it to attack."

"What about protection, then?" Andra asked eagerly. "Could you help me learn something of that sort?"

"Perhaps . . ." Setora paused, her eyes narrowing as she fell silent for a long moment. "Ah, I have an idea. Try this. Close your eyes, and imagine yourself standing in the center of a bubble."

Andra gave her an incredulous look. "A bubble?"

"Yes, yes," the witch said with a wave of her hand. "Stop questioning and just try it."

The girl obeyed.

"I want you to imagine yourself strengthening this bubble. See it in your mind's eye. See the thin, transparent walls growing thicker and thicker, stronger and stronger, until nothing can penetrate them. Are you doing it?"

Andra nodded.

"Good, good. Hold that image in your mind."

There was a brief pause. Then Andra felt a stone strike her in the center of the forehead. She let out a yelp and jumped, her eyes flying open in surprise. From where she watched nearby, Tiri let out a soft growl of agitation.

"She did not say she would start throwing rocks at you," the dragon remarked.

Before Andra could ask Setora if she'd gone mad, the witch

sighed, looking disappointed. "Your shield was supposed to stop the stone," she said.

"Oh." Andra could think of nothing else to reply.

Setora looked toward the sun, which was low on the horizon, casting red light over the desert, mountains, and forest. "You should return to the camp," she said. "I shall see you after your afternoon rations tomorrow."

The witch started to rise, but Andra interrupted her. "Wait."

The elder woman raised her eyebrows. "Yes?" she asked, settling back to the grass.

"I've been . . . wondering something," Andra said hesitantly. Though she and Setora had developed something akin to a comfortable friendship in the time she'd been training with her, Andra was still not certain this was a topic she should broach.

"And do you wish to continue wondering?" Setora asked with a wry smile. "Or do you wish to ask?"

Andra laughed quietly, then proceeded slowly. "Kael told me . . . that you were one of the desert tribespeople."

Setora nodded once. "I was."

"How . . . How did you meet Kael's father? I know he was a judge."

The witch sighed. "My father often traveled to Vereor to trade at the judges' manors on behalf of our tribe. I met Kael's father, Abbas, when I accompanied him on one of those journeys. And—" She drew a slow breath, a distant look coming into her gray eyes. "—I fell completely in love with him from the moment that he first smiled at me. When my father left the city a fortnight later, I remained behind. I was young and impulsive and certain that Abbas was my heart-song."

"Heart-song?" Andra repeated. She remembered the word that Kael had spoken that night in the seaside cave. He'd never told her what it meant.

"It is a saying among the nomads." Setora smiled. "They say that

198 · ERIN SWAN

every person's heart has a song, and it seeks the one heart in this world that sings the same, so that the two may sing together in this life and the next."

"That's lovely," Andra sighed with a quiet smile of her own.

Setora chuckled. "A bit sentimental perhaps, but I was always fond of it."

"What happened between you and Abbas?"

"Politics," Setora answered with a heavy shrug. "Abbas's father was a judge, and he refused to allow his son and heir to marry a . . . Well, 'desert *whore*' was his name for me," she said with a strong note of bitterness in her voice. "Abbas loved me, but he would not go against his father's wishes. But of course, the man cared less about who his son bedded, so he allowed my relationship with Abbas to continue until Caedo was born."

Andra saw Setora's hands clench around her skirts, her voice trembling slightly as she went on. "He took my infant son right from my arms. I listened to his cries as they dragged me from the manor and threw me out onto the streets."

"And Abbas did nothing?" Andra asked, feeling a pang in her chest.

Setora shook her head slowly, avoiding Andra's gaze. "Abbas was a kind and gentle man, but he was also weak in many ways. He feared his father. He would not dare to cross him. I took up residence at an herbalist's shop in the city, trying to stay close to my son, hoping Abbas would send for me. And when his father died, he did. He brought me back to the manor, and I finally got to see my Caedo again. He was nearly six years old then, and already a hard-hearted child. I often wonder . . ." Setora paused, looking down at her withered hands. "I wonder, if his grandfather had not raised him for those first years, if he might have been a different man."

There was a brief silence. Andra was at a loss for words, unsure of how to comfort the woman who sat before her.

Then Setora drew a breath and went on. "But, even with his father gone, Abbas still would not marry me. He now feared the retribution of the other judges as much as he'd feared his father. It would be an insult to them, he said, to marry a woman from the desert tribes—a people who refuse to acknowledge the judges' rule. But I loved him, and so I stayed, even though I was wounded. Kael was born, and I hoped for a moment that he would marry me then. But he didn't. He took another wife when Kael was barely a year old, and I was sent away again. Caedo was old enough then that he chose to stay in the manor. I didn't blame him. It was the only life he'd ever known. I took Kael with me and returned to the herbalist's shop. And it was there that I discovered witchcraft. It was . . . an escape from my pain."

"But Kael said he lived with his father, in the manor," Andra said.

Setora nodded. "When Kael was six years old, Abbas sent for him. Caedo had been passed over at the last Pairing, and Abbas's wife had never given him a child. But Abbas had begun to think that he might still have a Rider as a son through Kael. So he took Kael back into the manor, to train him and prepare him for the opportunity to be Chosen."

"Why did you let him go?"

The woman smiled weakly. "I was an apprentice at an herbalist's shop, sleeping in a back room with my growing son. He had the chance to live in a manor, to be groomed and trained, and perhaps Paired with a dragon. I could not keep him from the opportunity for such a life. Now—" Setora straightened, taking on her old, confident air. "—I believe I have done enough sharing for one evening. I'm afraid I must bid you good night, Andra."

Andra nodded. "Good night, Setora," she answered. "And . . . thank you. I know that it must not be easy to speak of things that pain you."

"Yes, I am certain you do know," she replied with a sad smile.

Setora stood, and Andra watched as the witch rounded the lake, headed back toward her hut.

"You should go have your supper," Tiri said as their minds touched. *"You've trained hard today."*

"Soon," Andra answered silently. *"I want to practice a bit longer. But it's been several days since you last hunted. You should go find yourself food."*

The dragon nodded and stood. *"I think I shall do that."*

"Be careful."

Tiri smiled at her, flashing white fangs in the dying light. *"I am always careful."*

With that, she threw her scaled body into the air and quickly climbed above the height of the trees. Andra watched her violet shape retreat, then disappear between the mountains. When the dragon was out of sight, she closed her eyes again and concentrated, trying to envision the shield around her, trying to touch that part of her mind where the magic lay.

But it eluded her. Setora's words continued to drift through her mind, distracting her. She hadn't known that the kindly woman hid such pain. And Kael . . . What had it been like for him, to be torn from his mother and forced into a household with a father and brother he'd never known?

Engrossed in concentration, Andra did not hear the footsteps that approached her until a quiet voice spoke from beside her. "You seem to be thinking very hard about something."

She jumped, her hand reflexively moving to the knife at her belt as she turned toward the voice. It was Kael, standing in a gray wool tunic that seemed to turn his eyes silver. Andra smiled, feeling that familiar warmth rise in her chest. She hadn't seen much of him over the last several days. She felt quite certain he'd been avoiding her. Seeing him now, the red light of sunset shining on his black hair, Andra realized just how much she'd missed him.

"I was just practicing something your mother tried to teach me today," she said as he sat beside her in the grass.

"And what's that?"

"A shield of protection."

Kael gave a satisfied nod. "Good. That's just the sort of thing you should be learning. Any luck?"

"Not yet," she said, shaking her head. "I'm quite good with the pebble, though," she added with a grin, holding up the tiny stone that she usually carried on her person.

She saw a half smile on his lips, and found herself yearning to see a true smile. A brief silence spanned between them, and she heard him draw a slow breath.

"Andra," he said slowly.

"Yes?"

"Do you remember what I asked you on the night you first trained with my mother?"

She nodded. "You asked why I stopped running. And if I would stay, if I had the chance to leave."

"Yes, well . . . I know you said you didn't know what your choice would be, but—" He turned toward her then, moving onto his knees as he faced her. "Andra, how much do you know about your contract collar?"

She touched the small lock on her neck, confused by the sudden change of topic. "I know it's bound by magic to my labor contract. When it's fulfilled, the lock is opened."

"And you know it is very difficult to remove the collar in any other way?"

Andra nodded. More times than she could remember, she'd been told that her collar could never be cut off or removed by magic. It was protected against such things.

"Well, I believe I found a way."

She watched him in confused disbelief as he reached into the pouch at his belt and pulled out a small roll of paper.

"This," he said, holding up the paper, "is a spell. There's a man in Thys who's known to be the best spell-breaker in all of Paerolia, and to our luck, he is a rebel. I sent word to him as soon as we reached Bellris and asked if he knew a spell to remove a contract collar. He didn't. But he created one that he believes will work."

Andra stared down at the little paper held between Kael's thumb and forefinger. Could such a small thing truly offer her freedom? Could the one thing that had been beyond her reach for nearly her entire life really be held between Kael's fingertips?

She opened her mouth, searching for words to say, but no sound escaped her. It was as if her voice were gone again. But now, hope was what held it at bay.

Kael spoke again, his voice soft, his eyes on her face, as if he were reading her thoughts. "Andra, if it works, you'll be free to go wherever you wish. I know Tiri would take you anywhere you asked. You'd have no collar marking you as a contract breaker. You'd be free to start any life you wished for, wherever you wished . . . with whomever you wished."

Andra met his gaze and saw the hesitancy in his eyes. He offered her freedom—and a way to leave him. But, looking at his expression, she felt certain that he did not want her to go.

"Please," she whispered, kneeling to face him, mirroring his position. "Please." It was the only word she seemed capable of speaking.

Kael nodded and unrolled the paper in his fingers. She thought she saw his hands shake ever so slightly. His eyes scanned the words of the spell once, memorizing them. Then he reached out with one hand and took the lock between two fingers. His hand grazed the skin of her neck, and he stared into her eyes steadily as he spoke, his voice clear and sure in the falling night.

"Casseram in serinno. Vintre ad linem. Liberse eius arint."

In the heavy silence, Andra heard the sound of a tiny, metallic click. Her breath caught, and Kael's hand pulled back, his warmth leaving her skin. There was a small, sad smile on his lips as he held his palm out to her. Resting in the center of his hand was the tiny silver lock.

Immediately, Andra grabbed at the leather around her neck. The small latch flipped open easily, and the band fell away from her skin. She dropped it to the grass, her hands feeling the bare skin of her neck, skin that had been bound in leather for nearly twelve years. A sharp laugh escaped her, and she realized that it sounded close to a sob.

She looked at Kael then, and saw now that he was smiling—a full, true smile that she had never seen on his face before. It softened the harsh lines and curved the scar above his lip into a tiny crescent. It made the gray eyes dance with life. It made him beautiful.

"Congratulations, Andra," he said in a gentle tone. "You're free."

Hurriedly, with a sudden certainty, Andra untied the knot that held the leather bracelet and slipped it off her wrist. Kael watched her with a veiled hope in his eyes. Without a word, she tied the bracelet around his wrist, just above his black Rider's glove.

Then she looked up at him. His gaze was heavy on her, a hint of a smile still lingering on his features. She spoke slowly, searching for words. "You told me once that my old life was behind me, that I have a new life, one where I can fight back. And you were right. But I've also been fighting to hold on to something, fighting to keep a part of that old life with me. That part of my life felt safer, more certain than this one, so I clung to it." She cautiously covered his hand with her own, her fingers curling around the leather of his gloves. "But . . . I don't want to hold on to it anymore. I want my old life behind me—every part of it. Because I want every part of this new life, no matter how uncertain it may be."

Kael's hand gripped hers with a warm and gentle pressure. His smile was sweet now, and soft on his face. "Every part of it is yours to claim, Andra."

She smiled too and, without thought, threw her arms around

204 · ERIN SWAN

his neck, the force of her embrace knocking him onto his back in the grass. But she did not release him. She lay there in his arms, holding him tightly, her face pressed against the warm skin at his neck, and she laughed. She laughed in wonder and disbelief and joy. She laughed as she had not laughed in all her life. And after a moment, she heard Kael laughing as well.

The rich sound seemed to carry in the night air around them. She could feel the vibrations of his laughter in his chest and through his neck as she lay half atop him in the grass. He smelled of trees and rain, and his laughter sounded of home.

Andra drew her face back from his neck and smiled down at him, feeling tears stinging at her eyes. "Thank you," she said. The words seemed horribly insufficient for the gift he had given her, but she said them again and again. "Thank you. Thank you. Thank you."

His smile softened to a mere curve of his lips, and he lifted a hand to her face. The back of his fingers grazed her skin, leaving a trail of tingling nerves in their wake. "You deserve freedom, Andra," he said. There was a deep sincerity in his voice, a tender passion she'd never heard there before. And she realized that, for the first time, she was truly seeing him. He had always worn half a mask, showing only a small part of who he was, what he thought, and how he felt. But now, it was gone, and all the Rider's soul seemed to be laid bare before her as he spoke. "You deserve freedom, and happiness, and so much more."

Andra felt his fingers slide softly into her hair, his hand cradling her face as he gazed up at her with those eyes that were somehow both soft as rain and penetrating as steel. She could feel his heart beneath her palm, and was surprised to find that it was beating nearly as quickly as her own. She felt the gentle pressure of his hand, not demanding, but carefully guiding her face closer to his.

And she found herself surrendering to it, wishing to know what it felt like to be kissed without anger or hatred or fear. Wanting to know what a real kiss—what *his* kiss—would feel like on her lips. A breath hung between them, and she felt the warmth of his skin as his forehead touched hers.

"Kael! Commander Kael!"

Andra jumped, springing away from the Rider, her heart racing—the cause of it unclear. Kael sat up, immediately looking alert, his eyes on the soldier who raced toward him. He was on his feet before the man reached them, and offered Andra a hand to help her to hers.

"What's happened?" Kael asked as the soldier drew up to them.

He was an elf, with long moonlight-blond hair and icy blue eyes. The sprint from Bellris hardly seemed to have winded him. "The Kingsmen's soldiers," he said hurriedly. "They're preparing to attack."

Kael's eyes narrowed. "Gathering in Vereor? Or already on the approach?"

"No," the elf said urgently. "They're here! In the north!"

Andra felt her heart become still, her breath stalling in her throat.

"How?" Kael demanded, his voice sharp, but she heard no fear in it. "Where?"

"In the northern pass."

A flicker of dread seemed to cross his eyes. "Near the . . ."

The elf nodded. "The supply cavern. That's how we found them. Colmen was sending men with supplies for the stronghold. It looks like they've been using the dwarf tunnels to travel."

"So we wouldn't see them coming," Kael breathed.

Andra stared at him for a brief moment, watching those eyes planning, analyzing, reacting. Then he nodded sharply.

"Gather those who cannot fight, and send someone to fetch my mother. Get them into wagons and on horseback immediately and send them east. Tell them to get as far away as possible. And tell the captains to gather immediately. We need every available moment to prepare our forces."

Without further instruction, the elf turned and ran back to Bellris. Kael immediately followed in the same direction, his feet flying across the grass, and Andra raced after him, leaving a length of brown leather and a tiny silver lock shining upon the grass.

22

Rebel Swords

When they reached Bellris, the camp was a flurry of panicked activity. People were darting frantically around the village, some pulling on pieces of armor, others laden with belongings. A single wagon stood by the fire, accepting whatever people threw into it. Four wild-eyed horses were yoked to the wagon, other livestock being herded around the area and letting out a raucous chorus of moos, grunts, bleats, and squawks, barely audible over the shouts of the Bellrisians.

"Freemen!"

The chaos quieted slightly at Kael's shout, as people's eyes turned to their leader. He leapt nimbly up onto the stone wall around the firepit and spoke in a loud, clear, calm voice.

"Those who will be staying to fight, find weapons and armor, and gather at the northern border of the village. Those who will leave, take only what you need to survive. Amala." The Healer stepped forward. "You shall lead the retreat. Everyone move quickly, but remain calm and follow orders. It's unlikely the

Kingsmen will attack before dawn, so we have several hours to prepare ourselves."

There was a brief silence as Kael took in the frightened faces stretched out before him. Andra thought she saw weariness and fear cross his face, but they were gone in a moment, and he stood straight and tall, confident and calm.

"We knew a fight would come," he said in a softer tone than before. "We knew it the moment each of us chose to become a Freeman. We may not be a great force, but we have great strength, because we fight for our own freedom and the freedom of every creature in this land." His voice rose beneath the trees, gaining strength as he went on. "Whether we stand or fall at the end of this battle, we will have given the Kingsmen something to fear! They shall know that we will not lie down and accept the new world they wish to build. We will not be subjects to the king they choose for us. We will fight them to our last breaths, and then others will carry on our fight. Whether we live free or die free, we are Freemen!"

A cheer erupted from the people. The fear Andra had seen on their faces was gone, replaced by a hope and determination that seemed almost absurd, given their circumstances. Each Freeman began to fall to his given task, and Amala began shouting directions to those who were gathering and loading items into the wagon. The square was a flurry of movement once again, but the panic and chaos were gone, replaced by purpose and direction.

Andra looked up at Kael as he hopped down from the wall. She opened her mouth to speak, but he spoke first. "Help Amala in directing the retreat," he said. "She's a good leader, but she'll need help with keeping everyone organized."

Her brows drew together, a feeling of surprise, anger, and disbelief rising in her. "What?" she asked sharply. "You want me to leave?"

Kael started away from the fire, toward the hut where the captains were gathering. Andra hurried after him.

"Your magic is strong, Andra," Kael said in a clipped, commanding tone, "but you have no control over it."

"But I am a better fighter than half your soldiers!" she shouted back at him.

"In sparring with a staff," he pointed out. "You don't know how to use a sword or a bow, and we'll be facing highly trained soldiers from the judges' armies. Do you really think your staff or dagger is going to be of any use against them?"

Andra caught his arm, forcing him to turn and look at her. She fixed him with a hard, determined look. "I can help, Kael!" she said, trying to keep the panic out of her voice. She wouldn't—she *couldn't*—let him fight without her.

He seized her by the shoulders, and she saw now that there was fear in his eyes again. "Andra," he said, his voice low and edged with strain, "I can't let you fight."

"But I have Tiri—"

"You can't Ride Tiri into battle!" he said loudly, his hands tightening on her shoulders. "You have no saddle, no training in dragon-mounted combat. Trying to fight on dragon-back would mean death for you, do you understand?"

"Then let me fight with the other soldiers!"

"No, Andra!" His shout surprised her, making her draw back from the fire in his gaze. He took a slow breath, closing his eyes briefly, and when he opened them again, he looked calm once more. "I know you are strong, Andra. And those who are retreating will need that strength. Other soldiers will be going with them, in case the Kingsmen somehow reach them. But I can't have you here."

"Why?" she demanded. "There are other women staying to fight—humans and elves. This is my home now. These are my people now! I have every right to defend myself and those I love!"

Hearing her father's words from her own mouth surprised her, but her determination didn't waver. She kept her eyes steady on his face. Pain darkened his eyes; then he ran a hand across his face and turned away from her.

"I have to go speak to the captains," he said in a deep, quiet voice. "I don't have time for this now. Speak to Amala and see if she can find you some armor and a weapon for the journey."

Andra watched him go, anger roiling inside her. Her mind reached out to Tiri. The dragon accepted the touch and opened her thoughts, immediately sending curiosity when she felt Andra's agitation. She relayed the conversation to the silent dragon and felt her agitation echo her own.

"What gives him any right to tell you whether or not you can fight?"

"He is the commander," Andra said with an internal sigh. *"If he told another soldier to accompany those retreating, I'm certain they would obey his orders without question."*

"Then why do you want to stay, Andra? Why are you so determined to fight in this battle?"

"All those I care about will stay behind," she said, her eyes scanning the crowds that continued to flow through the village. Her gaze settled on Alik and Syra in a tearful embrace; it was not a farewell she wished to have herself. *"Colmen, Kael, Alik, Eithne . . . and you."* Though Tiri hadn't said it, Andra felt certain that the dragon would stay behind and fight, and the feeling of determination she felt pressed against her mind confirmed it. *"Kael told me that in my new life, it is* not *fighting that can have terrible consequences. And I swore to myself that I would never run from another fight. I will never run if fighting could save those I love."*

"Then fight, Andra," Tiri said firmly. *"Fight."*

Andra paused for only a moment, her determination wavering with the realization that her choice could very well kill her. But a smooth, golden voice in her mind seemed to whisper, *"When the moment comes, you must stand, and you must fight."*

Finally, she silently replied, *"I will."*

Andra allowed another pair of soldiers to dress her in a leather breastplate and bracers that were too large for her slight frame. When they'd finished, Amala handed her a long dagger.

"We don't have many weapons to spare," the Healer said apologetically. "All the swords must stay behind with those defending Bellris."

Andra nodded in understanding and gripped the dagger, touching the hunting knife at her belt with her other hand. "This will be fine," she said. "I never really mastered a sword anyway."

Amala sighed, nodded, then turned to the waiting crowd. "Grab your packs, get together. We move out in ten!"

Andra's heart stuttered, and she swallowed hard. Her eyes fell on Kael and Colmen, who were emerging from the hut with the other army leaders. Kael's eyes found her instantly, and he and the elf strode to her through the crowd.

Colmen embraced her, holding her to him tightly. Andra put her arms around him and returned the embrace, pressing her face to his chest. He pulled back, holding her at arm's length, gripping her chin with one hand. He looked into her eyes, a kind but stern look.

"You keep your head up, understand?" he said. "Be safe, watch out for the others. You're a good fighter, Andra, and they need your strength. Above all, *be safe.*"

Andra swallowed again to fight back her tears, remembering those final words her mother had spoken to her. *Be good. Be safe.* She nodded and embraced him again. Then she looked at Kael, who stood close by, watching her.

She was angry at him, hurt that he didn't want her to fight with him. But she didn't hesitate as she rushed into his arms, holding him tightly, her hands clutching at the back of his tunic.

212 · ERIN SWAN

He held her with a desperation she had never felt before, as though he were afraid that if he let go, she would disappear like smoke. He pulled back, and his hand cupped her cheek, tilting her head upward. He kissed her forehead firmly, his lips warm on her skin. Andra closed her eyes at the touch, but it ended quickly.

Kael stepped away, turning toward his mother, who stood close by. Setora spoke a few quiet words to her son, and Kael nodded. Then he stepped away, straightening into the posture of the commander.

His hand fell to his sword, and he turned to look at Amala. He nodded once, and the Healer called, "Let's move out! Everyone move quickly, but remain as quiet as possible."

Without further instruction, the caravan of Bellrisians began to move east through the trees. Armed men watched them go, clutching their weapons as if they were a replacement for their loved ones. Kael looked back at her again, and his hand seemed to tighten around his sword. But he merely nodded at her.

"You should be guarding their flank," he said shortly.

Andra bit the inside of her lip, but nodded back at him and, with one last look at Colmen, Kael, and Alik standing together before the fire, she followed the line of retreating men and women.

Kael sat astride Eithne's back, his eyes on the dark sky. The first rays of dawn seemed to be touching the eastern horizon. Her quiet presence in his mind told him that she had neither seen nor sensed other dragons approaching. Kael felt certain that they would bring Riders, but he didn't know where they would be coming from. The dragons wouldn't have been able to travel through the tunnels, and nobody—not even dragons—ventured beyond the Last Mountains. So, his eyes remained on the sky.

But his mind was with Andra. He sensed disapproval from his

dragon at sending her away, but he obstinantly refused to question his own decision. She had received only a few weeks of combat training, and less than a fortnight of magic training. A battle like this would mean death for her—and that was not a sacrifice he could make yet.

Colmen stood in the grass beside Eithne's foreleg, silent, his usually jovial face somber. He looked up at Kael, reaching up to pat the Rider's boot.

"Gods be with you, brother," the elf said quietly.

Kael looked down at his friend, who had been by his side from the day he joined the Freemen. He nodded back, his lips pressed into a tight line. "And with you, my friend."

A sense of alertness suddenly touched his dragon's mind, and she immediately replaced his senses with her own. Against the dark shadow of the mountains, a pair of dragons suddenly appeared. Then there was the roar of a thousand voices, and in the trees, he heard the crashing of metal.

Kael felt his dragon's mind embrace his, feeling her determination, her readiness, and her love for him. He sent back the same, and then, with a furious roar, she threw them both into the sky.

23

Magic Within

In the growing light of dawn, Andra slipped deftly behind a tree, pressing her back against a trunk and remaining still, listening. Nobody noticed her. She silently moved away from the group that still walked briskly to the east, staying in the shadows. The roars of dragons reached her ears, and her heart leapt into her throat. The fear that had once paralyzed her now drove her forward, and her feet carried her west, racing back toward Bellris, toward the fight.

She felt Tiri touch her mind. *"They've brought two Riders,"* the dragon told her. *"I will have to fight. I cannot carry you back to the village as you asked me to."*

"I understand," Andra sent back. *"I can run back. Just be careful, Tiri."*

"And you, sister."

Then the mind withdrew, and Andra ran on. *What am I doing?* she thought to herself. Somewhere deep inside her, she knew this was foolish. She should turn back, return to her post with the caravan. But that voice continued to whisper in her mind, *When the moment comes, you must stand, and you must fight.*

And so she raced on, back toward the battle she'd been commanded to leave. She raced through the trees, leaping fallen branches and stones with ease, wishing for more speed. Above her, she began to see figures hidden in the trees. She heard the twangs of bows and the hiss of arrows. Then it was all before her.

It was chaos. Bloodstained chaos. Bodies were already strewn across the ground, arrows protruding from their chests, or deep wounds pouring pools of blood onto the dirt and grass.

Someone bumped into her from behind, and she jumped, spinning quickly around. One of the Freemen stumbled past her, bloodstained sword in hand, barely acknowledging her presence as he raced back into the battle. She drew her breath and followed him with determination. *I will not run.*

A man in silver armor and a deep blue tunic was heading quickly toward her with a sword in his hand. The blade arched toward her, and she stepped quickly to the side, turning her body out of the blade's path. She ducked fluidly under the soldier's reach, plunging her dagger into the exposed area under his arm.

He howled in pain and stumbled backward as she pulled her short blade from his body. She backed up as well, eyeing him as Kael had taught her, watching his movements, trying to find a weak spot in his defenses. He was clad heavily in armor. Well defended, but slow. *Your speed will be your greatest weapon,* Kael's voice said in her mind.

The man came toward her again. Andra darted quickly to the side, letting his thrust slide just past her. She turned and brought her knife down, drawing it as hard as she could across his arm. He howled again and his sword fell from his hand. He immediately scrambled for it with the other one, but Andra kicked it out of his reach.

Furious, the soldier dove at her legs, tackling her to the ground and crushing her beneath his heavy, armor-clad body. He grabbed at her dagger, trying to take it from her with his uninjured hand.

Andra reached for the well of magic in the back of her mind, demanding it protect her, imagining flames on her skin.

The blue-violet fire that had appeared once before erupted over her flesh again, and the man rolled away from her, screaming. Andra gripped her dagger and turned it on the man with a shout. It sank into the base of his neck. His eyes went wide and he made a choking sound. She pulled the blade out of his flesh, and he clutched at his neck, stumbling backward until he fell.

Andra forced herself to look away from him as she stood. Another soldier came toward her, and Andra's mind went blank as her body moved more quickly, killing more quickly. Dodge. Move. Strike. Kill. She killed with her knives and with her magic, never thinking, allowing her intincts and her need to fight to take over.

She never knew when her magic would work and when it would fail her. In one moment she would wish for protection, and an arrow would be deflected by a blue spark. In the next moment, she would try to summon magic to attack, and be left with nothing but her knives. But she continued to fight.

She felt Tiri brush her mind, ensuring she was still safe, and then the dragon withdrew again. Andra could only assume it was back into battle. She could hear the roars of dragons, but beneath the trees, she saw nothing. Briefly, she was grateful for their limited connection; if she fell, at least Tiri would not have to follow her beyond the Veil.

She caught a glimpse of Alik as his axe cleaved straight through steel helmets. His face was fierce and angry, and he looked once again like the man who had suggested that Kael kill her. Andra tried to call out to him, but he didn't hear her over the noise, and she was quickly distracted by another soldier.

Her body was screaming at her, her lungs burning with each gasping breath. After another soldier lay at her feet, she drew back from the battle, ducking out of the trees into the meadow. The majority of the battle remained clustered in the shelter of the woods, where the Freemen wanted it to remain. In the trees, they had an advantage, even if it was a small one.

Andra didn't know how many of the Kingsmen there were, but as her eyes darted over the bodies clashing beneath the canopies, she saw many more blue uniforms and shining metal than dirty tunics and leather.

She briefly examined her body for injuries. One long, shallow cut along her left arm. Another, deeper one on her right side. A small one across her cheek. With the sky open above her now, Andra scanned the area for the battling dragons.

The two green dragons spiraled and spat fire at the enemy they battled—a red dragon much larger than either of them. To the north, closer to the mountains, Eithne and Tiri battled a large blue serpent, and it was clear they were winning. Even as Andra watched, Eithne struck the creature from below, her teeth clamping into the blue scales.

She dug her rear claws into the dragon's underbelly, and Andra saw why Kael had told her battling aboard a dragon without training would mean death. She would never have been able to hold on amid the thrashing and spiraling descent that was now happening. And yet she saw blasts of magic being exchanged from the dragons' saddles, the two Riders still battling amid the manic thrashing of their mounts.

Just before the pair of dragons struck the trees, they sprang apart, wings snapping open, jerking them in opposite directions. And then the blue dragon fled. Streaming blood down upon the canopy, the enemy dragon took toward the desert, leaving the battle behind. Eithne barely paused before she and Kael turned to help face the second dragon.

Suddenly, Andra felt a chill race across her skin. Setora had taught her what that chill meant—there was someone with magic nearby. She turned her eyes and saw a sorcerer coming toward her. Their eyes met and Andra felt a pressure on her mind, like a clamp closing. She'd left her mind unguarded after Tiri's brief touch. She tried to throw the walls up around her thoughts but the clamp slammed closed, dividing her from the well of magic at the back of her mind.

The sorcerer didn't hesitate. He screamed a word that Andra couldn't catch, and a ball of fire flew toward her. She threw herself to the ground and rolled away from the flames, then sprang back to her feet, a blade in each hand. She charged forward, still struggling to reach the magic, but it remained behind a solid wall. She knew what she had to do. She had to break his concentration.

Her headlong charge at him seemed to catch the sorcerer off guard, and he leapt backward before conjuring a ball of black wind with another spell. Andra avoided this as well and rushed him again. Then invisible bonds seemed to snap closed around her. Her body went rigid, and she fell to the grass, sliding across its dew-soaked blades till she stopped at the sorcerer's feet. He looked down at her with a smile.

Andra reached out with her mind. *"Tiri!"* she screamed.

There was a furious roar, and Andra heard the snapping of trees as the violet dragon dropped from the sky, scraping the nearby treetops. The sorcerer stumbled back in surprise as Tiri swiped at him. Her claws grazed his chest, tearing his robes and drawing blood. And the bonds on Andra's body and mind fell away.

She sprang to her feet, rage burning through her veins. *Lightning,* she demanded, plunging her mind into the well it held. She felt the magic rush through her and she flung her hand outward. A bolt of pure energy shot from her fingertips and struck the man in the chest, throwing him backward across the grass, his robes smoldering.

Andra stared at him for a moment, feeling a sudden sapping of her energy. Her knees buckled slightly, and she placed a hand on Tiri's side for balance.

"On my back, Andra," Tiri said. *"Hurry!"*

Andra glanced around, realizing that the battle had left the trees; the Freemen were being forced from their sheltered areas of ambush and out into the open. The battle was being lost. Hurriedly, she scrambled up Tiri's side and onto her bare back. The dragon snapped and swiped at the advancing soldiers, but a blast of magic struck the pale lavender scales on her chest, and Tiri stumbled backward, then leapt into the sky.

Andra threw herself forward, clutching the spikes on the dragon's neck to keep from being unseated with the sudden movement. Tiri rose above the battle, circling over the lake, and Andra looked down to see that the Freemen were now in a full retreat, fleeing before their enemy. In the trees, she saw flames consuming huts and bridges, smoke rising into the sky. Calix and Egan were retreating as well.

Her eyes quickly scanned the area for signs of the other rebel Riders, her heart racing. On the desert sand, Andra saw a small green form lying still.

"Tiri . . ." Even in her mind, her voice broke.

Tiri emanated confusion; then her eyes seemed to find what Andra's had seen. *"Oh, dear Tildin . . ."* the dragon breathed.

"What about Janis? Do you see him?"

"Yes . . . I see him. He is alive. He is at his dragon's side . . . mourning."

Andra felt an ache in her chest, but she couldn't let herself become distracted. She turned her gaze away from the young dragon's body and back toward the battle. At last, she found Eithne. The red dragon was beating her wings at the tops of the trees, roaring furiously, trying to break through the thick canopy.

The girl threw her mind at the dragon, meeting a wall of distracted desperation. She beat against it until, finally, Eithne seemed to notice her mind.

"Andra!" she screamed, and Andra had never heard such panic in the dragon's silent voice. It rushed through her own mind,

overwhelming all her own emotions. *"Kael! Kael has been captured! I can't reach him!"*

"Tiri, put me on the ground!" Andra demanded.

"The battle is lost, Andra, it's not safe—"

"Now!"

Tiri obeyed, descending amid the chaos of the retreat, scattering soldiers. Andra leapt from her back as the dragon snapped and breathed fire, keeping the enemy soldiers at bay as Andra raced into the trees, toward where she heard Eithne continuing to batter at the canopy.

Then she saw him. Blood plastered his black hair to his forehead, running down his cheek. His hands were bound in front of him, and a man's hand gripped him by the back of the neck, forcing him forward.

She didn't know when he had left Eithne's saddle, or why, but there he was. The man holding Kael by the neck wore the same blue tunic and shining armor as the others, but he emanated magic from every inch of his body, making Andra's skin crawl.

Kael struggled against the hand that gripped his neck and pushed him forward, but the sorcerer simply laughed. The Rider's magic was bound, just as hers had been not long before. Raising one booted foot, the sorcerer kicked Kael firmly in the back of the leg, bringing him down to his knees.

Another soldier moved toward her. She hurriedly deflected his much larger blade with hers, just enough so that it split the air beside her; then she sank her little knife into the side of his neck, and he fell. She turned back toward Kael, hurrying to him, but she was too far away, and soldiers continued to block her path.

The sorcerer caught an axe-wielding soldier. "Bring me that barrel," the sorcerer ordered. "We were told to bring back his head. His body is optional." There was a sneer in his voice, and Kael fought once again to rise, but the sorcerer seized his hair, yanking his head backward as he dug a knife into the Rider's shoulder blade.

Above her, Andra heard a furious roar as Eithne continued to claw at the branches, tearing at them, trying to reach her Rider. Andra quickly killed another man, spinning back in Kael's direction as the sorcerer forced his head against the top of the barrel. The Rider struggled. The soldier raised his axe.

"Kael!" The name tore its way out of her throat, and she saw him jerk as he tried to lift his head to look in her direction.

Still several yards away, Andra hefted, then flung her dagger at the axeman. *Please, save him,* she begged, and once again, magic washed over her body with warmth and power. The knife seemed to surge forward suddenly, and the blade connected solidly, its entire length burying itself in the executioner's chest. The sorcerer looked up in surprise as the man in the blue tunic stumbled backward, dropped his axe, and fell.

Kael suddenly threw his weight to the side, catching the sorcerer off guard. They rolled across the ground until Kael pinned the startled man beneath him. Then he quickly took the sorcerer's head between his still-bound hands, and gave a sharp twist. Andra heard the crack and saw the body go limp, but she didn't look down at it as she raced to Kael's side. His magic now freed, fire filled his hands, burning away the ropes at his wrists.

They fell away as she reached him, panting breathlessly. "Kael!" she cried with mingled relief and terror.

He looked down at her briefly, his eyes startled and relieved and joyous at once. Then he caught her tightly in his arms for half a moment before clutching her hand and turning to pull her deeper into the woods. A few brave Freemen lingered. The archers in the trees, with nowhere to easily escape to, continued to send arrows at the Kingsmen, doing as much as they could in a battle that was already lost.

Kael hurriedly jerked his red blade from the dead sorcerer's sheath and straightened to follow the retreat. Suddenly, several soldiers appeared around them. The men circled them, swords in their hands. Kael tried to push Andra behind him, but they were surrounded on all sides.

"Come now, Kael," one of the men said. "Your men have all fled. Call off your dragon, and don't try any of your sorcerery, and we'll let you and the girl live—for now. They'll make a good example of you both when we get you back to Vereor."

She saw Kael's sword begin to lower, and anger surged through her. She would not surrender. And she would not let Kael surrender either. Andra ducked around Kael's arm, planting herself between him and the speaking soldier.

"No!" she screamed, her voice loud, furious, a sound more worthy of Tiri than the small girl. But as she screamed the word, anger coursing through her, she buried every part of her mind in the pulsing well of magic inside her. She drew out every last, burning piece of it and ordered it to save her and Kael.

There was a sound like an explosion, making the ground shake. A pulse of arching blue-violet light raced outward from her feet, spreading like a disturbance on the surface of a pond. The light sparked as it flew outward. It seemed to seize the soldiers in fingerlike strands of living power, and their bodies jerked before falling to the earth. It continued outward almost too quickly for Andra's eye to follow it, seizing soldiers, pulling them to the ground, while passing over the Freemen without harm. It spread away from her, dropping the Kingsmen to the ground, leaving the bloodied and bedraggled Freemen staring in bewilderment.

Suddenly, a wave of exhaustion washed over Andra, and her legs gave way beneath her. Kael caught her in his arms, and the light disappeared. Beyond where the ring of light had touched, the rest of the Kingsmen's soldiers stood frozen in surprise. The Freemen too were still.

Still held against his chest, she felt the vibration of Kael's voice as he screamed, "Freemen! To arms! To arms!" A few of those who had begun to flee caught up the cry, echoing it to those who had retreated, and rushed back into battle.

Andra didn't see any more. Her vision was hazy as Kael carefully lowered her to the earth, his face filling the shrinking space above her. His mouth moved and she struggled to hear him, fighting to focus on him.

"You need to draw in more energy, Andra." His voice was distant, hazy. "I know my mother showed you how. The earth. Use the earth."

Her mind growing foggier, Andra struggled to remember Setora's lesson. She reached out with her thoughts toward the ground against her back, feeling its warmth. She let her eyes close, wondering briefly if they would open again. Then the warmth of the earth began to rush into her body. It filled her so quickly that she gasped and pulled away, sitting up suddenly.

Kael caught her by the shoulders, steadying her. "You did too much," he said softly. "That's all. You'll be fine. Can you stand?"

Andra nodded, and he helped her to her feet. Sword still in hand, he regarded her, and she thought she saw respect and admiration in his gaze.

"Are you strong enough to fight?" he asked.

She nodded sharply, and a grim smile touched his face.

"Good. Then let's drive these bastards into the desert and let the Burning Sands finish them."

Andra smiled back at him, and they turned and charged into battle together.

24

The Fallen

Andra felt a strange sense of amazement and fear upon seeing Kael truly fight. Those gray eyes that were capable of looking on her with such tenderness burned with a fierce focus and merciless fire. Whirlwinds of flame flew out from his fingertips, devouring the fleeing Kingsmen in smoke and fire. His vision never wavered, his sword biting through flesh, the red steel dripping red blood after each swing.

She stayed at his side. The magic that pulsated from him made her skin rise with chills across her body, and it seemed to awaken a deeper awareness of her own magic. Now she reached into the well almost constantly, feeling how alive and powerful it was inside her mind. And the magic answered her call, as if it had been waiting for her to truly take command of it.

For each attack that Kael sent at the Kingsmen, Andra sent one of her own. Bolts of lightning for his streams of fire. Waves of arcing light for his trembling earthquakes. He pulled water from the ground at the soldiers' fleeing feet, and Andra filled it with coursing blue-violet light that made the men twitch inside their armor before collapsing to the earth. For a moment, Andra felt as if her mind was connected to his as strongly as Eithne's was. They fought without speaking, and yet their attacks seemed to be coordinated somehow, a perfectly choreographed dance of death.

Finally, the last Kingsmen fled into the desert. A cheer went through the bloodied, battered Freemen as they watched their enemy stumble across the sands, out into the merciless desert. Not many who had survived the battle would also survive the three-day trek across the Shesol Mal.

Andra cheered along with them, holding her bloodied dagger aloft. Tiri, Eithne, and Calix roared, their three voices making the earth tremble with the force of the sound. Beside her, Kael cheered as well, his red sword in the air, flashing in the sun. And Andra saw why he was the symbol of this rebellion. Not for his blood or his status, but for his heart. Because he was a leader who would fight to his last breath for those who followed him. And when they were victorious, he would shout his joy with theirs.

He caught her looking up at him and he smiled down at her, a triumphant expression. She felt his bloodied hand clasp her own, and she held it tightly as they both screamed their victory at the desert.

———◈———

The Freemen did not celebrate for long. When the last Kingsman had disappeared over the sandy dunes, they turned their weary eyes on the dead.

"Egan," Kael called, sliding his blade back into its sheath, "you and Calix bring back those who retreated. We'll need their help."

To Andra's surprise, the elder Rider nodded, gave a salute, then jumped onto his dragon's back before taking off toward the east. She looked at Kael to see if Egan's show of respect had caught him off guard as well, but there seemed to be an understanding in his eyes.

He looked back at her then, and she asked the question that had been at the back of her mind from the moment she'd entered the battle. "Colmen? Have you seen him? Is he all right?"

The Rider let out a breath, his gray eyes scanning the carnage around them. "I spent most of the battle in the air, and I didn't see him when I returned to the ground."

Andra felt anxiety clench a fist around her gut, but she nodded. All they could do now was search, as everyone else was doing. The Freemen wandered through the forest and field, searching for fallen friends and loved ones, their moment of triumph ended. Elves and sorcerers extinguished the flames that continued to devour what remained of the camp. Andra and Kael joined them.

Egan returned not long after, Amala behind him on Calix's back. The Healer leapt easily from the dragon's saddle after he folded his wings, and she hurried to where the wounded were being gathered around the central fire. A few magic-users gathered there as well, prepared to help with Healing wherever their skills allowed.

Kael stayed at Andra's side as they moved through the campsite, putting out any fires they came to, gathering the dead and wounded when they found them. Andra forced her mind to go blank as she grabbed the ankles of one dead man after another, carrying their bodies to the edge of the desert, where Tildin's sparkling green corpse still lay on the sand.

Janis was still beside his dead dragon, holding his mind-partner's head in his lap, stroking the scales between his closed eyes. Andra took a step toward the youth, wanting to comfort him, but Kael touched her arm, stopping her. He gave a small shake of his head, as if he knew that there were no words she could offer the young Rider, no comfort to fill the hole that now consumed his mind and heart. Without a word, they turned back to gathering the dead.

They approached another still form, unmoving on the edge of the grassy field, and Andra bent to pick up the boots as she had done dozens of times already. And then she heard Kael's sharp exhalation. She looked up as the Rider knelt over the unmoving body, his hands touching the pale neck, looking into the blank, staring, violet eyes.

Disbelief and denial held her for a moment, rooting her to where she stood. Then anguish gripped at her, tearing through her as it had not done since her mother's death. His body, though marked with shallow wounds, bore no signs of death, and she knew he had been killed by magic.

"No," she breathed softly, kneeling across from Kael. "No . . . please, not him."

Her hand hesitantly touched the elf's chest, resting over a still, unbeating heart.

"Colmen," she whispered. "Colmen . . ." She suddenly became aware of hot tears sliding down her cheeks, and she touched the moisture with a brief feeling of surprise. She had not cried in well over a year.

She heard an anguished moan and looked up to see Kael folding in on himself, as if his bones had become too weak to hold him upright. He crumpled, his body curling upon itself, hands seizing his black hair as a deep, keening noise escaped him.

Andra moved quickly around Colmen's body, her hands touching the back of Kael's blood-marked tunic. Without a word, he turned into her, his arms folding around her waist. He pressed his face into her tunic, and she felt his tears soaking the fabric. Her own tears fell more rapidly as she held him, her hands stroking his black hair even as her tears fell into it.

"I'm sorry," she whispered shakily. "I'm so sorry, Kael."

The Rider, who had always seemed so strong and immovable to her, shuddered with another sob, holding on to her as though she were all that kept him afloat in a sea of sorrow.

Through his anguished keens, she heard him say softly, "He was my best friend in this world. My brother. We swore to always defend one another. But I . . . I failed him. I was not there when he needed me."

Andra pulled him back from the desperate embrace, her hands framing his face as she forced Kael to look at her. His tanned face was streaked with dirt and blood and tears, his gray eyes—always so hard and calm—now filled with pain and loss that echoed in her heart.

"You did *not* fail him, Kael," she said firmly, trying to make her voice sound strong, trying not to let it shake as her tears continued to fall. "You did all you could. You fought. You defended the Freemen—his people. You led them to victory in an impossible battle. Colmen fought, and he died for this rebellion. You could never fail him, Kael. He loved you as a brother and as a leader. I know he would give his life for you and for this rebellion again if it were asked of him. You did not fail him. You did not fail any of us."

He embraced her again, this time pulling her against his chest. She felt his lips press against her hair, and she wrapped her arms around his back, clutching at the fabric of his dirty tunic as they both continued to weep for the elf who would never smile again.

———◦◦◦———

Andra stared at the pile of bodies in the sand, Kingsmen and Freemen alike. They lay together, straw and wood around them, Tildin's much larger form in the middle of them. She looked away from the pyre and toward Janis, who stood not far from her. His leg was in a splint, and his neighbors supported him on either side. He looked pale and sickly. Tears coursed down his already stained face as he stared at his dead companion.

Janis still hadn't spoken about what happened, but Egan had witnessed it. As they'd battled the red dragon together, the enemy Rider had struck Tildin's wing with a spell, knocking the young dragon from the sky. He'd fallen, evidently crushing Janis's leg in the process. The enemy dragon had followed, despite Egan's attempts to stall them, and when they landed beside the fallen dragon and Rider, Tildin had placed himself in front of Janis, protecting him.

The enemy Rider pierced Tildin's heart just as Egan landed to try to save him. And then Kael and Eithne had arrived, and the enemy was quickly dealt with. It seemed as if fighting together had forged a begrudging respect between Kael and Egan. Though there seemed to be no kindness between them, Egan followed Kael's orders without complaint.

Andra leaned against Kael's side, and his arm drew her more tightly to him. She forced herself to look down at the pale face nearest to her. The elf looked as if he were sleeping, only a few spots of blood marking his tunic as he lay beside the dragon's head, his eyes now peacefully closed. The crowd stood in a circle around the dead.

Kael's arm fell from around Andra's shoulders, and she looked up at him as he stepped forward, toward the pyre. Several others moved as well. Eithne, who stood on Kael's other side, took one large step toward the bodies. Egan separated himself from the crowd, Calix moving with him. Tiri, standing beside Andra, moved forward, but Andra hung back. The Riders lifted their marked hands, placing their free hands on their dragons' necks. The dragons opened their maws.

The crowd of mourners—all that was left of the Freemen—watched silently as fire poured from the Riders' hands and the dragons' mouths, consuming the straw, the wood, and the bodies together. Andra looked at Tiri, her flames seeming small compared to the older dragons'. Thinking only of wanting to be beside her dragon, Andra stepped forward and placed a hand on Tiri's neck.

One amethyst eye looked at her, but the dragon said nothing. Nor did anyone else as Andra silently lifted her hand. Sadness filled her chest, and blue-violet flames flowed from her fingers, spinning and spiraling as it mingled with the other flames. Kael looked toward her, but he remained silent as well. They all continued to pour fire onto the pyre, the blaze growing, twisting its fingers toward the sky. Andra's hand against Tiri's side began to tingle as she felt magic pulse through her and around her.

The bodies quickly burned to ash, the sand beneath them turning to glass in the heat of the flames. And still, fresh fire roared at the spot, as if they all knew there was more to be done. The glistening sand twisted, reaching upward like the flames. It twisted and bent, the glass rising and expanding, picking up the ashes of the dead.

Then the six sets of flames ceased together. The silent crowd stared at the spot where the bodies had been. The molten sand shimmered slightly, radiating its own heat as it cooled.

Someone from the crowd spoke. "It looks like an Ers Fehnar."

The words evoked in Andra memories of the Hall, of a room she had never been allowed to enter. But she had caught a glimpse of it once, passing when the doors were partially open. The room had been filled with glass orbs, carved with intricate images of dragons in flight, breathing fire, and fighting. They were the Ers Fehnars, the First Flames, of every dragon who had been Paired with a Rider.

It was tradition that, when a dragon first learned to breathe fire, the dwarves would carve a glass orb and deliver it to the Hall. The dragon would breathe a flame on the glass, and the enchanted orb would capture it, holding the flame inside so that it would burn on forever. Even the Ers Fehnar of Oriens burned inside that room.

Andra looked at the shimmering glass shape in front of her. It was not quite the same as those gathered in that forbidden room in the Hall of Riders. It was shaped of twisted glass, tendrils spiraling around one another until they had spun into a globe, the pieces still visible like twisted vines. The base of the glass was dark with ash, the color lightening until the glass near the top was clear. But it did remind Andra of the ones she had seen so briefly. Except it did not glow with the warmth of a dragon's breath.

"Tiri," Andra said, the words leaving her before she had time to think of them. "Give it one last flame."

Tiri blinked her heavy lids and looked at Andra questioningly. The girl simply patted her shoulder. The violet dragon turned her eyes to the glass globe and let out a small stream of fire. As she did, Andra pictured those glowing orbs in the Hall and touched the magic in her mind, guiding the flames to where she wished them to go. The fire passed through the shimmering surface and stopped in the orb's center, the flames flickering and spinning around themselves, casting a dancing light through the ash-filled glass.

Andra felt Kael reach out and seize her hand. He spoke not to her, but to the crowd. His voice was clear and steady, though his eyes were still reddened from sorrow. "This monument will glow in day and night for eternity," he said, "reminding everyone of the sacrifice the Freemen made to restore what the Guardians built."

Hundreds of pairs of tear-filled eyes watched the dancing flames for a long, silent moment. Janis was the first to move forward, his neighbors helping him. Silently, he kissed the tips of his first two fingers and pressed them to the glass. Those with him did the same; then they moved away. Others began to follow their example, kissing their fingertips and pressing them to the glowing orb before turning back toward the singed remains of Bellris. Andra stood with one hand still on Tiri's neck. Kael continued to hold on to her other hand, touching his own dragon's neck with the other palm.

The four of them stood, connected to one another, watching the Freemen file past the glowing glass orb. Soon, the two humans and the two dragons were the only ones left on the desert sand. Andra had thought that she cried every last tear within her, but she realized she was wrong. They began to come again as she stepped forward, kissing her fingers and pressing them against the glass. She left her hand there, feeling the warmth from the flames within.

"Goodbye, Colmen," she whispered, trembling.

Kael had followed her up to the glass, and he too pressed his hand against it. "Play for him," he said quietly. Andra looked up at him. There were tears in his eyes as he looked down at her. "Colmen was my best friend in this world," he said. "I know he would want you to play for him."

Andra looked down at the flute that hung at her waist, filling the place where the dagger had once been. She'd retrieved it from Colmen's quarters after they found him, and she hadn't allowed it away from her since. She pulled the flute from her belt, holding it in both her hands. Slowly, she shook her head.

"I don't think I can," she whispered.

"Please, Andra. For Colmen."

She took a shaking breath and put the flute to her lips. It took a moment for her trembling mouth and shaking fingers to coax a sound from the instrument, but the notes began to quiver across the desert. Kael recognized the tune at once, and he began to softly sing the words.

> Underneath the sycamore tree
> I'll wait for you if you'll come to me . . .

The lyrics seemed to rip through Andra's chest, no longer speaking of a young man waiting for his lover. She was pleading with Colmen, wherever he may be, praying that she would see him again, that he would wait for her beyond the Veil. It was uncertainty. It was loss. It was pain. She played through all three of the verses, and Kael sang right along with her, his bass voice shaking as much as the flute's notes. When the last note had fallen quiet, Andra returned the flute to her waist.

And the sobs returned. Kael pulled her into his arms as her body heaved with sorrow. It didn't last as long as it had the first time. Slowly, the agony dulled into a persistent ache, and the tears fell silently, with only the occasional tremor coursing through her body. Kael pulled back slightly, cupping a finger under her chin, lifting her tearstained face to his. She closed her eyes as he kissed her forehead, then the tears on her cheeks.

They stood in each other's arms for a long, silent moment, the flames of the glass pyre dancing over them in the growing darkness, alone except for their dragons beside them.

"Andra," Kael whispered. "Andra, I love you. I have loved you for far longer than I was willing to admit. But I can't deny it to myself any longer. Not when I have lost my dearest friend, not when I nearly lost you as well."

Her throat tightened in agony. "Kael . . ." she started.

"I don't care if you say you love me or not," he interrupted. "I just need you to hear me say that I love you. I need you to know that you have my heart. No matter what else may happen, you . . . You are my heart-song, Andra."

She shook her head, closing her eyes to hold back the tears. "You . . . You can't love me, Kael."

His hand touched her cheek, bringing her face up toward his again. "And why is that?" he asked softly.

"I'm . . . not what you need," she said weakly. "You deserve someone strong, someone whole, someone . . . unbroken. You . . . have enough burdens to bear. I won't become another one."

"Andra," he said quietly when she had finally stopped talking, "you must stop believing that what has happened to you makes you unworthy of love. If you were, then I must be just as unworthy, because I am as broken as you. We may be broken in different ways, but I *want* your burdens, your scars, your memories—the good and the bad. They're a part of you, Andra, and I want them. I don't expect loving you to fix either of us, but perhaps, if we try, we can fill some of the breaks that our lives have given us. Perhaps the pieces of me that are broken are made to fit with the broken parts of you. I love you, Andra. I love every part of you—and the broken pieces most of all."

Her heart ached with longing and uncertainty at his words. She wished she could say the same words to him, to assure him of her love. But she couldn't. Something inside her still held her back, a lingering fear that told her something like this could never belong to her.

Andra sighed and pulled away. Stretching up to the tips of her toes, she kissed Kael's cheek, tasting the salt of a tear as she did so. Then she wrapped her arms around his neck, and they stood in silence again, listening to the sound of each other's heartbeats.

25

The Art of War

Andra stood uncomfortably in front of hundreds of pairs of scrutinizing eyes, most of them still red with sadness and loss. Kael had set her on the crumbling ring of stones that surrounded what was left of the central firepit. He stood beside her, still holding her hand, the two of them standing above the rest of the Freemen. Andra could sense that Tiri was listening, as well as the other two dragons in the nearby field.

Kael was speaking. "By now, you have all learned of the unique bond between Andra and Tiri. They were destined to be Paired, but missed their opportunity. Still, Tiri claims Andra as her Rider. Today, many of you witnessed Andra fighting with the rest of the Freemen, returning to the battle after I had asked her to leave. In doing so, she saved my life, and the magic she used turned the battle in our favor. Without her, this rebellion would be over.

"You all stood witness as Tiri was honored with an Ers Fehnar like no other, and I don't believe any would argue that that dragon, who fought with us when the battle was not hers to fight, is undeserving of that honor." Kael paused as if waiting for someone to voice any disagreement. When the watchful crowd remained silent, he continued. "I only think it right that, in recognizing Tiri, we recognize the one she claims as her Rider. I believe that Andra has proved herself to be one of the Freemen, and I believe she has fought as bravely as any of us, and certainly as bravely as any Rider."

"No." Andra's eyes snapped toward the voice, the rest of the crowd searching until they found the speaker. Egan stood from where he sat on a stump, his eyes hard as he looked at Andra. He continued, "Andra did not fight as bravely as the rest of us. She entered the battle with less training than many of those who retreated. She fought with little understanding of her own magic, and only a dagger at her side. She is far braver than any of us."

Andra stared at the Rider, wondering at his words, so grudgingly spoken. When he spoke again, it sounded as if someone were forcing the words from his mouth. "Andra should be recognized as a Rider—and as a true hero to the Freemen."

There was a long silence. "I agree." Syra smiled at Andra.

Alik was quick to echo his betrothed. "I agree."

"Me too." Amala stepped momentarily away from the injured she was still tending to.

The votes came more and more rapidly. "Me too."

"Aye."

"Hear, hear."

"I agree."

"I agree."

Andra stared as the Freemen each spoke their turn, all of them voting to give her something she could never be worthy of. Every last rebel declared her the same as any other Rider in Paerolia. Conflicting emotions raged inside her. This was not how it should be done. She was not a Rider, not truly. Not like Kael.

Kael turned and looked down at Andra, a smile at the corner of his mouth. "It's decided," he said. "To the Freemen, you are now a Rider, Lady Andra."

Cheers and applause erupted around them, and Andra began to smile back at him. Movement in the corner of her eye made her look away from the Rider beside her. A single figure hobbled through the crowd, the others parting to make room for him, trying to help him along.

When Janis had reached the front of the crowd, he dropped a large black object before him. Andra looked down at the saddle, then at the young Rider's face, which was still ashen, his eyes still glassy with the loss of a companion who could never be replaced. The crowd fell silent again.

Janis's voice was a low murmur when he spoke. "You can have my things, Andra," he said. "You are now the Rider I cannot be."

Andra released Kael's hand and hopped down from the stones. "Janis," she said, "you are still a Rider."

The boy gave a hollow laugh. "What's a Rider without a dragon? I do not even fully feel like a person anymore, Andra, much less a full Rider. Half of me is dead."

Pity swelled inside her, and Andra unthinkingly embraced the boy. "But they're yours, Janis. They represent your Bond with Tildin. I cannot take them."

There was a soft *thud* beside her, and she looked up at Kael, who had jumped down from the stone perch as well. "She's right, Janis," he said. "A Rider's effects should remain with a Rider until his death."

"The saddle, then," the younger Rider countered. "She will need a saddle, and I will never need it again. I will keep my gloves and sword and jacket, but Andra should have the saddle."

Kael looked down at the black object at his feet, then at Janis and Andra. He nodded. "You're right. She will need the saddle."

Janis nodded once and looked at the girl. "The saddle is yours, then."

Andra embraced him again, and he halfheartedly returned the gesture. "I'm so sorry, Janis," she whispered. "I'm sorry for what you have lost."

Janis sighed, and she felt him shake as he did so. "Just remember him when you use it," he whispered back. "Remember Tildin for me."

"I will. I promise, I will think of both of you. Thank you, Janis."

The young boy released her and hobbled back into the crowd, his small form disappearing quickly among them as he returned to the groups of injured awaiting Healing. Another voice spoke from the sea of faces.

"What about the rest of her effects?"

Andra saw a hand rise in the crowd, and everyone turned toward it. An elven woman stepped forward. "I have helped to craft swords for Riders in Iterum," she said. "I will help to make Andra's."

Syra raised her hand as well and said, "And I can make her gloves and jacket. All I need is the leather."

Alik spoke immediately after her. "I can make her a decent belt and sheath for the sword."

Kael nodded in approval. "We can start preparing her effects immediately."

Another hand rose, a question this time. "Kael," a male voice said, "what will we do now?"

The Freemen looked woefully around at Bellris. To the south, only a few scattered huts remained standing, the rest still sending smoke from their ruins. Around them, though most of the quarters within the trees were still intact, burned bridges had fallen where they once connected the trees. Andra could tell by their faces that what came next was not something that the Freemen were yet willing to face.

But Kael sighed, and gave them an answer. "If there is one thing that we learned from yesterday, it is that the judges will waste no effort to eradicate us. They will not underestimate us again. And, as I'm sure we all know, they will be back, and this time with greater numbers of soldiers, sorcerers, and Riders. I doubt so many of us will survive if they do return."

"So, we run?" Egan asked. The sneer that would have been in his voice before was absent, replaced by a listless sense of defeat.

"No."

All eyes—even Kael's—turned to Andra at her single spoken word. She looked at them, the faces she had so quickly come to know and care about. She knew few of their names, but their faces meant something to her. They were the faces that had welcomed her into a life of freedom. And now, it was her turn to give them their own freedom.

She drew a breath and spoke loudly so everyone could hear her. "If it is Castigo that the Kingsmen wish to put on the throne, then we must remove him from the equation. If there is no man who would be king, then there are no Kingsmen."

"They could just choose another man to back," a voice in the crowd pointed out.

Andra nodded. "They may do so, but killing Castigo would bring about another change. With no Chief Judge and no heir to fill his seat, all the judges would need to be reelected. If we kill Castigo, we can put honorable, trusted men in the judgment seats, as the Guardians intended. The elves' Seer, Astrum, came to Bellris before and said that the key to ending this rebellion was the power that Ledo held. You believed that meant taking Ledo, but perhaps it means removing the power of Chief Judge Castigo altogether— the power he would have given to his son, the power he was already beginning to let him wield. Perhaps this is the answer that Astrum wanted for the Freemen. With the judges no longer pursuing us, we could fight *with* them to eradicate the Kingsmen from Paerolia."

As she fell silent, her eyes scanned the crowd, expecting someone to argue with her, to point out some flaw that she had not seen. Nobody spoke. Their gazes all turned to Kael, standing beside her. Andra looked up at him as well, and saw him watching her with an expression of quiet pride.

Then he looked at the crowd. "All in favor?" he asked.

Every hand rose into the air, and Kael nodded.

"Captains, gather to the hut to begin strategizing. Everyone else . . ." He sighed, his gray eyes looking around them at the destroyed settlement. "Gather what belongings you can."

"Where shall we go?" someone asked.

Kael looked at Egan, who was still standing in the middle of the crowd. "Egan will lead whoever chooses to follow him to the southeast. We have a small band of supporters who have settled near the base of the Mordis Range. Insarius?" The intelligence leader stepped forward. "Begin sending word to every supporter we have in every city and village. Tell them to gather at the Mordis camp as quickly as they can. When the Chief Judge falls, there will be chaos, and we will need to seize control as quickly as possible. We'll need every rebel we have ready to answer the call."

Insarius nodded, then turned and headed toward the dovecote.

Kael looked back at the crowd. "If you do not wish to join the Mordis camp, it will not be held against you. Every person here has already made great sacrifices for this rebellion. If you wish it, you may leave and find lives of peace wherever you wish. Now, let's get to work. We have a war to fight."

He hopped back to the ground and started toward one of the few standing huts, where the other captains were headed as well. He took several strides, then stopped and looked back at her.

"Are you coming?" he asked.

Her brow furrowed. "To the captains' meeting?" she asked.

Kael nodded. "You're a Rider now, and I think you've proved yourself worthy of the title of captain as well. And—" He paused, his jaw tightening slightly. "—we need someone to fill Colmen's seat."

Andra bit her lip, feeling fresh tears sting at her eyes. But she nodded without argument and followed him to the hut where the others gathered. Kael sat at the head of the table, and she took a seat to his left, across from Egan, with Janis beside her. Insarius's seat was empty, and two other men Andra didn't know well filled the other seats.

As soon as everyone was seated, Kael spoke. "There's no need for us to cover what has happened. We all know what we have lost, but that's in our past. I want us to discuss how we move forward. Andra has proposed a plan, and the Freemen have accepted it. It is our job now to make that plan work."

They fell into discussions immediately, each man proposing a strategy, another striking it down. After some time, Insarius joined them, and the debates began anew. Finally, one of the men Andra didn't know—an elf named Peregris—spoke.

"We must turn to the elves," he said. "King Vires is supportive of the rebellion."

"But relations with the human kingdom—" Egan started.

"Are tenuous," Peregris agreed with a nod. "But he will still offer shelter to those he can. I propose we send our Riders to Iterum. There, you will find sanctuary until you are prepared to make your attack on the Chief Judge."

"And you feel certain that King Vires will shelter us?" Kael asked.

Peregris nodded, his long pale hair shining in the torchlight. "I know he has done it many times. He often shelters new rebels on their way to join the Freemen. I don't believe this would be any different."

Kael drew a breath and nodded in agreement. "I second this strategy. Those in favor?"

Andra raised her hand, as did the others in the room.

"It's agreed, then."

"You don't plan to drag me along with you, do you?" Janis asked, his voice a low monotone.

"We agreed to send the Riders to Iterum," Kael said firmly. "Egan must lead the Freemen to the Mordis Range camp, but you are a Rider, Janis. You should go with us."

"I have no dragon," the young man said, his voice breaking on the last word. Tears began to fall down his cheeks as he continued, but he kept his voice steady. "Taking me would just be an extra load for one of your dragons to carry. I will follow with any elves who will return to Iterum, but you and Andra should fly ahead of us and begin preparing."

Kael was silent for a moment, regarding the boy's dark tearstained face. Then he nodded. "Very well, Rider Janis."

He seemed to add the title as a means of reminding Janis of who he truly was, but the boy didn't respond to it. He merely looked back down at the table, still shedding silent tears.

26

Broken Hearts

Andra lay awake in her bed, staring at the ceiling, tears streaming down her temples and into her hair. Her hand clutched Colmen's flute to her chest in the darkness as she fought to keep her sobs silent. Another woman slept in her room now, displaced by the fires that had ravaged the village, and she did not want to wake her.

The night was eerily silent, the woodland animals having fled from the fire and the smell of ash and blood. She knew she should sleep. Her body ached with exhaustion. But the aching of her heart overpowered it and kept her from sleep. Colmen's smiling face seemed to fill her mind, and she wept with the realization that she would never see his smile, hear his teasing voice, or feel his eager embrace ever again.

In the heavy silence that filled the forest, Andra thought she heard a soft sound. She held her breath for a moment, listening. It came again, the quiet, muffled sound of someone weeping and trying not to be heard. Silently, she slid from her mattress, leaving the wooden flute on her pillow, and crept from the room.

She stood outside her doorway, listening again until she heard the sound. And then she was certain from where it came. Andra's bare feet were silent as they crossed the wooden bridge, which had been patched together with rough boards. She paused briefly outside his quarters, then cautiously pulled the curtain away from the doorway.

At first, she saw nothing but blackness, but her eyes soon adjusted and she saw Kael, his chest bare, sitting against the wall, a fist pressed to his mouth to muffle the sobs that shook him. Without a moment's hesitation she rushed to him, drawing him to her as she had before. She held him, wishing for words that would comfort him, but no amount of wishing brought words to her lips. There was no magic that could mend this wound.

For a long time, the rebel leader wept, and Andra held him, accepting his tears. Gradually, the sobs seemed to ebb, and he released her from his tight embrace. But he did not draw back from her. He pressed his forehead against hers, his hand cupping her cheek and brushing away the tears that she had shed with him. His eyes were closed, as if he didn't wish for her to see the pain in them.

"Stay with me," he breathed, his breath warm on her cheek. "Andra, please . . . Promise me you'll stay."

Something in the way he said the words made her feel as if he meant more than this moment, more than this night. But still she nodded, her hands against the bare skin of his chest.

"I promise," she whispered in return.

Kael lay back on the mattress, gently bringing her to lie beside him, their faces still close. He wrapped his arms around her, holding her tightly, and she allowed her head to rest into the curve of his neck, just above his heart. Though sorrow still filled her, knowing that the man who held her shared in her loss offered comfort somehow. And, with his arms around her, she finally fell into a deep and quiet slumber.

———⋅◈⋅———

Andra tightened the last strap of Janis's saddle and stepped back from Tiri. The violet dragon was practically wriggling with joy. Her tail twitched excitedly from side to side, and she ruffled her wings occasionally.

"Try not to take off without me," Andra remarked with a smile.

Even across their limited bond, Andra could feel the dragon's jubilation. *"Today, we fly together as dragon and Rider,"* Tiri cried in her mind. *"People will see us together, see the sword of my colors at your side, and they shall fear us."*

"Soon, sister," Andra laughed, scratching the dragon under the chin. *"We will fly soon."*

Once again, she shifted the sword that hung at her side, still growing used to its weight and the feel of it against her leg. The Rider's attire that the Freemen had promised to her had been delivered in short time, and she wore it now, feeling like a mouse wearing the skin of a lion. She slid a few inches of the sword from the black sheath, admiring the shimmering amethyst color that so perfectly matched Tiri's scales. It truly was a sight to behold.

She let the violet metal slip back out of sight and looked toward Kael, who had finished saddling Eithne and was waiting for Andra with patient eyes. The Freemen had gathered to see them off; the rest of the rebels would begin their own trek across the desert at nightfall, but with no one else traveling with them, Andra, Kael, and the dragons could cross the Shesol Mal more quickly in the day, when the currents of air over the desert were stronger. Syra and Alik separated themselves from the crowd, stepping up to the two rebel captains. The older girl took Andra's black-gloved hands in her own and smiled at her warmly.

"You will be careful, won't you?" she asked.

Andra forced a smile of her own and nodded. "Of course. Our journey will be much swifter and easier than yours. You're the ones who must be careful."

Syra laughed a little, glancing at Alik. "Oh, I feel that I won't have much option but to be as careful as I can. Alik wouldn't allow me to step into danger even if I wanted to."

The large man gave her a loving smile, then looked at Andra. "I wanted you to know," he said, "that Colmen believed in you—in your strength, in your abilities. He told me that he thought you could be someone great. He would be proud to see you in that jacket and gloves, with that sword at your hip. He loved you as he loved his own sister."

Andra smiled tearfully up at the bearded man. "Thank you," she said.

To her surprise, Alik stepped forward and pulled her into a rough embrace. Then he turned to Kael, and the two men gripped forearms for a moment.

"Fly swift," Alik said. "Our hopes fly with you."

"I'll carry them as best I can," Kael said with a small smile.

A few others stepped forward to say their farewells; then Kael turned and mounted Eithne in a single swift movement. Andra followed suit, settling herself into the unfamiliar saddle, tightening her legs into the straps as Kael had shown her. Kael glanced at her, and she nodded her readiness. Eithne crouched and sprang into the air, her red wings beating heavily as she climbed into the sky. A moment later, Tiri followed, her smaller form climbing rapidly behind.

Andra held tightly to the straps, her legs clamping around the leather as they climbed. Soon, they leveled out, and she caught her breath, relishing the sensation of the cool air on her face, the steady beat of Tiri's wings on either side of her.

"It's so beautiful up here," she whispered, looking at the world stretched out below her. She leaned forward and pressed her cheek to the side of Tiri's sparkling purple neck. "I love you, Tiri."

She had never said the words before, except to her parents, and only as a child. But she felt certain that she did love Tiri, and that she had been destined to love her. She had gone almost seventeen years without this dragon, but the thought of any future without her seemed impossible. No, she knew without a doubt that she loved Tiri with all her heart.

She felt low vibrations coming from the chest beneath her, the gentle thrumming hum of a dragon. *"And I love you, Andra,"* Tiri answered. *"We are sisters in mind, heart, and soul."*

Andra turned her head, looking back at Bellris as it began to recede into the distance. In her mind, she said a silent farewell to the first place that had truly felt like home. Then she turned her eyes ahead of her, toward Kael, and toward Iterum.

27

Bounty

Andra's eyes shot open, her body rigid. A terrifying chill crept down her spine, the feeling of something cold and dark close by. She stayed perfectly still, not daring to move, not even breathing. Tiri and Eithne were both asleep, their warm breath filling the tent of their wings. Kael's arms were gently around her, and she was staring at his bare torso.

Inside the tent of red and violet dragons' wings, under that blanket she shared with Kael, everything was warm. But that terrifying cold was filling her mind and chest. Andra took several slow breaths, focusing more intently on that cold feeling in her mind. Her racing heart slowed as she tried to concentrate.

There were two other presences as well, drawing nearer as the dark, icy spot in her mind came closer. Suddenly, she realized what they were. People. Three of them, approaching her slowly and deliberately. And she knew that one of them was something less than human.

"Kael," she whispered, her voice shaking. He didn't stir, his features soft with sleep. "Kael," she repeated more insistently. "Kael, please wake up."

He jerked awake with surprising ferocity, immediately grabbing for his sword, which lay beside him, sitting up, and looking around. The dragons lifted their heads, blinking sleepily as Kael's eyes darted around for a moment, then rested on Andra.

"What is it?" he asked.

"Someone's coming," she responded, and even she could hear the fear in her own voice.

He was silent for a moment, and she knew he was searching for what she had felt. Then his face hardened, his gray eyes darkening.

"*What* is he?" she hissed, trying to restrain her fear of that dark presence in her mind.

He knew what she meant. "A Dark sorcerer," he answered quietly. "A powerful one."

Terror ran across her skin, gripping her stomach and setting her heart to racing again.

"We should run," she said quickly. "We can get in our saddles quickly and be in the sky before they have a chance to attack."

"A Dark sorcerer is not someone you can easily flee from, Andra," he said tensely. "He has enough power to bind a dozen dragons and their Riders if he wishes."

"Then what do we do?"

He looked down at her as she watched him expectantly, and she thought she saw a hint of panic in those gray depths. Tiri and Eithne were still and silent, watching them under their wings.

"Stay here," he told Andra sharply. "I'll speak to them. Perhaps I can lie our way out of this."

"*Kael*," Eithne said sharply, "*they will recognize you.*"

"Maybe," he responded, his eyes still on Andra, "but they'll certainly know that there are no female Riders."

"What will you do if they recognize you?" Andra asked anxiously.

"I'll figure something out," he said, pulling on his tunic and strapping on his sword. Then he paused, turning back toward her. His hand gripped her elbow as the other touched her cheek. "If they recognize me," he said sternly, "you get out of here, understand? Fight if you have to, then get on Tiri and get out of here."

Andra nodded, and Kael ducked under the edge of the wing and disappeared. She immediately slid on her belly to the edge of Tiri's wing. Cautiously, she peered under it. She could see Kael's boots striding quickly away from them, toward three figures that were approaching the two dragons. Two of the men wore thick leather armor, distressed from travel. The third wore a dark cloak, and Andra could feel cold energy radiating from him.

The other two both had heavy swords strapped to their waists, the buckles of their belts graven with the symbol of the judges—an olive branch crossed with a sword. Bounty hunters.

She held her breath as Kael approached them with an air of confidence. The three stopped and gave short bows to the Rider. Kael stood before them, his feet set wide.

"Can I help you with something?" Kael asked in a voice that clearly suggested he was unhappy with their presence.

"Just traveling, Rider," the sorcerer responded with an easy smile. Something in the smile made the hair on Andra's arms stand on end. "And you? The Hall is not but a few hours from here. Why sleep in the dirt when they would gladly accept you there?"

Kael didn't hesitate. "My dragon's old injury was causing her trouble, so we had to set down for the night before reaching the Hall."

One of the other men spoke. "Who's the other Rider?" he asked, and Andra saw him turn his head toward her, studying the two large forms and raised wings. She froze.

"Another Rider," Kael said calmly, dismissively. "Do you need to know anything more?"

The second sword-bearing man tilted his head to one side and frowned in Andra's direction. "But that's a purple dragon . . ." he mused. "There are no Bonded purple dragons."

Immediately Kael raised his hand toward the man. But the Dark sorcerer saw the movement and gave a deft twist of his fingers. The Rider's body shuddered, and he cried out in pain, collapsing on the ground. Both dragons snapped their wings open, turning on the three men with furious roars, fire pouring from their gaping maws. But the sorcerer raised one hand and slid it to the side, as if wiping fog from glass. The flames parted around him and his companions.

Eithne and Tiri changed tactics as the men continued unscathed, walking straight through the fire. They snapped at the men, lashing out with their front claws. The sorcerer calmly raised his hands, and the dragons reeled backward as if they had slammed into a stone wall. Now nothing was between Andra and the men.

She glanced at her companions. Eithne and Tiri were trying to struggle to their feet, but they were still reeling as if the earth were unsteady beneath them. Kael still lay on the grass, writhing as though he were fighting against invisible bonds. She looked back at the three men, who were studying her with three identical smirks on their faces.

Andra snatched her sheathed sword from where it lay in the grass. Kael had given her only two short lessons with it before they'd left Bellris, but she tried to maintain an air of confidence.

"Release the Rider," she demanded firmly, "and I'll let you leave in peace."

The men laughed at her, beginning to circle around her, regarding the small girl with the black jacket and gloves.

"Look at this," one of the armed men chuckled. "A little girl, masquerading as a Rider. Whose effects did you steal, girl?"

"They're mine," she snapped, her eyes darting among the three men, trying to watch all their movements at once. "They were crafted for me, and the violet dragon is my dragon."

"Lies upon lies," the sorcerer chided.

"It is not a lie," she spat back at him.

"Well, then," one of the soldiers said, "let's see your mark, eh?"

He stepped forward and seized her left hand with both of his, and Andra reacted instinctively. She twisted her arm away, then thrust her elbow into his nose, hearing the satisfying crunch as he stumbled backward, giving her enough space to draw her sword. She drew the blade from the black sheath, and the steel shone violet in the sunlight. The three men paused briefly, clearly surprised that she wielded a scale-colored sword; only elven magic could craft a blade tinged with dragon scales, and the elves rarely crafted them for anyone aside from the Riders.

The second soldier had drawn his sword and was the first to gather himself. Andra jumped back from the man's swing, then brought the amethyst sword down in a shining arc. The man screamed, dropping his blade as blood streamed from the bone-exposing wound.

Andra plunged her mind into the well of magic and directed her fury at the sorcerer, like a huntress setting her dog on a deer. She swung her sword through the air with a scream, and forked lightning streamed from the blade. The sorcerer's eyes widened with surprise and he raised his arms. Black, roiling smoke seemed to envelop him, and the lightning evaporated as it touched the blackness.

She didn't wait for him to recover from the attack. She raced to Kael's side, seizing his shoulders as he writhed on the ground. *Free him,* she demanded. Kael jolted as if he'd been struck, then scrambled to his feet, free of his invisible bonds. He looked at her for a brief moment, then over her shoulder as the swordsman and the sorcerer came racing toward them. The sorcerer's face was red with fury, shouting wildly as he drew back his hand. Andra could see a red glow growing around it.

She didn't see the dagger until it was too late. The swordsman had produced it from somewhere at his belt and flung it, end over end, straight toward Kael's chest. Andra had time for only one thing—a single step to the side. She stepped in front of him as the blade flew toward her. She felt Kael's hands on her shoulders, ready to push her away. The sorcerer had released his magic, and it followed just behind the dagger.

Protection, she thought, remembering the shield that Setora had tried to teach her to conjure.

Suddenly, there was a blue-violet spark on the dagger's blade, sending it spinning away in another direction. Light crackled briefly in the air. Then there was another spark, and the ball of fire exploded into harmless smoke. Time seemed to halt momentarily. Andra saw the surprised look that crossed both of the bounty hunters' faces.

The spell that had bound the dragons seemed to have broken as well, and Eithne and Tiri, with simultaneous roars of fury, charged toward the men. They didn't wait for the dragons to reach them. The men turned toward the trees and ran. Andra and Kael sent orbs of fire and lightning at their backs, but the Dark sorcerer managed to deflect them all. He gave a furious shout and threw one last spell over his shoulder as he disappeared into the trees.

A ball of darkness flew toward Kael, so quickly that Andra could hardly follow it with her eyes. Kael immediately lifted his hand to deflect it, but whatever spell he tried to use didn't seem to work. The darkness struck his hand. Andra expected some kind of explosion, a blast of sound and light. But it didn't come. Kael's hand seemed to absorb the shadowy ball, the writhing tendrils of shadow sinking into his skin.

Suddenly, Kael screamed, the sound tearing across the plain. Eithne let out a roar that sounded more like a pained howl, and both dragon and Rider collapsed on the grass, writhing in agony. Andra dropped beside Kael's thrashing form. Her eyes fell on his arm, and terror seized her.

From his hand to his shoulder, strips of his skin seemed to have been torn away, baring deep red muscle, blood spilling onto the grass. The smell of burned skin invaded her nostrils, and Andra covered her mouth with horror. Kael continued to scream, his body arching against the grass, and Eithne howled in unison.

"Tiri, what's wrong with him?" Andra shouted above the ear-splitting noise.

"Dark magic," Tiri responded, glancing between Eithne and Kael.

Andra's breaths became short and frantic, her eyes roaming the empty plains around her for some kind of aid. A sharp pain in her hand drew her attention away from her futile search. She looked down to see Kael's hand clutching hers, his entire body trembling with agony. His eyes were on her, his lips pressed together to try to hold back his own screams. Instead, he moaned, whimpering as tears slid down his cheeks. His eyes were desperate, pleading.

In that moment, Andra knew he would die. And she knew that he knew it as well.

28

Darkness and Light

Emotions raced through her, one after the other: Fear. Anger. Despair. Guilt. But she couldn't let any of them show. She had to be the strong one.

Andra shifted and lifted Kael's head into her lap, allowing him to continue to squeeze her hand, and wrapped her other arm over his shoulder and across his chest, trying to help him still the spasms of pain in his body. The gray eyes, clouded with pain, never left her face. Andra glanced up at the shredded skin of the arm, then bent her head toward his, trying not to look at it.

She pressed her forehead to his and whispered, "It's all right, Kael. I've got you. It's all right." She whispered those meaningless words over and over until they sounded like a prayer, an insistent demand. She gripped desperately at the magic in her mind as she continued to speak. "You *will* be all right. This will pass soon. You're going to live, Kael. I promise."

His trembling subsided, and Andra heard Eithne's agonized groans quiet. Kael closed his eyes with a sigh. The fierce grip on her hand went lax. Andra didn't stop speaking as tears began to fall down her cheeks. "You'll be okay, Kael. It's going to be all right."

"*Andra*," Tiri said softly to her mind.

She didn't want to listen. She didn't want to hear Tiri tell her that he was gone. That Eithne had gone with him. It couldn't be true. He couldn't leave her now. She kept whispering, muttering the same phrases to the closed eyes.

"*Andra*," the dragon said more insistently. "*Look.*"

She lifted her head slightly to see a blue-violet glow around her hand, which gripped Kael's limp one. The light seemed to trail across his skin in a stream that flowed over his arm and across his chest, then down the wounded arm, wrapping around it like a glowing ribbon.

Andra hardened her grip on the magic in her mind and urged it on. *Heal him!* The light flared brighter and the skin rushed to reunite with itself. The edges of the torn and burned flesh seemed to shift, drawing together over the exposed muscle, ceasing the blood flow.

Then the light began to withdraw, sliding back up over Kael's smooth, flawless skin, leaving it in a puddle of drying blood, gathering in a spiraling pool of light atop his chest, just over his heart. The light seemed to sink into his chest, absorbing into his skin as the dark orb had done. And then it was gone.

Andra hesitated for a moment, the meadow around them silent. Then, cautiously, hopefully, she pressed her ear to Kael's chest. She could faintly hear the slow, steady thudding of his heart. With a small laugh of amazement, she leaned close to his nose and mouth. His soft, warm breath caressed her cheek. Andra sat back and stared down at him, his face pale beneath the natural olive tones of his skin. Then she tilted her head back and laughed with relief.

There was a deep, rumbling groan, and Andra turned to see Eithne lift her head, blinking her bleary brown eyes at them. A moment later, she felt Kael stir, and she looked down as his eyes fluttered open. She laughed again, surprised to find tears of relief on her cheeks.

"You're alive," she breathed, speaking the words with a hint of disbelief.

Kael winced as he sat up. "Yes, and in a world of pain," he answered. He looked at her, his expression considering. "Andra, did you . . . Heal me?"

"I . . . I did," she answered.

"How?" he asked, his brow furrowing. "That was a Dark spell that struck me, Andra—one designed to kill. *No one* can Heal a spell like that."

Andra shook her head slowly, looking away from him. "I just . . . I knew I couldn't let you leave me, Kael. I . . . need you to stay with me."

She felt his fingers touch her cheek, and she looked up again to see him smiling softly. "I will stay with you, Andra, for as long as you will allow me to be by your side."

She hesitantly put her hand over his, meeting his tender gray eyes. How had she ever seen steel in them? She remembered with a vivid clarity that moment before the Kingsmen arrived in Bellris, when Kael had held her and she wished to know what his kiss would feel like. So much had happened since that moment, so much had been lost, but knowing how close she had come to losing him, the desire burned in her chest again.

Trying to still the trembling of her fingers, Andra raised one hand to Kael's cheek, drawing closer to him. His gray eyes watched her carefully, looking almost uncertain as he allowed her hand to guide his face toward hers. Their foreheads touched, and she felt his breath on her skin. His eyes were still watching her when she closed hers and allowed her lips to brush his, barely the hint of a kiss.

She felt his hand slide into her hair as the other pressed gently to the small of her back, drawing her to him, bringing his lips to hers again, more firmly now, with greater certainty. She returned it, her hand clutching his tunic, tasting the slow sweetness of his kiss, somehow both gentle and deep.

Finally, he drew back. His hands framed her face, and she closed her eyes again as he kissed her forehead, her nose, her cheeks, her eyelids. "I love you," he whispered between each kiss. "I love you."

She drank in the words, wishing to speak them, yet knowing that she wouldn't. *Soon,* she promised herself.

Instead, she turned her face toward his hand and kissed his fingers. "And you will never leave me?" she asked.

"Never," he swore.

And she believed him.

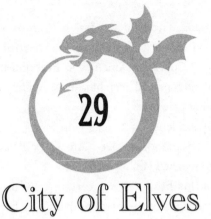

29

City of Elves

Andra sat in the palace at Iterum, staring around her in wonder. The pictures she had seen did not come close to the grandeur that surrounded her. The walls were of pure, dazzling white stone that seemed to rise up from the earth around her, sparkling in the lights of hundreds of glowing orbs. In the center of the spacious room stood a great tree, the likes of which Andra had never seen.

Its enormous trunk was dotted with open windows, and the branches reached up over the white stone walls, covering the room with a thick, green ceiling. The conjured balls of light hung from its branches, casting the room in a bright, sunny glow, though it was long past sunset.

A white stone walkway wound through the open palace to the tree at its center, which was the home of the royal family. But aside from the single path, the floor of the palace was lush, green grass bespeckled with flowers in vibrant colors. It was a palace crafted by nature itself.

Kael sat beside Andra at the low wooden table in the middle of the flower-filled grass. Across from her sat the elf king, Vires, and his wife, Camena. The king had dark hair under a golden circlet of leaves, and violet eyes. Something in his cheerful face reminded her painfully of Colmen. Camena was his opposite in coloring, with white-blond hair and deep blue eyes. A circlet of silver flowers rested on her pale brow.

"I'm deeply saddened to hear of your losses," King Vires said, his voice rich and smooth as velvet. "And you still have no idea how the Kingsmen reached you undetected?"

Kael shook his head. "We're certain they used dwarf tunnels. We found signs of their troops' passing when we searched the old tunnels in the Last Mountains. But they would have had to use inhabited tunnels to cross the desert, and we haven't yet made contact with the dwarves to discover why they would have aided the Kingsmen. They've always been our allies in this fight."

"Very strange," Vires mused. "I'll send word to Amiscan on the eastern cliffs. The dwarves' capital city lies beneath the village. Perhaps their king will have some answer."

Kael nodded. "Thank you."

"And now you plan to assassinate Chief Judge Castigo?" Camena asked, her voice soft, though her question was blunt.

"Yes," Kael answered. "It is the only choice we have."

"How will you enter the palace?" Vires asked. "Castigo has been very strict with his security since you killed his son."

Kael sighed. "We're not certain of that yet."

The queen touched her husband's arm. "Darling, perhaps you can help them."

He looked at her, his expression guarded.

She added hurriedly, "Not outright, mind you. That would be too dangerous. But if you send an ambassador to Castigo, perhaps under the guise of easing tensions between our kingdoms, Kael and Andra could smuggle themselves in aboard the carriage."

Andra saw Kael sit a little straighter at the idea.

"Perhaps . . ." Vires replied, tapping a finger against his lips. "If I can get you as far as the stable, can you do the rest?"

It was Andra who answered. "Yes," she said confidently. "I know Castigo's manor well. I can get us to a safe place where we can hide until nightfall. We'll put plenty of time between your ambassador's arrival and our attack, so no suspicion falls on you."

Vires smiled at her kindly and opened his mouth to speak, but he was interrupted as a shadow passed over them. Andra looked up, expecting to see a large bird fluttering among the enormous branches overhead. But what she saw was a small white dragon.

The creature circled lower, then lighted on the end of the table, examining the four of them with the same golden eyes that had watched Andra so keenly at the edge of the Shesol Mal.

"You . . ." she breathed.

The small dragon seemed to smile. "Hello, Andra," he said. "I did tell you I would see you again."

King Vires frowned at the dragon, then at Andra. "Have you met Astrum before, Andra?" he asked.

"The day before we crossed the desert," Kael said, realization in his voice. "We thought you'd imagined it."

Astrum ruffled his wings as he chuckled deeply. "I assure you, Kael, she did not imagine me. I merely visited Andra to offer her some important guidance." He turned his golden eyes back to the girl, who continued to stare at him with wide green eyes. "And, thankfully, she followed it. The battle for Bellris would have ended very differently if she hadn't."

Finally, Andra found her voice. "You're . . . Astrum?" she asked slowly. "Advisor to the elven monarchs? The Seer who gave the prophecy of the Guardians?"

Astrum dipped his white head. "I am."

Andra looked at Kael. "But you said Astrum had visited Bellris before you came to Vereor. You, Colmen, Alik—you'd all seen him before. Why didn't you recognize my description of him?"

It was Vires who spoke. "Astrum's form changes with each new monarch. When he visited the Freemen, Astrum was a stag, the form he took for my father."

"And when Vires ascended the throne," Astrum replied, "I took this form—an appropriate one for the first Rider to become king of the elves."

Andra stared at the small white dragon for a long moment, her mind spinning. She'd known of Astrum's ability to change forms, of course. In the time of the Guardians, he'd been a fox, and then a white wolf when Caelum's brother had ascended the elven throne. But she'd never imagined that he might have taken the form of a dragon.

Astrum spoke then. "But I am here now to tell my king that his presence is needed—or will be needed shortly—in Amiscan. There is soon to be some upheaval among the dwarves in Zwûrdgit Stöhl."

Vires sighed. "Seems that I won't need to send an emissary to the dwarves after all," he said. "I'll speak to the king myself, and hopefully will have a report of what happened in those tunnels by the time you return from your mission."

The king stood, and the others at the table followed suit. Vires reached across the table and shook first Kael's hand, then Andra's.

"Camena and my advisors will offer you every aid they can in your preparations. And when your mission is successful, I will welcome you back in my palace. I have many places that you and your dragons can use to stay hidden from the judges' men."

"Thank you, King Vires," Kael said. "For this, and for all you have done for the Freemen."

Vires sighed. "Would that I could do more, Kael. But the safety of my people must come first."

Kael nodded. Vires and Camena bade them good night, and Kael took Andra's hand, leading her through the palace, past the central tree, and out through a pair of oak doors at the rear of the room. They stepped out into a spacious courtyard, lined with two rows of trees.

He led her through a rounded opening at the base of the first tree they came to. The room was round and smooth, like those in Bellris, but the furniture within seemed to be grown from the tree, connected to the floor and walls. It was furnished like a sitting room, with a spiraling staircase at its center. They ascended the staircase together and stepped out into another round room, this one a bedroom, with a large bed framed of intertwining branches of wood.

Kael caught her other hand, turning her toward him, and he smiled softly down at her face. "This will soon be over," he said quietly. "It feels as if I've been fighting this battle my entire life, and now, the end of it is in sight."

Andra smiled back at him. "Soon," she agreed with a nod.

He leaned down and kissed her softly. "Good night," he said. "Sleep well, my heart-song."

"Good night," she answered.

Kael turned and left through another rounded doorway, crossing a bridge of woven branches to the tree on the other side of the courtyard. She watched him go, then lay back on the bed with a sigh.

Soon . . . she told herself.

30

Familiar Halls

Andra grabbed her cloak from her bed and followed Kael down the stairs into the courtyard. Eithne was already gone, taking a long route to avoid detection before finding a hiding place close to Vereor. But Tiri was waiting for them, her tail carving an arc of irritation into the crisp green grass. Andra stepped over to the dragon and embraced her tightly.

"Be safe, sister," Tiri whispered to her mind. *"Return to me quickly."*

"I will," Andra answered, because it was all she could say. Tiri would remain behind for this mission. Two dragons were too likely to draw attention, and Eithne was faster and stronger, so she would provide them with their means of escape.

Tiri turned her sharp eyes to the Rider standing nearby. *"Kael,"* she snarled, her voice in both their minds, *"I swear by every god there is that if something happens to her, I will—"*

"Kill me," he finished aloud for her. "I know."

Tiri surveyed him with narrowed eyes for a silent moment, then snorted, apparently satisfied that he understood her threat. She looked back at Andra. *"Be smart,"* she instructed. *"Stay close to Kael. End this madness as quickly as you can, understand?"*

Andra nodded and embraced the violet face again. *"I love you, Tiri,"* she said silently. *"My sister."*

Tiri hummed in her throat. *"And I you, dear one."*

She forced herself to kiss the dragon's forehead in farewell and turn toward the palace doors. She and Kael cut quickly through the large room and out the other side. A finely detailed carriage pulled by two white horses waited on the cobbled road for them. A fair-haired elf stood beside the carriage, waiting for them, dressed in a neatly cut suit. He nodded at them in greeting and opened the carriage door, indicating the hidden compartments beneath the seats, where Andra and Kael would hide once they entered Vereor.

"I will be in the palace for only a half hour at most. I intend only to deliver the missive King Vires gave to me, offer some condolences regarding his son's death, and then I'll return to the carriage. You will need to be out and in a safe hiding place by then."

Andra and Kael nodded in understanding, and as the elven ambassador climbed up into the carriage, a white shape settled atop the vehicle, drawing Andra's and Kael's eyes. Astrum regarded them silently for a moment, then drew a little breath and spoke. Somehow, his rich voice seemed different from before, sending a chill over Andra's skin that was reminiscent of magic at work. His words seemed to reverberate through the air.

> *From the bonds of former days,*
> *Brought to freedom never known,*
> *You now bring freedom to the rest,*
> *By sacrificing up your own.*
> *Into darkness you must go*
> *And face the fear and pain again*
> *To learn where darkness truly lies,*

And bring the shadows to an end.
A new captivity you must face
As you enter unknown halls
To bring light to the land again
And bring freedom to us all.

Astrum looked at her again, his golden eyes piercing her as she stared back at him. Then the little white dragon heaved a small sigh and flitted away.

She felt a crushing grip on her hand and looked down to find Kael holding on to it tightly, eyes fixed on the place where Astrum had perched. She studied his face, and saw fear written on every line of his features—fear that she knew she should feel as well. The Seer's words were ominous and forboding, and yet, Andra felt strangely calm.

"You should stay behind," Kael said, turning suddenly toward her. "I can do this alone."

"No, you can't," she replied with a small smile. "You know that you can't. You don't know the manor as I do."

He held her face between his hands, looking down at her with that fear in his eyes. "I'll find a way," he said, and she heard a desperation in his voice. He was searching for any excuse that would persuade her to remain in Iterum. "It may be a risk, but if your coming means—"

"Astrum said," Andra interrupted, seizing his hands firmly in both of hers, "that it would bring freedom and light to the land again, Kael. If I must endure some sort of pain or captivity for it, would you really choose to protect me, even if it meant failing to stop Castigo?"

The Rider was silent, staring down at her, his eyes searching and confused. "I . . . I can't lose you, Andra."

She raised herself on her toes and kissed him softly. "And we can't lose this battle, Kael. Astrum has just assured us that this is the path to victory. We must take it, no matter how difficult the path may be."

Kael sighed and pulled her into a tight embrace, his lips brushing the top of her head. When he finally released her, she found a determined expression on his face, and he held a hand out to help her into the carriage. She took it and ascended the stairs, Kael following close behind. Without any ceremony, the driver jiggled the reins and the horses trotted briskly toward Vereor.

———◦❈◦———

Andra held her breath in the dark box beneath the carriage seat, listening as the ambassador was escorted through the main entrance into the palace. After a pause, the carriage rattled forward again as the driver guided the horses and carriage to the stable yard. She gripped her sword as it lay atop her chest, and she thought for a moment that she must look like a dead soldier in repose for his burial. She quickly pushed the thought aside.

Finally, the carriage stopped again, and a moment later, she heard a hard rapping on the side of the hollow bench. She sat up, pushing open the lid and peering out from her hiding place. Across from her, Kael was doing the same.

"Hurry up," the carriage driver whispered urgently. "The patrol just left the stable yard. Go now, and you can make it into the manor."

Kael and Andra both scrambled out of the compartments and down from the carriage, belting on their swords. After a quick glance around the yard, Kael led the way to the servants' door at the back of the manor. They slipped inside, and Andra guided them to a hidden corridor used only by servants. She had been able to think of only one room in the manor that she knew would not be used. It was tradition to leave a person's room unchanged for a year after their death.

They slipped down the unused halls to the chamber doors that she knew too well. Cautiously, Kael pushed the doors open, then motioned to Andra that it was clear. She slipped inside and he followed behind her, closing the door without a sound.

Andra looked around her at Ledo's bedchamber. Everything remained exactly where it had been on the night of his death. It struck her just how close she had come to being in the room when Kael and Alik attempted to take him. If she'd still been there, would things have turned out any differently?

She felt Kael's hand on her shoulder. "What are you thinking about?" he asked.

Andra exhaled slowly. "Many things," she answered softly. "I thought it would pain me more, being here again, standing in his room. But . . . I feel as if it all happened to a different person. I am not that girl anymore. I'm not the girl who he hurt, who he forced into silence. I'm not the girl who was afraid. Not anymore."

She felt a strange warmth in her chest at the truth of her own words. Ledo had broken her, it was true. But those breaks were a part of her now—a part of something new and, if not yet whole, something that was beginning to mend.

She felt his lips press to the top of her head, and leaned against his chest with a sigh.

"How long do we wait?" he asked her.

"Until sundown," she replied. "Immediately after Castigo's family has taken their supper. That will be the safest time."

They stayed alert, watching the sun slowly set through the stained-glass window, their hands on their swords, ready should someone enter the room. Nobody did. As Andra had expected, they gave the room a respectful distance still. Finally, the sun began to sink below the horizon and Andra drew a breath.

"It's time," she said.

Kael nodded and followed her into the hallway. She led him from one dark corner to another, running through the old schedule in her mind. After supper, most of the servants would be in the kitchen, cleaning up. A few would be tending to the Chief Judge and his wife and their daughter. The wife and daughter always retired to their quarters immediately after supper if they didn't have company. But Castigo would be in his study.

The study was separated from the other rooms by a narrow corridor, giving the judge privacy and quiet while he worked. Though she knew guards would patrol that hall, they would have several minutes between each pass of the study—more than enough time to do what needed to be done.

As they neared Castigo's study, Andra heard the sound of approaching armor and voices, and saw a dim glow down the corridor; two soldiers were passing down the hall, one of them carrying a torch. Andra grabbed Kael's elbow and pulled him into a dark alcove occupied by the bulky statue of a former judge. His arm went around her waist, pulling her back to his chest, trying to keep both of them hidden behind the single statue.

"I don't know that he truly *does* support the Chief Judge," one man said.

"You're joking," the torchbearer chuckled. "Caedo is Castigo's most fervent supporter. He visits at every opportunity, always trying to bend the Chief Judge's ear. And he pledges all his own guards to every endeavor of Castigo's."

"But why does he have so many of his own guards?" the first asked. "It looks to me that Caedo is building his own army, not gathering men for Castigo's."

"You really think Caedo would try to usurp him?"

"I don't know," the soldier replied as their voices began to fade, "but with that sorceress always at his side, he would be a hard enemy to defeat."

Their voices faded with their footsteps, the light of their torch disappearing as they rounded a corner. Andra glanced up at Kael. There was a hint of suspicion in his eyes, but he quickly gestured

270 · ERIN SWAN

with his head and she followed the direction, moving out from behind the statue. They would have only a few minutes before the guards passed again.

They ran now, not bothering to muffle their footsteps in the empty corridor. Up ahead, a single wooden door was flanked by a pair of torches, casting a circle of light on the dark stone. Andra and Kael stopped outside the door, both of them breathing heavily. He looked down at her as he tightened his grip on his sword.

"Are you ready?" he whispered.

She nodded, and watched as he placed his hand against the door, then pushed. It swung open, and he stepped quickly inside. Andra followed, stepping into the study she'd cleaned a hundred times. The old judge looked up from the papers on his desk, illuminated by a lantern hanging from the ceiling.

Castigo's eyes widened at the sight of them, and he opened his mouth to scream. Andra instinctively raised her hand, as if to place it over the man's mouth, though he was on the opposite side of the room. The man let out a strangled gasp, his eyes bulging, struggling for breath.

Kael rushed forward and placed a hand over Castigo's gaping mouth. Andra saw a look of pain cross his eyes, as he touched the red sword to the old man's throat. "I'm sorry," he whispered. Then he slid the blade across the skin, and Castigo dropped to the floor with a gurgling moan.

The Rider looked at her, his lips pressed together in a tight line, his face somewhat pale. "Let's go," he said in a low voice. "Eithne's on her way."

Andra nodded, and turned away from the corpse and the growing pool of red around it. She led them down a nearby corridor, angling for the nearest exit—the library window. As they darted into the room, she heard a shout. Someone raising the alarm. She hurried to the window and struggled with the latch. Panic began to rise inside her. The window had been sealed shut.

"Stand back," Kael ordered.

She moved away from the window, and he raised his right hand toward the glass. A pulse of roaring wind rushed away from him, swirling Andra's hair around her face and striking the enormous window. The glass shattered into a thousand shining pieces, which made a sound like wind chimes as they fell to the grass below.

No sooner had the glass broken than the library doors were thrown open. A contingent of soldiers stood in the doorway, swords in hand. "The library!" one shouted. "To the library window!"

"Go!" Kael yelled to her, and Andra leapt from the windowsill, glass crunching beneath her boots as she hit the grass.

Kael followed immediately behind her, nearly landing atop her in his haste. They both scrambled to their feet and sprinted for the city wall, where Eithne was to meet them. They leapt the hedge of the manor's gardens, dashing through the paddock and rounding the rear of the palace.

And then a wall of soldiers appeared before them, pikes raised. Three men stood at their front, wearing white robes belted in blue, the judges' crest over their left breast—Castigo's sorcerers. Andra and Kael slid to a halt, simultaneously drawing their swords, amethyst and ruby metals glinting in the moonlight.

Andra glanced around them, trying to gauge the situation. Men were in front of them, with more beginning to flank them. At least a hundred soldiers, at least three sorcerers, and only one means of escape.

She looked up at the sky and saw an enormous shadow descending from above them. Eithne roared as she dove from the sky, her great jaws open, fire roiling between her teeth. The three men in robes looked up and raised their hands, shouting a spell together. The red dragon suddenly rebounded, striking an invisible wall. She drew back, blasting fire at the shield, but it held.

The soldiers rushed forward, swords drawn, and Andra pulled

a shield up around her and Kael. It shimmered in the now-familiar blue-violet color as the guards' swords struck it. Andra looked at Kael, watching his gray eyes dart from the soldiers encircling their tiny bubble of light to his dragon, trying to beat her way through the sorcerers' shield to them.

"We need to take out the sorcerers," he said, his voice taut.

"How?" Andra asked, her eyes scanning the shield around them, looking for weaknesses as the soldiers continued to batter at it with their weapons. "An attack can't get out of the shield, and I can't lower it or they'll hack us apart!"

Then they heard the roars of two other dragons, and Andra spotted their shadows, barreling toward the capital on swift wings. Kael growled under his breath, sword still at the ready.

Andra breathed in slowly, calming herself. "Kael," she said.

He looked at her, a flash of hope in his eyes, and she felt a pang of guilt. How he trusted her.

"When I drop the shield, can you use your magic to force the soldiers near us backward?"

"Yes, but not far, and not for long. There are too many of them."

"I only need a moment," Andra answered, confidence in her voice. "Press back the soldiers, and I'll incapacitate the sorcerers. It will buy us just enough time to escape."

It pained her to lie to him—even a partial lie—but she knew this had to be done.

"Ready?"

"Ready."

"Now!"

The bubble around them vanished, and there was a blast of wind so powerful that the armored soldiers nearest them flew backward, feet lifting from the ground as they collided with those behind them. Andra immediately lashed out toward where the three sorcerers stood, still holding Eithne back with their magic.

Three flashes of light burst to life before them, throwing them backward, and the shield above them disappeared.

Eithne came barreling down from the sky, roaring in anger and triumph. She landed amid the soldiers, scattering them as she snapped with razor fangs and swiped with dagger claws. She felt Kael seize her arm, starting to pull her toward the saddle.

She followed him to Eithne's side, and he scrambled up in a rush, then reached down for her. But she knew it wouldn't work. The sorcerers would soon be on their feet again, and the two other Riders would arrive in moments. But Andra could delay them just long enough.

Kael seized her forearm and began to haul her upward, but she did not allow herself to be pulled into the saddle. She slid a hand behind his neck, grabbing a handful of his black hair, and pulled his mouth roughly to hers. The kiss was brief and desperate, and she pulled away long enough to look into his gray eyes.

"I love you," she said, barely loud enough to be heard over the roars of the approaching dragons. Then she leapt away from him. "Go, Eithne!" she shouted as her feet struck the ground.

Eithne's mind pressed against hers, pleading for Andra to find another way, but Andra pressed back, and she knew the dragon would not delay for long; her Rider's life was at risk. She heard Kael scream her name, desperate and afraid, and she had to force herself to not look back at him. She felt the wind of Eithne taking to the sky, and Andra turned to face the enemies that awaited her.

31

Judgment

The sorcerers rose to their feet, and Andra saw them all turn toward the red dragon that was soaring low, hurrying for the city wall. She swung her sword through the air with a shout, and blue-violet fire arched from its edge. It tore through the line of soldiers closest to her, setting their uniforms aflame before striking the three sorcerers. The men howled in pain, thrashing briefly before extinguishing the fire with a spell.

She brought the sword down then, striking the earth between her feet, and there was a crack like thunder. The advancing soldiers were thrown backward, clearing a circle of several yards around her. And then the Riders were upon her.

They swooped low, racing toward where Eithne had disappeared over the wall with Kael. Andra screamed in fury, and a mass of swirling gray clouds and crackling lightning materialized before the dragons. One of the creatures drew back, careening away from the sudden storm. The other flew into it, and Andra heard the dragon roar in pain as energy raced through the pair.

She gritted her teeth, focusing on the remaining Rider. She

could feel that well in her mind dwindling, flickering with only the smallest amount of energy, but she gripped it, demanded for it to give every last trace of itself to ensure Kael's escape. A fierce whirlwind spun to life before the dragon as it tried to cross the stone wall. It veered away, but the cyclone followed, twisting around the dragon and Rider, pinning the serpent's wings to its side as they both screamed.

The dragon crashed into the wall, crumbling the stones to the earth and causing the ground to shake. And then Andra felt the magic leave her. The energy raced out of her limbs, the edges of her vision going black, and she fell. She felt the softness of the grass, smelled the cool dirt, and heard the shouts of soldiers surrounding her. Then there was nothing.

The minute Eithne's feet touched the grass outside the elven palace, the small violet dragon let out a furious roar in the darkness and rushed at her. Eithne rose onto her back legs, buffeting the younger dragon aside with her legs and neck, keeping her fury away from the Rider still on her back.

"Where is she?" Tiri's mind demanded.

Eithne snarled and snapped at Tiri's neck, forcing her backward as Kael jumped down from the saddle. He turned hurt, accusing eyes on his dragon.

"What have you done, Eithne?" he shouted. His hands were curled into fists at his sides, and fire glowed around his form.

"This was your doing?" Tiri snarled, blowing a cloud of smoke over the other dragon's face.

"I had no choice," Eithne answered sharply.

This didn't appease either of them. "Why would she demand to be left behind?" Kael snapped.

"She knew we wouldn't escape unless she remained to delay them. If

the sorcerers didn't bring us down, the Riders would have pursued us. We all would have been captured."

"We could have done it!" Kael yelled at his dragon. "With my magic and hers, we could have escaped!"

Eithne sighed, and he felt her own heartache in his mind; it had pained her to leave Andra behind as well. *"If that were true, Kael, she would have come with us. You know as well as I do that there was no hope of us all escaping from that fight."*

Tiri roared again, but this time, the sound was edged with pain. Eithne saw her crouch, prepared to leap into the air and no doubt fly to Vereor. Eithne threw her shoulder against the smaller dragon. The force sent her violet body rolling sideways.

Eithne dug her claws into the ground, bracing herself as Tiri shook her head and rose back to her feet, snarling like a rabid animal. *"You cannot go after her, Tiri,"* Eithne tried to reason. *"If you go crashing in there, they could kill her just to ensure she doesn't escape."*

The young dragon didn't listen. She roared, and a jet of flame burst from her maw. Eithne turned her body, ensuring that Kael was shielded behind her, tucked her head down, and closed her eyes, allowing her scales to absorb the heat from the angry blast. She waited, ready, for the inferno to end. The moment it did, she threw herself forward.

Tiri was unprepared, and the weight of Eithne's much larger form sent them both tumbling across the grass. The other dragons in the field jumped out of the way, watching the skirmish with impartiality. Eithne twisted her head to the side as they tumbled, and carefully clamped her teeth around the violet neck, taking a firm hold, while being certain not to draw any blood from beneath the hard scales.

Tiri let out a pained bugle as they stopped tumbling. She thrashed against the red dragon's weight on top of her, but Eithne's fangs held her in place. Finally, she went still beneath her. Eithne continued to hold her neck in her jaws.

"*Choose your battles more wisely next time, hatchling,*" Eithne snarled with her mind. "*Your anger will not help you win against a dragon nearly a decade older than you.*"

Tiri growled again, but didn't move.

"*Will you let there be peace?*" Eithne demanded.

Tiri thrashed once more, and Eithne bit down harder, making her go still again. Finally, Tiri begrudgingly answered, "*Yes.*"

She released her hold on Tiri's neck and stepped away from the young dragon, placing herself between Tiri and Kael. The violet dragon continued to lie on the grass for another brief moment; then she sat up, shook her head, and stood, giving Eithne a distasteful look. When Tiri maintained her distance, Kael stepped around his dragon.

"Eithne's right, Tiri," Kael said. "We can't go flying blindly back into the palace. Right now, they are on the alert, searching for us, rousing every soldier and Rider near Vereor to hunt for me and Eithne. Attempting a rescue now would get every last one of us killed, including Andra. We need a plan if we're going to get her back."

"*But we* are *going to try?*" Tiri asked.

"Do you truly believe that I would simply leave her behind?" he demanded in a low voice. "I love her, Tiri. I love her as much as you do. I would die before I would leave her."

Tiri nodded. "*Then what is your plan, Rider?*"

Despair racked him, and he made a noise somewhere between a sigh and a groan as he leaned against his dragon. He ran a hand through his hair, feeling hopelessness fill his chest. "I don't have one," he whispered. "I have none at all."

Andra groaned as she slowly returned to consciousness. Her body felt as if she'd been dragged behind a horse for thirty miles. Slowly, she opened her eyes, wincing against the bright light that streamed through a window nearby. She looked around herself, confused and disoriented. She remembered clearly her battle with the judges' men, her brief farewell with Kael. She had expected to wake in a dungeon—if she awoke at all—but the room she found herself in was far from a prison cell.

The room was not very large, but it was beautifully furnished, with plush chairs and sofas occupying the majority of the space. She lay on a soft bed with a down comforter and far too many pillows. Instinctively, she reached for her magic, but something stood in her way.

A wall seemed to separate her from the well of power, which was still dim from her fight with the soldiers. But this wall felt different from the one that had briefly bound her magic in Bellris. There was a coldness about it that sent chills across her body. She tried for a moment to batter her way through the wall, but it held strong.

Suddenly, the door opened. Andra jerked her head up to look at the figure that stepped into the room. She knew him in a moment. She had seen him many times before in his frequent visits to the Hall of Riders, but she'd paid him little mind then. Now, however, she watched him carefully, wondering at the similarities to his younger brother. The young judge had the same jet-black hair, the same gold tint to his skin, the same sharp jaw. As he stepped closer, she saw that his eyes were blue, but there was a hint of nomadic gray around the irises.

"Caedo," she spat.

He raised his dark brows, so like Kael's, and smiled at her. "You know me, do you?"

"Where am I?" she demanded, ignoring his question.

"The guest quarters of my manor," he replied, calmly striding forward. "All the judges in Vereor were summoned to the Chief Judge's palace the moment you were captured. It was agreed that

I, as Castigo's interim Chief Judge, should take responsibility for you. Not a burden I expected when he named me to the position after Ledo's death, but one I will gladly shoulder."

"And how long shall I be your 'burden'?" she questioned sharply. She held no illusions about why she was still alive; she knew they had some purpose for keeping her.

Caedo chuckled as he sat in a chair close to the bed. "Until we learn what we wish to learn from you."

"I won't tell you anything."

"They always say that," he sighed, the same cold smile on his lips. "For now, let's talk about what I already know." He began to tick items off on his fingers as he spoke. "You were with Kael, the rebel leader, and helped him to assassinate the Chief Judge. You carried the effects of a Rider. You somehow fought off three of Castigo's sorcerers, over a hundred of his soldiers, and two of his dragon Riders with your magic. And . . . you chose to remain behind so that Kael could make his escape." His smile broadened at this last statement. "All very interesting facts, wouldn't you agree?"

Andra stayed silent, staring at Caedo, hating that his face reminded her so much of Kael.

"And now, let's talk about what *you* know," Caedo went on.

She clenched her teeth together, determined not to speak.

"Do you know who I am?"

The question surprised her, and after a pause, she nodded. "You're Caedo, one of the judges in Vereor."

"And you know who my brother is?"

"Kael."

"Very good, girl," he said with a condescending smile. "And who are you?"

She remained silent.

"I could wager a guess," he went on. "Your hair is short for a girl, and there is a circle of slightly paler skin around your neck. You were indentured, weren't you? Did Kael free you? Remove your contract collar somehow? Is that why you are so loyal to him?"

She bit the side of her tongue and held back her retort.

"Why do you carry what appears to be a Rider's sword? You are clearly no Rider."

Andra glowered at him.

"How did you become so strong? Even Tormina is having trouble containing your magic, and she is quite a talented sorceress."

"Perhaps not so talented as you think, then," Andra answered bitterly.

Caedo laughed at her, a strange and gleeful sound. "Now, *that* is a tone that I recognize. Tell me, girl, did that weak-minded rebel brother of mine teach you such impudence?"

Andra felt a flare of hatred for the man before her, and reflexively she threw herself toward him. He easily caught her wrist, turning and throwing her to the ground. She grunted as the impact sent fresh pain through her bruised body. Caedo knelt and gripped her face tightly in one hand.

"Now, let's be reasonable," he whispered dangerously. "I have very kindly kept Castigo's good widow from hanging you by your pretty little neck. I am allowing you, for the moment, to stay in a room that should be for guests. I am a judge—the *Chief* Judge, for now. Speak to me like that again, and I will teach you a lesson you won't soon forget. Do you understand me, girl?"

She glowered at him, clenching her teeth to keep herself from spitting in his face. He seemed to take her scowl as acquiescence, because his mocking smile returned.

"Wonderful," he said. "Now, you must be hungry. Guard!"

The door opened at his call, and a soldier stepped in bearing a tray of food. The man set it on the low table beside the sofa, then bowed and left without a word. Caedo stepped over to the table and took an apple from the tray. He sat and leaned back into the sofa cushion as he bit into it. Andra stood where she was, watching him mistrustfully.

"Well?" he asked. "What are you waiting for? Come on, then. If you ruin my good mood, I'll take it away."

Part of her wished that he *would* take it away, remove the temptation. She didn't want to accept anything from him. But her stomach growled angrily, and her feet carried her forward against her will. Her hand reached quickly out and grabbed a slice of warm bread and a piece of freshly cooked meat from the tray. She backed up again as she bit into the food, eyeing him. Caedo chuckled as his eyes roved from her booted feet to her tangled hair.

"You can sit, you know," he said, gesturing at the empty space on the sofa. "I'm not going to hurt you. I just want to talk."

"I have nothing to say to you," she answered quietly.

His eyebrows began to pull downward into a scowl, but he quickly smoothed his face again. "All right, then, why don't you ask *me* a question? Anything you want."

Andra narrowed her eyes suspiciously. But she figured that, if he was going to torture her, asking a question wouldn't make a difference. "Why are you keeping me here? What do you think I can tell you?"

He leaned forward and answered in a falsely sweet voice, "Why, my dear girl, isn't it obvious? I want to know where they are. All of them. Every last rebel who was in that camp north of the desert. We know they fled, but we haven't been able to track them. And, of course, I want to know where that fool brother of mine is."

"The Veil take you," she spat.

Andra braced herself to be struck, but Caedo simply tilted his head back and laughed at the ceiling. When his mirth had subsided, he shook his head, still grinning. "You know, I find your desire to protect him very intriguing." His eyes were calculating, the grin slowly turning into a sneer as he studied her face. "Especially given your noble sacrifice to ensure his escape last night. Castigo's men saw that heart-breaking farewell kiss, you know."

Andra felt her heart flutter. "I don't know what you're talking about."

"Actually," he said quietly, stepping toward her, "I think you do. If you won't tell me where Kael is, at least answer me this: Do you love that murderer? The one who betrayed his father and his brother, who betrayed all of Paerolia?"

"Shut up!" Andra screamed angrily. "You are the traitor! I know you wanted to make Castigo into an emperor. I know you murdered your own father! You're—"

The strike finally came. She heard the crack of his hand against her cheek before she felt the sting of it. The slap made her gasp, jerking her face to one side. Before she even had time to turn to look at him again, he seized her firmly by the chin and yanked her face back in his direction, squeezing it tightly in his hand once more.

He was smiling at her, lips drawn back over his teeth, his eyes glinting with mad amusement. "You think I would want to put that fat, weak, old man on a throne? Then you are as foolish as my brother." He shoved her away, making her stumble against the arm of a chair as he laughed. "Do you think I didn't *know* he'd have spies in the manors? It was a child's game, planting those lies among his eyes and ears. Kael might have won the heart of my father when he won that blasted dragon, but that mark on his hand doesn't make him any less of a fool.

"Castigo wouldn't have the courage to send an army of men against the rebels in the north. Castigo—the half-blind, half-dead Chief Judge! Do you really think he would inspire the other judges to rally around him and make him an emperor?"

Caedo shook his head, still chuckling. "No, no, no, you dull, daft girl. When you and my brother entered the Chief Judge's manor and killed Castigo, you were not cutting the head off a snake. You were biting the worm on my hook. You killed the last man standing in my way." His blue-gray eyes were alight with glee, and Andra felt the blood drain from her face. "The rebels have just cleared my path to the throne. By the first frost, the Kingsmen will have made me emperor."

A Dark Place

Kael sat on Andra's bed, his head buried in his arms. It was his fault. He shouldn't have asked her to go with him. He shouldn't have let her go back. Gods only knew where she was now, and what was happening to her. He groaned and ran his hands across his face, not fighting back the tears in the emptiness of the room.

He swore at himself aloud, throwing her pillow across the room, then dropped back onto the mattress, tearing at his hair. He should have pulled her straight into the saddle. He had let himself get too easily distracted. Distracted by her kiss, by her words. He heard them ringing in his ears now: *I love you.*

"We will think of something, Kael," Eithne promised in his mind.

"When, Eithne?" he demanded angrily. *"They could kill her! Every moment we're delayed is a moment when they could be torturing her!"* He pressed the heels of his hands against his eyelids until he saw stars.

"Your spies are gathering information as we speak," she answered soothingly. *"As soon as we know where they have taken her, we will find a way to get her back."*

Kael sighed, allowing the calm of his dragon's mind to wash into his own body. After a long pause, he asked, *"How's Tiri?"*

"Furious, terrified, distraught. Everything you would expect of a dragon whose Rider was in danger."

"Are you keeping an eye on her?"

"Yes. She keeps pacing around the meadow, but she doesn't seem to intend a rescue attempt at the moment. She knows that it could put Andra in more danger."

He heard a voice call his name and he sat up, looking across the bridge to his own quarters. "Here," he called to the figure searching his room.

King Vires looked toward his voice. "Ah, there you are," he said, and crossed the bridge, stepping into Andra's room.

Kael ran a hand through his disheveled hair and stood, trying to look collected as the elf king approached. He gave a short bow, then asked, "How was the journey from Amiscan? What news from the dwarves?"

Vires sighed. "It seems the dwarves did not willingly allow the Kingsmen to use their tunnels to reach Bellris."

"They were attacked?" Kael asked, his brow furrowing.

The elf nodded. "The Kingsmen took the tunnels and cleared away any dwarf who attempted to stop them. The dwarves were unprepared for the attack. Hundreds were killed. King Lineal is in quite the temper, raging about men defiling their halls with dwarvish blood."

Kael felt hope rise within him, and his hand closed around the hilt of his sword. "Does he wish to fight?" he asked.

King Vires's violet eyes crinkled with a small smile. "He does. As do I."

———◆◆◆———

Caedo tried to persuade her into talking for three days. He kept her in the guest chambers, visited her often, and provided her with food and drink as often as she needed. Andra lived more comfortably in those three days than she had in her entire life. But each time Caedo visited her, she would smile bitterly at him and say nothing.

It was almost as if her voice had fled her again, but now, it was a choice. Ledo had taken her voice from her, taken all desire to fight out of her. But now, her silence *was* her fight. She accepted Caedo's rich foods and fine wines. She even sat and listened to him as he tried to persuade her into betraying the location of the Freemen. And each day, Andra smiled at him and said nothing.

"I've had enough!" Caedo finally screamed, standing so quickly that he knocked the tray of food to the floor in front of him.

Andra looked down at it, then up at him with a raised eyebrow, her face a mask of calm.

"Tormina!"

A breath of air seemed to pass through the room, and a woman with long brown hair suddenly appeared. To the eye, there was nothing remarkable about her. She was clad in a dress of deep gray, crafted of a soft silk that gave off a gentle shine in the torchlight. Her brown hair fell in soft waves down to the small of her back, and her round face was pale and somewhat plain, with large dark eyes and a small, mouselike nose. But the presence around her sent a shiver down Andra's spine and set her skin to crawling. The Darkness that seemed to emanate from the sorceress was the same Darkness Andra sensed in her own mind, blocking her from accessing her magic.

"Yes, my love?" the sorceress asked lazily.

"The girl has made it quite clear that our guest chambers do not suit her," Caedo spat. "Please, ensure she is shown to more appropriate accommodations."

Tormina gave a small smile and waved her hand toward the chamber doors. They banged open, making the guards outside jump in surprise.

"Guards, escort the girl to the dungeons," Tormina said in a voice that assumed obedience.

The guards stepped into the room, each taking Andra by an arm. She didn't fight them. She'd known Caedo's patience and diplomacy would run out eventually. The guards led her down the halls with Tormina trailing behind, keeping that ever-present wall of Darkness between Andra and her magic. They reached a wooden door and stepped through, descending the stone steps into the damp coldness of the dungeon.

"Put her in that cell. And chain her to the wall."

The guards obeyed Tormina without a word, shackling Andra's wrists and ankles with the chains driven into the wall. Then they retreated from the cell, closing and locking the barred gate behind them. Andra stood in her shackles and met Tormina's gaze calmly through the bars.

The sorceress's lip curled as she studied the girl before her. "It is only a matter of time before Caedo yields," she hissed. "I told him his persuasion wouldn't work, but the silly man insisted on trying. You'll be mine soon enough. Then you will sing like a bard on a feast day."

Andra smiled and curtsied mockingly without a word. She heard the woman let out a feral sound close to a snarl; then she turned and glided from the room, black dress billowing behind her like smoke. The door at the top of the stairs closed, and the dungeon was plunged into complete darkness. Andra blinked, waiting for her eyes to adjust, but there was nothing for them to adjust to. There was no hint of light. It was utter blackness.

288 · ERIN SWAN

She sighed and sank down against the wall, her chains tinkling musically in the dark. A line of Astrum's parting words to her came into her mind. *Into darkness you must go. . . .* She'd known when she heard the Seer speak that she would not be returning from the mission. But she had not been afraid.

Not because she wanted to be a hero. Not because she wanted to help Kael complete the task that he'd given the last five years of his life to. She'd been unafraid because she'd known that the reward would be much greater than her sacrifice. Because the Freemen deserved to truly be free, and surrendering her own freedom—or her life—for theirs was not something she feared.

33

Plans

Kael hurried through the palace to the rear courtyard, skidding to a halt when he saw the young man sitting with his back against one of the guest-quarters trees. His arms were wrapped around his legs, chin on his knees, light hazel eyes staring blankly at the grass.

"Janis!" Kael called, trotting up to the young Rider.

The boy's eyes slid up to Kael's, looking hollow and haunted. "Hello," he said flatly. "Been wondering if I'd see you. I arrived yesterday, but you weren't here."

"Yes, I know. I've been meeting with informants at the Hall, trying to determine where Andra's being kept."

A look of pity passed over the blankness in Janis's eyes. "Someone told me she was captured," he replied.

"I'll find a way to get her back," Kael said briskly, confidence in his tone. "But that's not why I'm here." He was surprised to find himself smiling, heart pumping with more excitement than he had felt in years. "Janis, they want to fight with us. The elves *and* the dwarves. They're going to help us."

For the first time since his dragon's death, Janis's eyes brightened with life. "Truly?" he asked, pushing himself up to his feet. "They'll fight?"

Kael nodded.

"With the elven army *and* the dwarves, we can . . ."

"We can actually fight," Kael finished. "No more lurking. No more scheming. No more trying to manipulate things from the shadows. We have an army now, Janis. It's time to take the fight to the Kingsmen."

"When?" Janis asked.

"We need our people here first. That's why I came to you. I want you and two elven messengers to go to the camp at the Mordis Range." He handed Janis a scroll sealed with a drop of wax. "This will instruct them on when and how to begin departing without drawing attention. Ensure it goes directly to Egan. Vires has already sent word to the other elven cities, and their soldiers will begin gathering here. King Lineal is sending all dwarves who are willing to fight with us to Iterum via their tunnels. In just over a fortnight, we'll have twenty thousand men, elves, and dwarves to fight at our side."

Janis smiled, an expression Kael thought he would never see on the boy's face again. "Kael . . ." he breathed. "With twenty thousand soldiers . . ."

The rebel leader nodded, a smile rising to his own lips. "We could actually win."

⟡

Andra didn't know how long she sat in the dark before the door opened again. A guard appeared, rattling a set of keys and carrying a lantern. She stood as he set the lantern on the ground and unlocked the cell. Without a word, he stepped forward, unlocked her shackles, then seized her by one elbow.

She swung the flat side of her hand at him, striking him in

the throat—an attack Colmen had shown her in training. The guard let out a choking sound and released her arm, and Andra sprinted through the open door. Her feet carried her up the stone steps, and she threw open the door, bursting out into a tiled corridor.

A guard jumped back in surprise, but she didn't stop. She ran, the shouts of men beginning to echo behind her. She didn't know where she was running. She didn't know these halls. But she ran, praying that she would find an exit.

Suddenly, with a sound like a dying breath, Tormina appeared in the hall before her. Andra slid to a stop on the tiles, nearly colliding with the sorceress. There was a pause as the girl stared at the black-garbed woman, and scrabbled against the wall in her own mind, trying to grab her magic. Tormina merely smiled at her and raised a hand in Andra's direction. Her pale fingers curled slightly.

Agony ripped through Andra's body, every cell alighting with pain. She screamed, the sound tearing its way from her throat as her body crumpled to the floor. She thrashed and writhed, trying to escape the demon that seemed to be clawing its way out of her skin, tearing at her mind.

"That's enough!"

Abruptly, the pain stopped, and Andra lay panting on the cold tiles, staring at the gilded patterns on the ceiling. She tasted blood in her mouth, and tentatively touched her tongue to her cheek. She'd bitten through the skin. With a groan, she rolled onto her hands and knees, spitting blood onto the creamy colored tiles before looking up.

Caedo was striding down the hall toward them, looking somewhat disheveled. "I told you, no Dark magic!" Caedo snapped quietly. He caught Tormina by the arm and turned her toward him, but it was not anger on his face. He looked concerned. He touched the sorceress's cheek gently. "Not here, in the open. If anyone witnessed you using such magic, do you know what they would do to you? There are already rumors of your powers, my darling. I could not bear to lose you should someone discover the truth."

Tormina smiled at the young judge, but Andra saw resentment clearly in the expression. "As you wish, my future king."

"Emperor," Caedo corrected her with a small smile. "And you shall be my powerful empress."

They kissed, and Andra felt her lip curling in disgust. But before she could struggle to her still-trembling legs, the judge and the sorceress turned back to her. Caedo's expression darkened as he regarded her.

"I asked for you to be brought to my quarters so that I could attempt to talk sense to you again. But it is clear to me now that there is no driving sense through that thick, rebel head of yours."

Andra spat again, the red spray speckling the tiles at Caedo's feet. He looked down at it, then back at her.

"Tormina," he said calmly. "Take the girl back to my chambers. I shall join you shortly."

Without a word, Tormina stepped forward and gripped Andra's forearm. She started to pull back against her, but before she could even begin to struggle, the world around her vanished. For a brief moment, she seemed to hover in blackness, in a cold so sharp that it felt as if her skin were on fire. And then the blackness was gone. Air rushed into Andra's lungs and she gasped it in with a feeling of relief.

Tormina smirked down at her. "Jarring the first time, isn't it?" She chuckled in her throat, brushing her long hair back over her shoulder. "You grow used to it rather quickly, though."

Andra forced herself to straighten and drew a hand across her mouth, clearing away any sign of blood. Her eyes scanned the room she now stood in—an elaborately furnished bedchamber with a fireplace large enough to roast a horse. She took several slow, steady breaths as she took in her surroundings. She could not show weakness, no matter what was coming.

The sorceress seemed to notice Andra's efforts, because she smiled at her with a dark humor in her brown eyes. "Putting on a brave face, little girl? How wonderfully predictable. They always start with brave faces on, but they never last long." She leaned close to Andra, her dark eyes peering directly into Andra's pale green ones. For a moment, Andra thought she saw a swirl of black move across the irises. "Do you know what Dark magic can do, girl? Do you know the powers I have over your very body? That little demonstration in the corridor was only the beginning. I can turn your blood to ice inside your veins. I can make your mind believe your skin is crawling with insects until you claw your flesh into ribbons. I can turn your mind against yourself until you surrender to the Dark and beg it for mercy."

Andra met Tormina's gaze steadily, and finally spoke. "What spell do you have him under?" she asked. "I know you're using Dark magic to make him love you."

The smile slid off the sorceress's face, and she sneered. Tormina turned away from her with a scoff. "I don't need to put any spell on Caedo to make him love me," she snapped. The woman crossed her arms and stared into the enormous fireplace, one finger tapping against her elbow in agitation. "It is my power that Caedo loves, the only part of me that he truly desires."

Andra heard the bitterness in Tormina's voice. "But you love him, don't you."

The sorceress looked back toward Andra, her face impassive. "I love what Caedo can offer me—a throne and a crown. I wield my magic for myself, not for him."

Andra didn't believe her. The door to the room opened, and both women turned their eyes toward Caedo as he stepped inside. He shut the doors behind him, drawing a lock into place before turning to face them. He stood erect, head high, hands clasped behind his back as he took slow but purposeful steps toward them.

"I've stationed two trustworthy guards outside my door, and

several down the corridors to ensure everyone stays out of ear-shot." He drew to a halt in front of Andra, regarding her. "I *did* want to avoid this, girl. I tried to be diplomatic. I hope you'll re-member that. But I can't afford to have my little brother gather-ing an army against me when I am finally *so close* to having the throne I deserve."

"The only thing you deserve is a sword in the belly."

Caedo raised his eyebrows, as if surprised that she had spoken. "Is that so?" he asked, his mouth quirking slightly.

"I know what you are, Caedo," Andra spat. "You're a power-hungry, murderous bastard who would kill his own father for just a drop more power. You would bed a snake just to have its venom in your purse," she continued, casting a glance at Tormina, who stood by his side. "And you would kill your own brother simply because he has the power of a dragon Rider. He has Eithne, when you were passed over at your Pairing. He has magic, when you are completely ordinary. He has men who raised him to leader because of his strength and goodness, while you lie and scheme and mur-der to try to force men to make you their ruler. You are half the man your brother is, and you loathe him for it."

Finally, the back of Caedo's hand struck her across the mouth, landing with such force that she stumbled backward a step. She heard him inhale and exhale deeply once.

Then he said in a tight voice, "Well, when you finally decide to speak, you certainly can get going, can't you. . . ." He turned toward the woman at his side, touching a finger to her chin. "Tormina, my love, why don't you see if you can keep this new, talkative trend of hers going, won't you?"

Tormina looked at Andra with a vulpine expression. "It would be a great pleasure."

The woman's hand seized hers in a tight grip, and Andra screamed as pain devoured her body.

34

Blood of Ice

"Why not wait until the armies are here?" Vires asked, studying the map Kael had drawn, which was stretched out on the table before them. "In less than a fortnight, you'll have twenty thousand at your command. Retrieving Andra will be simple then."

"It will never be simple," Kael replied, shaking his head. "Not with my brother involved."

His spies had finally come back with the information he needed. Andra was not being kept in the Chief Judge's dungeons, as he'd thought she would be. She'd been taken to Caedo's manor on the other side of the city. Caedo, the interim Chief Judge, was given responsibility for the rebel prisoner until the formal election could be held to fill Castigo's judgment seat.

Kael didn't doubt that Caedo would take the seat. He knew his brother had enough ways of manipulating the other judges into giving it to him. And, since Castigo had named him to be interim Chief Judge in the event of his death, it was clear whom Castigo had intended as his new heir. It was unlikely that the other judges would go against those wishes.

Kael went on. "Caedo will no doubt have his Dark sorceress questioning Andra, trying to find where the Freemen have gone. And he won't let her far from him. Andra used magic like I have never seen on that night she helped me escape. Over a hundred men witnessed it. He'll know about her power, and he won't let it go easily. Caedo loves power . . ." he muttered under his breath.

"You think he'll try to turn her?" Vires asked.

"Perhaps," Kael answered. "But Andra won't turn. I know her."

"She may have no choice, Kael," the elf king replied hesitantly. "You know how Dark magic can infest the mind."

He did know. If a person were tortured by Dark magic, it could embed itself in the person's mind like an infection. It could take over a person so completely that they were left with only two choices: surrender to the Dark or die. Kael knew which one Andra would choose.

"And that's another reason we can't wait," he said. "Andra is strong, but if Caedo's sorceress applies enough Dark magic, she could kill her. I know where she is now. I know that manor. I can get her out."

"But you don't know *where* in the manor she's being kept," Vires pointed out.

"I'll be able to sense her mind," Kael said confidently. "I know her presence like I know Eithne's, Vires. If I can get close enough to the manor to sense her mind, I will be able to find her. Eithne and I will leave tomorrow. We'll take a wide route so Caedo won't see us coming. We'll land outside the city wall, here." He touched a spot on the map. "We'll approach on foot to stay out of sight, then I'll go over the wall into the manor." He traced the short path from the wall to where his brother's manor lay. "I'll find Andra, get her out, get back over the wall, and fly back here."

"You refuse to take any of my men with you?"

Kael shook his head. "The less attention I draw to myself, the better. If I can, I want to get Andra out without being spotted. An attack from elves on Caedo's manor would put the judges on high alert for the election, and we want them unprepared for our attack."

Finally, Vires sighed. "Very well. If there is any aid I can give . . ."

"Thank you," Kael said definitively. "But I'll have everything I need once I get Andra back."

———◦❦◦———

Andra grunted and raised an arm to shield her eyes as a lantern-bearing soldier opened the door to her cell.

"C'mon, girl," he said gruffly. "Judge Caedo wants to see yeh again."

She whimpered quietly and lowered her arm, curling around herself on the cold stones. The man let out an exasperated sigh and bent down, pulling her roughly to her feet.

"Come on, now," he grunted. "Don't make my job more difficult than it needs to be."

He pulled Andra along beside him, her feet shuffling weakly. Her body still ached from the previous day's torment, and the nightmares Tormina had planted in her mind had kept her from sleep through the night. The images of Kael being murdered again and again still played through her mind in a horrible, bloodstained array of images.

They arrived at Caedo's chamber doors, and the guard rapped once. She heard the judge's voice call out, and the soldier opened the door, escorting her inside.

"The girl, as you asked, m'lord."

"Thank you," Caedo said with a nod. "You may return to your post."

The man exited the room, the doors banging shut behind him.

Andra was left standing in the bedchamber, Caedo and Tormina regarding her from where they lounged together on a sofa, bodies slightly entangled.

The sorceress sighed as she stood, straightening her hair and running a hand over her dress to smooth it back into place. Caedo stood as well and strode slowly to Andra's side. She raised her eyes to his, but she couldn't force defiance into her gaze. She felt only weariness.

"You don't look well," Caedo said, concern in his voice. But there was amusement in his eyes. He looked over his shoulder at Tormina. "Darling, do you think you could Heal the poor girl? Perhaps give her a little energy for today's activities?"

Tormina walked up behind him, draping an arm over one of his shoulders and resting her chin atop the other. "I could. But it seems silly to strengthen her when she's so clearly near breaking."

Andra clenched her teeth. "I am no nearer breaking now than I was when I fought off Castigo's entire guard."

Tormina chuckled, sliding around Caedo to stand in front of her. "Yes, but then you had your magic, didn't you." A thoughtful look came over her face. "Such remarkable magic, really," she said. "I can always feel it, pulsing with such pure energy, even as I hold you back from reaching it. I'll admit, it feels even more powerful than the power I can summon from the dead." She glanced at Caedo, who had a thoughtful expression on his face. "Are you certain I can't just try that experiment I mentioned to you? It would be lovely to try to tap into that power myself."

"As I recall," Caedo said with a chuckle, "a possible outcome of that experiment is the girl's death. If that were to happen before she told us where Kael and the other Freemen were, that would be most unfortunate."

Tormina sighed. "A pity."

"Indeed. But, for now . . ." He raised one hand, gesturing toward Andra in an indulgent manner.

Tormina smiled and stepped forward. Andra steeled herself, forcing her feet to stay in place, and not back away. The sorceress's hand closed around her arm, and Andra shrieked as she felt her blood turning to ice, freezing in her veins. Frost trailed from where Tormina's hand touched, freezing the skin as the blood burst from Andra's veins in frozen threads of red.

"Where is Kael?" Caedo asked calmly.

"Far from you," Andra spat between clenched teeth. Tormina's grip tightened, and she screamed again.

"Where are the Freemen?"

"Gone!" Drops of frozen blood began to fall to the floor, shattering like red glass.

"What are they planning?"

"To put your head on a pike!"

Andra's skin began to turn black, threads of white frost creeping over the skin. And then the pain was gone. A tingling sensation rushed over Andra's arm as Tormina Healed her, renewing the dead flesh, sealing the burst veins. Andra let out a sharp breath at the feeling of sudden relief.

Then Tormina touched a finger to her forehead. White-hot flames shot through her mind, burning across every nerve. She shrieked with agony, her voice turning raw from the scream. The pain disappeared as suddenly as it had come, and she distantly heard Caedo's voice, repeating the same three questions they had been repeating for several days. And she answered none of them.

Andra lay in a heap on the floor, her breaths coming in ragged gasps, listening to Tormina's footsteps retreating from the room to fetch Andra's escort back to the dungeon. Caedo's boots appeared in her vision, striding slowly toward her. He crouched, bringing his face into her line of sight.

He touched her cheek, turning her face upward to look him more squarely in the eye. He made a pitying *tsk-tsk* under his breath as he began to smooth her hair away from her face, as if stroking an animal. "It's quite tragic, really," he mused, almost to himself, "to see such a beautiful, powerful creature brought so low over the love of one like *Kael*. Like seeing a dragon beaten in defense of a mongrel dog."

Andra's lip curled in hatred, but she couldn't even muster the strength to spit at him. Instead, she groaned softly in pain and closed her eyes.

"I'm going to make you an offer, girl," Caedo said. "I know your magic can be stronger than Tormina's. Abandon this foolish attempt to defend my brother. Pledge yourself to me, help me defeat what's left of those Freemen, and I will make you empress over all of Paerolia. With you at my side, I could bring the elves to their knees and send the dwarves scurrying back into their holes. The entire land would be ours to rule. You shall be showered in jewels and riches beyond your imagining. You shall be worshipped like a goddess. I will care for you in ways that Kael never could. All you need to do is say yes."

Andra opened her eyes again, looking up into Caedo's face. Through her haze of pain, for a moment, he looked like Kael, and her heart ached to touch him, to see him once more. Not this hateful, soulless mimicry of him.

"No," she rasped. "Never."

Caedo's gaze hardened, and he straightened. "You're a great fool, girl. Your love for my brother will be the death of you."

Andra smiled up at him weakly. "So be it."

35

Into the Light

The moment Kael was near enough to the manor to cast his mind toward it, he searched for the brilliance that was Andra's consciousness—that bright spark of life he had come to recognize so easily. His heart began to drop as he leaned against the outer wall, searching the manor with his thoughts. She should have stood out immediately, but he didn't sense her. And then he brushed the dim presence of a mind, nearly passing over it before he felt the warm familiarity of it. It was she, but something was wrong.

Kael struggled to touch her mind, but he couldn't. A thick black fog surrounded her. Andra remained completely unaware of him.

"Someone powerful is blocking her mind," Eithne said from beside him.

"The sorceress," Kael remarked. *"The snake in Caedo's bed."*

"She'll be keeping a close watch on Andra's mind, Kael. You'll have to move quickly, get Andra far enough from here that she can break the sorceress's hold, before the sorceress can follow us."

"I know. You'll have to be ready to fly quickly."

"I will be ready. You be safe."

302 · ERIN SWAN

"I will."

Kael cast a long look down the length of the wall, making sure no one was nearby. Then he carefully placed one boot on Eithne's nose. She lifted her head until he was able to scramble over the wall and drop down to the other side. Once over, Kael didn't pause to see if anyone was looking at him. He darted immediately into Caedo's gardens, hiding himself behind a high-growing hedge.

He crouched there for a moment, listening, but no one approached. He drew a slow breath, settling himself, as he peered through the branches toward the manor. In the light of early morning, the doors to the kitchen were opened, letting in the early autumn breeze and letting out the smoke from the cooking fires. He counted only four kitchen workers; breakfast was a simple meal, and there were not many to serve here. He spotted no guards.

Kael waited until all the servants were out of sight, far from the doorway; then he darted out of the gardens and hid himself behind the open kitchen door. The manservant disappeared through another door. One of the women carefully stirred something in a pan; another continued to squat beside the oven, watching the last few minutes of the bread's baking; and the third grabbed a broom.

He held his breath. The two cooking were intent on their work. He just had to wait for the sweeping woman to go the other way. She swept in front of the open door, just feet from where Kael hid, for what felt like hours. Finally, she worked her way down the length of the kitchen, and disappeared behind the stone oven. He immediately darted out from his hiding place and ducked into the kitchen, staying close to the wall where there were crates and boxes neatly stacked. When he reached the door that connected to the manor, he pulled it quietly open, peered through it for half a moment, then slipped inside.

There was no one in the corridor to the kitchen, so Kael stopped wasting time with stealth. He ran at a full sprint down the corridor and rounded a corner before skidding to a halt and darting back around the corner. He peered out again cautiously; the guard had not seen him. But he was standing right in front of the door to the dungeon, where Andra's mind dimly glowed.

Kael paused for a moment, eyes scanning the area. Then he very carefully focused his magic on the guard, summoning only the smallest amount of it; if he used more than just a thread of power, it would send up a beacon for Caedo's sorceress to find him. He lifted one hand in his direction, then slowly closed it, willing the air to draw away from the man. A startled look came over the soldier's face, and he made a gagging sound. His eyes began searching around frantically, either for his attacker or for help. After a while, his body sagged, and he slipped to the ground.

Kael raced around the corner and immediately pulled open the door to the dungeon, dragging the limp body inside as the heavy door slammed shut behind them. He could see absolutely nothing. Quickly, he sent up a small ball of light, just enough to see by.

His eyes found her immediately. She sat with her knees pulled to her chest, her head resting against the stone wall behind her. Her eyes were closed, her feet and hands shackled inside the locked cell.

Kael hurried to the cell door and channeled a thread of fire into the lock. It melted under his magic, and the door swung open. Andra still didn't move, curled against the wall of her cell as if she slept. He knelt beside her, cautiously touching her arm.

"Andra," he whispered, his heart aching as he looked at her. Her face was pale and dirty, marked with bruises. The skin of her arms was a strange, mottled color of black-and-blue amid the pale flesh. Her fingers were bloody, as if she'd been clawing at the stones or her shackles, trying to escape. "Andra, it's me. It's Kael."

Cautiously, she turned her eyes toward him. They were glazed and bloodshot as she blinked at him, taking him in. She gazed at him for a long moment, as if she expected him to vanish. Then she gave a mangled, muffled cry and threw her arms around him, her body shuddering with choked, quiet sobs.

He put his arms around her, embracing her tightly, relishing the feeling of her body in his arms again. But only for a moment. He forced her arms from around his neck and softly touched the tears on her cheeks.

"I'm going to get you out of here," he whispered.

He turned his eyes to her wrists, raw from the metal shackles that were tight around them. Kael touched the shackles. He focused, carefully summoning fire into the black keyhole, as he'd done to the cell door. It began to glow red; then the shackles fell open. He repeated the magic with the bonds around her ankles, then took her by both hands, pulling her to her feet.

She embraced him again, her hands clutching at the back of his tunic as if she needed to hold him there, to keep him from vanishing like smoke in a windstorm. "You're really here," she whispered, her voice cracking with tears. "It's really you. You're here."

"Yes, Andra," he answered, kissing her matted hair. "I'm here." He stepped back and clasped her hands in his again. "Are you hurt?" he asked. "Or can you run?"

She swallowed and dashed away the tears on her cheeks, smearing away dirt as well. Her expression took on a determined look as she nodded once. "I can run."

"Good. We need to go quickly. Follow me."

Still clasping one of her hands, Kael led the way up the stairs, past the unconscious guard. He opened the dungeon door, looking out for only a moment before rushing out the door and down the nearby corridor. Andra followed him on silent feet, her breath already sounding labored.

A pair of guards approached, and Kael shoved Andra through a doorway, tumbling in after her and shutting the door quickly behind him. They both held their breath, listening as the chatting guards passed by. Kael exhaled, then peered out for a moment, seized Andra's hand, and continued their mad dash toward freedom.

They burst through the kitchen doors, surprising the workers, but they didn't pause. Their feet were on grass now, racing faster, covering the ground to the wall. Kael felt Eithne on the other side, waiting for them in the clearing, her mind pressing against his with anxious urgency. They drew up to a low-growing tree, its branches reaching over the stone wall.

"Climb," Kael ordered hurriedly.

Andra did, scrambling up the trunk and across the branches onto the top of the wall. Kael followed. On the other side, Eithne waited, nose at the top of the wall. Andra stepped gently on the dragon's nose, then shimmied carefully down the spikes of her neck to the saddle on her back, Kael close behind her.

He drew on Eithne's energy and every ounce of magic within himself, creating a powerful ward around them all. The sorceress was going to notice Andra's movement soon enough. He settled into the saddle, wrapped his arm around Andra's waist, and signaled his readiness to Eithne. The dragon crouched, then threw herself into the air, barely clearing the nearby treetops as they raced away from the city wall.

Kael felt something strong and icy cold batter against his ward, and he strengthened it further, sweat beading on his forehead as the force continued to pound against his mind. Beneath his legs, Eithne shuddered slightly from the force of the attack, but flew dutifully onward. Kael looked back and saw a woman in black standing atop the wall, a look of fury on her pale face. He smiled to himself as they climbed higher, flying farther, and the sorceress disappeared from sight.

36

Darkness Within

Andra felt the moment that the wall inside her mind broke. It shattered into a thousand icy pieces, and the warmth of her magic seemed to burst to life within her. Tears of joy filled her eyes, and she laughed aloud at the sensation, wondering for a moment how she had ever been unaware of this well of power that was so bright inside her.

But even as the warmth of magic flowed through her, something cold seemed to rise up against it. Like the ice Tormina had put in her veins, her body seemed to flare with resistance against her own magic, ice battling fire beneath her skin. She doubled over in the saddle with a groan, her stomach roiling from the pain, her vision blurring.

"Andra?" Kael asked from behind her, his arm tightening on her waist, keeping her from slipping out of the saddle. "Andra, is something the matter?"

She didn't answer, her body shuddering against the battle that continued to rage in her mind.

"Hold on," she distantly heard him say. "We're nearly to Iterum. Hold on, Andra."

Sweat began to bead on her brow, her breaths coming in rasping pants. Eithne's form trembled slightly as her feet landed heavily on the grassy field outside the elf city. Andra felt Kael lift her from the saddle, carefully sliding down Eithne's foreleg and onto the grass with her in his arms.

Something warm, familiar, and strong pressed against the coldness that tried to embrace her mind. *"Andra,"* Tiri's worried voice whispered through the black fog. *"Andra, fight against it. Push it back. I will help."*

Somehow, the dragon's thoughts seemed to pierce through the cloud to the place where Andra's magic pulsed. She grasped at Tiri's powerful presence as though it were a piece of flotsam in a stormy sea.

"Fight it!" Tiri urged, her voice louder, stronger in Andra's mind.

She felt the jostling of Kael running with her in his arms, racing through the city to find the Healer. Andra clung to Tiri's thoughts as she grasped at the well of magic, drawing on the power of both. The two seemed to grow brighter in her mind, forcing away the encroaching darkness. Fire began to melt the ice in her veins, light driving out darkness like the night at dawn.

"Fight!" Tiri roared silently.

With a last mental push, the pulsing light flooded her mind, sending warmth from her scalp to her toes. Andra sat up with a gasp, just as Kael settled her onto a mattress inside a hut. The Rider jumped back in surprise, and Andra found an elf woman looking down at her in confusion.

"Are you . . . well?" the elf asked.

Andra took several breaths, trying to slow her racing heart. "I . . . I think I am," Andra said.

The elf looked at Kael, raising an eyebrow. Kael's brow

furrowed. "She was . . . She was beginning to display the signs of a Dark fever. I recognized the symptoms. I've read about them before. The shivering, the sweating, the pain."

"Were you tortured with Dark magic?" the elf asked, looking at Andra again.

She nodded.

"Did you feel Darkness infesting your mind? Like a cold blackness trying to claim your thoughts."

"Yes. The moment the sorceress's barrier against my magic broke."

The elf continued to nod. "They say the Dark fever can be triggered by a person's magic touching the remnants of Darkness in the mind. And how do you feel now?" she asked curiously.

"I feel fine," Andra answered. "In my mind, at least," she added, forcing herself to acknowledge the pain that still pulsed through her body.

The elf gave her a bewildered look. After a moment, she asked, "May I delve you?"

Andra nodded again, and the woman placed two fingers on either side of Andra's head. She closed her blue eyes, and Andra felt a foreign presence touching her thoughts. She allowed the presence to enter, to explore the recesses of her mind to a point that the intrusion began to feel uncomfortable. Then the elf's thoughts withdrew.

"There is no sign of Darkness," she said quietly. "It does sound as if it was the beginning of a Dark fever, but . . . for you to be free of the Darkness so suddenly, without very complex Healing, is completely unheard of."

"Tiri helped me," Andra remarked. "She helped me to fight it back, to drive it out."

"Even still," the elf said, shaking her head, "it is a miracle."

"So she doesn't need Healing?" Kael asked. Andra heard both confusion and relief in his voice. "She's fine?"

"As far as any Darkness in her mind is concerned, she is completely Healed. There are still many bodily injuries," the Healer went on, "but most seem to have been caused by Dark magic, and I cannot Heal that. We will simply need to wait for it to pass. Keep an eye on her, though. If anything begins to seem amiss, she'll need to come here immediately." They both nodded, and the Healer left, stepping out of the hut and into the sunlight.

Kael held a hand out to Andra and pulled her to her feet. She rose and, for the first time in weeks, looked on his face in the light, truly drinking in the angles and contours of his features—the high cheekbones, the sharp jaw, the scar above his full lips, the long, dark lashes above misty gray eyes. How she had missed that face.

She lifted a hand and touched his cheek softly, caressing the golden tones of his skin. He turned his face into her palm, kissing the scar she'd earned when she caught the arrow intended for his heart.

"You're truly here," he whispered against her skin. "I thought I . . . I feared . . ." He looked down at her, taking her face between his hands now, indifferent to the dirt and the bruises that marred her skin. "I was so afraid that I would never see you again," he breathed.

She felt his hands draw her face to his, and she obeyed the gentle guidance, rising to meet his lips. They were just as she remembered. Warm, gentle, soft, and oh-so careful. She sank into his kiss, her fingers closing around the front of his tunic as her senses drank him in. The taste of his lips. The warmth of his hands. The smell of his skin.

When he finally drew back, his thumbs caressed her cheeks, and she realized that tears had begun to fall, tracing fresh paths through the dirt on her face.

"I missed you," she said, her voice barely above a whisper.

A pained expression crossed his eyes, and after a pause, he asked, "Why did you do it, Andra? We could have escaped together."

She shook her head slowly. "You know we couldn't have, Kael. We never would have escaped. I needed to hold them back."

"We could have tried," he insisted.

"Kael," she said firmly, "you heard Astrum's words before we left."

"And I heard his words when I first planned to enter Castigo's palace," Kael interrupted her, his eyes taking on a fervent look. "I didn't see it until you were taken from me, Andra, but . . . *you* were the power within the manor, the power that Ledo held. You were the reason Astrum sent us there. Your power, your connection to Tiri—" He paused, trailing his fingertips across her cheek as he gazed down at her. "—my need for you . . . You were always the key to this, Andra. I should have seen it sooner, and I never should have put you back into harm's way."

Andra was silent for a moment, taking in what he'd said. Could he be right? Could Astrum have sent Kael, Colmen, and Alik to free her from the manor? She forced herself to push those thoughts aside. All of that was in the past now, and they needed to direct their attention to more important matters.

"But, Kael," she said, taking his hands in hers, "I *needed* to be taken. There *was* a purpose for it."

"What purpose?" he asked, his interest clearly piqued by the rising fervor in her voice.

"We did not stop the Kingsmen by killing Castigo," she said fervently. "He was never a part of their uprising. He was a puppet, a façade they used to distract us. They were never going to put him on the throne, Kael. Caedo was feeding us lies, misleading us intentionally. *He* is the true leader of the Kingsmen. *He* is the one they wish to make an emperor. And they plan to do it at the election."

"In thirteen days," Kael said quietly.

"Yes."

She saw his jaw tighten, and she furrowed her brow in response.

He saw the question in her eyes and said, "We have an army coming to support us, Andra. The dwarves and the elves are going to fight with us." Excitement began to rise in her, but before she could even smile, he added, "But the numbers we'll have . . . It would be enough to catch the judges unaware, but if Caedo is going to have an army of Kingsmen at that election . . ."

She didn't know the numbers they would have, but she could see in his eyes what he didn't want to say aloud. "We won't have enough," she whispered.

Slowly, Kael shook his head. "No, Andra. I don't think we will. Caedo is going to be emperor."

37

Captains and Riders

Egan arrived five days later, flying discreetly by night aboard Calix, Janis in his saddle with him. The two Riders dismounted in the dark predawn hours, their boots hitting the grass silently. Kael and Andra waited in the trees along the edge of the clearing as Egan quickly unsaddled his dragon, and Calix immediately took back to the sky, heading for the cave behind the waterfall, where Tiri and Eithne had been hidden for the majority of the time since Andra's return.

When Calix had left, Kael sent up a brief flash of light from his palm. It attracted the other Riders' gazes, and they hurried to the trees where Kael and Andra waited.

"What word?" Kael asked.

Egan huffed, shifting the saddle in his arms. "We received your pigeon about the Kingsmen's coup. I can't believe we fell for that slimy serpent's lies—"

"And our numbers?" Kael interrupted, cutting off Egan's mutterings.

"The same, more or less," Janis put in with a shrug. "We've

picked up a few new recruits as the companies have journeyed, but it's difficult to gain members while remaining discreet, Kael. If we try to bolster our cause at every village we pass through, the Kingsmen will descend on us well before we reach the Hall."

"I know," the rebel commander muttered.

"What about the dwarves?" Andra asked. "Could King Lineal send us more men?"

Egan shook his head. "The dwarves don't have an army, Andra," he said. "A few hundred guards for the king himself, but no true soldiers. Lineal won't force anyone to fight for us who doesn't wish to. All dwarves who have chosen to battle with us are already on their way."

"So we will still be outnumbered," Kael said, a hint of desperation in his voice.

Andra silently slipped her fingers into his and gripped his hand tightly. She felt him return the pressure.

"Why must the dragons hide?" Egan asked, abruptly changing the subject. "I don't much like Calix having to cower behind a waterfall."

"Caedo has been searching for us since Andra escaped his manor," Kael answered. "His men have been here several times already. I think he suspects Vires, but he can't accuse him outright without proof that he's hiding us. We don't want to give him any more reasons to suspect."

Egan nodded in understanding.

Kael went on, redirecting the conversation back to their plans as he began to lead the other Riders toward the palace. "The elven soldiers from the other cities should arrive in a few days' time. They can travel more openly, since Vires is free to summon his men whenever he wishes, but they are attempting to keep from drawing attention to themselves."

"What about Riders?" Janis asked. "Have any others joined us?"

"The elven Riders who can join us have all stated their support of the Freemen, and their agreement with Vires's choice to fight alongside us. We will have their support when we arrive at the Hall, but there are many who will be unable to fight alongside us. If all of the elven Riders were to begin leaving their posts, the Kingsmen would surely begin to suspect something. But the Riders who are pledged to the judges will remain an uncertainty until we arrive."

"So we just charge into the Hall and hope that all those human Riders decide to side with us?" Egan asked.

"More or less," Andra sighed.

"Brilliant."

They entered the palace to find Vires and six other elves waiting for them at the long wooden table that rested in the grass beside the winding stone pathway. Orbs of light hovered over the table, illuminating the papers strewn on the surface. Andra sighed, bracing herself mentally for the long days ahead.

Egan deposited his saddle in the grass, and brief formalities ensued as Egan and Janis were introduced to the Riders who had pledged themselves to Vires and the rebel cause. Andra was briefly aware of the fact that she was the only woman in the group, and the only one who had not been Paired with a dragon. But she pushed the thoughts aside. She had a role to play here, and a mark on her hand would not make that role any more vital.

They all took seats around the table, and without ceremony, they began to plan their path into the battle that would end the rebellion—one way or another.

———— ◈◈ ————

Through the windows of the palace, Andra saw the sun rise and climb the sky. The men around her bickered, picked at details, made minute changes, and argued over the smallest affairs—all of which could tilt the battle in their favor. Knowing little of strategy, she wasn't clear on many of the things they discussed. But even without a military vocabulary, Andra understood that they were standing on the edge of dagger. The smallest shift in numbers, alliances, or positioning could make the difference between victory and defeat.

As the men talked around her and the sun began to set again outside the palace windows, a single thought continued to circle through Andra's mind: Someone needed to persuade the human Riders. But how? They couldn't send someone in to openly discuss the impending attack on the Hall. But if they charged into the election, the Riders would likely see them as an invading force, and they would fight against them, not with them.

"I need to speak to them," Andra said.

Kael looked down at her, his brow furrowing. It was clear that he had been the only one to hear her quiet statement, as the Riders around them continued to talk.

"Speak to whom?" Kael asked.

Andra raised her voice, drawing the attention of the others. "I need to speak to the human Riders," she said loudly.

The others fell silent and looked at her.

"What are you talking about?" Kael asked sharply.

Andra released his hand, which she'd been holding beneath the table through most of the meeting, and stood. They all watched her, silent, curious, and clearly skeptical.

"We can't expect those Riders to choose to fight with men who charge into their Hall and attack the men they call their leaders. Many of them don't even know the Kingsmen exist. They don't know what Caedo is planning, or that the judges are going to support him in becoming emperor. They only know that they've been pledged to serve the judges, and if we attack, then they will defend. All of you would do the same."

Several of the men around the table nodded in agreement.

Andra went on. "We need to give them an opportunity to

choose, before open battle begins. They need to know that there is another side to this fight, and that the side they stand on is not so righteous as it pretends to be."

"So you're just going to . . . tell them?" Egan asked incredulously.

Andra leaned over the table and drew a large map of the Hall toward her. It was already marked in countless places from the day's strategizing. "The Freemen's forces can begin to gather in the dwarf tunnels as we discussed," she said, tapping the different marked tunnels on the map. "We only need a few men here, here, and here." She indicated spots around the Hall. "And one man inside the meeting. The man inside can signal the others when Caedo has entered for election to the Chief Judge's seat. Then Tiri and I will enter through the main arena doors."

"What?" Kael interrupted, voice tinged with anger and disbelief. "You're just going to charge into the Hall by yourself?"

"Well, not by myself," Andra said in a calm tone. She'd expected his outburst. "I said Tiri would be there as well, didn't I?"

"And what will your charging into death's embrace accomplish?" he snapped angrily.

"Kael," Vires interrupted, holding up a hand, "let the girl finish."

Andra gave the king a nod of thanks and went on. "I'll raise a ward to protect myself against immediate attacks, and I'll enter the Hall and demand the right to speak against Caedo before he's elected."

"Only Riders have the right to speak against a judge," one of the elves pointed out.

"And that's why I'll need Tiri," Andra said with another nod. "I may not be marked, but she's claimed me as her Rider. That may be enough to persuade them to listen."

"And what if it's not?" Kael asked.

"Then we fight," Andra said simply. "Then we proceed with a direct assault on the Hall as discussed. But if they do let me speak,

Kael . . ." She looked at him, her expression determined and fervent. "I can tell them the truth. Every Rider in that Hall will know what Caedo is and what he is planning. Then they can choose who to fight for."

"It's not worth the risk," Kael insisted, standing from his chair as well. "If they don't listen, and we have to attack the Hall with you right in the center of our enemies, you will be killed, Andra."

Andra opened her mouth to protest, but Egan interrupted. "It's not a bad plan, Kael," the Rider said with a shrug, slumped back slightly in his seat. Kael fixed him with a scowl, but Egan didn't seem to notice. "If they allow her to speak, and even one Rider is turned to our cause, it can make the difference in this battle. Right now, our intelligence tells us that fifty human Riders will be attending the election. It could be more. We have thirty Riders. I know I don't have to tell you how much of an advantage twenty Riders can give the Kingsmen. Any Rider and dragon that Andra can persuade to our side could be the thing that tips the scales in our favor."

"I'm sorry, Kael," Vires put in, "but I have to agree. This is our best hope of bringing the Freemen the support that they need."

Andra looked at Kael as he regarded the faces around the table, taking in their obvious agreement with her plan. His hand clenched at his side and his jaw tightened. Then he dropped heavily into his chair.

"Very well," he said quietly.

Vires nodded, then looked out the palace window, which was growing dark with evening. The king sighed and rubbed at his eyes, standing. "I believe that we have been at this long enough for now. Everybody get some rest. We can reconvene tomorrow."

The men around the table stood, parting with few words to one another, dragging weary feet toward their quarters. Andra looked down at Kael, who had remained seated, staring moodily at the papers on the table.

"You're angry with me," she remarked, leaning against the edge of the table and looking at him.

Kael didn't raise his eyes, but his hand covered hers where it rested atop the wood. "No," he answered. "I'm not angry with you." Finally, he looked up, and she saw anxiety in his tired eyes. "How could I be angry with you for finding the one path that could lead my people to the victory we've fought for for so long? I know that you're right, Andra. I know this is our best hope of success, but—" He sighed and stood, moving to stand in front of her, taking her face gently between his hands. "—sometimes I think I would sacrifice the Freemen if it meant protecting you, Andra. I know I shouldn't think that way. I'm their leader, and I should put this cause before all else, but . . ."

He closed his eyes and pressed his forehead to hers, and she let her arms go around his back. "If I had to choose between the rebellion and having you, Andra . . ." he breathed. "I don't think I could give you up."

Now Andra sighed, and she leaned into him, pressing her lips softly to his, feeling the tenderness of his kiss. She pulled away and let her head rest against his shoulder, his arms tightening around her, as if he could hold her there through this final battle.

"Kael," she whispered, "you are more than I ever thought I could have. But—" She drew back, placing her hands on his chest to look up at him. "—I don't think you are mine to claim yet."

"Why not?" he asked, and she was surprised by the frustration in his voice. "I have given everything to the Freemen for the last five years. I have sacrificed for them again and again. Why can't I have this one thing? Why can we not have each other, Andra? Don't we deserve that?"

She sighed once again and ran a hand wearily over her face. Then she looked up at him and took his face firmly between her hands.

"Kael," she said in a calm and sure voice, "all of this will soon be over. In barely more than a week, we will fight the last battle of this rebellion. We can dedicate one week more to the Freemen. That is all they are asking of us. One week more of putting our own happiness aside. Just one week, and then we can claim the life we want."

"And you want that life to be with me?" Kael asked.

"Of course," she answered with a smile.

"Then marry me, Andra."

She felt her smile widen, and her heart thrilled within her. Though she had long been certain of his desire to remain with her after this was over, hearing him speak those words made her skin come alive with pleasure.

"Of course, Kael," she answered. She drew his face to hers and kissed him warmly, but he quickly pulled away, surprising her.

"No," he said. She looked up at him in confusion as he removed her hands from his cheeks, clasping them tightly in both of his. His expression was eager, a note of pleading in his gray eyes, as if he felt certain his request would be denied, but still held on to hope. "Andra, I don't want a promise of 'someday, when this is all over.' I want to marry you now. We don't know what this battle will bring. And I can't go into it without knowing that our souls have been bonded for this life and the next. Marry me here, Andra. Marry me today."

38

One Night

Andra stared at him, a sharp breath catching in her throat, heat rushing up her neck and into her cheeks. "What?" she choked out.

Kael smiled down at her, all eagerness and sincerity. "Marry me, Andra," he said again. "Why must we wait?"

"K-Kael," she stammered, slowly finding her tongue again, "we must focus on—"

"I know," he interrupted. "This battle must be our priority. But do you really think they would begrudge us this one night? That's all I ask, Andra. One night for our happiness to be our own. One night to think only about us, and not about wars and rebellions and successions. One night not to be captain or commander or Rider or leader. One night just to be me, just to be yours, just to be happy. Is that too much for me to ask?"

Andra was silent, staring at those eager gray eyes that continued to pierce into her heart. She knew how much Kael had sacrificed for this rebellion. He'd shouldered the leadership of the Freemen when he was barely old enough to be considered a man.

But it was not until this moment that she truly saw the weight of his sacrifices. Not once in all the years that he'd led them had he ever stopped to think of his own happiness. And now he was—for just one night.

Slowly, Andra brushed her fingers over the planes of his cheek and nodded, a smile rising to her lips. "After all you have given to this cause, after all you have given to me," she whispered, "I believe we deserve for this one night to be ours."

A smile, brighter and purer than anything she had ever seen, lit up Kael's features. He swept her into his arms and crushed her to his chest briefly, then pressed his lips firmly to hers. Andra smiled against the kiss, joy seeping down to her toes, her heart trembling with excitement in her chest.

Abruptly, Kael pulled away and caught her by one hand, pulling her at a run toward the tree at the center of the palace. "Vires!" he called. "Vires!"

As they approached the doorway at the base of the tree, the elf king and queen peered out at them, brows furrowed. A look of obvious agitation was on Queen Camena's face at having their supper interrupted.

"Something the matter?" Vires asked, his voice weary.

"No," Kael answered with a soft laugh. "For once, there is nothing wrong." He looked down at Andra, pulling her closer to his side before looking back up at Vires. "We wish to be married. Tonight. Would you do us the honor?"

Vires gave a sharp laugh, looking between them for a moment in apparent disbelief. "Tonight?"

Kael nodded once. "Yes. As soon as possible."

"Well, I . . . Very well, then," he chuckled. "We'll need rings. And someone to stand as witness."

"I'll bear witness," Camena chimed in, her look of irritation gone, replaced by a delighted smile. "If that is all right with you both," she added.

Andra nodded, as did Kael.

"I'll find a smith," Kael said, releasing Andra's hand. He kissed her quickly and darted toward the palace doors.

"And change into something decent!" the queen called after him. "It's your wedding, for the gods' sakes!"

Andra heard his laugher ring briefly through the room before he disappeared through the large wooden doors. She felt someone grip the hand that Kael had just released, abruptly drawing her attention away from the doors.

Camena smiled broadly at her. "And we can't have the bride in the same tunic she's been wearing for nearly two days, now, can we?"

She laughed quietly. "I . . . suppose not," she answered.

"Come with me. I'm certain I can find you something."

The elf queen pulled Andra into the enormous tree. The inside of the space was much the same as Andra's own quarters, but on a much larger and grander scale. The round room's intricate furniture grew from the walls and floor, with woven tendrils of wood that blossomed with real flowers. Camena led her up the curving staircase at the center of the room, past several more open doorways, before stepping out into a large bedroom.

Camena released her hand and hurried to a wardrobe that stood against the wall opposite the large four-poster bed. Andra stepped up beside her, her eyes widening at the array of stunning gowns before her.

"Now, let's see . . ." Camena mused. "Riders always wear their dragons' colors to a ceremony, even if he is the groom. I suppose the same should apply to a Rider who is a bride. Luckily, the color of the elven royal family is also violet, so I have plenty we can choose from." The queen sifted through the hanging silks and velvets adorned with embroidery and jewels. Finally, she pulled out a silk gown in a rich violet color. She turned to Andra with the gown draped over her arms.

"I think this will do nicely," she said, holding the dress up against Andra's form. "Faemil! Ciala!"

Andra heard the sound of swift steps on the staircase, and a pair of elven women appeared—one fair haired, one raven haired. They curtsied briefly to the queen.

"Rider Andra will be married tonight," she announced to the servants. "Let's ensure she shines for her groom, shall we?"

The young elves smiled brightly and immediately set to work. Andra was forced into a chair, and she sat in stunned silence as the elves flitted about her like hummingbirds around a particularly fragrant flower. Her head was tipped back and her hair washed in a basin of warm water, then magically dried in a flurry of wind. She was stripped and scrubbed as well as possible in the absence of a tub, and an oil with the soft scent of lilies was applied to her skin before they wrapped her in a robe. One of the elven servants began to braid her hair, and the other expertly powdered and painted her face.

After some time, Vires reentered the room. He smiled in pleased surprise at Andra. "Kael has managed to find a set of marriage bands for the ceremony. He's dressing now, and said he will meet you beside the river, near the waterfall, so that your dragons may be in attendance without drawing attention."

Andra nodded in eager agreement.

"Is there anyone else you would like to attend? I can retrieve them for you," the king offered.

She paused. Yes, there were so many she wished could attend. Alik, Syra, Amala, and Setora, who were with the Freemen. Her mother and father. Colmen . . . Andra swallowed and shook her head.

"No," she whispered, forcing a smile. "Just Eithne and Tiri."

Vires nodded in acknowledgment, then left the room.

"And now for the dress," Camena said, pulling Andra gently but briskly to her feet.

The bathing robe they'd covered her with was removed, and the servants helped her to step into the gown. The smooth silk slid over her skin with a soft, whispering sound, and Andra slipped her arms into the tight sleeves, which came to her wrists. Camena turned her to face a floor-length mirror as the servants worked on the laces at the back.

Andra caught her breath as she looked at herself. The silk bodice was snug around her torso, but flowed like liquid amethyst from her waist to the floor. The neckline dove in a sharp V below her neck to a point between her breasts. The fabric sparkled with silver thread, which danced across the bodice in intricate embroidery, accented by shining white jewels. Her hair sparkled as well, dotted with bejeweled pins that shone in the light from the orb on the ceiling.

"Camena . . ." she breathed. "Your Majesty, you have been far too kind to me."

The queen laughed and placed a hand on Andra's shoulder, standing beside her in the mirror. "Nonsense. You and Kael will help to finally end this cold animosity between our kingdom and the human government. It is what the Guardians intended hundreds of years ago, and you are restoring their great work. A dress is certainly the least I can do for you. Now," she said, taking Andra's hands, "I am certain your groom is waiting for you, so let's be on our way."

Andra followed Camena down the staircase and out of the palace, carefully lifting the hem of the dress, which was obviously tailored for the taller elf queen. They wound their way out of the city proper and into the uninhabited woods. It wasn't long before Andra heard the rushing of the river and the crashing of the waterfall ahead.

Soon, the queen's step slowed, and Andra saw the glow of moonlight reflecting off the river. She drew a deep breath, smoothing her hands over the silk to keep them from trembling. She felt the familiar touch of Tiri's mind, and she opened her thoughts to the dragon.

There was a thrum of happiness in her mind, and Tiri spoke, *"Your mind is bright with joy, sister. I have not felt such happiness in you before."*

Andra let out a breath of laughter. *"And do you feel the fear as well?"* she asked jokingly.

"Yes," Tiri answered, *"but it is not true fear. There is no desire in you to flee. There is no uncertainty in your mind."*

"No. I suppose there isn't."

"You fear only an unexpected change," Tiri said.

"Are you certain we're not Bonded?" Andra asked with a mental laugh. *"You see into my heart far too well."*

"No," Tiri chuckled, *"we do not share a true Bond. But I am beginning to think that the bond we do share is just as strong as any other dragon and Rider."*

Andra smiled and sent as much love through their mental link as she could muster. It was returned to her with a hum of happiness.

At last, the trees parted and Andra stepped out onto the rocky bank of the river. Before her, Eithne and Tiri stood at the edge of the churning water, the waterfall crashing behind them, sending up a spray of silver in the moonlight. Beside their moonlit hides, Vires stood, hands clasped before him. Kael stood beside him.

Andra stopped as her eyes fell on the dark-haired Rider. His black trousers and boots echoed the midnight tones of his hair, and his tunic was a deep red in the growing dark. The weariness was gone from his eyes as he looked at her. They were alight with joy, shining nearly as silver as the moonlight that fell around him.

Vires raised a hand, gesturing Andra to continue forward, to where Camena had moved to stand beside her husband as witness. Andra drew a breath and stepped slowly forward, her hands still and calm. Kael's eyes never left her face, and she never looked away

326 • ERIN SWAN

from him. When she reached him, he took both her hands in his and smiled warmly down at her.

The king spoke, finally drawing their eyes from one another. "I suppose," he said with a smile, "that I shall not delay you with any flowery words. Please, join your hands."

They turned to face Vires, and Andra rested her hand atop Kael's.

"Kael," Vires said, "do you take Andra to be your wife, to defend and protect, to honor, care for, and love through all your days?"

"I do," he answered immediately.

"And will you give everything for her, and promise to be true, and strive to bring her happiness throughout your life together?"

"I will."

Vires's eyes turned to Andra. "Andra," he said, "do you take Kael to be your husband, to honor and care for, and to love through all your days?"

"I do."

"And will you be true and faithful," Vires continued, "and stand beside him in all trials, and strive to bring him happiness throughout your life together?"

Her answer was easy. "I will."

The king produced a pair of silver rings. He took Andra's hand from Kael's and slid one on her middle finger. She looked down at it and could faintly distinguish a silver moon carved into the band. He then slid the other band on the middle finger of Kael's right hand, and she saw that it bore a sun. Vires placed Andra's hand atop Kael's again.

"As the day is not complete without the night," Vires said, "you shall not be complete without one another. By my power as king of Iterum, I declare your two souls to be one, bound for this life and the life to come. Kael, you may kiss your wife."

Andra turned toward her husband with a thrill of excitement.

She barely had time to register his smile shining in the darkness before he pressed his lips to hers in a full, deep, burning kiss. His hands pressed her body to his in shameless desire, and she felt heat course through her veins.

Finally, he pulled away, leaving Andra searching for breath as he turned toward the king and queen. "Thank you," he said with a smile. "Thank you both for doing this."

"It was our pleasure," Vires chuckled. "Now I'll reiterate what I said before: Get some rest. We still have much to do tomorrow."

Kael nodded. "At sunrise, we shall be at your beck and call, Your Majesty. But for one night—" He turned back to Andra, his fingers brushing her cheek. "—I answer only to her."

The queen smiled at his words and took her husband's hand. "Good night to you both," she said with a nod. "We must be on our way."

She led Vires back into the trees and out of sight, leaving Kael and Andra with their dragons. Eithne nosed gently at Andra's shoulder, and the girl turned to her with a smile, stroking the scaled snout.

"*Thank you,*" Eithne said in Andra's mind. "*Thank you for bringing such joy to my Rider's heart.*"

Andra embraced the dragon's face, but turned away as Tiri's snout touched her back. She turned and wrapped her arms around the violet scales as Kael stepped up to his dragon.

"*I wish you every happiness, Andra,*" Tiri said softly in her mind. "*I know that Kael will guard your heart well. It brings me great peace to know that your future is far brighter than your past.*"

"*I hope you're right, Tiri,*" Andra answered, her mind drifting briefly to the battle ahead, and the uncertainty that came along with it.

Tiri felt the direction of her thoughts. "*None of that,*" she said. "*Tonight, you are only a happy bride. Leave thoughts of uncertainty for when the sun has risen.*"

Andra drew away and found Kael waiting for her. He smiled at her, and held out his hand. She took it, their fingers entwining, the silver of their bands touching, sun and moon joining together. For a moment, Andra thought she saw a white, winged shaped flit through the tree branches above them, but it was gone in an instant, and Kael was turning her toward Iterum. Neither of them spoke as they strode through the quiet forest and down the cobbled streets of the city. They passed silently through the palace and out into the courtyard, ascending the steps to Andra's quarters.

She sighed with relief and dropped onto her stomach on top of her bed, kicking her shoes off her feet as she did so, and pressing her face into a pillow. She sank gratefully into the bed, her exhausted body finally relaxing.

She heard Kael laugh, and she turned her head to look at him as he sat in a chair to pull off his boots. "Tired?" he asked.

"Extremely," she answered. Her eyes stayed on him while he stood and stripped off his tunic. Bronze skin turned silver in the light of the full moon outside and she smiled to herself. He disappeared from her line of vision as he walked around to the other side of the bed. She felt the mattress shift with his comforting weight.

She didn't turn her head toward him as she felt him draw closer to her. His lips softly kissed the curve of her neck as his fingers ran down her back, then up again. She lay perfectly still, soaking in his touch, until she felt the laces at the back of the gown begin to loosen.

He kissed the skin of her back as the laces parted, his lips warm. She lay still, barely breathing as his mouth moved lower, kissing between her shoulder blades, down to the small of her back. Slowly, she turned, lying on her side, and he moved to lie beside her. His eyes seemed to reflect the moonlight as he looked at her, reading the hesitancy in her expression.

He touched her cheek softly. "Andra," he said quietly, "I love you."

"I love you too."

"I told you once that I would wait for you to say those words to me. Do you remember?" His eyes were earnest and tender as he spoke.

She nodded. "I do."

"I will always wait for you, Andra," he whispered.

She drew a breath, looking into those stormy eyes. For a moment, she hesitated, painful memories swirling through her mind. But she pressed them down. She'd left that life far behind her. It could not control her now—not tonight. She ran her fingers through his black hair, allowing her hand to come to rest at the nape of his neck.

"We have waited for one another for far too long already," she answered.

His smile echoed hers, and he kissed her. The kiss was slow and deep, and Andra's heart fluttered as she tasted him. All other thoughts fled. The past was gone. The rebellion was gone. All that they had been through and would soon endure was far away and distant. The only thing that existed was the feeling of Kael's arms around her—for one night.

39

A Time of Action

Kael's brow furrowed against the sunlight as it fell across his face. He stretched and sat up, looking around him in mild confusion. Then he remembered. Remembered the million miracles that had happened the day before. The bed beside him was empty, but he found her quickly.

She was standing on the bridge, the sunlight reflecting tones of red off her brown hair. She was already dressed in a tunic and breeches, a brown leather jacket buttoned up against the brisk autumn air. She was leaning against the bridge railing, staring thoughtfully off into the distance.

He slipped quietly from the bed and padded softly across the room, trying to sneak up on her. But she heard him before he had even reached the doorway. Her face turned toward him and smiled reflexively.

"Finally awake?" she asked, moving to meet him as he stepped out onto the bridge.

He gave a small grunt of a response and pulled her into his arms.

He kissed her softly, and felt her lips smile against his. He pulled back and asked, "What time is it?"

She chuckled. "Let's just say that it's closer to lunch than it is to breakfast."

His dark eyebrows rose. "I thought Vires would've sent for us long before now."

"He did," Andra replied sheepishly. "I told him we'd join them as soon as you awoke."

"You didn't need to do that," he said, still holding her tightly against his chest. "You could have woken me."

Andra sighed, resting her head against his shoulder. "Allowing you to sleep was only a small part of the reason I delayed it," she answered.

"And what was the larger part?"

She paused briefly, then answered in a soft voice, "I didn't want our one night to end."

Kael exhaled heavily and rested his cheek atop her sun-warmed hair. "Neither do I," he whispered back. A brief silence stretched between them, and he closed his eyes, soaking in the warmth of her body, encased in his arms. Finally, he forced himself to draw back. "But we made a promise—to the Freemen and to ourselves." He looked down at her, his hands resting on her shoulders. "We must see this through," he said.

"I know," Andra answered with a nod, her expression hardening with determination.

He brushed a strand of hair from her forehead. "One week more," he reminded her. "Then we can have as many nights for us as the gods will allow."

She smiled softly and rose to her toes, kissing him warmly. Kael allowed his fingers to grip her waist, pulling her closer, heat rising in his veins as her fingers brushed over his bare chest. Then she pulled away, making him groan in disappointment.

"Get dressed," she laughed. "The Riders will be waiting for us."

Kael noticed how she didn't say "the other Riders." Despite all she had done and all she had accomplished for the rebellion, Andra still did not refer to herself as a Rider. She accepted it when others said it, and did not argue with Tiri when the dragon referred to her as her Rider, but she would still not say it herself. He wondered briefly what it would take for her to see herself as the Rider that everyone else saw.

Pushing the thoughts aside, Kael quickly dressed, then followed Andra down the staircase and through the doors to the palace. They rounded the central tree, and the men seated around the table turned to look at them.

"Ah!" Vires called with a smile. "Kael, I see you've awoken at last."

"I apologize," Kael replied as he and Andra took a pair of empty chairs at the table. "I hope I didn't cause too much delay."

"Not at all," Vires replied. "Captain Raelia was just giving me her report."

Kael looked at the elf to whom Vires had gestured and found that there were several new faces at the table, all of them elven. The armies of the elven nation had arrived. The captain in question, Raelia, nodded at Kael, sizing him up with sharp amethyst eyes. Her long, black hair hung in a braid over her shoulder, and her pointed ears were cuffed in metal in the fashion of the Nidus elves from the west.

She looked back to Vires and continued speaking, evidently feeling no obligation to rehash whatever Andra and Kael may have missed. "There are still two companies from Nidus that are journeying here, each with a hundred soldiers. They will be the last of the elven army to arrive, and they should reach Iterum within a day."

Vires nodded. "Excellent."

"And what of the Freemen and dwarves?" Kael asked. "Any word from them?"

Egan spoke. "We received a runner from our people only an hour ago," he said. "They are making good time, with the dwarves guiding them through the tunnels. The first of our soldiers should arrive two days from now, with the remainder reaching the tunnels below Iterum in four days."

"And the election is in seven days," an elven Rider remarked. "We should begin stationing our troops near the Hall as soon as possible."

"Agreed," Vires said. "Since my troops have begun to arrive, I shall have my captains begin taking up discreet positions in the forests, here." He leaned forward, his slim finger tracing a curve of forested ridges just north of the Hall. "I shall send several of my Riders with them."

"Won't they draw attention, gathering that close to the Hall?" Andra asked.

"It's breeding season for the dragons," another Rider replied. "We'll keep our dragons unsaddled and arrive individually or in pairs. They'll pass for wild ones gathering to breed."

"We can place additional battalions here and here," Vires went on, touching two spots south of the Hall. "With a proper ward, they can avoid detection for several days in those woods."

Kael nodded, eyeing the map, envisioning the troops' movements. Where would Caedo place his men? He mentally noted several strategic positions on the map, including the ridges north of the Hall, which Vires had indicated. Of course, Vereor was only four miles to the west. It would be possible to position a small strike force close to the Hall, and have the majority of his troops move in from the human capital. If he chose that approach, the Freemen could secure victory by simply being closer to the Hall. Capturing the Hall would give them a firm defensive position and a strong advantage over any attacks from Caedo's Kingsmen.

"Any news of movements around the Hall?" Kael asked, looking

334 • ERIN SWAN

up at the faces around him. "Any sign of the Kingsmen preparing themselves for the coup?"

One of Vires's men shook his head. "None yet. We have several spies in the forests around the Hall, maintaining a watch. They haven't spotted any troops or suspicious movements among the Riders. Though preparations have begun at the Hall for the arrival of all eleven of the remaining judges, everything else remains as usual."

"And the tunnels beneath the Hall? Caedo used dwarf tunnels to attack us in Bellris. He may use them again to attack the Hall."

"No movement there either," Egan answered.

Kael fell silent, musing over the map. His brother was far more calculated than this. Caedo would be planning, preparing, positioning himself in any way he could to assure his victory. Caedo left nothing to chance. But he did have that sorceress on his knee. Perhaps she would provide him with some way to move his troops in quickly. But Kael had no way of predicting what that might be.

With a sigh, he forced himself to focus on another issue at hand. "What of the Riders' dragons?" he asked.

"There will be too many Riders present for all their dragons to be at the Hall," Janis said. "Our sources tell us that the dragons will rest here, in the caves of the southern cliffs." The young man indicated the southern edge of the continent, which was fifteen miles south of the Hall. "When the battle begins," Janis went on, "we will have some time before any of the Riders' dragons arrive."

Kael mulled this over for a moment. They could attempt to intercept the dragons, but there would be no way of knowing which of them would be coming to fight with them and which would be against them. But letting them all descend on the Hall at once was a desperate roll of the dice—one they had to take.

"Well," Kael sighed quietly, "it seems as if all our plans are in place."

Vires nodded slowly once more. "Indeed it does. The time for talking has ended. Now it is time for us to take action."

40

The Violet Flame

The Freemen began to arrive in two days, as scheduled. On the day of their arrival, Kael escorted Andra down a long, steeply declining tunnel that carved its way through the earth. An orb lit the path ahead of them, gliding on through the tunnel, tethered to Kael's magic.

They descended deeper and deeper into the earth until the sounds of hundreds of voices began to reach her ears, echoing off stone and earth. Finally, up ahead, Andra saw the glow of fires, torches, and more hovering orbs. They stepped out of the narrow tunnel into a large, open chamber.

Before her sprawled a bustling army camp. Tents were pitched around glowing fires; horses were stamping their hooves, impatiently awaiting their supper. Men and women shouted to one another, and soldiers sparred in an open space near the back walls. A deep, rough voice called out, and Kael stopped.

She followed his gaze and found three short, broad-chested men approaching them, bearing hammers and spears. Beneath their gleaming metal helms, unkempt beards sprouted from ruddy faces, spreading across their mail-covered chests. Though each of the three dwarves was well outfitted in armor with sturdy hammers and short spears, Andra could tell that they were not comfortable carrying the weapons. Dwarves were experts at crafting armor and weapons—not using them.

"Identify yourselves," the dwarf in the lead barked at them.

"Riders Kael and Andra," Kael replied with a brisk nod.

The dwarf seemed to recognize the name, because he immediately straightened and saluted them with a clenched fist to his forehead. "Commander Kael. Captain Andra. It is a great honor to fight with your people."

Kael returned the salute. "We are grateful for the support you've given to the Freemen, Captain . . ."

"Solrek," the dwarf provided. "I was captain of the king's guard, and I now lead the dwarves who have chosen to fight and claim vengeance for the dwarven blood that these Kingsmen shed in our halls."

Kael nodded. "I assure you, you shall have justice for the kinsmen you lost."

"Come, this way," Solrek said, turning toward the camp. "I'll take you to the rebel leaders with this contingent."

Andra and Kael followed the three dwarves between the tents to a central fire, where there were several humans gathered. One of them looked up, and Andra felt a thrill of joy at the familiar face.

"Alik!" she called.

The burly man smiled back at her and approached them. He roughly accepted Andra's embrace, then clapped Kael on the shoulder. "It is good to see you again, brother," he said.

"And you," Kael answered, gripping the man's forearm.

Alik looked down at Kael's hand and raised an eyebrow. "Is that an elven wedding band I see?" he asked.

Kael smiled and drew back his arm, looking down at the sun-carved ring. "It is," he answered.

Alik's brown eyes darted down to Andra's hand, and he smiled. "I'm glad to see it," he said. "It seems that this battle has hastened many things along." He held up his own hand to show a thick, roughly hewn band around the fourth finger of his left hand, in the human tradition.

"Is Syra here?" Andra asked eagerly.

Alik nodded. "She is. She's with Amala, receiving additional training in treating wounds. She'll be acting as Amala's assistant during the battle."

As much as Andra wished to find her friend, she and Kael had not come to socialize.

"Have you sent any men on to scout the tunnels beneath the Hall?" Kael asked.

Alik nodded. "They left a few hours ago. It will still be some time before they return. They're doing a thorough sweep before we begin sending our troops into position."

"Good," Kael answered.

"How much training have the dwarves received?" Andra asked, glancing at the short, thick men who strode through the camp.

"As much as we've been able to give them while on the move," Alik sighed. "The king's guards are fair hands at battle, and all dwarves are quite strong. They can take a hit better than any man or elf I've seen. But there's not much strategy to their fighting."

Kael nodded, his face thoughtful. "We'll pair each of our battalions with a small contingent of dwarves. Hopefully our magic-wielders and more experienced swordsmen will give them enough advantage in the battle to put those hammers to good use."

There was a brief silence, and Alik fixed Kael with a considering look. "And how much advantage do you think we have in this battle, Commander?" he asked grimly.

Kael's answer was quick and sure. "We have one advantage, Alik. Only one." He turned his eyes on Andra, eyes filled with confidence—confidence in her. Confidence that she could not share.

———◦◦◦———

Andra rubbed one of her arms against the early morning chill. The air was crisp and sharp with the deepening autumn, and the leaves were bright with a splendor of colors. The same reds and yellows and golds that she had watched from so many windows over the years surrounded her in blazing color. She thought of how she had watched the trees drop their leaves in years past, drifting one by one to the earth, finally leaving the trees bare.

She had watched the snowfall from those same windows, had touched the cold glass and wished she could simply stand in the snow for a moment, feel the flakes kissing her skin. And she realized with a pang of regret that she may not live to experience winter outside the walls of a judge's manor.

Her hand rested on the hilt of her Rider's sword. One of their spies in Vereor had managed to retrieve Andra's effects from where Caedo had stowed them. It turned out that some of the judge's guards were quite easy to bribe for such things. It felt good to have it at her side again, to have the familiar black leather on her hands and her jacket over her back. She felt . . . safer with them, somehow.

Tiri's snout touched her shoulder, and she looked up at her violet face. *"Your mind wanders, Andra,"* the dragon said. *"You should be focused on the battle ahead of us."*

Andra sighed, her breath leaving a cloud of fog in the air before her. *"I know,"* she answered silently.

Her eyes scanned the faces that had gathered in the field around her. There were hundreds of soldiers—human, elf, and dwarf— and several dragons. This was to be their strike force. In a few moments, Andra and Tiri would leave them behind and charge into the Hall, unprotected, and hope that the Riders gathered there would listen to the words of a girl who sat astride a wild dragon.

"I will protect you, sister," Tiri promised in her mind.

"I know you will, Tiri," Andra replied, pressing her cheek against the dragon's forehead. The scales were chilled with the cold of the night. *"I just . . ."* She sighed aloud. In the battle for Bellris, Andra had felt some comfort in knowing that Tiri would not fall with her, should she be killed. But somehow, with this new fight looming before her, she felt only a deep desire to have the dragon's mind connected to hers, to feel her presence through every moment of what they were about to face. *"I feel that this would all be easier, that I would feel safer and stronger, if I shared a true Bond with you."*

She felt the dragon's yearning pressing against her mind. *"I wish the same,"* the dragon answered. *"With all my heart, I wish it were so."*

A feeling of warmth, love, and longing enveloped Andra's mind, making her heart ache, and she pressed the feelings back upon the dragon's thoughts. Tiri thrummed deeply in her throat, and in the back of her mind, the well of magic thrummed an answer.

Andra gripped the shining magic in her mind and the warm presence of Tiri in her thoughts, holding fast to them both—her two sources of strength. She looked down into Tiri's shining amethyst eye, and something in the dragon's gaze caught her, transfixed her.

She felt a hand touch her shoulder. "Andra," Kael said softly. "It's time."

But she didn't turn toward him. She stood, her hand on Tiri's snout, her eyes gazing into the bright jewel of the dragon's eye. Tiri continued to thrum in her throat, and the magic in Andra's mind continued to hum an answer. Andra gripped the vibrating magic tighter, drawing on it, though she did not know what she was trying to do. She knew only that she wanted that power to touch the warmth of Tiri's presence in her mind.

She felt Tiri's thoughts pressing forward as well, feeling the dragon's desire to bring their minds closer, to sense every part of the girl's thoughts. *Please,* Andra thought, her body beginning to tremble with the effort of drawing on her magic. *Please, let us be one.*

There was a sudden burst of light, illuminating the gray twilight in a flash of brilliance that would have stood out on the brightest day of summer. A searing sensation sprang to life in Andra's hand, where it rested on Tiri's snout. Her body tensed, but she could not pull her hand away. It was as if her skin had been joined to the dragon's scales.

The burning raged up her arm, invisible flames seeming to sear at her flesh, sending pain along her palm and forearm, climbing up her skin to her elbow. Andra tried to scream, but her lips would not part. She stood frozen, rigid, as her magic blazed brightly in her mind, mingling with a clear and powerful presence that touched her thoughts.

A sequence of images began to flash through Andra's mind— memories that were not her own. The first ray of light as she began to crack through the hard shell of her egg. The pale face of a girl on the rafters high above her, a feeling of yearning to reach that face. The feeling of the wind under her wings as she spread them and rose into the sky for the first time. The sensation of flames burning across her tongue as she breathed her first flames. The images and feelings came faster and faster until they began to blur together in Andra's mind, mingling with her own thoughts, becoming a part of her. She was wild and temperamental. She was loyal and passionate and stubborn. She was Tiri.

Then, suddenly, the images and feelings ended. The blaze of light vanished, and Andra dropped to the grass, drawing in a shuddering gasp. She gripped her forearm to her chest, groaning in pain, her head pounding.

"Andra!" she heard someone call over the ringing in her ears. "Andra!" She blinked, and the spots cleared from her vision to reveal Kael kneeling above her. "Andra, are you hurt? What happened?"

She blinked again, sitting up as the pain in her arm began to ebb. She continued to cradle it to the leather armor she wore as she sat up and looked at the dragon beside her. Tiri turned her eyes on the girl, and Andra felt a clear flash of confusion.

The clarity of the emotion surprised her, and almost immediately, her sense of surprise was returned to her in another flash of feelings that were not her own. In rapid succession, emotions rebounded from her own mind to the dragon's, and within seconds, she knew that Tiri had experienced the same flood of memories and feelings. Without having to form her thoughts into words, Andra shared her brief confusion, surprise, and then a feeling of clarity.

Tiri sent one word across their link, and it echoed clearly and powerfully in Andra's mind. *"Bonded."*

Slowly, Andra pulled her arm away from her chest and looked down at it. There, reflecting the light of the rising sun in an array of violets, was a flame. But it was not the flame that other Riders bore. The purple fire began in the center of her palm and spread out over her forearm, curling tendrils of flame winding across her skin like a breath of fire from a dragon's tongue, reaching up her arm.

Kneeling beside her, Kael took her arm gingerly between his hands. He looked down at it for a long, silent moment, then up at Andra's face. "Andra . . . Are you . . . ?"

She let out a sharp laugh and sprang to her feet, rushing past Kael and throwing her arms around Tiri's face. The dragon's happiness sang through her mind, their silent laughter mingling in Andra's thoughts, sounding as one.

Kael was suddenly at her side again. He gripped her right wrist and, without a word, raised it over their heads. The eyes around them took in the shining violet flame briefly, and then a cheer began to rise from the crowd. It echoed in the quiet of the morning, growing louder as every voice in the field chanted it, fists thrusting into the air.

"Veholum! Veholum! Veholum!"

Beside her, Tiri bugled triumphantly at the sky. In a nearby tree, Andra spotted the white form of Astrum, perched above the crowd, watching with approving golden eyes.

Andra laughed, feeling the dragon's strength and certainty and power flooding into her body, becoming her own. The chant continued around them, rising with the dawn. She sent her thoughts, filled with joy and confidence, to the dragon's ever-present mind.

"We are one, Tiri. We are sisters of mind and heart. We are Sky Riders."

41

Words

Andra and Tiri had only a handful of minutes to process the sudden change in their bond, and no time to seek an explanation for it. Not that Andra thought there would be one. She knew that what had just happened between them was unprecedented in the world of Riders. Even Astrum had offered no words of explanation for how this could have happened.

The immortal Seer had simply nodded at Andra once before saying, "May the gods be with you." And then he'd darted from his perch and disappeared above the trees.

With Tiri's mind shining brightly in her thoughts, Andra climbed into the saddle on the dragon's back. She looked down as she felt someone grab her boot, and found Kael stepping onto Tiri's foreleg. He pulled himself up high enough to reach her face, then drew her lips down to his. She expected a deep, passionate farewell kiss, but the touch was slow and soft, and somehow, she felt that she could taste sadness in it.

Kael pulled back and looked up at her, his eyes filled with worry.

"I will follow you as soon as I can," he promised quietly. "Be safe, my love."

Andra nodded. "I will see you soon," she said, forcing certainty into her voice.

He stepped down from Tiri's leg, and with a last glance back at him, Andra signaled her readiness to the dragon. She felt the muscles beneath her coil, sensing the tension in her mind, and then the moment of release as Tiri sprang into the sky, wings opening and beating, pulling them into the sky and above the thick covering of clouds, remaining out of sight.

"Our first true flight as dragon and Rider," Tiri said in a quiet, contented voice.

Andra smiled briefly to herself. *"It feels very different,"* she remarked. *"It feels . . . easier, somehow. I know every move you're about to make before you make it. I know every movement of your tail, every shift you sense in the wind. It almost feels like your wings are my own."*

"They are *your wings, Andra."*

Andra felt the words more than she heard them, and she smiled yet again at the warm feeling of companionship that spread through her. Soon, however, Andra knew they must be drawing close to the Hall. Tiri dipped below the clouds, catching a glimpse of the brown stone towers rising above the treetops. Then she pulled back above the clouds again.

The election would be starting soon. They simply had to remain above the clouds until their man inside gave her the signal that Caedo was present. Tiri circled lazily on an eddy of wind, her sharp eyes scanning the sky around them. It would be unlikely for a Rider to be flying this high while approaching the Hall; they tended to remain easily visible on their approach, so as not to appear a threat. Still, Andra felt her dragon's alertness.

As the minutes ticked by, her heart began to race in her chest. What would she say to these men? How could she persuade them to fight alongside a rebellion that they may not have even known existed?

She felt Tiri's emotions press against hers, radiating confidence and calm. Before, the emotions would have just touched Andra's mind, letting her know what Tiri felt. But now, they seeped into her thoughts, the emotions becoming her own, slowing her heart and steadying her hands.

"Thank you," Andra whispered in her mind.

"This is our best hope," Tiri told her. *"I know that you shall succeed in bringing Riders to the Freemen's aid."*

"I hope you're right," Andra answered.

Before the dragon could respond, a streak of light shot up through the clouds, bursting above Andra's head in a rainbow of color—the signal that Caedo had arrived. Immediately, Tiri's wings closed to her side, and she pointed her nose to the ground. She didn't slowly circle downward as she normally would have. They needed speed and surprise. So the violet dragon dropped like a stone from the clouds, making Andra's heart rise into her throat and her stomach churn violently again. Her eyes watered from the rush of air against her face, and she squinted to see the grass racing up to meet them.

At the last moment, Tiri gave a powerful backward thrust of her wings, and she landed with a heavy *thump* just outside the doors to the Hall. They both glanced quickly around them once. Someone was staring at them—a serving woman with a bucket in her hands—her eyes wide and her lips slightly parted. They ignored her and turned their eyes to the massive doors in front of them.

She felt Tiri's muscles coil underneath her, and Andra braced herself in the saddle, touching her magic and drawing up an invisible shield around her. Then Tiri rose onto her hind legs and, with a furious roar, slammed her front feet against the wood, sending them both hurtling into the large, crowded Hall.

Andra heard shouts of surprise, which quickly turned into gasps of wonder as the hundreds of eyes fell on the deep purple hide of the dragon. It was exactly how Andra remembered it, when she had climbed the rafters and spotted Tiri for the first time from above. For a breath of time, their memories of that moment flickered between their two minds, and Andra felt the yearning that Tiri had felt while trying to reach her, so high above.

Then they both forced themselves to focus. The seated spectators had fallen silent, staring at Andra and Tiri, as if waiting for some kind of explanation for the interruption, and for the presence of a violet dragon in the Hall. In the center of the arena, Caedo was standing on the steps of a wooden platform. They had interrupted him just as he was preparing to present himself to the gathered Riders. His blue-gray eyes were narrowed slightly, taking in the slim form in the saddle, surprise and disbelief mingling in his expression. Tormina stood at the base of the platform, her unremarkable face contorted into a sneer.

Andra felt something slam against her mind, making her wince in surprise and mild pain. But her shield held, and Tormina's face went red with fury. Tiri's roar had long since died away in the echoing room. No breath ruffled the air. In the silence, Andra slid down from the saddle and stepped toward the platform. Tiri followed behind her, her angular head low, her lips curled backward in a snarl, a warning.

Andra regarded the gathering of Riders, all in identical black jackets and cropped gloves, swords belted at their waists. Most of them had one hand on their sword hilts, their expressions tense and uncertain. The other ten judges were present as well, blinking in surprise at Andra and Tiri's sudden appearance. The remainder of the Hall was empty, save for a few servants and contracted workers, who peered curiously out of corners and doorways at the commotion.

One face caught her eye, nearly making her stumble at its familiarity. Talias watched her from a narrow corridor, his eyes wide with disbelief. She met his gaze and felt a pang in her chest. He and the other servants would be in danger when battle broke out around the Hall.

Her thoughts found his, unguarded and filled with wonder, and she allowed a tiny crack in her shield. *"Servants' quarters. Barricade,"* she said in his mind.

Andra saw the young man's lips part in surprise at her silent voice in his thoughts, but she quickly slammed the walls down around her mind again, before Tormina could force her way through the crack in her defenses. After a moment, Talias nodded, then disappeared down the corridor.

Andra breathed a small sigh of relief, then cast one long look at Tormina as she passed her. The sorceress's face was nearly purple, and Andra felt a sharp pressure against her mind as the woman tried to pierce the shield she'd raised. But nothing more. She gave her a small, satisfied smile, then turned toward the steps. Caedo was frozen there, halfway up to the platform, his face a mixture of fury, surprise, disbelief, and amusement.

Tiri continued to press calm confidence into Andra's mind, keeping her steps steady, her chin up, her expression certain. "Excuse me," she said quietly as she stepped around Caedo's still form and climbed onto the platform. Tiri crouched beside the wooden structure, her fangs still bared, her eyes darting around the room, searching for a threat. Andra stared out at the Riders, their eyes suddenly focused on her and her alone, none of them certain of what to expect from the small woman arrayed in full Rider effects who had dismounted an amethyst dragon.

She glanced briefly at Caedo, and saw him looking at Tormina with a furious expression. It was clear on his face that he wanted the Dark sorceress to do something, but the woman clenched her jaw and shook her head sharply. She could not touch Andra, no matter how hard she tried.

Andra looked away from them and down at her own hands.

Despite Tiri's efforts, they were beginning to tremble. Slowly, methodically, Andra pulled off her gloves. She looked at the shimmering flame on her right hand and forearm, then drew a deep breath and looked up at the Riders.

Ledo had once taught her about the power of her words. And now, she would put that lesson to good use. She was no longer a servant girl, scared and silent. She had found her voice. And her words now would hold more power than they had ever held before.

She swallowed and spoke. "I know why you are all here," she said. Several of the Riders leaned forward, straining to catch her words. She raised her voice and continued, "As Riders pledged to Vereor, you are here to give your sustaining vote to your new Chief Judge, Caedo." She glanced over her shoulder at the man. He had climbed the final steps up to the platform and stood on the far end from her, his scowl deepening.

She ignored him and turned back to the Riders, who were beginning to look intrigued. "Before the Riders provide their vote, however, the law dictates that any Rider who wishes it may speak against the new Chief Judge. You see, despite all the laws and traditions, I too am a Rider." She held out her marked hand so that they could see the flame, and a soft murmur went through them at the strangeness of the mark; but none could deny what it was. She gestured at the violet dragon below her. "Tiri is my dragon. Nearly two years ago, an amethyst hatchling was removed from the arena before she could be Paired. It was a series of fateful events that led to her egg being in the arena on that day, but we were destined to be Bonded. Though we missed the allotted time to be Paired, Tiri found me again more than a year later. And now, she has been able to mark me as her Rider.

"And, as a Rider, I oppose the election of this man. My reasons are many, but I ask you to hear only two. One, you may have heard rumors of. His mistress, Tormina, is a Dark sorceress." A few Riders turned and whispered to one another, but Andra continued

350 • ERIN SWAN

on. "I was a victim of torture at her hand, by the power of Dark magic, and at Caedo's bidding. And, as you know, the law states that no man who condones the use of Dark magic may sit in judgment over Paerolia."

"Shut up!" a furious voice shouted. Every eye in the room moved away from Andra, and she turned to stare at Caedo, his face contorted with rage, his fists shaking at his sides. "You lie! You are a filthy, lying rebel! Somebody seize this girl!"

Nobody moved. The Riders and soldiers in the arena continued to watch Andra with interest, ignoring Caedo's outburst.

Andra looked back at the Riders and continued as if the man had not spoken. "I can't prove what she is. But I believe some of you may be able to sense it about her, the coldness of her magic. It is not truly evidence, but you know in your gut that there is Darkness in her."

"Without proof, you cannot oppose me!" Caedo snapped, stepping toward her.

Beside the platform, Tiri snarled a warning, and the young judge took a hasty step backward.

"There is a second point that I wish for you all to bear in mind," Andra said. "Caedo does not intend to be contented with the seat of Chief Judge. He would have, instead, a throne—as emperor of Paerolia. He leads a band who call themselves Kingsmen, and if you place him on the judgment seat today, he will use his armies to turn that seat into the throne he desires."

She steadied herself with a breath, then continued once more. "Riders . . . my fellow Riders, I ask you now to truly consider the vote you are about to cast." She held her right hand out to them again, pleadingly, showing them the mark that they shared. "I know that my bearing a mark is not something that any would expect. Perhaps some of you oppose it. But I do bear it. I am bound to Tiri as surely as you are bound to your dragons. And I ask you, as a Rider, to see what I can see. To recognize that the man standing here for your vote is not worthy of it, nor worthy of the judgment seat.

"This day will not end with your vote. A battle is at our doors, even now. And I ask you—I beg you—to cast your lots with us, the Freemen, and help to bring Paerolia back to the peace and freedom that the Guardians worked so hard to create for us."

A deep hush fell over the arena. The Riders were exchanging glances, eyebrows raised or drawn together in confusion, lips pursed in thought or pressed in a tight line. They made no move to vote, or do anything else besides look at each other, waiting for someone to speak.

Finally, one of the elder Riders stepped forward. He glanced at Caedo's furious face, at Andra and Tiri, and finally turned to face the other Riders. He cleared his throat. "Riders," he said loudly, "my brothers of flight and flame. The time has come again for us to give our allegiance to the Chief Judge. In doing so, we pledge ourselves to his service, and declare before all the land that we find him worthy to lead us. If, for any reason, you do not believe that he is worthy of the power that comes with his seat, do not give your vote." He paused, as if thinking through the final words of the traditional speech. Finally, he said, "All in favor?"

Andra held her breath, her eyes frantically scanning the faces of the nearly sixty men and boys in front of her. She knew, somewhere in the Hall, their spy waited to signal their troops. This vote would tell them how many—if any—Andra had brought to their side of the battle. The Riders glanced at each other nervously, looking to see what the others would do. Slowly, one of the elder Riders lifted his hand. Those of his generation of Riders followed. A few more hands began to rise as well. Andra's heart began to sink.

Then she saw arms crossing over chests, firmly refusing to give their allegiance, young faces hard as they scowled at the Riders who lifted their hands. The newest Riders, the twelve-year-olds from the Pairing she'd interrupted, crossed their arms as well. The hands stopped rising, and Andra quickly counted the hands in the air. Twenty-seven. Joy swelled inside her. Only twenty-seven.

"Any opposed?" the eldest Rider asked. He paused, then raised his own hand.

Andra watched happily as the rest of the Riders, the majority, refused to give their allegiance to Caedo, refused to allow him to retain the judgment seat, and cast their lots in with the rebels. A small laugh escaped her.

"Now!" Caedo screamed furiously. "Tormina! Bring me that girl's head!"

A sudden flurry of shouts and movement filled the arena as men rushed from hidden corners, seeming to appear from the shadows themselves, charging forward with swords raised. There was a burst of living darkness, and black shapes raced at the Riders. The men shouted, raising shields and swinging swords at the shadowy attackers. Several of them were enveloped in the shapes, screaming in agony as they were pulled to the ground.

Andra saw with a shock that the Riders were beginning to turn on one another. Those who had pledged themselves to Caedo turned against those who had sided with the Freemen; colored swords clashed against one another, and bursts of magic exploded in the arena. Andra leapt from the platform and landed in Tiri's saddle as the arena doors flew open. The sea of blue tunics told her immediately that these were not her Freemen.

With a flash of panic, Andra threw a powerful shield around all the Riders, unable to separate those who were her allies from those who were her enemies. A transparent, blue-violet bubble appeared around them all, encasing the battles that raged between them, but keeping the incoming soldiers and Tormina's magic from touching them. The Freemen needed those allies. She had to protect them as best she could.

She pressed her intentions against Tiri's mind and the dragon responded instinctively, turning toward the doors and releasing a jet of flame. The soldiers immediately ceased the forward charge, raising arms and shields to deflect the inferno, but they were unnecessary. A cold wind roared across the arena, dispelling Tiri's fire, protecting the troops.

Andra turned her eyes on Tormina, who stood at the side of the arena, a snarl on her face. Andra felt a growl rising in her throat even as Tiri growled beneath her. As much as she yearned to face the sorceress directly, Andra knew she had to delay the incoming troops, who seemed to have appeared immediately outside the arena doors, until the Freemen could arrive. She turned her eyes away from the black-clad woman and focused on the wave of armored men who now raced at her.

She touched her magic and the thrumming power that was Tiri in her mind. And, after a deep breath, the battle truly began.

42

Battle of the Hall

A crack of lightning bolted down from the ceiling, sending waves of energy through the air as it struck the center of the incoming horde. Men screamed as they were thrown through the air or burned in their armor. Andra attempted to pull down another bolt, but Tormina was prepared this time. The lightning disappeared into a cloud of blackness that seemed to completely devour the bolt of power.

Andra sent waves of fire roaring toward the men. A few struck, driving the soldiers backward several feet before Tormina managed to intervene once again, wicking away the flames like a candle in a strong wind. The sorceress still could not touch her directly; Andra's shield held firm. But Tormina was doing all in her power to make Andra completely impotent.

Andra pulled up a wall of earth, holding the men back, close to the doors. Tormina ripped it down with a wave of blackness. Andra summoned a ring of fire to encase the soldiers. Tormina snuffed it out as easily as she had the other flames.

Frustration welled up inside her as the soldiers reached the ward she'd raised around the Riders. Inside, the Riders continued to battle one another, but the soldiers pounded against the shield, still held back. Andra felt their blows in her mind and knew that she would not be able to maintain the shield and her own ward for long.

Then she felt something familiar touch her mind. A warm, loving caress against her thoughts. She couldn't allow her mind to open to it without exposing herself to Tormina's incessant mental blows, but she knew immediately who it was. Kael and the Freemen had arrived.

She heard voices rising outside the Hall and the roars of dragons. Then, from above the arena seats, men and elves in green and brown tunics began to appear. Armored dwarves dotted their ranks, waving enormous hammers and axes above their heads. The Freemen quickly descended the steep steps, surefooted elves leading the charge.

The Kingsmen, startled to be attacked from within the arena, turned their attention away from the Riders and toward the new threat. In the open doorway, Andra saw blue-clad soldiers turning to the rear, facing another attack from outside the Hall.

"Secure the Hall!" Caedo was shouting. He'd retreated to Tormina's side, hiding half behind her like a child behind its mother's skirts. "Drive them out! Hold the Hall!"

"Drop the ward!" another voice bellowed.

Andra looked down to see that a Rider was shouting at her, beating a fist against her shield. Many of the Riders within had fallen, but they continued to fight one another. Roars of fury echoed above and around the Hall, and she saw flashes of fire through the windows. The Riders' dragons were beginning to arrive. She quickly dropped her shield, and the Riders charged away from one another, racing toward the doors, shoving soldiers aside with body and magic.

She then turned toward where Tormina and Caedo had stood,

bracing herself to deal with the Dark sorceress. But they were both gone.

"*They vanished,*" Tiri remarked. "*They were both here a moment ago.*"

"*No time to search for them,*" Andra replied. "*We'll be needed outside with the other Riders. Let's go!*" Tiri immediately charged forward, racing headlong into the wall of men before her. Soldiers dove out of her path while others were plowed under clawed feet. The Freemen's foot soldiers would have to face the Kingsmen within the Hall. The sky was where Andra was needed.

She pushed back as many soldiers as she could with her magic, but she could feel the well of power beginning to drain already. She had to conserve her strength as best she could. Andra and Tiri charged through the open doorway, and the violet dragon leapt quickly into the sky, swooping over the heads of battling Kingsmen and Freemen. Above them, the sky was a chaos of fire and magic as Riders and dragons battled with one another.

"*How do we know who fights with us?*" Tiri asked, anxiety pulsing in her mind.

Then Andra saw the blue sigil that seemed to glow on the breasts of some of the Riders—a sword crossed with an olive branch. They had marked their own allegiances with magic. Dragons darted across the sky, clashing and rolling, roaring and snapping, claws scraping over scales and tearing at wings. Andra's heart clenched with pain.

"*Dragons should not turn against their own like this.*"

It took her a moment to realize that the thought and the accompanying pain had been Tiri's.

"*Nor should Riders,*" Andra answered. Riders had not fought against one another since the Guardians had created peace between the races. This went against all that the Guardians had built. And yet, it was necessary to restore what they had built as well. Andra steeled herself, and Tiri responded by charging into the battle with a furious roar.

Immediately, a blue dragon, its Rider bearing the glowing symbol of the judges, turned toward them, releasing a jet of flame. Andra raised a shield before Tiri, and the fire parted around them in a cone of heat. The violet dragon flew headlong into her opponent, ending his jet of flame as her jaws clamped around his neck.

Andra clung to the saddle, barely retaining her seat as they careened toward the ground, the dragons snapping and clawing as they fell. The ground raced up toward them, and Tiri finally sprang away, both dragons rising suddenly back into the air. At a silent signal from Andra, Tiri doubled back, darting away from their enemy, allowing Andra to reorient her spinning vision. Kael had not been exaggerating when he told her that fighting aboard a dragon was like saddling a desert sandstorm.

The blue dragon began pursuit, but was suddenly cut off as a snarling red beast crashed into him from above. As the pair collided, the Rider aboard the red dragon released a ball of magic that struck the other Rider, sending him careening toward the ground. The blue dragon sprang away from his enemy, chasing down his Rider.

The red dragon drew up close to Tiri, and Andra looked at Kael's hard face, gleaming with sweat. She felt his mind touch hers, and she allowed his thoughts in. He gave her a small smile, and she returned it before they charged back into battle together. The red and violet dragons flew close beside each other, climbing, circling, and spiraling as four other dragons chased them across the sky.

Andra's mind was only one of four parts of a single mind. Her thoughts mingled with Tiri's, Eithne's, and Kael's all at once. She knew that it should have been a confusing chaos, but it wasn't. She knew in an instant what Eithne would do next, and felt Tiri's immediate response as she followed the more experienced dragon's instruction. Andra could hear Kael speaking to her as well as to

Eithne, giving instruction. They spoke more by instinct and feeling than by words.

"*Split*," Andra thought. She felt Kael's reluctance to leave her side, then his agreement, followed by both dragons' understanding. Less than a second later, Eithne and Tiri dropped in a steep dive toward the trees. At the last moment, they pulled in opposite directions, making themselves parallel to the canopy at the same moment.

Their four pursuers seemed confused for a moment; then three followed the larger Eithne, one continuing its pursuit of Tiri. Andra glanced back at the winged creature behind them. It was larger than Tiri, and Andra could already feel the sharp pressure of a more experienced mind pressing against her own.

Suddenly, Tiri jerked hard to the left, nearly throwing Andra from the saddle. She glanced frantically around and saw that two more Kingsmen Riders had entered the airborne flight, flanking the one dragon that had been in pursuit. One of the dragons shot hot flame at Tiri's wing. Andra threw her mind outward just in time to rebuff the flickering tendrils of fire.

Tiri darted around the massive shadow of the Hall, trying to lose some of their pursuers, but to no avail. "*Getting tired,*" the dragon panted in Andra's mind. "*They're gaining on me.*"

"*Higher. Into the clouds. Rejoin Kael and Eithne.*"

The other dragon and Rider heard her thoughts, and they both climbed quickly into the clouds, the two dragons once again flying close together, a mass of six others now pursuing them. Andra's thoughts were quick as they darted into the minds of Eithne, Tiri, and Kael. Then Tiri broke away again, and their three followers were close behind. The violet dragon circled and twisted above the Hall, then looped around back onto their former path.

Ahead of them, Andra could see Eithne barely managing to avoid the attacks of her three pursuers. She urged Tiri forward, and the young dragon put on another burst of speed, jerking away from another enemy's snapping jaws. As she drew up behind those that followed Eithne, the elder dragon suddenly dropped downward and slipped back in a barrel roll, sliding underneath one of the enemy dragons just as Tiri closed in above it.

Eithne snapped at the dragon's legs from underneath, making it jerk upward, right into Tiri. The young dragon clamped her jaws around the dragon's neck and shook violently, making the other cry out in pain. Andra clung to the saddle as her mount writhed in the sky, falling with their enemy, claws raking against scales. Then Tiri kicked away and jerked them back up into the sky as the other dragon crashed through the trees, slamming into the ground with an earthshaking rumble.

Andra could feel Tiri's sides heaving beneath her legs, and her own lungs burned from the dragon's exhaustion. Where were the other Riders? The number of Riders who had pledged themselves to the Freemen outnumbered those who fought for Caedo, and the Freemen had the elven Riders. Why did it feel as if they were horribly outnumbered?

As Tiri circled back toward the Hall, she saw the cause of the Freemen's trouble. Atop the enormous brown building, a pair of figures stood. One stood back from the edge, shouting and gesturing, obviously trying to direct the tides of the battle. But the second figure didn't seem to be listening. Her black dress flapped around her in the swirling winds of dragon wings, her brown hair whipping across her rage-filled face. Tormina's hands were raised, and hulking black shapes soared around her, tangling with roaring dragons.

"What are those things?" Andra asked of the three minds that mingled with hers.

"Dragons," Eithne answered, her thoughts taut with rage and fear.

"*Dragons?*" Andra repeated with disbelief.

"*The summoned spirits of dead dragons,*" Kael added. "*Dark magic can force the dead—any of the dead—to do the summoner's bidding.*"

As Andra watched the shadows move, fighting with the living dragons, she caught glimpses of the creatures' true forms. Black, smoky wings cutting through the air. Flashes of black teeth and claws. A glowing black eye. There were at least twenty of the creatures, each one of them tangling with a Freemen Rider, leaving the Kingsmen's Riders free to attack in groups and wreak havoc on the Freemen's foot soldiers below.

"*We need to stop her,*" Andra said, her thoughts forceful.

"*I'd be happy to hear a plan,*" Kael answered tensely.

"*Just follow my lead.*"

43

The Shadow's

Embrace

Eithne and Tiri rose above the clouds, their remaining enemies still in pursuit. The moment they passed through the misty grayness, Andra seized it with her magic and pulled it into a thick wall of fog around the two dragons. Her mind sent a flash of command to Kael and their mounts, and they followed.

As the first dragon pierced the fog, Eithne descended from above, crashing into the dragon's wings and crumpling one to the creature's side. The dragon roared in pain, his Rider echoing the sound with a scream as they began to fall. The second dragon penetrated the clouds, and Tiri struck, claws digging into the larger dragon's underbelly, ripping at the softer scales as Eithne gripped their enemy's neck in her jaws.

A burst of magic from the dragon's Rider finally forced the pair away from his mount, but the damage was done. Blood poured from the torn flesh, and the dragon and his Rider dove out of reach before turning west and flying away from the battle. Only three remained, but they were quickly closing with Andra and Kael.

Andra submerged her consciousness into the magic that pulsed inside her dragon, and knew that Kael did the same. She felt a tingle across her skin as he released a jet of flame from his palm, and Andra raised her own flame-marked hand. Tendrils of light crackled down the mark and flew from her fingertips, mingling with Kael's fire. In a swirl of flame and lightning, the magic struck the first Rider's shield. Andra felt the resistance from the ward, and shoved against it.

The shield gave, and the flames and lightning connected with the Rider. He flew from the saddle, writhing in the air as his dragon screamed, thrashing her head in agonized fury, tumbling after her Rider, though she had not been hit.

The remaining two Riders darted away from where the magic had struck, circling wide of Andra and Kael. Andra drew a breath. One for each of them. This was doable. Eithne and Tiri split, each diving headlong into their own battle. Tiri climbed rapidly skyward, her enemy giving chase, and the two spiraled and climbed around one another in a series of flaming breaths and raking claws. They climbed until Andra's lungs began to burn and her head began to spin.

And then Tiri dove for the ground again. Andra closed her eyes against the burning wind as it howled past her, gripping the straps of the saddle Janis had given her. As the ground raced ever closer to them, she braced herself for what she knew Tiri was about to do. At the last moment, the violet dragon spun, turning on the enemy above her. Her claws dug into his underbelly, and she opened her wings, spinning again, forcing him to his back.

Andra saw the enemy Rider jump away from the saddle just before the dragon under Tiri plowed into the earth, the spines of his back ripping up the grass, his body digging a gaping trench in the earth. Tiri jumped away from the dragon and lowered her head at him with a hiss. The larger creature let out a groaning sound and turned over as his Rider rushed to his side. They were both alive, but Andra didn't think either of them would be rejoining the battle soon.

She turned her eyes upward to see Kael and Eithne quickly descending. Eithne landed heavily on the grass, and they both turned toward Andra. They looked weary, and bore many marks of battle, but there was determination in both their faces.

"Now," Andra said, "I deal with Tormina."

"She's strong, Andra," Kael replied, his eyebrows drawing together. "You can't face her alone."

"You're needed here, Kael," Andra answered, looking around them at the battle that raged on. Dwarves, elves, and men were still fighting on the field around the Hall. There were screams of pain and rage and death around them. The field was littered with corpses of all races, and the heaping bodies of dragons stood like mounds around the Hall where they were hatched. "This needs to end, and quickly. I can handle Tormina," she said, her voice filled with Tiri's confidence. "Rally our people. Ensure that we hold the Hall. Most of their Riders are down, but our footmen are losing. They need you."

Kael hesitated, looking between the battling men and Andra. Then, finally, he nodded. "Be safe. I beg you. Please, return to me."

Andra nodded. "I will," she said. She could see in his face that they both knew the promise was an empty one. But Eithne still turned away, enormous strides carrying her and Kael to the battle that continued for possession of the Hall of Riders.

Andra lifted her eyes to the top of the stone parapets, where she saw bursts of darkness and shadow continuing to rain on the men below, the black shapes of dead dragons still battling their living brothers.

"*Tiri,*" she said, her voice soft even in her own mind. "*I am afraid.*"

"*Great courage always begins with great fear,*" the dragon answered her.

Andra swallowed and nodded once. *"Let us finish this, whatever the cost."*

Tiri released a furious roar that sent vibrations through Andra's body, then leapt into the sky once more. Andra could feel the ache of her dragon's muscles, the weariness of her body, but Tiri's confidence was as fierce as it had been when they charged into the Hall. Andra latched on to that feeling, allowing it to flood through her own body, to give her strength and courage.

They crested the wall, and in an instant, Tormina was before them. She'd seen them coming, and a deluge of shadow suddenly rained upon them. Andra raised her arms over her head reflexively, drawing on her magic. The shadows seemed to strike a dome of light, and they burst into mist, dissipating in an instant, sapping away at Andra's lingering strength.

Tiri alighted onto the roof of the Hall and released a jet of fire that seemed to part around Tormina and Caedo without any effort from the sorceress. Andra leapt from the saddle, unsheathing her sword for the first time since the battle had begun. She gripped its amethyst-studded hilt, feeling the black leather beneath her fingers as she strode forward.

The dragon's flames ended, and Andra charged forward, bringing down her sword in a shining arc of violet. Tormina raised an arm, and the steel struck flesh. But the flesh held. It was as if the sorceress's skin were made of iron. Tormina smiled at Andra's startled face, then shoved her other hand forward.

A burst of shadow exploded against Andra's gut, sending her arcing through the air. She struck the rooftop, the wind rushing from her lungs as she tumbled over the stone several times. When she finally stopped, she scrambled quickly to her feet, feeling the blood streaming from her temple, her left shoulder screaming in pain.

Andra held her left arm to her side and charged back in, giving extra strength to her shield. Another burst of shadow flew at her, stopping her in her tracks as it collided with her ward. The shadow seemed to press against the invisible force for a moment; then, with a mental shove, Andra forced the darkness aside.

With a shout, Andra swung her sword through the air, channeling her magic through her mark and down the length of the blade. A stream of blue-violet light burst from the steel, cutting across the air toward Tormina. The sorceress raised her arm to deflect the magic, but her shield wasn't powerful enough. The light struck her, and she tumbled over the stones, colliding with one of the parapets.

Andra looked around briefly, realizing that Caedo was nowhere in sight. He had fled, leaving his sorceress to do his work for him. She looked back at the woman, who was beginning to struggle to her feet.

"We don't need to do this, Tormina," Andra called to her, staying close to Tiri's side, drawing on the dragon's magic for extra strength. "Caedo has abandoned you to fight his battle for him. He does not care about you. You are no more than a sword to him. End this, surrender, and I will let you go free."

Tormina laughed as she stood, wiping blood from the corner of her mouth. She pushed her disheveled hair back from her scraped and bleeding face. "I know what Caedo's feelings for me are. Do you really think me so stupid? I knew when I first laid my eyes on him that he could only ever love me for my power. So I made myself more powerful. I learned Dark magic. I became what he wanted, so that he would want me as I had wanted him. It may only be my power he loves, but I don't care," she spat. "If I defeat you, he will still be mine. I shall still be his empress. What does it matter if he loves me, so long as he belongs to me and so long as I sit on a throne above Paerolia? I may never truly have his heart, but I *will* have him. I won't let you take him from me, girl. I won't!"

At the sorceress's shout, a wave of pure blackness surged up around her, rising as it rushed toward Andra and Tiri. Andra froze, staring in terror as the churning shadows came for her. In the blackness, she thought she saw the shapes of screaming faces and reaching hands. And then the shadow crashed down around them.

Andra threw her arms up over her head, ducking in close to Tiri's side as the dragon curled her head and neck around her Rider. The shadow seemed to consume them, wrapping them in a cocoon of darkness that was filled with screams of pain and terror.

Andra pressed her hands over her ears, trying to block out the sounds, but they seemed to pierce her mind. Cold hands seemed to claw at her back amid the black whirlwind, shredding her armor, raking her skin. She could feel madness burrowing into her mind, making her scream aloud, demanding for her to surrender to the shadow's embrace.

"Hold fast, Andra," Tiri whispered in her thoughts. *"Hold fast to me. As you did before."*

Andra's mind reached toward that whisper, grasping the dim light that was Tiri. They clung to each other, two candles somehow still burning in the midst of a stormy black sea.

Suddenly, another voice was in her mind. *"Draw on me, Andra. Use my magic."* It was Kael, his voice firm and clear through the blackness. *"Mine and Eithne's. Use us."*

Andra felt her body tense as she tried to cling to the four burning lights in her mind—Tiri, Kael, Eithne, and her own well of dimly pulsing magic. They were tiny flickers amid the black, barely enough to hold to. But she pulled on them, drawing them to her through the darkness that filled her mind.

She pulled their magic into her, drinking it in like life-giving nectar, feeling herself growing stronger as it flowed through her. With a shout, she flung her arms outward, and the shadow that embraced her burst away from her in a halo of light, sending tendrils of fog curling into the sky, harmless as smoke.

Andra stood, panting, atop the roof, staring at Tormina, who was staring back at her with wide eyes. Eyes that were filled with fear. Andra saw in the sorceress's face that she had used nearly all her strength to summon that wave of shadow. And it had failed.

Andra gripped her sword and stepped forward. Suddenly, Tormina spun. Her dress seemed to swirl around her, enveloping her in shadow, swallowing her until she simply disappeared from existence. Andra stared at the spot where the Dark sorceress had disappeared for a long moment.

Then the sounds of shouts reached her ears. She rushed to the parapets and looked down at the field below her. The shadows of dragons were trailing away into dark mist. Blue-clad men were fleeing into the woods while men, dwarves, and elves raised weapons in the air, giving victorious shouts. The Hall had fallen to the Freemen.

What Remains

Andra leapt aboard Tiri's saddle, and the dragon carried them to the ground, landing beside the cheering troops. Her eyes scanned the crowds; then she saw Eithne limping around the northern edge of the Hall, Kael at her side. Andra rushed to them, throwing her arms around Kael's torso. He embraced her tightly, but she could feel that his body was trembling from exhaustion.

She pulled back and looked up at him. "Are you hurt?" she asked.

He smiled weakly and shook his head. "Not badly. But when I said to use our magic, I didn't say to use all of it. You nearly drained us both."

Andra let out a short laugh and took his face between her hands, kissing him deeply and warmly. "You saved my life," she said as she pulled away. "If you hadn't given me your magic . . ."

He brushed a lock of hair from her dirty, bloodied face. "I know," he said quietly. "Our minds were still touching. I . . . felt you . . . dying." She saw him swallow and he shook his head. "It was all I could do to reach your mind and pull you back from the edge."

"Tormina and Caedo both fled," Andra told him.

"Well," Kael sighed, "Caedo tried. Our men captured him making for the woods. He's already been locked in the dungeon. But I doubt we'll see his sorceress again anytime soon."

Andra nodded, and looked around them. The initial shouts of victory had died away, and the jubilant atmosphere died with it. She saw many among the Freemen who already began to weep as they took in the destruction and death that surrounded the revered Hall of Riders. At least a dozen dragons had fallen in the battle, and the howls of their Riders rent the air.

Above their wails, a deep keening noise reached Andra's ears, and she turned toward it to see a red dragon, head bent over the corpse of his fallen Rider. Even as Andra watched him, the dragon's keens died away, and he laid himself on the grass beside his Rider. In a few moments, he was still.

Andra turned her face into Kael's leather armor, feeling tears falling down her cheeks. They had done this. They had brought this death to the Hall. They had turned these Riders against one another.

"We did what needed to be done," Tiri reassured her in her mind. But through the words, Andra could feel her dragon's own pain and sorrow at the death of so many of her kind. *"It would have come to this someday, Andra, with or without us. Someday, Caedo would have begun another war with the elves, or hunted every Rider who supported the Freemen. Riders would have killed Riders in greater numbers than this. We did what needed to be done."*

"We need to secure the Hall," Kael said quietly, drawing back from her slightly, "gather our forces, and ensure that the remaining Kingsmen can't reclaim it from us."

A disheveled, bloodstained elf pressed through the crowd, clad in a Rider's attire. It took Andra a moment to recognize him as Vires.

"My men have found and secured the rest of the judges," he told them. "They're being held in the arena until we can determine which of them supported Caedo, and which were blind to the plan to place him on a throne. And the Hall has been cleared of Kingsmen. We had some . . . unexpected help."

The elf king turned his head and Andra followed his gaze to see a disheveled young man with dirty blond hair striding toward them, that same crooked smile on his face, as it so often was.

"Talias!" she called, a disbelieving laugh rising in her throat.

The kitchen boy strode toward her and pulled her roughly into his arms, crushing her to his chest. She returned the embrace for a long moment. Then he pulled back, holding her at arm's length and grinning down at her.

"You're a Rider!" he laughed.

"And I have you to thank for that," she replied.

"Me?"

"It's a very long tale."

"So you're Talias?" a gruff voice said.

Andra and the kitchen boy both turned toward the voice, and Kael thrust a hand between them. Talias took a step back, his brow furrowing slightly, but he gripped the offered hand, looking down at it as he did so.

His head cocked to the side for a moment, then he said, "Interesting bracelet."

Kael released Talias's hand, glancing down at the braided leather that cuffed his glove. "It was a gift," he answered.

Talias's eyes turned to Andra, a look of confusion in them.

Andra swallowed and stepped up to Kael's side, taking his hand. "Talias," she said, "this is Kael . . . my husband."

The young man raised his eyebrows, but as always, he was quick to put a smile on his face. "Oh. Well, that's . . . Congratulations, Andra."

Nearby, Vires awkwardly cleared his throat, drawing their attention. Then he said, "Young Talias here led the servants and contracted laborers against the invading Kingsmen. Taking the Hall would have been much more difficult without their aid."

Talias nodded sharply. "Once I knew which side Andra was on, it was easy to know which I would fight on."

"I told you to barricade everyone in the servants' quarters," Andra said, raising an eyebrow at him.

He grinned at her. "All you said was, *'Servants' quarters. Barricade.'* You didn't say everyone needed to be in there. I gathered everyone I could find to the servants' quarters, then told them what was happening. As I saw it, we had a choice to make, and everyone who chose to fight came with me. The rest barricaded themselves in, exactly as you asked."

"Exactly?" she repeated with a laugh.

"Well, perhaps not *exactly*," he confessed.

Kael turned and spoke to Vires. "Can you find Insarius? He has a copy of a spell I need." Then he looked at Talias again. "Tell every contracted worker in the Hall to gather in the arena, and their collars will be removed immediately."

Talias looked at him in disbelief. "Truly?"

Kael nodded. "Truly."

A bright smile lit up Talias's face, and he turned on his heel without further question, racing back toward the Hall. Kael watched him go.

"He seems to be a decent sort of fellow," he remarked, his tone begrudging.

"He is," Andra replied, leaning into his arm. A brief silence passed between them, then she added in a quiet voice, "I don't think I ever truly loved him."

"No?" Kael asked.

"No. He was just . . . an ideal. A hope that I held to. I loved the idea of him, the idea of being free to love him. But I don't believe I ever truly loved *him*."

Another silence held them for a moment, and Andra felt that an understanding passed between them. Finally, Kael looked down at her and said, "I know you're tired, Andra. But there is still work to be done."

Andra nodded, straightening and dashing away her lingering tears with the black leather of her gloves, smearing away blood as well. "I know. We'd best begin."

———◌◈◌———

Kael sat in the council meeting, head pounding from exhaustion. He hadn't slept more than three hours at once since the battle at the Hall two weeks prior. Since then, he and Andra had been trundling back and forth between Vereor, the Hall, and Iterum, acting as emissaries for the Freemen. As it turned out, rebuilding a government was just as taxing as overthrowing one.

Seven of the other ten judges had had a hand in Caedo's attempt at the throne. Most had been bribed or threatened into it in some way, but they were all removed from their seats, and were each awaiting their own judgments. Caedo had already received his. Many had expected Tormina to appear and attempt a rescue, but the execution proceeded without complication. He forced thoughts of his brother's swinging feet from his mind and focused on his new responsibilities. For now, this council led Paerolia, and Kael had the unfortunate responsibility of leading it.

After a fortnight of meetings, they'd released every indentured worker in Paerolia from their contracts, rewritten the laws surrounding the labor contracts, established clearer laws for the succession of judges, and—the most important of the tasks in his mind—eliminated the limitations on candidates for Pairing. At the next Choosing, elves and humans would be permitted to send any six candidates they deemed worthy, regardless of age or gender. Andra had laughed with tears in her eyes when he'd told her the week before.

"I don't care if they didn't have a hand in the attempted coup," a blustery man was saying, his face red with anger. Kael forced himself to refocus on the man's words, and the other council members around the table. "I don't trust a single one of them, and I want none of them sitting on judgment seats!"

"Mayor Eurus," Kael said wearily, pressing two fingers to his temple, "if one of your advisors committed a crime, would you surrender your place as mayor of Thys?"

The rotund man blinked, making a spluttering sound. "Well, I— That, that's entirely different!"

"It isn't, actually," Kael answered bluntly. "And until you're willing to answer for the sins of your fellow leaders in your city, you cannot ask those judges to answer for the sins of their fellow leaders. Judge Aecus has been in Thys with you for the last year. Do you have reason to believe he was conspiring with Caedo from halfway across the continent?"

"No, I—"

"Very well, then," Kael cut him off. Eurus had been talking incessantly for nearly a fortnight, and Kael was entirely finished listening. "Is there anyone with *good* reason to remove the three remaining judges from their seats?"

The men and women around the table remained silent.

"Good. Then we're agreed. Those three will be the beginning of our new government. I shall invite them to join the council tomorrow, when we'll begin submitting candidates for the remaining judgment seats."

"What about you?" a woman asked. Kael recognized her as the representative from the house of merchants.

"What about me?" Kael asked with a barely suppressed sigh.

"Would you consider taking a judgment seat?"

He looked at her, his brow furrowing. "No," he answered shortly. "I am, first and foremost, a Rider. I will perform a Rider's duties, and nothing more. If there are no other questions, we'll dismiss and reconvene tomorrow."

Kael didn't wait to see if there actually were more questions; he gathered the papers on the table before him and left the council chambers, quickly exiting what had once been Castigo's manor. Eithne waited for him on the vast lawn.

"It would not be a bad idea, you know," Eithne said as he climbed into her saddle. *"With a judgment seat, you could ensure that things are done the way they should be—the way the Guardians intended for them to be done."*

Kael sighed heavily as his dragon took to the sky, preparing to carry him back to Iterum once again. *"This is not the life I want, Eithne,"* he told her. *"I know that I cannot abandon leadership entirely. That is something I accepted when I became your Rider. But to be a judge like my father and brother were? To be confined to endless councils and hearings? That is not what I want."*

He could feel her understanding, her warm contentment as she sensed what he *did* want. *"We shall have that life soon enough,"* she told him.

Kael smiled and patted her neck. Soon, they were descending above Iterum, and he felt a thrill of excitement as he spotted Tiri on the field, Andra removing her saddle. She had been in Thys for three days, dealing with a small band of looters who had taken advantage of the chaos that came after the judges' fall.

He leapt to the ground the moment Eithne's claws touched soil, and raced to her side, forcing her to drop the saddle as he swept her into his arms. He kissed her full on the mouth, relishing in the taste of her as he lifted her boots from the ground. He felt her arms go around his neck, her fingers familiar in his hair as she returned the kiss.

When at last he pulled away, she smiled up at him. "I missed you too," she laughed.

"You told me we needed to give them only one more week," Kael grumbled, pressing his face into her neck.

"What?"

"Before the battle at the Hall," he said. "The day we were married." He drew back, looking down at her again, taking in her own tired eyes. "You said the Freemen asked us to delay our own happiness for only another week. And yet, here we are, nearly a month later, our lives still at a standstill."

Andra sighed and ran a hand across her face. "I know," she said quietly. "But we *are* Riders, Kael. There will always be duties for us to perform."

"Do you know what those duties normally are, Andra?" Kael chuckled.

She made a sheepish face. "Range Duty?" she asked hesitantly.

"Yes," Kael laughed. "One year of Range Duty for each Rider. But aside from that, a post. A simple post, assigned to a city, where you patrol, provide aid to the city guard, and advise the city mayor or the judge who sits in that city. Duties, yes. Power, yes. But Riders still have lives of their own. They marry, they have homes, they have families."

Andra pulled him close, tightening her arms around his back as she looked up at him. "Soon," she promised. "Once the new judges have been decided and the Chief Judge elected, we shall receive our assignments. We'll have that life, Kael. We will build it together, from the remains of the life we leave behind. It will be ours. Soon."

Andra stood before the twelve seated figures in the judges' chambers in Vereor. She was arrayed in her Rider's attire, sword strapped to her waist. The walls of the room were lined with men—other Riders who had fought with the Freemen.

"Rider Andra," the Chief Judge said in a deep, warm voice. He had black hair that curled close to his head, like the wool of a lamb, and richly dark skin. His eyes were a warm brown, and she knew him to be the former judge in Thys, Aecus. "Do you know why you've been called here today?"

"No, my lord," she answered respectfully.

"The men around you were summoned because they broke their vows to the former judges. They came to receive a formal pardon, and to reaffirm their oaths to the capital of Vereor. A formality, of course, given the former judges' corruption, but a necessary one to uphold the letter of the law. But you, Andra, have never made any such oaths, is that correct?"

"Yes," she answered, nodding again. "My only vows as a Rider were to the Freemen."

"Seeing as the Freemen are no more," Aecus went on, "we thought it only proper that you receive the opportunity to pledge yourself and your dragon to the service of the judges, as every Rider has done since the age of the Guardians. Will you make this vow?"

Andra hesitated, taking a moment to feel her dragon's mind, to sense her thoughts on the idea. *"My only pledge is to you, Andra,"* Tiri said. *"If this is what you wish to do, then you may do so."*

"And if I choose not to?" Andra asked.

The other judges looked startled. "Well . . ." the Chief Judge said slowly, "we would not be able to permit you to enter any city without express permission from the city's mayor or sitting judge. We can't allow a rogue Rider to come and go as she pleases—especially one with such power as I've been told you hold. But if you do not pledge yourself to protect and uphold the human kingdom, you shall be permitted to leave in peace, and find a place for yourself and your dragon away from the cities in our control."

Andra glanced to the side of the room, to where Kael stood among the ranks of Riders. His brow was furrowed as he considered her words. Minutes before, he had renewed his own pledge to the judges, speaking the same words he'd spoken as a twelve-year-old boy. And he'd received his post—Amiscan, a small city on the eastern coast, the only place where humans and elves lived in equal numbers.

"And if I do pledge, I'll receive my own assignment?" she asked, looking back up at Aecus.

"Yes." He nodded. "Your talents would be put to good use, training young Riders at the Hall."

Andra bit her lip and glanced at Kael again. She could see in his face that he'd expected them to receive assignments together. But she'd feared this would be the case.

"Amiscan is technically in elven control, is it not?" Andra asked.

Aecus raised his eyebrows. "It is . . ." he said in a careful and deliberate voice. "King Vires would make a final decision on whether or not you would be permitted to travel freely in his realms. But our government does maintain a presence in Amiscan, and we keep our own Rider there—your husband. However, we could not keep you from entering a neutral city like Amiscan."

Andra thought she saw a glint of amusement in the Chief Judge's eyes as he steepled his fingers together, regarding her over his fingertips. He knew the reason for her questions, but there was no anger or disappointment in his gaze. For a moment, she wondered if he'd expected this of her, if this was why he'd assigned Kael to the one place where she would be able to be with him.

She had been under other men's control for her entire life. She'd always answered to one ruler or another, and she had left that life far behind her long ago. She wouldn't answer to the beck and call of any judge again. For the first time in her life, Andra was really and truly free, and she would not surrender that for a vow of loyalty to any man.

Andra drew her sword and laid it on the ground at the judges' feet, as she'd seen the other Riders do when they renewed their vows. She knelt beside the sword and bowed her head, catching a glimpse of Kael's raised eyebrows and slightly parted lips.

"I, Andra," she said loudly and clearly, "Rider of the dragon Tiri, do vow my sword and my dragon to the protection of the land of Paerolia, to the defense of all kingdoms that mark her shores. In times of great need, I will rise and fight for this land." She gripped the hilt of her sword and slowly stood, lifting her eyes to look upon the face of each judge, ending with Judge Dusan, who had retained his seat after the coup.

"But," she continued on, "I shall do so on my own terms. I will fight when my conscience dictates it. Be it for men, elves, or dwarves, my dragon and I will decide for ourselves when to fight. We will be our own masters. But we will be a force you can call upon whenever you are in need. This is the only vow I will make to the judges."

The judges began whispering among themselves with furrowed brows. Along the walls, Riders began to murmur as well. No Rider had done this before. Each was pledged to either the human or the elven kingdom. But Chief Judge Aecus met Andra's steady gaze calmly, a small smile playing over his lips.

After a moment, he raised a hand, and the room fell silent. "This is . . . certainly not customary," Aecus said thoughtfully. "And yet, it is not a surprise to me, I must admit. You've served this land well already, Rider Andra, even without a vow. And, to be entirely candid, I don't feel I need more from you than what you have just given. I accept your decision, and your pledge, and I wish you peace and happiness in pursuing your own free life."

Andra smiled at the man and bowed deeply. "Thank you, my lord," she said.

"Thank you, Rider Andra. Now I bid you to leave in peace. As for the rest of you," he added in a louder voice, addressing the other

Riders in the room, "report to your posts within a week. You are dismissed."

The Riders immediately began to file from the room, but Kael hurried to Andra's side. She turned to him with a smile as he ran his hand down her arm until their fingers laced together, their rings touching above their riding gloves.

"It would appear it's time for me to report to my post," he said quietly.

"And I must leave all human cities at once," Andra replied. "Do you think Vires would allow me to stay in one of the cities under his command?"

"I think he may oblige you," Kael chuckled.

"Good. Because I've always fancied living somewhere close to the sea."

ACKNOWLEDGMENTS

When I wrote *Bright Star,* it was for my own enjoyment, and perhaps the enjoyment of a few online readers. And, if not for some truly incredible people in my life, it wouldn't have gone any further than that.

First, I want to thank my husband for his never-ending support and encouragement. I had all but given up my love of writing before he came into my life and pushed me to keep that spark alive. Thank you for believing in my dreams more than I did, and for helping them come true.

I would also like to thank the rest of my family. As much as I tried to hide my writing from them, they have always supported my passion. My amazing parents and sisters have cheered for me throughout this process, and it means the world to me. No matter what happens, I know I have so many amazing family members behind me, rooting for my success. Thank you to all of my beloved family for listening to my ramblings, always asking for updates, and genuinely caring about my writing. It is everything to me.

And of course, as with any writer, I could not have come to this point without some incredible teachers. While there have been several that have influenced and guided me, there is one teacher I want to thank by name—Susan Nunan, a woman who has always been more than an English teacher to me. You pushed me in ways nobody else did, and I wouldn't have become the writer I am without the two years I was blessed to spend as your student. Thank you for your guidance, your lessons about English and about life, and your incredible example of strength, grace, and positivity.

There are truly no words I can write that will express the depths of my gratitude to Ali, Linda, and the rest of the team at Inkitt. They are the ones who dug up *Bright Star* after years of it gathering dust. They brought it into the light, and made the publication of this book a reality. I want to thank each of them for their support, the hard work they put into promoting me and my story, their personal tutelage throughout this process, and the incredible amount of faith they have in this book's success. You have all truly transformed my life, and made my dream possible.

Finally, I want to express my humble gratitude to the team at Tor Teen for taking a chance on me and on *Bright Star*. Thank you, Whitney, for bearing with me through the major and exhaustive rewrites, and for your help in working through some of the stickier issues. Thank you, Elayne, for helping me to fine-tune the book and for championing it through the final stages to publication. And thank you to the copy editor whose name I never got to learn, who did such incredible work in helping me to perfect my book.

I know there are so many others who I have not named who have made this book possible. You know who you are. Just know that the support and aid you have offered me has had such incredible meaning to me, and if not for those little steps and bits of encouragement along the way, this book never would have happened. From the bottom of my heart, thank you.

ABOUT THE AUTHOR

ERIN SWAN was born in a small farm town in Oregon, and spent her childhood on United States Air Force bases around the country. A graduate of Brigham Young University, Erin lives with her husband and their daughter in Utah, where she works as a marketing copywriter and a novelist.